THE
LIGHTNING
HORSE

AN EMPIRE AT TWILIGHT NOVEL

N.L. HOLMES

WayBack Press
P.O.Box 16066
Tampa, FL
⚱

The Lightning Horse

Empire at Sunsettm 2020

Cover art and map by StreetLight Graphics. Author photo by Kipp Baker.

Dedicated to my husband.

CHAPTER 1

T HIS IS WHAT IT MEANS *to be a charioteer*, thought Tiwatipara in awe. *Not a diplomat—an emissary— but a driver of horses.* A charioteer was a man who cracked the whip, and a pair of powerful, perfectly trained animals sprang forward, devouring the earth before them with a roar like a clap of thunder. How their manes streamed behind them, rippling like battle flags! How their hooves beat the black earth, throwing clods and tufts of dry grass at the spectators! *Wasn't the god of lightning, Tarhunta Pihasshasshi, the first charioteer?*

The sight of a team swallowing the black earth in a furor of speed never failed to swell the heart of Tiwatipara son of Pawahtelmah. His eyes followed the vehicle as it made the turn, his father bent over the leads. "It's like riding a lightning bolt," he said to his friend Zidanza at his side, trying not to sound too much like the little child jumping up and down inside him. "Their power. Their nobility. You can't imagine horses doing anything ignoble, can you? I wouldn't be happy in any other profession."

"I don't know," said Zidanza vaguely, his gaze on the

galloping animals. "It's rare that I get to take a team out, and even then, it's only for the distance of a few *iku*s. But I do love being around them." He gave his amiable grin. "Feeding them isn't quite as dangerous as driving them." Zidanza was a groom of the royal stables even though he was a prince of sorts, descended from the great Tudhaliya. He was a mild young man with a round face and sleepy eyes that held a curious mixture of lassitude and anxiety. By and large, he was slow moving and even lazy, which nicely balanced Tiwatipara's crackling energy. They had been friends since childhood.

Tiwatipara dragged his eyes away from the team that thundered past him. King Hattushili was testing out the new horses he had bought from Hurrian merchants in Karkemish, and Tiwatipara's father, the *hashtalanuri*—the king's own driver—was in the box. The young man's family had served the king in the honored post of charioteer as long as there had been a king of Hatti Land, since the first men of Hatti had come forth from Kusshara and established themselves in the old capital of their predecessors, defying the curse on Hattusha to make it the heart of a mighty empire. Tiwatipara took pride in that heritage. Only the cream of Hatti's aristocracy could touch these priceless horses, even to serve them their mash or brush their sleek, glistening coats. A job that might seem menial became an act of high ceremony when performed for the royal horses. Many of the drivers—and even the grooms—were, like Zidanza, princes of the blood.

Tiwatipara continued to assemble the royal chariot, forcing the two tall wheels onto the axle slathered with sheep fat and hammering in the cotter pins while Zidanza held it steady. Tiwatipara dropped his mallet into the toolbox on the ground, and Zidanza pushed it aside with his foot. The charioteer laid the long draft pole, with its fixed double yoke, out before the vehicle. With one eye still on his father's headlong course around the field, marked by a great plume of dust, Tiwatipara set the harness leathers on the floor of the box until he could bring the horses from their stalls. Not far away, their backs to him, stood a crowd of grooms, drivers, and royal princes, all watching, with excitement, the test of the first pair of horses. The king's three oldest sons, young men about Tiwatipara's age, were among them, including Prince Nerikkaili, the *tuhkanti*—or crown prince—and Tiwatipara's employer. Hishni, the third in age, cried eagerly, "Look at those demons fly! I've never seen such power!"

But Tiwatipara smiled to himself. They hadn't seen the best team yet.

He headed back into the royal stable, and the thunder of hooves and the roar of the crowd faded. It was always quiet, hushed in a nearly religious sense, inside the long, stone-walled barns that housed the king's horses. High-spirited lightning bolts though they might be on the field, the stallions were tranquil and well-mannered in repose—except perhaps when the mares were in heat. Pihasshasshi's boys were so perfectly trained that Tiwatipara would have trusted them to step over his prone body. In fact, every day, he entrusted his body to them as he did now, entering the box of Storm Cloud of Tarhunta. The big beast rolled his eyes and jerked his head away but only to be contrary. He knew the appearance of a human holding a bridle signified, *Go have fun. Run! Run fast!*

9

"You know what this means, don't you, my beauty?" cooed Tiwatipara in his horse-calming voice. He ran a hand over the horse's dappled hide and down his muscular chest and long powerful leg, which darkened into silvery black along the cannon as it approached the hoof. The horse's skin shivered at Tiwatipara's touch, as if in umbrage at the familiarity, and the youth laughed, his voice rich with affection. "Yes, we're both a little touchy, aren't we? You're my soul mate, young man. I may never have a chance to drive you"—*not until Prince Nerikkaili becomes king, at least*—"but you and I understand each other, don't we?"

He slid the bridle into the horse's mouth and pulled the straps back behind the animal's head, pulling each ear through with a little felty pop. At the age of twenty-two, Tiwatipara loved everything about his life. He had worked in the royal stable since he was old enough to toddle at his father's side with a bucket of barley, and he couldn't imagine doing anything else. He loved the smell of horses, warm and pungent, the feel of their muscular movement through the sleek pelt, and the challenge of their often crafty intelligence—the emotional connivance that let a mere man direct these immensely more puissant creatures who were, nonetheless, fearful and in need of reassurance. Tiwatipara led Storm Cloud out into the corridor and tied the stallion to a ring in the wall until he had bridled the animal's teammate, Silver Lightning. Then he took the pair of them back outside, accompanied by the counterpointed clopping of eight hooves upon the hard ground.

On the practice course, Tiwatipara's father, Pawahtelmah, was just pulling up to the knot of observers, reining in his overstimulated team gently and insistently.

There's a man who knows how to drive, thought Tiwatipara, his heart swelling with pride. His father wasn't a tall man, but he was solid, with a strong pair of shoulders hewn by a lifetime of driving these high-strung beauties, powerful arms, and broad, calloused hands in perfect control of the leads. The pair of big bay stallions—running pace for pace with one another—slowed, their heads up, nostrils round from exertion, stately and beautiful in a cloud of dust. A groom reached for his reins, and Father leaped down from the back of the box, his face red and glistening with exhilaration.

"What do you think, Pawahtelmah?" cried the king, grinning broadly. "Did I get taken, or are they worth the price?"

At his side, Hattushili's friend Benteshina, the former king of Amurru, said with an exaggerated moue, "They'll do." He seemed incapable of speaking seriously about anything.

"Well worth it, My Sun, whatever you paid for them. They're a magnificent pair," agreed Tiwatipara's father.

"There's more and better to come. Where's the other team? Ah, Tiwatipara. It's you hitching them up, hah? Show your father these beauties, my boy."

Beside the king, Tapala-tarhunta, Tiwatipara's grandfather, laughed and clapped his grandson on the shoulder. He had been the king's driver in his youth and, more recently, during the war for the throne. Tiwatipara led the two dappled stallions forward for his father's admiration. Pawahtelmah ran his hands over their legs, opened their lips, and eyed their teeth.

"Well matched," he commented. "Impressive

conformation. Let's see what they've got. Hitch 'em up, Tipa."

"I'm going to join you on this run," said Hattushili, still grinning. He turned to his eldest son, Nerikkaili, who had drawn closer to see the two stallions. "Tell your stepmother to come on out if she wants to see something beautiful." He turned to Tiwatipara's father. "I saw them run in Karkemish, Pawahtelmah. You can hardly believe how they seem to think with one mind."

The men were still talking and laughing behind him as Tiwatipara led the horses back to where the king's chariot sat parked. It was a massive war car with a three-man box of bronze-bound scarlet wood and wheels as tall as a man's hip—at least for a fairly short man such as he was. To pull a vehicle like that at breakneck speed was a real test of a team's stamina. But that was what they had to do on the battleground.

Zidanza stood beside the chariot, leaning against the box with crossed arms as he watched the activity on the field. He blinked sleepily and stepped back as his friend approached with the horses. Tiwatipara winked at him, scarcely able to contain his high spirits.

"Show Our Sun what you're made of, boys," Tiwatipara told the pair as he pulled first one and then the other alongside the draft pole and, nudging them toward the center with his chest, lowered the yoke over their withers. Automatically, with the expertise of one who had been harnessing horses since childhood, Tiwatipara laid the saddles and checks in place, tied up all the straps, and ran the lines through the terrets as he listened with one ear to the king and his men in the distance. He gave an extra pull to the breeching strap and tug just to be sure. He was a cautious lad who had been trained by cautious men. Then he made sure the blinders cleared the animals' eyes, and he led them back to the practice field, Zidanza in his wake.

Their coming was met with whistles of appreciation and a babble of excitement. Tiwatipara saw his father and grandfather grinning at the king, and Hattushili's three oldest sons exchanged something hastily.

"They're making bets," Tiwatipara said, amused, to his friend. "I wouldn't trust that Lurma-ziti not to cheat."

"After you, My Sun." Pawahtelmah gestured to the king, and Tapala-tarhunta made a stirrup of his hands for Hattushili to mount the box. The king—a tall, thin, middle-aged man, his ugly face lit with boyish eagerness—hauled himself up. He laughed at his sons and Benteshina on the ground below. Then Pawahtelmah jumped up beside him and took his place on the king's left, shortening up the leads.

"Tapala-tarhunta," cried the king in his rough voice. "Come join us for old times' sake. It's not a real test unless they're pulling three men."

Tiwatipara's grandfather heaved himself up without further coaxing. He would play the shield bearer at the rear.

Pawahtelmah had just eased the animals into a walk to turn them onto the practice field when a pageboy came running from the direction of the stable. He shot toward the field after the chariot, his footsteps making little puffs of dust in the tattered dead grass. "My Sun! My Sun!" he cried, waving his arms. The men on board turned as the driver drew the team to a halt.

"What is it, damn it?" yelled the king.

The boy trotted up to the vehicle, panting. "The *tawananna* said to tell you there's a messenger from Karduniash, My Sun. She said it's very important and that you need to hear him and formulate a reply."

Hattushili stifled a curse and squinted around as if he hoped someone could rescue him from this interruption. Finally, he said, "All right. Tell her I'm on my way." He aimed an elaborate shrug at his sons. "All bets are off, boys." Then he clapped Tiwatipara's father and grandfather on the shoulders and let himself laboriously down from the box.

"Should we wait for your return, My Sun?" asked Pawahtelmah.

"No, no. Go ahead. Impress the others. I've seen these gorgeous fellows in action." The king gave Storm Cloud an affectionate slap on the rump as he passed, then Hattushili strode off toward the stable on his long legs.

"So, show us what they've got, Pawahtelmah," called Prince Nerikkaili from the sidelines in his smooth baritone. Hishni and Lurma-ziti stood beside him, the latter smirking.

"Tipa? Do you want to join us as the third man?" called Pawahtelmah.

Tiwatipara had just begun to run eagerly toward the vehicle when Nerikkaili stopped him. "Did you finish repairing that collar you were working on, Tiwatipara?"

"No, my lord," he admitted, dreading what was coming.

"Then I'd rather you did that. I need it tomorrow."

"Yes, my lord," he replied, lowering his eyes with a pang of disappointment and even resentment that his prince couldn't wait while he, Tiwatipara, had the ride of his life, sharing such a moment with his father and grandfather—three generations of charioteers in one box.

"You coming, son?" called his father.

"No. I have things to do," he replied with a forced smile. He was a soldier, and orders were orders. He would never admit the depth of his disappointment.

Pawahtelmah clucked the team up into a trot, and already, one could see how perfectly matched the pair were, not only in appearance but in spirit as well. Usually, one horse would pull hard while the other was content to come along—much like Tiwatipara and Zidanza—but Storm Cloud and Lightning seemed to exult in the competition, each springing ahead against the load of two men and a heavy wooden car. Tiwatipara watched, holding his breath in admiration, as the vehicle disappeared toward the other end of the field in a storm of hoofbeats and dust. Then he made his way, with a deep sigh of resignation, toward the stable.

It was silent inside. Everyone was at the field, watching the new horses. Only an occasional ruffle of equine breath or the scrape of hooves disturbed the heavy golden quiet of the place, with its straw-covered floors and mote-filled air. Tiwatipara snuffed the sweet, hay-perfumed atmosphere as he made his way to the tack room and took down the collar he had begun to repair. It was part of Nerikkaili's ceremonial harness; he would indeed need it for the next day's festival procession. There was a rip in the seam, but Tiwatipara saw that he had almost completed restitching it. A few minutes' work remained, no more, and it wasn't altogether clear to him why one of the grooms couldn't take care of it. Normally, such things were their job, but the ultimate responsibility was the charioteer's, and Tiwatipara was a perfectionist, often choosing to do things himself.

For this, I missed a chance to test the new team with my father and grandfather. He heaved a mighty breath as he laid the collar down. He found a big curved needle and threaded it with a length of thin gut. Then, sitting on the only bench in the tack room, he proceeded to stitch carefully through the old holes.

From off in the distance, Tiwatipara heard the faint thunder of wheels and hooves as the team approached the near end of the field again and the whistles and shouts of the onlookers. But he wasn't one to rush a job. He finished it at a meticulous pace then put away his equipment before hanging the collar with the other pieces of the harness.

At last, Tiwatipara jogged back out to the field. The king had returned from his diplomatic distraction and was joking with the men, even as the royal eyes stayed fixed on the thundering team and the two men in the chariot, their heads low, their long hair flying behind them.

"Faster!" Hattushili shouted, and the crowd joined in the cry. "Faster! Faster!"

Tapala-tarhunta shook his fist as if brandishing a spear, and the team pounded around the curve, barely slowing. From the horses' lips, foam slung out at the onlookers, and Nerikkaili laughingly wiped his cheek. Tiwatipara saw his father's face, wild with the joyous thrill of the speed, before Pawahtelmah completed the turn and sped away. Now the length of the field stretched before the chariots. Pawahtelmah laid his long whip with a crack upon the eager backs of the horses. The animals, who were already flying like the wind, seemed to find within them some secret reserve of power as if their feet had sprouted wings. Their stride lengthened impossibly, and they shot forward like the very horses of the Lightning God. Tiwatipara was so moved by the sheer beauty of it that his nose began to burn. Zidanza, at his side, was as tense as a drawn bow.

Then something happened. There was a lurch of the box. The chariot rocked and fell to the ground on one side with an infernal screech and a crash. A wheel spun off drunkenly across the field. Tiwatipara's grandfather catapulted out between the horses' backs. The chariot flipped sideways on top of him and kept sliding. His father, thrown likewise over the rail, still had the lines in his hands as the dragging car braked the animals brutally. They fell against one another, their legs in the air, and rolled and kicked against the weight of the box as it slid into them. The draft pole splintered. Pawahtelmah was plowed under the chariot and the horses' bodies as they screamed in pain and fear, striking out desperately with their hooves.

All this happened in an instant, surely, but every action was printed in agonizing detail in Tiwatipara's sight, as if time slowed down for those few terrible beats. His heart seemed to stop. A great cloud of white dust surrounded the wreck. A massive furrow, smeared with blood, followed the slide of the chariot, whose one wheel spun helplessly in the air. The horses' shrieks rose in the unashamed terror of injured animals, but the two passengers were silent, buried under the overturned chariot and the struggling horses. Zidanza gripped Tiwatipara's arm and sucked in his breath, aghast.

Among the spectators, no one moved for a horrified instant. Then everyone ran at once, Tiwatipara bursting into the lead. He pounded down the field, his heart in his mouth. "Father! Grandfather!" he shouted.

What happened? Was it something I did—or something I left undone? Why did the chariot throw a wheel?

Storm Cloud struggled to right himself, but he hadn't the strength. His blood was pumping out, saturating the harness and ground. His big eyes rolled in mortal fear. He bared his teeth in a scream of uncomprehending agony. Tiwatipara squatted beside the overturned car and tried to heave it up off the animal, but it was too heavy until someone lent a shoulder at his side. It was the king, his lips drawn back from his crooked teeth in a grimace of effort. The box fell to its base with a crash, and the other wheel fell off. Tapala-tarhunta lay where he had been mown down by the heavy wooden box, flat on his face, covered by his tangle of hair, his legs at unnatural angles. Bloody. Unmoving.

"Dear gods," moaned Tiwatipara, sinking to his knees. Everything seemed strangely sharp and sparkling. His hands were quivering like poplar leaves in the breeze. He wondered if he were going to faint.

An infinitely remote voice said, "Who's got a knife? Put these horses out of their pain, man."

I should be the one doing that, he thought. But he seemed incapable of movement. The horses' screams stopped abruptly, one after the other. The men cut harness straps and dragged the dead animals out of the way. Storm Cloud had been impaled on the splintered pole. Both of them had broken legs, perhaps ribs. Priceless. Wonderful. Dead. Tiwatipara was dimly aware of Zidanza throwing up beside him.

Under the horses lay his father, his tunic half ripped from him by the abrasion of the earth. Pawahtelmah was a bloody, mangled pile of something less than human, crushed by the weight of the animals and the bashing corners of the wooden vehicle. Tiwatipara crawled toward him and fell on his face at his side, and suddenly, the sobs that had trembled within him came pouring out in desolate howls. This man had raised him all alone for twenty-two years, after the death of Tiwatipara's mother in childbirth. He was all the young man had.

"Father! Father! All you gods! What did I do wrong?" Tiwatipara sobbed into the dry grass, fearing to touch his father, nonetheless, as if it might increase his pain. But Pawahtelmah felt no pain. Pawahtelmah son of Tapala-tarhunta was clearly dead. At last, not caring that he was covered with Pawahtelmah's blood, Tiwatipara fell upon his father's back. Men of Hatti Land weren't supposed to cry, but he wailed unashamedly.

He felt a heavy hand on his shoulder. Raising tear-blurred eyes, Tiwatipara saw the king kneeling over him, his long gray hair hanging in a curtain around his sorrowful face. "It's not your doing, son. The gods have permitted it for their own reasons."

And from somewhere behind the youth, a voice cried in astonishment, "My Sun! Tapala-tarhunta is alive!"

"Don't try to move him. Get a board to carry him on. Nerikkaili, call a doctor," Hattushili directed, rising to his feet. Men shot off in all directions. The field became very still except for the distant cries of grooms.

Overhead, an eagle sailed silently, and Tiwatipara craned his head to stare upward through his tears. *Pawahtelmah* meant "eagle's eye." Perhaps it was the spirit of his father planing above his ruined body.

Tiwatipara sat back on his heels, drained and unfeeling, as if he, too, had died. "I should have been on board," he murmured through his tears. "Why? Why was I spared and my father taken?"

His father was forty years old, a man in his prime. He was endowed with exceptional gifts as a horseman, but even more, he was a gem among men. Kind, principled, and humorous, he had been both a firm father and a tender mother to Tiwatipara. Grandfather was austere, a hard old soldier in manner and inclined to expect a boy to do things his way or do them over. But Pawahtelmah had let his son make his own mistakes and find his own way. He had taught Tiwatipara by example, and the youth loved him beyond life itself. *Perhaps too much*, he realized, desolate. *Perhaps anything one loves so much will be taken away by some jealous god.*

At last, the grooms returned with a door, upon which they placed Tapala-tarhunta and carried him away. The stable boys left Tiwatipara kneeling at his father's side while they dragged away the carcasses of Storm Cloud and Lightning, picked up the broken bits of harness, wrestled away the splintered chariot box and retrieved its wheels, and raked the bloody, gouged earth of the practice field.

It was nearly sundown when Nerikkaili laid a hand on Tiwatipara's shoulder. "You've got to go now. The Old Women need to take Pawahtelmah to wash him and prepare him for cremation."

Tiwatipara got unsteadily to his feet, which had gone dead from sitting on them for so long. He felt as if a lifetime had passed since the accident. He looked blankly at his tunic and his twitching hands, which were black with his father's blood. Beyond the city walls, the sun was sinking into a pool of gore. The day grew suddenly chill, as it did at sunset on the high plateau, even in summer, and he shivered. Above them in the royal citadel, torches had been lit. The Upper City, sparsely inhabited except for the stables, sank into darkness and cricket song. Tiwatipara stared with tear-boiled eyes and empty heart at his father's body, stretched out still and motionless before him as it would lie upon the funeral pyre.

"I guess I need to tell my grandmother…" he began, a terrible reluctance making its way through the numbness that blanketed him. *Tell her that her only child is dead and that her husband is at death's gate. That I was the one who put together their chariot. That I have killed them with my carelessness—I, who was supposed to be on board with them but wasn't.* He wasn't sure he had enough courage. He felt as exhausted and without resources as some ageless, insensate stone.

But Nerikkaili said, "The *tawananna* has told her. She'll take care of the funeral arrangements. My father said the festival tomorrow will be put off for a day." He took hold of Tiwatipara's upper arm and stared him in the eye. The prince was tall, and Tiwatipara had to look up at him, his lids feeling almost too heavy to lift. "My condolences, Tiwatipara. This was a tragedy." The *tuhkanti* wasn't a particularly warm man, with his smooth diplomatic smile that didn't always touch his eyes and his powerful, polished voice, but he was decent. And despite his sarcasm, Nerikkaili was kind in a rough way—if he liked a fellow.

Tiwatipara nodded, grateful but unable to respond. Everything was sparkling in his tear-blurred sight as if there were a gauze between him and the world of the living. Around them, the Old Women, priestesses of the Queen of the Underworld, flowed in their black cloaks and veils. Two silently laid a shroud upon the ground and prepared to move Pawahtelmah's body. Another bore a censer, and the sickly, penetrating smell of incense mingled with blood rose up into Tiwatipara's face. The young man saw that flies had already gathered on his father's corpse, and he could hardly repress a gag.

A red wave of anger suddenly blasted through him at the sickening waste of death. He tore himself from his employer's grasp and stalked away, lurching like a drunk. No one stopped him. Zidanza seemed to have left with the others, and perhaps that was for the best. His sympathy might have been more than Tiwatipara could bear.

He made his way toward the barn, aware that it was pointless. The marvelous horses were dead. They would be fed to the king's hunting dogs or perhaps burned with Pawahtelmah. *My soul mate*, Tiwatipara thought with a bitter, silent laugh. *Both of us have died today, Storm Cloud.*

Where, then, should I go? Home, he decided. He and his father lived with his grandparents in the big ancestral house not far away, itself in the Upper City. He would go home to a sickbed and a corpse to be laid out and an old woman crushed by tragedy.

By the time he arrived, lamps had been lit throughout the house. Puduhepa—the *tawananna*—and some of her women were there, helping the household slaves prepare. Hattushili's young wife was Pawahtelmah's first cousin; Grandmother was her aunt, a Hurrian from Kizzuwatna, of a priestly family that had been royal back when Kizzuwatna was an independent kingdom. Tiwatipara could hear the queen's bright, efficient voice calling out orders, consoling in her brisk way, getting things done. He heard the wails of professional mourners, the *taptara* women. Behind him at the door, there was a stir as the Old Women arrived with his father's body, but Tiwatipara couldn't look at him again. He charged up the stairs as if he needed some momentum not to stop and flee into the night.

On the landing, he encountered Puduhepa. Her eyes were red, but she greeted him with a smile, holding out her arms. "My dear cousin," she cried. "Your father has made the Great Journey. I'm so sorry for you. May Lelwani, the Night Sun, give you strength." She folded him in her embrace. Any other time, he would have enjoyed finding himself in the arms of a beautiful woman like his cousin, who was only three years older than he—the same age as her husband's eldest son. Tiwatipara smelled her perfume, a piercing scent of roses, but it only added to his nausea.

"Where's my grandfather? Is he still alive?" Tiwatipara said, brusque to the point of rudeness. His stomach was revulsed and knotted. He could just keep control of it if he limited himself to a minimum number of words.

"He's alive," said Puduhepa somberly, "for now. Your grandmother is with him. Come."

She took him by the hand, led him to his grandparents' bedchamber, and pushed the door open gently. By the dim light of a lamp, Tiwatipara saw the bandaged, disfigured face of his grandfather, the drooping shadow that was his *hanna*—his grandmother—sitting at the bedside, her hands over her eyes, and all around, priests and doctors. Tiwatipara knelt at his grandmother's side and put an arm around her silently. He could feel her thin ribs swell and collapse as she drew a tremulous breath, but she said nothing and didn't uncover her eyes. He wasn't sure she even knew he was there. She had retreated to somewhere far away. She must have been bargaining with the gods.

The air was heavy with chanting and prayers along with the smoke of aromatics and the metallic-sweet stench of blood. One of the doctors was washing his hands. He turned at the entry of the two relatives.

"This is his grandson," said Puduhepa.

"We've tried to splint the broken limbs, but there's not much to be done if there are internal injuries." The doctor was grim, his jowls a mastiff-like puddle of flesh, his eyes deeply circled. "He's in the hands of the gods, young man. I've tried to explain to your grandmother, but I'm not sure she hears." He turned to the *tawananna*. "I've left a potion for her, too, my lady. She should take it before going to bed to help her sleep. And you, young man—watch out for fever or red around the broken skin. You don't want the demons to attack him while he's weakened. If there's a problem, call the Old Women. They know the proper prayers and sacrifices to make." He heaved a sigh and lumbered toward the door as if he couldn't wait to be gone and turn this hopeless case over to someone else.

Tiwatipara stood staring after his broad, stooped back with the longing of a child. *Make this be all right*. But it wasn't going to be so easy.

To see Tapala-tarhunta, the stoic old soldier, helpless and suffering was an inversion of the order of the world. Tiwatipara couldn't face his grandfather any longer, let alone the immobile statue that was his grandmother. Tiwatipara staggered to the door and down the stairs, unnaturally conscious of the clatter of his feet on the planks. *Hoofbeats.* He thought of the priceless horses and their dying screams. That was the noise he would make if he weren't a man, hemmed in by all the strictures of society. *Don't show fear before a battle. Don't cry when your father dies.*

Don't think about the fact that you were the one who put together the king's chariot and harnessed his team... He longed to let loose that wail of raw, animal anguish.

The Old Women had Pawahtelmah laid out in the salon, but mercifully, they had covered him with a piece of tapestry, his bow cradled on top where the crook of his arm would be. Tiwatipara preferred to remember him as he had looked alive—his face radiating the thrill of speed, the joy of flying, hair in the wind, feet braced, like a god riding down the lightning bolt. Yet only moments later... the irony was unendurable. The youth's nose burned, and he gripped his lip between his teeth to hold back the tears.

Tiwatipara dropped to a seat on the floor, his back against the wall, his arms crossed on his up-angled knees. The *taptara* women wailed and rocked, tearing at their hair, clawing their cheeks. It angered him that they were permitted such a display when the dead man had meant nothing to them. Where were the family members? His grandfather lay upstairs, probably dying. His grandmother seemed already to be dead, deaf to the world of the living. His cousin the *tawananna* organized things somewhere, and for that, he was grateful. Tiwatipara himself felt incapable of any rational thought or powers of organization. He wanted only to bawl out his fury at the injustice of the universe.

Wannumiyash. Fatherless. He had no father. The word *wannumiyash* seethed with meaning. It meant he was an object of pity. A disgrace. He was cursed. The gods had struck him to the ground, taken away from him his greatest treasure upon the black earth. He had never known his mother. Lots of people lost a mother, and that was sad enough. But a man without a father had no protector, no model, no name. No identity.

A shuffle at his side made him look up. Instead of taking a stool, Puduhepa had seated herself beside him, tucking her skirts neatly around her feet. She laid a gentle hand on his arm but said nothing. They looked at the draped outline of the dead man on the bier before them.

"Where do the dead go?" asked Tiwatipara dully. His cousin was a priestess; she would know.

"Pawahtelmah was a nobleman, so he will surely go to the Liliahmi, the meadows of the blessed. It will be like earth only far more wonderful, Tiwatipara. There will be horses, I'm certain." She looked at him with sweetness and pity, and she was so beautiful that he could have taken her right there on the floor in front of his father's body. A powerful desire not to die gripped him, a desire to cast his seed and create a past for some future being. Instead, he hung his head.

"Our Sun said he will officiate at the funeral tomorrow." She waited to see her cousin's reaction, and when he started, she said, "That's a profound honor. He esteems your family greatly and not just because your grandfather is my uncle. He's spoken many times about how he trusted and valued your father and Tapala-tarhunta before him— their skill with horses but also their intelligence. Their

26

integrity." Suddenly, her lip trembled. "Everybody loved Pawahtelmah."

The sight of tears was more than Tiwatipara could bear. He began to weep in deep shuddering sobs and buried his face in the hollow of his arms. "Forgive me," he struggled to say. "I ought to be a better soldier…"

But Puduhepa just squeezed his arm. After a moment, he heard the queen get to her feet. She said quietly, "You should marry, Tiwatipara. Keep the family line going."

Some time later, Tiwatipara heard hesitant footsteps enter the room and the rustle of clothing as someone seated himself beside him. He looked up through bleary eyes to see Zidanza at his side, the groom's face desolated with weeping. "Tipa, your father shouldn't have died," he stammered, before dissolving into tears. The two young men each put an arm around one another and sat side by side in grieving silence except for an occasional sniff. Finally, Zidanza gave his friend a squeeze of the shoulders and climbed to his feet with his usual awkwardness. Without another word, he made his way out with unsteady steps.

Night had fallen when the princess Lalantiwashha and her handmaids appeared at the door. Tiwatipara bounded up, ashamed to be seen in such a state of helplessness but not quite functional enough to conceal it. "My lady," he stammered. She was the king's daughter and Nerikkaili's full sister, a genteel adolescent with a delicate long pale face and a neck like a swan. "We're honored."

She took his hands. "My father told me of your family's tragedy, Tiwatipara. I wanted to assure you of my prayers," she said, but her heavy-lidded eyes were tenderer than mere courtesy demanded. She and Tiwatipara had watched one another with longing for years, ever since she was old enough to find boys interesting. They had exchanged few words and were rarely alone, but he realized suddenly that he loved her and that if any human comfort could ease him, it was hers. The princess couldn't stay long; it wouldn't be seemly at this hour. Still, behind the discreet curtain of her long hair, she leaned forward and kissed him. Her lips were light and cool and innocent. He clung to the memory of them as the one beautiful hope of this black night.

Almost immediately, the king entered. He must have accompanied his daughter. He said nothing, just folded Tiwatipara in his embrace and stood for a long time with his arms around him. The king's chest heaved in a slow, sad breath. Then he tousled Tiwatipara's hair with rough compassion and turned to pay his final respects to the dead man. After a long beat of heavy silence, Hattushili turned away, the muscles around his mouth bunched with the effort to control his lips. He and his daughter and servants departed without a sound, and Tiwatipara was alone once more.

Tiwatipara kept vigil that night. The charioteers and grooms came and went one by one. Prince Nerikkaili. Prince Zuzuhha, weeping aloud in broken sobs. At some point, Tiwatipara's grandmother drifted in and sat down, but she didn't seem to understand what was happening. She kept talking to her son in a puzzled tone as if he were alive. Then she drifted out again. Tiwatipara had the feeling that something terrible had happened to her—even worse than what had befallen her husband and son—and his stomach constricted.

He was afraid and alone. Exhaustion had eaten away

at his anger until nothing was left but a big void of dully throbbing loss. He would never see his father again. He tried not to indulge his memories, because that only made the pain more intense, but he couldn't help thinking of the great battle that had put the king on the throne three years before. He, his father, and his grandfather had all driven that day, each in a different chariot, the whole male population of their dwindling family offered to Runda, the god of chance, on a single throw. Grandfather had ridden with Prince Hattushili, for old times' sake, Tiwatipara with the pretender's eldest son, and Father with Nuwanza, an unranked brother of Hattushili.

Before the battle, Tiwatipara's father had told him—with his serious smile, full of love—that one of them might die that day, but it would be a death of honor and courage in the service of the rightful king. The Lord Wurukatte would accept it as a sacrifice, and it would make the survivors strong. They had all lived. They had been victorious.

How different a man was his grandfather. Tapala-tarhunta was a little stiff and old-fashioned. Who nowadays would call their son Pawahtelmah, the name of the father of Hatti's very first king? Tapala-tarhunta had about him something of the fatalistic courage of the horses themselves. He didn't ask questions or get anxious about things. If people died, they died. He had scolded his grandson more than once for worrying, wondering, asking about the afterlife, or crying over a dead horse. "You're a soldier, son. Just go fight. You live or you die. The gods have their reasons."

Tapala-tarhunta could be gruff. He *was* a soldier, a man who went to life as he went to war, and his creed left no room for hesitation, states of the soul, or what he considered softness of any kind. Tiwatipara wondered if his grandfather found him disappointing in some way or thought him unmanly because tears came so readily to his eyes. Or perhaps that brusqueness was just part of who Tapala-tarhunta was. Pawahtelmah had always buffered their interactions with his humor and clemency. But that was over—if Grandfather lived.

This endless day would be the dividing point of his life, Tiwatipara knew. Henceforth, everything would fall Before the Accident or After the Accident.

CHAPTER 2

Three Years Later

Pʀɪɴᴄᴇ Nᴇʀɪᴋᴋᴀɪʟɪ ᴅᴇᴄɪᴅᴇᴅ ᴛʜᴀᴛ ᴛʜᴇ southern vassal kingdoms in midsummer were only marginally more attractive than the Tenawa, the grim underworld where most people would spend their afterlife. Amurru wasn't the worst of it. It was hot, but its coastal location earned it some pleasant sea breezes, despite the humidity. They had made a long detour to Tsumur, the kingdom's capital, en route to Nuhasshe to arrest Urhi-tesshub, the ex-king of Hatti. And Nuhasshe was where he found himself at the moment. It was surely the most miserable place upon the black earth.

Passing by Tsumur had required some rather delicate diplomatic obfuscation, since the prince's interpreter on the journey was Benteshina, the former king of Amurru, who had been deposed for going over to Mizri years ago, just before the great battle at Kinza. Shapili, the man who now sat on the throne, had been placed there by Nerikkaili's uncle, and Benteshina—barely Nerikkaili's present age at the time—had been carted off to Hakpish, where he became Hattushili's honored prisoner and, eventually, friend. Or perhaps jester—the eccentric little Amurrite seemed to tickle his father's sense of humor.

The two of them made a laughable pair, in fact. Hattushili was as tall as any man in his kingdom and wonderfully ugly, with his equine face, suspicious hooded eyes, long nose, and mobile, muscular mouth. Benteshina, by contrast, was a really handsome man in the southern way. Even in his forties, he had thick dark hair. His eyes were big and black and twinkling with irreverent mischief in a triangular face enhanced by the cut of his close-trimmed beard. His smile was a gift from the gods for the ladies. But although strong and wiry and graceful as a fox, he was really small, even by Amurrite standards. Their companionship just proved that he and Hattushili had no vanity.

Benteshina had kept a prudently low profile during their sojourn at Shapili's court. He had not been introduced by name, and apparently, after fourteen years' absence, no one recognized the interpreter who spoke Amurrite like a native. He was probably in the city illegally. The situation was really quite amusing. Nerikkaili wondered what was going through the man's head as he found himself back in his own capital under such circumstances.

But after Amurru, they had crossed the mountains and the River Arantu eastward and northward into Nuhasshe, a formerly independent vassal kingdom now directly under control of the Hittite viceroy at Karkemish. Urhi-tesshub, having been kicked off the throne of Hatti, had been assigned to serve as its governor.

And that was where the desert heat had really struck

them. It was blindingly, sickeningly, murderously hot in the sun there. Nerikkaili and his men, in their woolen uniforms, had had to spend much of their time resting in the shade as soon as they passed the crest of the mountains that cut off the coastal winds. Their progress was slow; the prince thought he was going to lose men to the terrible breath of the Sun Goddess. He'd had to send messengers ahead to notify Urhi-tesshub of their approach to be sure water and food would be ready for them and their animals when they entered.

That had turned out to be a strategic mistake. Nerikkaili ground his teeth. *I had to provide for my men, didn't I?* He pictured himself saying that to his father, but he knew Hattushili wouldn't even give him a chance to explain when he appeared before him without Urhi-tesshub in tow. Because of course, by the time they had reached the capital, Urhi-tesshub had disappeared into the trackless desert, like the piece of treacherous shit he was. And the king was going to be extremely, incandescently angry, as only he could be.

The *tuhkanti* sighed with the bitterness of a young man who respected his father but didn't always agree with him. *What was Father thinking?* Urhi-tesshub was the nephew whose throne Hattushili himself had taken by force, and instead of eviscerating the deposed ruler and hanging him up as a warning somewhere, Hattushili had made him governor of Nuhasshe. From there, the ex-king had connived with the kingdom's allies—Karduniash, Mizri, even neutral Asshuriya—for support to regain his throne. Father had said he didn't want the Zuwalli Gods, avengers of violently ended life, coming after him—meaning, a lot of his supporters would be scandalized if Urhi-tesshub's handsome young blood was on his hands, maybe enough so that they would abandon the usurper. Because no matter how one couched it, that was what Hattushili was: the usurper.

Nerikkaili exhaled a cynical snort, and Tiwatipara, sipping a cup of the local wine at his side, looked up. "You say something, my lord?"

"Just snorted, Tipa. I was thinking of how that ass turd Urhi-tesshub came to be in Nuhasshe in the first place."

"Would that he were still there, eh?" The charioteer smiled humorlessly and considered the depths of his cup.

"Listen, friend. Go easy on that stuff," warned the prince. "It's stronger than beer. And I don't want you throwing up all night, because we need to get an early start."

"Where to, my lord? No one will admit to knowing where the pretender went."

"We'll find someone; don't worry. I sent Benteshina out with a bag of gold." The *tuhkanti* smirked. With the help of Runda, god of the hunt—and luck—they'd find him, all right.

His smile chilled when he looked back at Tiwatipara, who sat with his head low over his goblet, his face drawn and grim, his hair pulled back in a long braid against the heat. He had the look of an old man whose world had drained out around him. *Dear gods, the fellow is only twenty-five. What happened to all the twinkling good cheer and laughter that so endeared him to everyone?* Nirikkaili's driver had changed in some dreadful way since his father's death three years before, growing hard and impenetrable, he who had once been so open and innocent. Nerikkaili hoped that the pain of that terrible accident would someday wear away.

Even the hardest rock ground down with time. Meanwhile, a man who had once been a pleasant companion three years younger than himself slumped like a dour old vulture at his side.

Suddenly, the vulture said, "My lord, may I ask you something personal?"

"Why not?" the prince replied, taken a little aback. "If I don't want to answer, I won't."

Tiwatipara looked up at him, and there was a kind of vulnerability in his melancholy face. "Does Our Sun have any special plans for Lady Lalantiwashha?"

"Plans? You mean marriage? Probably, but I've never heard him speak of it, although she's nearly twenty. Why do you ask?" But then the obvious reason dawned on him, and Nerikkaili suppressed a smile. "Interested in her, are you? Ask the *tawananna;* she seems to be in charge of making matches. I'm sure my father would give her to you." His other second-rank full sisters had been married to local aristocrats. Puduhepa seemed to be saving most of the international alliances for her own daughters. All the honors fell to her children. The pattern was enough to lead a man with an *eshertu* mother—a second ranker, a *pahhurzi*, like him—to feel resentful. His stepmother was a desirable little piece, but it wouldn't take much to make him hate her.

Finally, he rose to his feet. "I'm going to grab a siesta. It's impossible to sleep at night with this heat. Don't drink yourself into a stupor." Nerikkaili turned away from his driver and was heading for the door of the common room of his apartments when his aide-de-camp appeared at the outer door.

"My lord," the man announced breathlessly. "There's a scout here from the viceroy's troop who says he's seen Lord Urhi-tesshub. He asks for an audience."

"Send him in, by the thousand gods. The sooner the better. And call Benteshina; we may need him to translate." *At last!* The prince returned to his seat at the table. Tiwatipara looked up at him, his bloodshot eyes asking for orders, and Nerikkaili told him, "You can stay. You'll be driving the route to wherever he's gone."

The scout was a sweaty, panting, wrung-out rag covered in dust that whitened him to the knees. He dropped in a reverence, fists to his chest, but Nerikkaili cut off the ceremonial greetings. As soon as Benteshina had slipped into the room, the prince urged the scout, "Speak, man. Where did you see him?"

The soldier reported at length and rapidly, and then Benteshina repeated, "He followed him into the desert, my lord, as you had commanded. But as you know, he lost him. Only soon thereafter, quite by chance, he saw a cloud of dust heading southwest, out of the desert, and sure enough, it was Urhi-tesshub, traveling with a very small party, maybe a half dozen men."

"Southwest?" cried Nerikkaili, relieved. "Then he's not heading to Mari. Or worse, to Asshuriya. Thank the gods; it must have been a ploy." Nerikkaili and his men would not have to track Urhi-tesshub across the Southern Desert in the full heat of summer. Besides, if he'd gone that route, and they hadn't caught him in time, he might have taken refuge with an unpredictable, ambitious neutral power that would no doubt think of many ways to make use of a disaffected Hittite prince. "Where, then?"

Benteshina transmitted the question then relayed the man's reply. "He thinks they're planning to rejoin the coast and head south into Egyptian territory, maybe crossing back at Qatna or Qadesh—Kinza, he means. Although they may go due south on the east side of the mountains and descend into Mizri through Amka. But that will be a harder journey and keep them in Hittite territory longer, so he'll probably cross the border near Gubla, on the coast."

"Good. Tell him he's dismissed. And give him this." Nerikkaili slipped off his bracelet and offered it to the scout, who accepted with eager gratitude. It was only silver, but it would still bring him a tidy sum.

As soon as the man had left, the crown prince said, "Well, gentlemen, what do you think? Will he go down through Amka or turn to the coast? Where do we stalk him?"

Benteshina mimed throwing the oracle sticks. "If I were on the run, I'd rejoin the coast. It's more densely settled, easier to lose oneself in. Six men isn't a big party; they can join any merchant's caravan and become invisible."

"Tiwatipara?"

The driver looked up openmouthed, no doubt not having expected to be consulted. "I would go down the east side of the mountains, my lord. They can make good time at twilight, when the heat is less, and hole up during the day. It's virtually empty desert, and nothing would stop them from flying."

Nerikkaili chuckled dryly. "This is why kings end up making unilateral decisions." He flattened his palms on the table with a decisive bang. "Here's what we'll do. We'll send the viceroy's men to the coast to await him somewhere south of Batruna, fingering every caravan. If he's planning to cross at Gubla, they'll get him, unless he's disguised in some way. I'm hoping he's too vain to resort to that. We, on the other hand—you and I, Tiwatipara—will watch the roads outside of Qatna and Kinza. Maybe we can split the men to cover more ground. The terrain is open. We should be able to see any group approaching, especially at speed. And all eyes alert at twilight."

Tiwatipara bowed and left, more or less steady on his feet. Nerikkaili called Benteshina back.

"You know this part of the world, Lord Benteshina. Do you think the locals are likely to help Urhi-tesshub—hide him, feed him, whatever?"

The little man grinned, white teeth fully deployed. "For gold, my prince, they'll trim his toenails and wipe his bum. But in their hearts, I think the southern kingdoms have no great love for the former king. His policies fell heavily on them, whereas your father is quite well-thought-of. He hasn't had time to irritate them."

"And that means, in practical terms, that if I pay them more, they'll betray Urhi-tesshub, right? He can't have much in the way of gold. We've interviewed his treasurer; he wasn't party to the governor's plan to escape."

"They'll betray him, all right, my lord. You can't trust these people."

Benteshina's expression was so comically smug—even though he was one of "these people"—that Nerikkaili laughed in spite of himself. Only a moment afterward did it occur to him that the Amurrite might be mocking the self-satisfied men of Hatti.

"Maybe I should send you with the viceroy's men. You

could dress up as an old beggar or something and watch for my cousin. I doubt if the viceroyal troops know what he looks like. Although," he added by way of good-humored revenge, "he'll certainly be taller than 'these people.'"

"That would be a pleasure, my lord. My *small* talents have lain idle for too long."

"To it, then, friend. Tiwatipara and I will take a few men to cover the border of the desert. We'll leave this evening. Urhi-tesshub will have gotten well ahead of us in any case."

The little Amurrite bowed and bounced out like a puppy too long enclosed, eager for the sheer joy of mischief. Nerikkaili called his aide-de-camp. "Tell the men to harness up. We're moving out as soon as the chariots are ready."

The horses stamped and blew, swishing their tails against the flies, cropping the poor, salty desert vegetation with rustling lips. Tiwatipara, the worse for his late hours, leaned on the rail of the chariot, but his fists were alertly closed around the lines. At his side, Prince Nerikkaili, shading his eyes with a hand, stared into the corrugated russet distance. The air was already shimmering with heat at this early hour. To the east, the Sun Goddess appeared, enormous, firing the rusty sky with brightness. Tiwatipara greeted her glumly. *Lady Wurushemu, you who see all, my father will never again look upon your face.* Apathy covered him like a heavy woolen blanket so that he seemed to wade through life. The constant heat was draining, and he had a headache from his overindulgence the night before. It was almost a permanent condition these days. His father would not be proud of him. His grandfather certainly wasn't proud.

Against all likelihoods, the old man had lived. It had taken Tapala-tarhunta a long time to get back on his feet again. He was still badly crippled and always would be, hauling himself around with laborious determination on crutches. The strong, straight, handsome old soldier he had been Before the Accident was no more, yet in more important ways, Tapala-tarhunta was unchanged. Tiwatipara supposed that was a measure of his grandfather's honesty—he was so ruggedly himself all the way to the core that even the ruin of his body, his pride, and his manhood hadn't destroyed him. Whereas Tiwatipara… he hardly knew the man he had become. There seemed to be nothing left of the fun-loving boy. Nowadays, he took even his pleasures grimly. He and Zidanza made a joyless pair at their seats in the garrison inn—the charioteer glowering and his friend slumped and dull, like a dog with his tail drooping. Tiwatipara heaved a sigh, which he hoped the prince would interpret as physical weariness and not weariness of life.

"Look, Tiwatipara," Nerikkaili cried suddenly. "Over there, to the left. There's a cloud of dust. Can you see what it is?"

They were on a high slope of stony ground with a long view of the undulating desert, rock strewn and inhospitable. To the right lay the foothills of the eastern mountains. Somewhere in that direction were the Arantu River and the necklace of border towns grown rich off inland caravans— Tunip, Qatna, and Kinza. The pale traces of desert roads scratched the ground here and there. Far away, almost as far as his gaze could stretch, there was indeed a mist of dust that marked some movement. Tiwatipara could hardly believe the former king had not made it farther before his pursuers caught up to him. He squinted to sharpen his vision, regretting the night's debauch. "It could be a herd of goats… but no, they're larger. Dark things… horses, my lord. Surely horses." He turned to Nerikkaili. "It must be them."

"Catch them, Tiwatipara. If you can possibly overtake them, do it."

The prince signaled to the men behind him to move out, and Tiwatipara yelled and clucked the team into action. The ground was rocky and rippled, full of little runlets where spring's rare storms sent floods washing over the hills. Its surface was pocked with small, tough grasses and wiry tufts of silver-leafed plants. Chert gravel strewed their path, sharp as potsherds, slipping and clattering beneath the horses' hooves as they picked up speed. Down the slope they flew, no road beneath them but just the treacherous breast of the desert. The beasts were strong and sure-footed. Urged on by their driver, they knew but one law: *Run! Run like the wind!*

The ground below them was growing level. Tiwatipara leaned into the rail, head low, and loosed his whip over the horses' backs. *Run!* The chariot rocked and rumbled, bouncing over stones and washes, but the charioteer's crouching legs took the shocks, and his balance was that of an eagle on the wind. A strange sense of exaltation crept over Tiwatipara—not just the usual exhilaration of speed but also an intuition that if he could just drive fast enough, he might pierce the wall between this world and the next.

All his sorrows might end in a glorious strike of lightning, and he would see his father again.

He couldn't make out their quarry so far ahead, now that the ground was lower, but their pursuit had fallen away in the charioteer's mind. He was dimly aware of Nerikkaili at his side, crying, "Shaushga's tits, man! Slow down!" but he didn't slow. Far from it. He poured his will into the horses; their strides lengthened, and they ceased to touch the ground. They flew. They flew. He whipped them again, his hair lashing, his eyes glazed and blind. *Run! Fly! Strike!*

"Slow down, I said!" roared the *tuhkanti*, and he fought the whip out of Tiwatipara's grip one-handed, hanging onto the rail. The chariot lurched off balance as the driver struggled; the horses began to throw their heads and slow.

"No!" cried Tiwatipara in anguish. "Faster!"

But Nerikkaili backhanded him across the face and jerked the lines out of his hands. Tiwatipara fell to his knees, stunned by the pain, and fear fluttered in his stomach as he struggled for balance, clutching at the struts. The horses were bouncing to a stop; the chariot wheels hopped over rocks and dropped to the ground again. Tiwatipara climbed to his feet, breathless and dazed, the throbbing of his cheek like a rope that dragged him back to the moment once more. He seemed to see the desert around him for the first time.

Nerikkaili, his face crimson, his eyes wide with terror and fury, reined in the team brutally. As soon as they ceased moving, he turned on his driver. His powerful voice loosed itself on the younger man like the lash of a whip. "You bastard. What was that all about? You could have gotten us killed."

Tiwatipara didn't know what to say. He seemed to have fallen from a height and was breathless and confused. "I… I… something came over me."

"*Something* indeed. By the thousand gods, Tiwatipara, you must be mad. I've seen you take some pretty dangerous chances in recent years, but that was folly of the first rank." Nerikkaili jumped down from the box, quivering with rage and the tension of death narrowly averted. "I know I said to catch Urhi-tesshub—but at the cost of our lives? What sort of stupidity would that have been? Damn it, man, I thought I could trust you." He was breathing hard, avoiding his driver's eyes.

Tiwatipara stood limp in the box until his wilting legs could no longer bear him. He sat down on the edge and put his face in his hands. "I don't know what… I just wanted…" His eyes were suddenly blind with tears. "I just wanted to see my father. If only I could go fast enough, if only…"

"If only you could die?" finished the prince in a blanched voice.

Tiwatipara nodded brokenly, sobs shaking him. *What was I thinking? Dear gods, forgive me. Pihasshasshi, my lord, forgive me.*

No one spoke. The horses blew their warm breath into the desert air and cropped grass. The cicadas razzed, uncaring. Tiwatipara's sobs gradually ceased and gave way to sniffs. "Forgive me, my lord," murmured the charioteer to his patron god and to the prince. He mopped his face on his forearm. "I could have killed the horses…"

"You could have killed you and me." Nerikkaili's anger was ebbing, his voice no longer raw with fear. Tiwatipara looked up at him and saw that his face, while still red, was

43

troubled, his arched eyebrows crooked. "What's wrong with you these days, Tiwatipara? You haven't been yourself for a long time. Since the accident."

"Forgive me."

"You're forgiven, you're forgiven. But I don't know that I want to be in the box with a driver who wants to die. Doesn't it honor Pawahtelmah more to live and carry on his name?"

A huge knot of shame choked Tiwatipara, and he fought to get past it, to say what he needed to say without letting his voice shake too badly. He tried to sound like a good soldier, not hiding his guilt but admitting it honorably. "I caused his accident, my lord. I harnessed those horses. I put together Our Sun's chariot. I should have been on board with my father and grandfather—"

"But I sent you off. I saved your life. Is this my gratitude?" The prince turned away pensively. "The Gulshesh didn't want you to die, Tiwatipara. Isn't that clear? Your thread wasn't ready to be cut."

"I killed my mother, too, my lord," the charioteer continued in a flat, trembling voice. "She died bearing me. Both my parents, dead at my hands. How can the Lady of Arinna bear to look upon me? The gods should wipe me from the face of the black earth." He sat, head hanging, looking at his hands as if he'd never seen them before. His shoulders sagged with the crushing weight of his guilt.

Nerikkaili demanded, "Who are you to give the gods orders? If they—"

A thundering of hooves and wheels behind them made the prince and his driver look up. Only now had the other two chariots caught up with them. "Have we lost them, my lord?" called one of the soldiers as they drew abreast in a storm of gravel and dust.

"Probably," said the prince in a level voice, trying to pull his wind-tangled hair out of his face with his fingers. "Go a little farther to see if you can spy them, but I'm afraid they had too much of a lead to catch."

"Sorry, my lord. We just couldn't keep up."

"No sane man could. Go." They clattered off, and Nerikkaili and his charioteer were alone again.

There was a strained silence as the two men mounted the box. Tiwatipara took up the leads with a questioning look at his employer, wondering if Nerikkaili trusted him to drive. He wasn't sure he could trust himself anymore. *Perhaps my life as a* hashtanuri *is over.* This thought, which lay like a leaden rock under his heart, paining him at every breath, had haunted him for a while. But what else could he do? Driving horses was all he knew. He couldn't read or write and therefore had no future in the chancery. Who was this pitiful wreck of a man who had actually considered asking for Lady Lalantiwashha's hand? Grandfather would laugh him to shame.

"Take us back to Nuhasshe, Tiwatipara," said Nerikkaili dryly. "Alive."

When they reached the governor's palace in Nuhasshe, Nerikkaili discovered that Benteshina had returned as empty-handed as he and Tiwatipara. The little Amurrite had lost his beard; even the backs of his hands had been cleared of hair. Clean-shaven, he was as handsome as a small, mischievous god.

"What happened to you, Benteshina?" The prince smirked. "Get caught in an abrasive dust storm?"

"Just a bit of disguise, my lord. I figured no one would suspect a woman selling buns. I heard quite a lot but nothing about the passage of anyone who might be Urhi-tesshub." Benteshina bared his pretty white teeth and pretended to simper like a girl. "Buns also make very good… you know." He held his fists in front of his chest.

The prince snorted, unable to keep a straight face. "You're too convincing, except for the shadow on your jaw. I hope no one subjected you to ungentlemanly behavior."

"Not at all. This girl knows how to fight."

"Well, welcome back to your life as a male. You didn't see Urhi-tesshub because he was headed down the eastern side of the mountains, through Amka. Unfortunately"—Nerikkaili grew grim as he thought yet again of how his father was going to receive this news—"he was too far ahead of us to catch, despite Tiwatipara's breakneck efforts. And I mean *breakneck*."

"Any way to stop him at the border?" Benteshina asked.

"I sent some of the viceroy's men down there to try, but he has a huge lead by now. He's gone into Mizri's territory for sure. Won't they be delighted, the sheep fuckers."

"I believe it's cats they fuck down there, my lord. And crocodiles."

Nerikkaili stifled a snort of laughter, not wanting to egg on his father's friend any further. He let the thought of Hattushili's wrath chill his merriment. Settling into diplomatic pomposity, he said, "Then we're homeward bound, Benteshina. Pack up your dresses, and let's go."

Prince Nerikkaili stood in his father's antechamber, upright and, to all appearances, relaxed but by no means easy in his heart. He fully anticipated a scouring at the king's notoriously ungentle hands. The prince had failed in his mission. Urhi-tesshub had escaped him. Nerikkaili's thumbs were hooked in his belt in a gesture of manly insouciance. Still, he couldn't prevent his fingers from breaking into an uneasy tattoo against the studded leather from time to time.

Needing air, he heaved a deep breath. Behind him, the outside door opened. The prince turned, his heart beating suddenly faster. His father stood framed in the opening.

The king's brows contracted when Nerikkaili caught his eye. "Well, Nerikkaili," he growled in his rough voice. "Where is the pretender? Chained up in the stable? A prisoner in my bedchamber? Playing knucklebones in the soldiers' mess?"

Nerikkaili's stomach clenched. He dreaded what this sarcasm predicted. He took another deep breath and said frankly, "He got away, Father."

"So I'm told," the king snarled. He drew near to his son with the carnivorous grace of a grizzled old lion. Nerikkaili saw, with a mental cringe, the green fire in his father's eyes. The prince straightened and dropped his hands to his sides as if at a military review. Hattushili stopped almost nose to nose with him, his long jaw outthrust, watching him murderously from under heavy lids.

"Was it so difficult a task, son? He was the governor of a province. Could you not see him in audience and take him prisoner? You outrank him; his men wouldn't have opposed you."

"That may be true, Father, but in fact—"

"In fact, you gave him warning of your intention, and he had time to flee before you arrived."

Nerikkaili marveled—not for the first time—at how his father seemed to know exactly what had happened thousands of leagues away before he, the perpetrator, had even made his report. He had a suspicion the source, on this occasion, was Benteshina. *I should have known the little jester would be sent along as a spy*, he thought.

Aloud, he said with a sigh of resignation, "That is unfortunately true, My Sun."

"I'm 'My Sun' now, hah? No more 'Father dear,' I see." The king's ugly mouth twisted in disgust. He turned away and drifted over to the ewer of water that sat on a chest against the wall. Nerikkaili watched uneasily as his father poured a goblet of water and lifted it to his lips. "I counted on you, son. When I send you out to accomplish something like this, it's as if I go myself. When you fail, it's me the world sees failing. Can you grasp that?"

"Yes, My—Father."

Nerikkaili jerked in surprise as the king dashed the goblet's water in his son's face and roared, "Is it too much to ask of you to bring back one rotten prisoner? Where do you think he's off to now, hah? Mizri? Karduniash? How do you propose to get him?" Hattushili stalked toward the prince and leaned over him, shouting in his face until the younger man had to shrink away. Nerikkaili ground his teeth with the effort to take his correction like a soldier and not shout back. He let the water drip down his face, resisting the urge to wipe it out of his eyes. "That means that my failure—your failure—has made me the laughingstock of my peers. This must not happen again, Nerikkaili. Do you understand? My position on the throne is too precarious to risk destabilizing it by making stupid mistakes. This must not happen again."

"I understand… Father." The prince swallowed with difficulty.

"And *will* it happen again?"

"It will not, Father."

The king drew back, his face still scarlet, his expression still dangerous, but Nerikkaili reckoned the worst of the storm had passed. He had acquitted himself pretty well, even though his heart was still hammering with the humiliation. At least he hadn't succumbed to the temptation to make excuses for himself. That was the biggest mistake of all, the thing his father couldn't abide.

Hattushili poured himself another cup of water, and this time, he drank it to the bottom with a lip smack of satisfaction then turned to his son once more. His features had relaxed into their normal state of wry evaluation. "So, give me a complete report."

The prince risked wiping his face and dared to breathe. He recounted his visit to Nuhasshe, the scouting expedition of Benteshina, and the precipitate journey through the desert with Tiwatipara. The king's features took on a peculiar expression between pride and sorrow at the latter news. He said with a sigh, "He feels he has nothing to live for."

"He admitted as much. He said he had killed his father and his mother and there wasn't much reason for him to darken the face of the black earth." Nerikkaili thought he could probably ask for a new driver at this point without looking cowardly. He wanted to keep the request well separated from the failure of his mission. "I told him that whoever he was carrying shouldn't be much of an asset to the battle if they didn't get to the battleground alive."

The king tugged thoughtfully at his nose.

"So," Nerikkaili continued, "I'd like to ask for a new driver, at least until he works this out."

Hattushili pursed his lips. "Of course. It's only prudent. I may be able to put an end to his gloom—or not. But at least I've got an assignment for the lad so he doesn't feel he's been put out to pasture." He looked up at his son and clapped him on the shoulder, all rancor forgotten. "You can tell him that."

"I will, my father," said Nerikkaili, relieved that his moment of disgrace had ended.

They both turned as the outer door creaked. Hattushili opened his mouth to blast the newcomer, but it was Benteshina. The little man looked quickly back and forth between the king and the *tuhkanti*. "Oh, sorry. Didn't mean to interrupt. I'll come back."

"No, no," Hattushili reassured him. "Come in. I'm my own doorkeeper this morning." He shot his friend an evil grin and held his fists up before his chest.

Benteshina advanced, smiling demurely and tilting his head like a girl, a coy finger to his lips. He nodded to Prince Nerikkaili with a knowing sparkle in his black eyes and curtsied to the king. Then, his normal self again, he asked, "All is well?"

The prince gave him a frigid smile. *No thanks to you,*

you little fox. Aloud, he said coolly, "Yes. I just reported to Our Sun the results of our mission to Nuhasshe."

"It seems our dear nephew has gone over the border to Washmuaria's friendly bosom." The king chuckled darkly. "Where he has no doubt just begun his machinations with our fellow kings abroad. If he had shown himself this clever while he was in the arms of Halmashuit, he might still be there."

Benteshina protested with an extravagant gesture of his hands. "Oh, no, My Sun. The Lady Shaushga wanted you on the throne. Nothing Ulmi-tesshub could've done would have prevented the will of the gods from being accomplished."

Nerikkaili watched the little man with a mixture of disgust and grudging admiration. The ex-king of Amurru certainly knew how to play the fawning courtier. The prince found it hard to believe that his father, no fool, would fall for such transparent flattery.

In fact, Hattushili observed dryly, "No, not even if I had sat on my hands, hah. The *lupanni* would have dropped from heaven right onto my head."

"It would indeed, My Sun. And the *kalmush* forced its way into your hand."

"You little piece of dog shit!" The king let out his hearty, gurgling laugh. "I can't figure out why I put up with you!"

"I make everyone around me feel smarter, My Sun." Benteshina winked impudently at Nerikkaili.

But the king laid a hand on his friend's shoulder and grew suddenly serious. "All jesting aside, Benti, we need to think about getting you back on your own throne now. That turd Shapili, whom my brother put in your place, hasn't proved to be much of an asset. Wouldn't you have thought he'd have had some inkling of the whereabouts of Urhi-tesshub, right there on his doorstep?"

The other men agreed, although Nerikkaili wasn't sure he liked where this was leading. He didn't have much confidence in Benteshina, even though the Amurrite's loyalty seemed to be beyond reproach. *But then*, the prince thought, *why am I ambivalent about the fellow's capabilities? He's certainly smart enough. Have I let myself fall for his buffoon act? One might even say that it's political brilliance on the rascal's part to let himself be so underestimated.*

Benteshina was smiling smugly. He had to be happy to think his fourteen-year exile was ending. The king's eyes sparkled back at him. He slapped Benteshina on the back and, leaning over him, said in a small, juicy voice such as one might use with a young boy, "How would you like that, little fellow?"

The Amurrite clapped his hands like a delighted child, but he was no doubt serious when he said, "I would like that very much, My Sun. I think I've more than paid for my costly bad decision."

"Well, then, we'll get this going. And my girl Gasshulawiya is coming of age. We can marry you to her, and then your heirs will be princes of Hatti. That should settle your legitimacy." The king turned to Nerikkaili. "How old are you now, son?"

"I'm twenty-eight, Father," the prince replied in his silky baritone.

"Time you were married, too. Past time." Hattushili poked his son's ribs in good-natured malice. "Sorry to put an end to your bachelor adventures, my boy, but we have alliances to make."

A flutter of hope lifted within Nerikkaili's breast. He had been waiting for years for his father to say this—for twelve years, ever since he'd come of age. He knew his father was scouting for just the right princess who would knit just the right family ties. Marriage was the surest guarantee of alliance, after all. *Will it be with Karduniash? The Egyptians don't marry their daughters out, but they've been known to send a court lady upon occasion. Will it be Alashiyah? Ahhiyawa? Less important, of course, but links could still be useful. Or even Asshuriya?*

"Benteshina," said the king. "What would you say to marrying one of your daughters to my firstborn?"

Nerikkaili's jaw dropped, and his heart went cold as a clinker. He almost cried aloud in protest.

"It would be a great honor, My Sun. Ummi-hibi is seventeen and a beautiful girl who is sure to please the *tuhkanti*." Benteshina beamed at Nerikkaili, who struggled to control his expression. Disappointment threatened to rise up and drown him. *Benteshina's daughter?* The daughter of a vassal would sit upon the throne of Hatti with him and in time become the *tawananna*? He felt as if his father had slapped him in the face. His cheeks were burning.

"What do you think of that, eh, son?" said the king, watching him closely. "A beautiful girl of seventeen."

A fucking Amurrite vassal. What do you think I think? But Nerikkaili bowed as if honored, saying nothing and just managing to keep his suave mask in place. He had a terrible feeling that this had something to do with his failure in Nuhasshe. He was being punished. His father had lost confidence in him.

"Whom else do we have unmarried? How old is Lalantiwashha now?"

"Twenty," said Nerikkaili stiffly.

"I'm thinking of giving her to Manapa-kurunta in Sheha-River Land. He's a widower. But the *tawananna* will need to pass on that." The king elbowed Benteshina with a knowing chuckle. It flittered through Nerikkaili's mind that he should say something about Tiwatipara's suit at this point, but he was too upset and wasn't sure he could keep the rancor out of his voice.

The king turned to Nerikkaili. "We'll talk later, son. I assume Benti came here for a reason, so let us palaver, hah? Your stepmother will be in her element with all these marriages to arrange."

The prince felt as if he carried a great frozen stone in his stomach. "My father." Nerikkaili bowed formally. "Lord Benteshina." He tried not to imbue the Amurrite's name with the fury it inspired in him at the moment. He rose from his reverence and exited with dignity.

CHAPTER 3

WINTER HAD FALLEN UPON THE high plateau where the kings of Hatti Land ruled from their aerie in the rocks, although the position of the sun said it was only fall. Hattushili's campaigns were over for the year, shut down by the early snow. Now he could turn his attention to the political details that kept his kingdom strong and himself on the throne.

It was relatively rare to find the king's wife in the women's quarters by day, because the *tawananna* spent her daytime hours at work as a man would. Anyone looking for Puduhepa might well try the chancery, her office, the council chamber, one of the numerous audience halls, or maybe even the king's apartment in a tête-à-tête with him. Or perhaps she would be managing the royal nursery, where her own children and others of the king's begetting—plus young aunts and uncles and endless ranks of cousins born of cadet lines—were brought up.

In short, Hattushili's wife was never idle, and he loved that about her. She was a busy little bundle of energy and ambition and emotion—a white-hot drop of ball lightning rolling through the halls, making people's hair stand on end. Hattushili laughed at the mental image. In fact, Puduhepa was closeted with their eldest daughter that morning. Gasshulawiya had come of age, and her mother was instructing her in all the things a sheltered thirteen-year-old needed to know about life and marriage. The king was curious about the process itself, so different from the way in which royal sons were introduced to adult life—a ceremonial visit to the garrison brothel—but he also wanted to give Gasshulawiya the news about her betrothal to Benteshina.

He brushed aside the hovering eunuch chamberlain and let himself into the *tawananna*'s apartment. It was warm and dark and cozy as a womb inside, the shutters drawn, the braziers crackling cheerfully against the wintry morning chill. The two women were sitting knee to knee in the middle of the room, where it was freest from drafts. They both looked up, and Hattushili recognized with pleasure the light that sprang into their eyes as they saw him.

"My Sun!" cried Puduhepa.

"My father!" cried Gasshulawiya at the same time, and they simultaneously rose to their feet.

"Morning, dear girls." He pecked his daughter on her cheek with a fatherly one-armed embrace and gave his wife a heartier squeeze. "So, your mother is teaching you all the secrets of womanhood, is she?"

"Yes, my father." Gasshulawiya grinned and blushed, dropping her eyes.

They must be juicy secrets, the king thought affectionately. His daughter wasn't the girly, blushing sort; she was a steady, thoughtful young personage with the good sense of a much older woman. He gazed at her fondly. She was his spat-out image, alas—big-boned, tall, and thin with a long, homely face and hooded eyes. Almost all his children looked like him. Their resemblance was so conspicuous that when the *tawananna*'s second boy was born with his mother's beauty, the king had teased, "Who was this one's father?" But in fact, he trusted his wife's fidelity implicitly. He might feel insecure about his legitimacy on the throne but never about his manhood.

The king tried to picture tall Gasshulawiya at little Benteshina's side and suffered a small twinge of conscience. He didn't want either of them to feel ridiculous, but political necessity took precedence over the sensitivities of individuals. Puduhepa herself looked tiny beside her barely pubescent daughter—and extremely desirable, with her perfect face and voluptuous curves. The Lady Shaushga had certainly done well by him...

The thought of his naked wife had distracted him. Forcing his mind back to the moment, he addressed his daughter. "I have some excellent news for you, my dear. You'll be married to Benteshina this summer and go with him to be queen of Amurru."

Gasshulawiya's drab face brightened touchingly— Benteshina was a handsome little bastard—but the *tawananna*'s expression of expectation froze into reproach.

"Oh, thank you, Father," cried the girl. "I promise I'll do everything in my power to be a good queen."

She threw her arms around him, and he hugged her, overcome with tenderness. *I may have my vices, but I do love my children, as the gods are my witnesses.*

Puduhepa was making *Why?* gestures behind the girl's back, but Hattushili pretended not to understand. "It's a very important kingdom, a key to our foreign policy. Both of you will be my eyes to the south. You'll watch over the border with Mizri; you'll look out for that misbegotten turd Urhi-tesshub if he should show his nose in our territory, and you'll keep our shipping lanes open. I can't be sure of Ugarit, with their boy king. It depends on who's advising him and his mother." He glanced up at Puduhepa, whose eyes were bright with anger, her lips compressed. *Storm brewing in the east*, he thought with a silent chuckle. She was irresistible when she was furious.

"So, Gasshulawiya, my love, I need to have a word with your mother. Can you leave us for a bit? We'll talk more about your marriage, all right?" Hattushili kissed the top of her head perhaps for the last time; she was a woman now, and as soon as she married, she would be capped with the *kurasshar* and veil. He hugged her again, and she hustled away. "Wonderful girl," he said proudly.

But Puduhepa, not to be deflected, cried, "A vassal? Why, Hattushili? She's the Great Lady, by the thousand gods." Her cheeks blazing, she stalked over to the king and stared up, quivering, into his eyes, so far above hers.

"My dear, he's also my best friend and a singularly important figure in our foreign policy."

"He's crazy," she spat. "He's worse than a juggler at a festival, always prancing around, talking in funny voices—"

"He's hilarious. For that reason alone, Giya should enjoy her marriage."

"But she's a serious girl, and your miniature friend is a buffoon."

58

"Then they'll be perfect together. Complement one another."

"You have an answer for everything, don't you?" she snapped, turning away in disgust. Her cheeks were lit with red flames. "You've been planning this all along without telling me—"

"Because I knew you'd object, frankly." He grinned at her back.

As if she felt his eyes upon her, she whirled. "If only you'd bothered to consult me beforehand, my dear, we could have done so much better by her."

He was *my dear* again, he saw with approval. The king extended a hand and drew his wife to him. She fit neatly beneath the arm he draped around her shoulder. "Let me repeat what I said to her: Amurru is extremely important to us right now. Let the two of them breed some Hittite kings down there, and I, for one, will breathe a lot easier."

Puduhepa's anger was abating. She grumbled, "He's in his forties, and Giya's only thirteen," but she looked up at him contritely as soon as the words came out of her mouth.

"And I was in my forties when I married a fourteen-year-old. Was that so bad? Hah?" Hattushili asked, challenging her with a suggestive arch of his eyebrow. "This alliance is important, as you'd realize if you didn't dislike Benteshina so much. So important that I'm giving his daughter to Nerikkaili."

She stared at him, digesting this, a smile starting to grow on her lips. "Shaushga bless you, my husband. *That* was brilliant." They laughed together uproariously. "How did Nerikkaili take it?"

"He bowed obediently and never said a word,

which means he's furious." Hattushili bared his teeth in amusement, then he grew suddenly sober. "Poor lad. He's starting to figure out what's going on, and I think he believes it's because he let Urhi-tesshub escape. I don't want him to feel I've demoted him because I'm disappointed in him."

"He'll be *tuhkanti* for years yet. Why shouldn't he be married into such an *important* vassal dynasty?" She was beaming now. The replacement of Nerikkaili with her own son as crown prince would be her triumph. Hattushili had in mind to wed Tashmi-sharrumma into the royal family of Karduniash, a vastly more prestigious match. But not until the boy was older, of course. That would be the public revelation of his destiny.

"Pleased, are you, my love?" he teased, tipping her face up to him.

"Yes, thank you, My Sun." She melted against him, and he felt Shaushga's power stirring in his loins.

He kissed her roughly. "This is a victory for your little boy, isn't it?"

"*Our* little boy," she chided him. "You love him, too, don't you?"

"Of course I do. But I also love Nerikkaili. The issue isn't who I love most. It's who will make a stronger successor—who will secure the most support when I go down the Great Way. Half the kingdom will oppose either one of them just because they're my sons. That dog shit Arma-tarhunta's spawn, for one, will reject anyone I've so much as looked at."

Puduhepa drew away, all business now. "You're right, of course, and that's precisely why it has to be Tashmi-sharrumma. He's first rank."

"I know, I know. That's why a lot of people supported me over Urhi-tesshub."

"And then there's our Ulmi-tesshub…" she said uneasily. "He and Tashmi have to stay friends. And no one must tell him his rank."

The king stared into space, suddenly thinking of another royal secret. But he said only, "Speaking of Tashmi-sharrumma, my dear, I want him to take driving lessons."

Puduhepa's eyes widened. "Already? He's not even twelve."

"He's strong for his age. He can do it. And I want him to drive for Ulmi-tesshub when he's old enough. Ulmi is of an age to go to war now."

The *tawananna* pursed her lips dubiously. "Not even sixteen…"

"But he will be soon. Almost a man." He shrugged. "That's what king's sons do, my dear. He certainly has no aptitude for the chancery."

"I just hope we aren't training him to take arms against Tashmi-sharrumma." Her eyebrows crumpled in anxiety, and she wrung her hands. That was not a gesture typical of Puduhepa.

"This is why I want 'em in the same chariot as soon as possible. Let 'em face death together, relying on one another. A man and his driver form an unbreakable bond."

Then Hattushili thought of Nerikkaili and how he had asked to have Tiwatipara transferred. Normally, that would have fallen under the jurisdiction of the chief groom, Zuzuhha. But Nerikkaili must have observed that his father had a particular guilt-fueled relationship with the orphaned young charioteer and wanted to guide his career—although the *tuhkanti* didn't know the real reason why.

Puduhepa's mouth pursed a little mutinously, but she mastered herself. "If you think it's time, then do it, My Sun."

"I'm going to have Tiwatipara teach him."

She stared up at him, mouth ajar. "I thought you said he'd been acting strange since Pawahtelmah's death. Nerikkaili said he tried to get them killed in Nuhasshe."

"He had a good cry with Nerikkaili and let out all the guilty feelings he's had. He thought he was responsible for Pawahtelmah's death. I'm sure he'll be calmer now. And he won't be driving at a breakneck speed across the maquis with the boys. They'll just be trotting around the field with a couple of well-trained mares."

She bit her lip and fell into silence. Hattushili put his two forefingers into the corners of her mouth and pulled them up into a smile. Puduhepa pushed him away, grumpy at first, but she finally laughed. "If you think it's safe, My Sun, do what you have in mind."

"Walk back with me, my love, and we can talk. I have a meeting with the council after lunch, and I assume you'll be there." He steered her to the door, and they passed together into the court of women.

It was damned cold, and his eyes began to water as soon as the wind hit them. He wrapped an arm around the *tawananna*. They were a mismatched couple if there ever was one. A eunuch barreling in through the gate fell precipitously to his knees when he saw the king and queen making their way toward him like a lopsided quadruped. Hattushili gave a low chuckle. Maidservants here and there dropped as they passed, murmuring a ragged chorus of "My Sun, My Sun," to which the king responded with an amused nod.

"Is this what you want for our son, my dear? He seems like a shy lad; I can't imagine that he'll enjoy it." He had to hold back his long stride to match hers, and that, with the nose-freezing wind, left him a little breathless.

"Not like you do, my love, I'm sure," his wife said primly to the clicking of her little steps. "But then, one isn't a king for one's pleasure, is one?"

Nerikkaili sat, glum, at a corner table of the inn, where he could see those who entered. Mostly, it was the usual cheerful crowd of officers, grooms, charioteers, and an occasional scribe from the chancery seeking companionship and good beer after a long day of work. He nodded, lifted a hand, and smiled distantly at his acquaintances, but everyone left him alone as he desired. None of these people was of a rank to sit down beside the crown prince without an invitation, and he didn't want to talk to any of them. He might have welcomed a few companionable words from Tiwatipara, but the lad was nowhere to be seen. And anyway, Nerikkaili would have found it too trying in his present raw condition to maintain a polite fiction with his charioteer, knowing he had asked to have the fellow transferred.

He nursed his pot of beer slowly, far from drunk but a little blurred nonetheless. It occurred to him to hire a girl for the evening, but he was too tired to make the effort. Then he saw his two brothers enter. Hishni, squat and rugged, a soldier's soldier, fit right in. Lurma-ziti, two years younger than Nerikkaili, looked like a weasel that had sneaked into the poultry yard. His sharp face swiveled, searching for someone whose secrets he could pry loose. When his eyes landed on Nerikkaili, Lurma-ziti gave Hishni a poke in the ribs with his elbow and pointed, and the two of them made their way between the tables toward the *tuhkanti*.

Nerikkaili was not in the mood to deal with his brothers. He put on a pained expression for Lurma-ziti's benefit, but the latter's black eyes refused to acknowledge it. Instead of going away and leaving Nerikkaili alone, Lurma-ziti swung his leg over the bench and seated himself across from the crown prince. He leaned his forearms on the table and stuck his face into Nerikkaili's with his usual malicious grin. Hishni seemed to debate which side of the table to settle on, as if it were a statement of political alignment that required all his deliberation. He finally took a seat next to his eldest brother and held up two fingers for the serving girl.

"I'll take another one," said Nerikkaili, and Hishni raised another finger. The *tuhkanti* glared at Lurma-ziti. "What brings you here?"

"Beer and girls," Hishni volunteered cheerfully.

Lurma-ziti just grinned. He had their father's anarchic teeth. "I heard you and Father had a little row today."

"You did, did you?" Nerikkaili asked, trying to sound neutral. "Listening at doors again?"

"I have my sources."

"He's been fucking Our Sun's chamberlain." Hishni snickered, but the laughter died on his lips at the withering glare Lurma-ziti fixed upon him.

"What is it you find so attractive about other people's misfortunes, *huwalpant?* I swear, you get off on it."

"Shut up, Nerikkaili."

"I'll bet you masturbate while someone whips your slaves."

"I said *shut up*." Lurma-ziti's narrow face had grown crimson, and his eyes were starting to bug from his head. Nerikkaili reined in his humor, knowing that in a minute, his brother would be on the table on all fours, screaming at his elder until he foamed at the mouth. Well, two could play the taunting game. And if it came to blows, Nerikkaili could break Lurma-ziti in half. He wasn't sure whose side Hishni would take.

"So, is that why you're here?" Nerikkaili said with a smirk. "To pick a fight?"

The serving girl appeared with three pots of beer in her arms. She set them down on the table, transferred the *tuhkanti*'s straw and filter to his new pot, and took away the old vessel.

Lurma-ziti chose not to answer his question. "Our father is disappointed in you. I wonder how he knew what happened before you reported to him?"

"I bet you told him, eh? And how did you know, I wonder? You're fucking Benteshina?"

Lurma-ziti's face darkened, but he chose to ignore the insinuation. "No, I didn't tell him. I've been busy working with Nuwanza on a new system of flag signals, haven't I, Hishni?"

"He has," confirmed the youngest brother.

"But you're getting warm with Benteshina," Lurma-ziti said. "He was there in Nuhasshe, after all."

"And he had no better sense than to talk to you about what happened on a royal commission before the official report was made? You must be very good in bed." He pinched his brother's fleshless cheek. "Or listening at doors, as I suspect."

"And from what I've been told," Lurma-ziti said as if his brother hadn't spoken, "Our Sun is thinking of replacing you as *tuhkanti*." He looked up from his beer and fixed Nerikkaili with a smug, avid black-eyed stare. His eyes were so damned black they were like holes in his white face.

At the sight of him, a wave of burning anger scalded Nerikkaili. He could feel his smile growing sharp-edged and brittle as if his lips had become blades. With the greatest of efforts, he suppressed the desire to throttle the younger man's skinny neck. It was almost more than he could manage. He glared at Lurma-ziti for a long space, reminding himself that dismembering a sickly weed like his brother would be a less-than-glorious display of strength. But someday, someone needed to teach the dog turd a lesson.

Finally, he said sarcastically, "And I suppose you're next in line. You'll make a great king, Lurma-ziti. Father has made a splendid choice."

Lurma-ziti grinned. There was that gap where his left canine should have been. Nerikkaili had knocked it down his throat when he was thirteen and Lurma-ziti was eleven—back when he could indulge his more violent reactions to the hunchback's nastiness without qualms of conscience.

"Let's say that the chosen heir is someone with a very

powerful advocate." Lurma-ziti sucked placidly at his beer and belched.

Hishni chuckled.

Nerikkaili turned to him. "Oh, you're still here?" he said dryly.

"Still here," the younger man agreed. "You two are better than a bullbaiting. I'd pay silver to see you go at it."

"Well, I have more important things to do, gentlemen. Lurma-ziti can entertain you with his repertory of barks and growls." Nerikkaili swung his leg over the bench and slipped out. He stood up and stretched, finding he was less than steady on his feet.

Suddenly, Hishni shot out toward one of the house girls who had passed through the room. His broad back disappeared up the stairs in her company. The two brothers stared after him for a moment.

"Now that the audience is gone," said Lurma-ziti, his eyes demurely fixing on his pot of beer, "perhaps you'd like to talk more seriously."

"Not likely," Nerikkaili said, but then thought his condition might be improved by eating something. He had put away quite a lot of beer on an empty stomach. He dropped back onto the bench and called out an order for bread and olives. The serving girl brought it immediately and set it before him.

"None for me?" said Lurma-ziti, tilting his head in that mocking, almost feminine way he had.

The *tuhkanti* sneered. "I thought you already satisfied your appetite." He ate in silence while his brother, clicking his straw around in the beer as he stirred it, watched him.

"Here's what I think," Lurma-ziti finally said. "I think

you should stand up for yourself. Our Sun's position is precarious on the throne. It would be foolish to risk everything for a row over the succession. Let him know that you'll fight for it. That'll make him reflect twice before demoting you."

Nerikkaili looked at him, suddenly dead sober. "And here's what I think. I'd be a fool to start a civil war over a rumor mongered by a black-hearted weasel who loves to see people fight." He fixed his brother with a skewering stare. "You should be a little more loyal, I think, my prince," he said pointedly. "Someone might overhear and report you—someone who cares enough to save you from yourself. And that wouldn't be me."

Nerikkaili got to his feet, and this time, he was steady. "Good night, *huwalpant*." He could feel Lurma-ziti's resentful eyes on his back as he made his way through the room.

It was a relief to emerge into the cold night air and the twinkling stars. Above him, he could make out the deeper darkness of the citadel, an occasional watch fire glowing on its walls, the flame-lit, ember-spangled smoke drifting upward into the vast black of night.

As he trudged through the dark streets of the Upper City, Nerikkaili reflected on what his brother had revealed. His father intended to replace his firstborn with another son as *tuhkanti. Is this all about the search for Urhi-tesshub? Did I fail so egregiously?* The prince sank into a wordless pit of pessimism that scarcely deserved the term *thought*.

But then, there was no telling if the *huwalpant* was even telling the truth. Nerikkaili wondered what Lurma-ziti hoped to gain by encouraging his elder brother to rebellion, because he would never have suggested such a course of action if it didn't somehow benefit him. Lurma-ziti was incapable of pure brotherly benevolence.

And who was the replacement with the powerful advocate? Certainly not Lurma-ziti himself. A hunchback on the throne was unthinkable; the augurs would wet themselves in a frenzy of denunciation. Tashmi-sharrumma? For sure, Lurma-ziti would be unhappy to see Tashmi-sharrumma going up to the High Place. He had made the boy's life such misery with his mockery, tricks, and lies that the *huwalpant* could expect a truly terrible vengeance should the lad ever come to power. Tashmi-sharrumma was a nice little boy, if a bit slow—although, dear gods, he was not even twelve years old, whereas Nerikkaili was a grown man trained in diplomacy and military command. He was well-thought-of by the army and the chancery alike. If there were a showdown, as Lurma-ziti seemed to envision, the confrontation would surely play out as it had six years before for their father, with experience and connections defeating youth.

Except for that one imponderable factor—the bronze will of the *tawananna*. If the *tawananna* decided she wanted her son in the arms of Halmashuit, the divine throne, Nerikkaili could see it happening.

The *tuhkanti* ground his teeth. He had a sudden desire to fuck her till she screamed.

The king's council had finished their morning session, to which Tapala-tarhunta had been summoned to offer his expertise on the Luwians. He had, after all, served for ten years in the diplomatic corps in the West. By ones and by twos, the men had departed until Tapala-tarhunta alone was left. As usual, he preferred to make his laborious way out without the benefit of an audience. He heaved himself to his feet and arranged his sticks under his armpits before risking any steps. The old charioteer resisted a grunt of effort; he had too much pride to go heaving and sighing at a little pain. He thanked the gods he was alive. That was the attitude to take.

A sound at his back made him turn, almost unbalancing him. Hattushili had stepped back into the room through his private entrance. He stood in the doorway of the darkened space, a tall, elongated shadow.

"My Sun." Tapala-tarhunta clapped a fist to his chest in salute. He dared not remove the other from his supporting stick. But the king shook a hand at him to let him know he need not bother. He came forward out of the darkness, moving quietly for such a big man. "Sit down, Tapala. I wanted to let the others leave so I could talk to you alone."

Tapala-tarhunta lowered himself carefully to a stool, clenching his teeth against the effort. The king sat on one of the other stools at his side and waited, watching the *hashtanuri*'s face closely, as Tapala-tarhunta settled himself and laid his crutches on the floor. Once he had his breath back, Tapala-tarhunta said, "I'm at your service, My Sun."

"How are things going, old friend?" asked the king quietly, his greenish eyes dark with concern. "How is Mashuhepa? The *tawananna* has asked about her."

"As well as she'll ever be, My Sun. She talks to Pawahtelmah a lot, as if he were in the room. She has the servants set him a place at table for every meal and inquires whether he likes his food." A cold weight of misery sat upon Tapala-tarhunta's chest at the thought. He had effectively lost his wife of forty-four years after the accident. He would never have her back. The loss of Pawahtelmah had broken her. After all those years of trying to bear a live child, all the anguished prayers, and finally the knowledge that, after the difficult childbirth, she could never have another, she had put all her hopes in their boy, and they'd been smashed to pieces along with his body.

Hattushili muttered a sad oath and sat for a moment in silence. "Puduhepa will be sorry to hear it. She's fond of her aunt."

"We treasure her concern, My Sun."

The king cleared his throat uncomfortably. "Listen, Tapala. I need to talk to you about Tiwatipara." His voice trailed with reluctance.

A colder breath of gloom blew down the charioteer's back. *This can be nothing good.*

"Nerikkaili reports that he's become more and more reckless in the box. From a prudent young driver, he's turned into a daredevil. Nerikkaili said he's afraid the lad's jeopardizing the horses. And his passengers, too, of course. My son's no coward, but he was frankly afraid for his life in Nuhasshe." The king's long, ugly face was drawn with heartfelt sorrow.

Tapala-tarhunta's shoulders sank in shame to have troubled his old friend and sovereign like this—he who had always been so good to Tiwatipara, opening opportunities for him and seeing to his promotion. The charioteer hung his head and let a sigh escape him. "My Sun, my heart is heavy at this news. I had hoped it was only I who saw this change in him."

"Tapala, old friend," Hattushili continued, his gravelly voice low, "Nerikkaili said the boy told him that in a certain sense, he wanted to die. He wanted to die with Pawahtelmah in a chariot accident. He's... he's trying to kill himself."

Tapala-tarhunta felt the sting of tears in his eyes, and he wasn't sure he could hold them back. He clenched his jaw until its trembling became yet another sign of weakness he couldn't control. He was too old, too broken. *It was I who should have died...* The king laid a heavy ringed hand upon his shoulder, and the two old men sat silently side by side in shared pain.

Finally, the *hashtanuri* said in a voice flat with hopelessness, "My Sun, I wouldn't for anything upon the black earth jeopardize your heir. If he's uncomfortable with my grandson as his driver, demote Tiwatipara." He swallowed with considerable effort. "I will tell you this, but not to excuse him—he feels he's at fault for the accident and thus for his father's death. He feels he has killed his father and his mother, in fact, and bears the hatred of the gods for a parricide."

"That's what Nerikkaili said. But why would he be responsible?"

"Because it was he who harnessed the horses, My Sun. It was he who assembled your chariot. He wakes up screaming that the wheel has come off, sobbing that he didn't mean to be careless, that Tarhunta Pihasshasshi should punish him."

"Dear gods." The king's mouth stretched in a grimace of pity. Then his face grew predatory and keen. "But it wasn't his carelessness at all, Tapala. The chariot was sabotaged. Has no one told you that?"

"What?" Tapala-tarhunta looked up, his heart stopping dead within him. "Sabotaged? Surely you don't think Tiwatipara—"

"Not at all, man. I'm saying someone tampered with it after it had been assembled. The axle had been sawed partway through underneath the carriage, where it couldn't have been seen without a minute inspection. Remember, *I* was supposed to ride in that chariot."

Someone might as well have thrown Tapala-tarhunta flat to the ground, knocking all the wind out of him. He goggled at the king. "Someone was trying to kill you?"

"Imagine." Hattushili gave a deep, bitter snort of a laugh. "I have enemies."

"I wasn't supposed to have been in the car at all. It was supposed to be you…" The *hashtanuri* could scarcely believe the picture that was emerging, but it was agonizingly clear. Somehow, the Sun's words lit a new flame of meaning beneath an event that had seemed cruelly random. His son had died *for the king*. He himself had been crippled *in the king's place*. Was this not the glory of any soldier—to hurl himself between his sovereign and the thrown spear? It had not been an accident at all, but an act of war. "May I tell Tiwatipara, My Sun?"

"Absolutely. He has to know. This may change everything for him." The king looked pensive, his jaw sliding sideways. He murmured, as if to himself, "There's something else that may change everything for him, but not yet, I think."

"Oh, My Sun," cried Tapala-tarhunta with the orgasmic

73

relief of a man whose companions had just lifted from him a great rock that threatened to crush him. "How can I thank you for this news? Maybe now Tiwatipara will want to live, if only to avenge himself on the real murderer of his father."

"Pawahtelmah deserved such a son," said the king in a weary voice. He laid a companionable hand on Tapala-tarhunta's thigh then rose heavily. "Your family has borne the terrible burden of your fidelity to me, old friend. Go home to Mashuhepa, and tell Tiwatipara that he's exonerated of parricide."

With an effort, Tapala-tarhunta bent, seized the king's hand, and pressed it to his lips. "We are your men, My Sun."

He had arranged his crutches and begun to make his way to the door when the king called out, "Oh, Tapala, I almost forgot to tell you. I have another assignment for Tiwatipara, now that he needn't feel he has to die. I'll tell you about it shortly."

It was late when Tiwatipara forced himself to leave the inn and make his way home. His home—once a haven of love and security, filled with his father's laughter and the gentle sweetness of his grandmother—had become a place he dreaded. He never passed through the salon without remembering his father's broken body laid out under a mercifully concealing tapestry, his bow alongside him.

That was the last mercy the house had offered Tiwatipara. It had become a house of the dead, where the Zuwalli Gods, the dark avengers of unspeakable crimes, lurked, mocking him, sending him nightmares that threatened him with the fate of the parricide. Once when he was a child, he had dared Zidanza to enter a silver mine with him. The air within had seemed heavier than normal, as if it were crushing him to the ground, as if he'd weighed many times more than a normal boy, had been remade of lead. That was what he felt now every time he entered his childhood home.

The doorkeeper admitted him with an uneasy smile.

"What?" the charioteer demanded with the suspicion of the slightly drunk.

"Nothing, my lord. Your grandparents are in the salon. I'll tell them you've arrived."

Tiwatipara didn't know what all these formalities were about. He didn't wait to be announced. He followed the slave into the room, which was heated unendurably by several blazing braziers. Grandfather and *Hanna* were sitting face-to-face at the table, an austere supper before them, barely touched. They both looked up, and *Hanna* cried in a warbling little voice, "Pawahtelmah! You're back, my son." She held out her thin arms to Tiwatipara, tears welling in her eyes. "Mother's so glad to see you again. I knew you'd come back to us."

Tiwatipara's heart sank. This had happened nearly every night since the accident, and it never failed to overwhelm him with a kind of superstitious horror. Was his father really present somewhere invisibly, or did his grandmother's desperate need to see her son paint his features on every face?

His grandfather, his mouth a compressed slit, lowered his eyes.

"It's Tiwatipara, *Hanna*. Your grandson." Resigned,

Tiwatipara approached his grandmother and kissed her forehead.

She clung to him, stroking his face with her fluttery hands, murmuring, "My son!" Her eyes never quite seemed to meet his, as if she were looking at someone behind him. Tiwatipara disengaged himself gently. Gloom sat upon him in a suffocating cloud. This house of broken old people, overheated and smelling of cabbage and medicine—it was like a shaming finger wagged under his nose day and night, saying *guilty, guilty, guilty!* His little grandmother, as vague and transparent as a ghost, and his stoic old grandfather hauling himself around on sticks, his face white with pain he refused to express with so much as a sigh—they were his victims. They were his accusers. Tiwatipara wanted to flee, but where could he run that his own guilt could not follow him? He pulled out a stool and sat glumly, thinking he would have some beer with his grandparents then go out and eat in the soldiers' mess or perhaps go back to the inn. *Anywhere but this house of the dead.*

The young man readied himself for the next part of the evening ritual—the moment when he'd hear, "You've been drinking again, Tiwatipara?" from his grandfather's disapproving lips. But instead, Tapala-tarhunta looked up at his grandson with a forced smile and said, "I have something to tell you, son."

Tiwatipara greeted the prospect with indifference. The only news that would have moved him would have been, "The Gulshesh have changed their minds. That day never happened." But he was, at the bottom, a dutiful young man for whom family was more important than anything. He said, pretending to care, "What's that, Grandfather?"

"I was at a council meeting with the king this afternoon, Tipa. He spoke to me afterward about… about you and Nerikkaili—"

"Do we have to talk about that, Grandfather?" Tiwatipara interrupted with the quick anger of a man who'd had too much to drink. He started to push out his stool.

But his grandfather held out a temporizing hand. "That's not what I wanted to tell you. That wasn't all he said." Tapala-tarhunta locked gazes with him. Despite his sixty years and the terrible things that had befallen his body, he was still a handsome man, square jawed and eagle nosed. An indecipherable light had started to burn in his dark eyes. "The chariot, Tiwatipara—"

"I'm going back to the inn," the young man said, trying once more to rise. There was only the one *chariot*, and he had no desire to roll yet again in the exquisite horror of that day. He was too tired.

But his grandfather held out a hand once more to catch his sleeve and cut him off. "Wait." The old man spoke in a rush, as if he feared his grandson wouldn't hear him out. "He said the chariot was sabotaged. It was nothing you did, son. Someone cut halfway through the axle so it would come apart after a few circuits. They were trying to kill the king."

Tiwatipara sat in silence with his mouth open, unable to speak. Time seemed to swirl around him with a roar as if all the voices, all the screams, all the grinding of wood and metal that had haunted him for three years were draining out through a hole in his heart, flowing out faster and faster into some hideous septic pit of memory, far from sight.

"S-Sabotaged?" he repeated stupidly. "Someone did that on purpose?" *It wasn't me?*

"Remember, Our Sun was supposed to have been on board. It was only by accident that he was called away. Somebody wanted to assassinate him." Tapala-tarhunta's smile was growing real now as he saw his grandson take in the truth. "It wasn't a pointless accident that killed your father. It was an attempted assassination. Pawahtelmah died for his king. He was a hero."

Tiwatipara could hardly process these words of absolution. He could feel tears of cleansing relief rising up inside him. It was too much to absorb. He stared at his grandfather with the dazed, god-blinded eyes of a man whom the lightning bolt has spared.

"The king told you this?" he murmured, afraid to let himself believe that his long punishment was over.

The old man nodded. "He thought I knew long ago, but I guess I was still unconscious when they found out, and no one ever remembered to tell me."

The young man sat for another silent moment, poised on the crest between fear of a trick and the monumental tide of release. Then his face buckled, and the tears jetted from his eyes, a purifying flood. He threw his head forward until his crossed arms cradled his face, and he wept loudly, unashamedly, with all the bone-deep easing of an ejaculation. But it was his soul that was emptied—of three years' worth of guilt and shame and self-loathing.

He felt his grandfather's hand heavy on his back and heard his grandmother ask in genteel curiosity, "Why is he crying?"

Tapala-tarhunta replied, "He's happy, my love. He's happy to be back with us."

And because Tiwatipara was—yes, at last—happy again, he wept. After what seemed like years, he raised his tear-stained face to his grandfather. His voice was hard, but it was the voice of a living man. "Who did it?"

"No one's sure, Tipa. Our Sun has many enemies."

"I'll find him," said Tiwatipara grimly. He wiped his nose on his wrist. "I'll find him, and I'll make him pay."

CHAPTER 4

"**A**ND SO IT WASN'T ME after all, Zidi. It wasn't me after all!" Tiwatipara was scarcely able to contain the grin of sheer happiness that split his face. He was flushed and sweaty despite the cold of the day. They were standing in the stall of one of the king's stallions while Zidanza curried the animal after a morning of target practice from a moving vehicle. Tiwatipara held the pieces of tack his friend had removed from the horse, and he watched Zidanza brush out the wet marks the saddle and checks had left in the creature's russet hair.

"That's a huge relief, I suppose," said Zidanza, bending to brush the horse's leg. Tiwatipara couldn't see his face, which was covered by the curly mass of his hanging hair, but his voice held a surprising lack of intensity.

The charioteer said in his own defense, "Maybe that sounds like nothing, Zidanza, but the horrible thought that I was guilty of my own father's death has curdled the last three years. You know how I've changed since the accident—the drinking and all. I felt like I'd never be happy again. As if losing your father weren't terrible enough, to think you were responsible…"

Zidanza straightened up, his face red from being bent over. He reached out, still holding the brush, and cuffed his friend's head affectionately. "No, it's not nothing, Tipa. I know how you've suffered. My heart is lightened for you, my friend." But there was a curious sadness in his eyes. Tiwatipara wondered if Zidanza was having trouble at home. His father, a priest, was impossibly demanding, filled with the importance of being descended from the great *labarna* Tudhaliya. Zidanza, the youngest son, never seemed to come up to his expectations.

Zidanza smiled, although his dull eyes remained untouched by it. "Do you want to suck down a little beer this evening after work? I was thinking of heading to the inn, maybe finding a girl."

"Yes. I feel the need to celebrate… whatever it is I'm celebrating. Not being a parricide. Not having the Zuwalli Gods at my heels, for a change."

The two young men walked together to the tack room through the alternating sunlight and shadow of the corridor, and Tiwatipara handed off one piece of harness at a time for his friend to hang.

"Seems like you didn't much care if you lived or died there for a while," Zidanza said, his eyes on his work as he hung each piece of leather and metal on its peg. He moved with a kind of trailing slowness, as he always did.

Tiwatipara blew out a deep breath, much like a winded horse. "It was a nightmare, Zidi. I just wanted to be out of my pain. Every time I saw my grandmother or grandfather, I'd think, 'That's my doing.'" He looked more closely at

Zidanza, who seemed to be avoiding his gaze, his mouth tight. Suddenly, he felt ashamed of himself, so wound up in his own happiness. "And you? Are you all right, friend? You don't look very happy."

Zidanza shrugged and forced an indifferent parting of the lips. "I'm fine. You know my father…" Then he tossed his head a little and said with a brighter smile, "At least he's alive, right? What have I got to complain about? See you tonight, Tipa."

Zidanza was already seated at their favorite table when Tiwatipara entered the common room of the inn. The upper air of the room, under the low, blackened beams, was foggy and acrid with smoke from the central hearth, where scullions turned a goat on long spits. The smell of wet wool and sweaty men mingled with that of roasting meat, spilt beer, and a muskier, suggestive odor from the brothel above. Princes Lurma-ziti and Hishni sat in the corner, absorbed in conversation, but Tiwatipara's employer was nowhere visible. He wanted to make an apology to Nerikkaili if the *tuhkanti* came around—tell him he was back to himself and would be a better driver.

But that could wait. He made his way through the crowd of soldiers and stable personnel to join his friend. Zidanza pushed a pot of *tawal* beer toward him with a smile. "Sorry I didn't seem myself this afternoon, Tipa. Things are a bit grim at home."

"Say no more, friend. If there's anything I can do, speak the word."

Zidanza nodded gratefully and stirred his beer. He

looked tired, listless, but he was never very energetic. "So what does your life look like from here on out? Feeling guilty kept you pretty busy. What now?"

"Vengeance," said Tiwatipara without hesitation. He could feel his features grow hard as he pronounced the word, as if he had begun to transform into some dire bird of prey. He certainly didn't have the aquiline visage of his father and grandfather, but his thoughts were suddenly those of an eagle—hard and cold and unpitying. "I'm going to find whoever did it, and I'm going to crack their bones one by one, like my father's. I'm going to flay them and drag them through the dirt until they die slowly and in agony."

Zidanza looked at him uneasily, his round face paling. He said quietly. "Don't let this make you as hagridden as the guilt, Tipa. Finding the killer won't bring Pawahtelmah back."

Tiwatipara laughed, but his laughter had a stony edge. "Sorry, Zidi. Didn't mean to sound so grim. Don't worry; there will also be plenty of room for happiness." He tapped the groom on the chest. "Maybe the time has come to ask the *tawananna* for Lalantiwashha's hand. What do you think?"

"Sure, Tipa. Do it."

The charioteer put a fraternal arm around his friend's shoulders, and Zidanza's arm moved to encircle his waist in reciprocal affection. Zidanza wasn't much of a leader, but he was a devoted follower, always ready to support. "What would I do without you, my friend?" Tiwatipara said, his heart clenching with tenderness. "You're the brother I never had."

Tapala-tarhunta, who had been invited to report on the situation in the West, was already seated when the councilors arrived. All together, they rose for the *labarna* and *tawananna*. Puduhepa bustled to her place at the king's right hand. She was so young and pretty that it was easy to overlook how powerful she was and how much influence she wielded over the king... and any other male with whom she had so much as a conversation.

Hattushili took his throne, and the others sat. "My lords. Let us speak of Piyamaradu," said the king in his rough growl. "He's finally decided he wants to offer us his submission. Kulana-ziti, tell us what's going on in Arzawa." Kulana-ziti, an unranked brother of Hattushili, was the ambassador in Taruisha. He and Tapala-tarhunta probably knew more about the Luwian-speaking peoples of the West than any other two men in Hatti Land.

"The *former* Arzawa," the *tawananna* corrected primly.

The king's brother said, "He claims he wants official recognition as a vassal of Hatti Land."

"And what country does he rule?" inquired Nerikkaili in his most supercilious diplomatic voice.

"He's a country unto himself. A peripatetic country—like my great-grandfather." Benteshina began to tick off on his fingers. "He's the king; he's the vizier. He's the chief scribe of the wood tablets. He cleans the latrines."

The queen rolled her eyes, but her husband chuckled. The Amurrite's great-grandfather had indeed been a kind of bandit king, ruling a nomadic population of refugees, outlaws, and escaped deportees. Eventually, he had become so powerful—and such an embarrassment—that the Egyptians had recognized him as a vassal and let him set up a proper kingdom. It wasn't a bad analogy at all. Benteshina was no fool, despite finding it useful to behave like one.

The *hashtanuri* spoke up. Although he had not returned to his post in the West since the accident, he still had his sources and collected their reports for the king. "He claims he represents all of the Luwian-speaking West, My Sun. In short, the Arzawan Confederacy reborn."

Nerikkaili gave a bark of dismissive laughter. "What do the real kings, like Kupanta-tarhunta, have to say about that? They're already vassals."

"More precisely, protectorates in some cases, my lord," Kulana-ziti said. "But their reactions vary. Some laugh him off as a victim of delusion; others are waiting to see how successful he is. And if they perceive him as having some power of negotiation with us, they'll probably hitch themselves to his cart. For good or ill."

"Do you agree with this analysis, Tapala?"

"I do, My Sun. Although it's been a few years since I lived among them, I know the men of the West. We must deal very carefully with this Piyamaradu. If he sets himself up at the head of some small state and submits to a proper vassal treaty, he could be an excellent example to the others—to places like Hapalla, which blows hot and cold, or Karkisha, which has always stayed outside our sphere of influence."

Kulana-ziti took up the relay. "But if he's just using this demand to taunt us and make a mockery of us—if he continues harassing our real vassals while claiming he wants to become one, just to stay our hand—then he's very dangerous. We don't need to lose our dignity in the West."

"Again, like my great-grandfather." Benteshina made a plaintive face.

"So," asked the king, "what do we do in practical terms?"

One suggested this, another that. It was clear to Tapala-tarhunta, as it had to be to the king, that there was no good response to Piyamaradu. Whatever the council did, they risked being undercut and made to look foolish by the renegade prince, who roamed with his ragtag followers like an ill wind—promising much, delivering little, chastising those who didn't take him seriously, then disappearing to the islands where the Sun's men couldn't touch him. What gave him cachet among the disaffected Luwians—always looking for someone to reunite them against their conquerors—was precisely the fact that he was able to embarrass the Hittites in ways great and small. It was difficult to believe his sudden longing to become their underling was sincere. But they could not afford to ignore it.

The morning stretched on. It was hard to deal with any other issues, so heavily did the specter of a revived Arzawan Confederacy under the rule of Piyamaradu weigh on them.

The king and Tapala-tarhunta were the last two men left in the council room after the meeting. His hips beginning to stiffen painfully, the charioteer gathered his crutches and prepared to rise, but the king folded himself onto a stool at his side and motioned for him to stay.

"Thank you for your insights, my friend," said Hattushili. "Those puppies have their ideas, but it's the old dogs who speak wisdom." The king clapped his friend on the shoulder, and his hand remained heavily there for a moment. "We'll probably end up going to war against that bastard Piyamaradu."

"Probably so, My Sun, despite all your efforts to deal with him peaceably."

"I envision leading the troops myself, at least at some point. If we send Manapa-kurunta against him, as my brother suggested, we risk giving a vassal more power than is prudent. I'm half-afraid Manapa-kurunta will go over to the blackguard's side."

"I agree, My Sun, as I said in council. But perhaps the crown prince—"

"But why, Tapala? I'm a better general than he is, although the whelp isn't half-bad. Surely you don't think I'm too old! Why, I'm younger than you!" The king grinned wryly, his eyes twinkling. Then he looked away, his gaze fixed in space. "It's been six years since I took the field in anything more exciting than a skirmish, and I miss the thrill of battle."

Tapala-tarhunta made himself smile, but the pain was almost insupportable. He, too, missed the thrill of battle. But while the king could don his coat of scales anytime he wanted, Tapala-tarhunta's life in the box of a chariot was over forever. He'd be lucky to be reassigned to a diplomatic post. The war to put Hattushili on the throne had, it seemed, been his own farewell to the life of a *hashtanuri*.

"Do you remember Kinza, old friend?" asked the *labarna* quietly.

"How could I forget, My Sun? It was a moment of glory for the chariotry of Hatti Land."

No, he would never forget that day seventeen years ago,

below the walls of Kinza on the Arantu. Even after all this time, the thought of it stirred Tapala-tarhunta's heart and filled his soul with pride. Hattushili's brother Muwatalli had confronted the young king of Mizri, Washmuaria Riamashesha. *Dear gods, such a thing was unheard-of—two Great Kings in hand-to-hand combat!*

At the suggestion of Hattushili, the Hittites had sent out false scouts for the Egyptians to "catch," feeding them an erroneously optimistic idea of Muwatalli's whereabouts. Then, as Washmuaria, in the arrogance of his youth, set up camp before the rebel vassal city, the forces of Hatti Land—three thousand chariots strong—had fallen upon them from hiding, crushing the Egyptian barricades, smashing their lines, and surrounding their king.

Ah, Lord Wurukatte! What a ransom it would have brought had we captured the king of Mizri, lord of the land of gold! But the undisciplined mercenaries with whom Muwatalli had fattened his manpower had become distracted by their rapine and let Washmuaria get away. Still, the Hittites had broken the siege of Kinza and chased the Egyptians back into their own borders in inglorious flight. It had been a day of triumph. A day of glory.

And Hattushili and Tapala-tarhunta had been there. The former, then only king of Hakpish, led the troops of the Upper Land. Tapala-tarhunta had driven the chariot, lashing his team into the fray like an avenging bolt of Lord Tarhunta's lightning.

The charioteer realized he had drifted away from the present moment and looked up. The king was fixing him with an intent gaze of pride and affection. "How would you like to relive that, my friend? How would you like to be in the box again?"

Tapala-tarhunta replied uncertainly, "It's a beautiful dream, isn't it, My Sun?"

"I'm not talking about a dream, Tapala. Do you want to drive for me in the West? Do you think you're up to it?" Hattushili bared his crooked teeth in a grin that was boyish in its eagerness.

Tapala-tarhunta's stomach wedged in his throat so that he could hardly speak. Longing invaded him, an aching flood. But he was also afraid. He could feel the sweat spring on his temples at the thought. *How can I balance on the bouncing leather floor of a car—I, who can scarcely stand up with crutches? How can I control the might of two plunging stallions with these arms I can barely lift? Is there enough left of me?* And what if he fell or crashed? He couldn't go through all that again at his age. He did not have much acquaintance with fear, but he was almost mastered by it at the thought of mounting the box again. He could only see *the chariot* tumbling and sliding, crunching, screeching, banging, with him and his son beneath it and the screaming, broken horses on top.

His lips were forming the words "I cannot," but because he was, above everything, the king's man, he forced them to say instead, "Whatever My Sun commands." He was almost faint with fear.

"Ah, old friend," cried the king, laughing in relief. "How that gladdens my heart! I wouldn't have anyone but you or your son beside me on the dancing floor of Wurukatte!" He rose and helped Tapala-tarhunta up, handing him his sticks. "Let's give it a practice turn, hah? Just to be sure you've had enough healing time. There's no shame if you want to change your mind."

Together they crossed the court, the king holding back his long stride to match that of his friend. They mounted litters at the outer gate of the citadel and descended the steep-stepped, log-paved road of the causeway. *Thank the gods that Hattushili had this causeway built*, Tapala-tarhunta thought, *or I could never have made it to the council meeting at all.* The royal enceinte crowned the cliffs above the Upper City like an eagle's nest, inaccessible to mere humans.

The bearers took them through the rocky, half-inhabited Upper City to the stables, and Tapala-tarhunta could feel the old eagerness building. Since the accident, he had not returned to this place that had been the heart of his life for so many years. Once again, he smelled the horses—tart and warm and rich—along with leather and beeswax and straw and sweat. The godlike calm of the great calm beasts transfigured the grooms and drivers who passed him, busy with their daily tasks, into celebrants of a stately liturgy. He saw a round-faced young groom, his grandson's friend, lead a chestnut stallion out one end of the stable and start down the row between buildings. Tiwatipara himself had to be there somewhere, but Tapala-tarhunta didn't think he could face the boy, because the old charioteer could fail. He could fall.

The king swung his long legs out of his litter and called for a groom. A middle-aged fellow well known to Tapala-tarhunta came running up. His eyes widened with surprise and delight at the sight of his former colleague, but he bowed to the king.

"Help Tapala out, and hitch us up a pair of well-seasoned horses, my man. We're going for a drive."

It was a fine, cold early-winter day, a sky as blue as lapis stretching overhead, unmarred by any cloud. A pair of hawks circled curiously. Tapala-tarhunta waited at the king's side, drawing in deep breaths of the scent of his former life. The fear was still there, ticking in his belly, but the tranquility and courage of the horses had begun to mellow it. With all his will, he desired to do this thing.

The groom led out a fine team of gentle geldings suitable for a carriage, but they were harnessed to a real chariot. Terror flared momentarily in the depths of Tapala-tarhunta's body as the scene of the accident flashed before his eyes yet again. But the king was saying, "Help him up." The groom had placed a stool at the rear of the box, and he held Tapala-tarhunta's arm as the old charioteer pulled himself up with both hands, using all his willpower, teeth gritted with the effort. And then he was in the chariot, breathing heavily, concentrating lest he make a false move and unbalance himself. He held onto the rails and turned himself around, using his arms' strength, not that of his legs, to move to the front of the box. The floor, woven of leather strips, was springy beneath his soles. He could hear Hattushili climbing in behind him. *Dear gods, is the king riding, too? Does he really trust me so much? What if I fail?*

"Whenever you're ready, Tapala, take us on out," the king said calmly at his side.

Tapala-tarhunta shook the leads and urged the team into a walk. He almost staggered as the chariot lurched into motion, but he felt Hattushili's supporting arm move around his waist. Forward the two horses plodded, their heads bobbing in unsynchronized nods as they crossed the trampled snow. Some knowledge deeper than his tensely concentrated mind began to direct Tapala-tarhunta's movements. His weight balanced itself securely, his arms found their positions, and his fingers melted into the leads. He had no whip, but he clucked with his tongue, and the horses obediently sprang into a trot. There was only the rust-red leather-banded length of their backs, the slim necks with the line of their roached black manes, and the alert ears bouncing along before him. He heard the rumbling of the wheels, the clopping of eight hooves, and the jangling and creaking of harness. The rest of the world had ceased to exist. The fear was gone. The memories were gone. *There is only this.*

"Take 'em to the field," said the king beside him.

The charioteer trotted the animals onto the field, in the middle of which several targets for spear practice were still set up. Dimly, some part of his mind told him that something terrible had happened there. But the past no longer existed. *There is just this.*

"Let 'em fly, man."

Tapala-tarhunta gave a shout, and the geldings opened into a canter. He leaned against the forward rail⬛as a driver shouldn't, but he couldn't take the shocks in his legs, and this gave him stability. He felt solid as an oak. The horses' shoulders churned back and forth with their strides. Their tails streamed out at him. The chariot bounced, but the ground was level and well cared for, the snow carefully cleared; the movement was the rocking of a cradle. They galloped down the length of the field, and although the speed wasn't great—they were only carriage horses—Tapala-tarhunta's hair lifted off his neck, flying like the animals' tails. He was just a part of them. And he knew their joy. *Run! Run fast!*

They leaned into the turn, and he felt a momentary thrill of fear as his body listed, but between the rail and the king's arm, he kept on his feet. Up the field they pelted to the methodical rhythm of the horses' hoofbeats. Tapala-tarhunta was peripherally aware of several men standing at the edge of the field, bulky in layers of woolen clothes, watching.

"Bring 'em in now, Tapala," Hattushili said, and the driver could hear the grin in the king's voice.

He drew back gradually on the lines, and the team bounced to a stop. Tapala-tarhunta's face was flushed and hot once the wind stopped. His heart was pounding, his feet vibrating with the memory of motion. He shot a triumphant look at the king, and the two of them laughed in sheer joy.

Unaccustomed tears trembled in the *hashtanuri's* eyes. He thrust out his jaw. "Thank you, My Sun, for your confidence in me. For… for—"

"Purely selfish, Tapala. Purely selfish."

The king and then the driver descended to the stepstool the groom had set in place. Tapala leaned on the groom and risked an unsupported step at the bottom. It was always harder to go down than up.

Someone handed him his crutches, and as he took them, he looked up and saw that it was Tiwatipara. The lad's eyes were swimming, and on his face were all the feelings Tapala-tarhunta himself had experienced—fear, pride, and exaltation. "You're back, Grandfather. May the gods be praised." He threw his arms around the old man and hung onto him fiercely.

The soldier in Tapala-tarhunta mastered his emotions, and he smiled as he said into his grandson's ear, "This is life, isn't it?" He held the boy at arm's length and gazed at him for a lingering moment before he turned away. Tiwatipara was a handsome, honest-looking lad with warm brown eyes under straight brows, a long nose, and a wide smile that dipped down in the middle like a flying bird seen against the sky. His shaven forehead, the mark of an active charioteer, gave him the big brow of a child. He was the picture of his mother. His grandfather hadn't seen such an expression of undiluted joy on Tiwatipara's face in three years—he who had once been so full of mischief and laughter. Maybe this was a step back to life for him, too.

Tapala-tarhunta hauled himself along beside the king, grinning at the other grooms who had gathered—Tiwatipara's curly-haired friend and the older one—along with some charioteers and stable boys.

"You can drive me in the upcoming festival, Tapala," the king said. "That won't be taxing, just a stroll. But that way, you can work your way up to a battle charge. You know, I don't see why we couldn't install a little seat of some sort so you can brace yourself with your own butt. Who said *hashtanuri*s have to stand? Coachmen don't."

"Not a bad idea, My Sun," said Tapala-tarhunta. But he suspected that as he built muscle again and his bones continued to heal, he wouldn't need a seat. *At last*, he thought as a great weight spread wings and took off from his chest, *I am a man again.*

CHAPTER 5

IN HIS OSTENTATIOUSLY SHABBY WHITE tunic, the augur priest Armatalli son of Arma-tarhunta stood before the *labarna*. He positioned himself a little too close, pushing at the edge of protocol, trading on the fact that he was a blood relative of the king. Hattushili didn't like the man, and not only because Armatalli's branch of the family had supported Urhi-tesshub. The augur was arrogant and impatient, quick to brush lesser mortals out of his way, and Hattushili—who didn't have much patience either—couldn't endure that sort of self-importance.

The king was aware of his wife, the *tawananna*, sitting silently and observantly at his side. He knew what she thought of the wily old birdwatcher.

Hattushili growled, "What is it, my friend? Birds not flying according to your liking?"

The priest dipped his shaven head in acknowledgment, his round, ruddy face all professional pomposity. "I felt it was important to warn My Sun as soon as the auguries were clear. There is a source of displeasure for the gods in My

Sun's household, a potential source of pollution that could bring misfortune down upon the *labarna*."

How you wish it would, thought Hattushili, but he just cocked his eyebrow. "And what would that be, Armatalli?"

"My Sun, it came to our attention at the recent festival that your charioteer is a lame man, an *ikniyant*. The gods seem to view this as a violation of the sacrosanctity that surrounds the Sun of Hatti Land. As you are certainly aware, even the badly scarred cannot serve in the king's presence, and this man is severely—"

"I point out that *this man* was injured in the king's service, Armatalli. If we banned every officer who bore honorable scars, we wouldn't have an army left." He felt the heat rising to his face. Puduhepa must have seen the telltale flame in his cheeks, because she put a quiet hand of warning on his arm.

"I only repeat what the gods have revealed to us, My Sun." The augur clasped his hands smugly across his broad belly.

"And since augury requires the practitioner to ask a yes-or-no question first, I wonder what question it was that you asked, cousin."

Armatalli looked slightly flustered, his plump moon face beginning to flush like the king's. "I can certainly show My Sun the record of the consultation…"

"Which god is so displeased by the service of a loyal man who sacrificed his body for his king, if I may ask, hah?" Hattushili narrowed his eyes.

"We have yet to ask that, My Sun. I thought—"

"I'll bet," growled the king in a dangerous voice. Puduhepa's knee nudged his unobtrusively. Hattushili realized he was leaning forward over the priest. Even seated, he was tall enough to use his height and the riser of the dais to intimidate Armatalli. He straightened up and said noncommittally, "I'll take this under advisement. You're dismissed."

The augur bowed and backed away from the king's presence, this time scrupulously observing all the niceties of protocol. He could see, no doubt, that the king's notorious temper was aroused. The priest's nostrils were white with the effort to control his own anger. Armatalli liked to be obeyed, not brushed off.

When the door had closed carefully behind his cousin, Hattushili turned to his wife, his jaw grinding. "The sheep-fucking bastard. You saw what he was trying to do, didn't you?"

She stared her husband in the eye, her lips compressed in outrage. "Get rid of a loyal man, clearly."

"More than that, my love, more than that. Once he has 'proof' that the gods are offended by a lame man in the king's chariot box, it's an easy step to the idea that they're offended by a man in imperfect health on the throne. Armatalli's still pushing old Arma-tarhunta's agenda. He pretends to accept me, but he's constantly looking for excuses to declare me illegitimate, damn it. Like father, like son. At least his brother is honest enough to have come out and declared openly for my nephew."

Puduhepa raised her little dimpled chin in a gesture of stubborn righteousness. "Well, Shaushga herself has justified you, My Sun. The Sun Goddess herself has blessed you and given you strength."

"You and I know that, my dear. May she strike that fat

impostor down. May… may a bird fly up his sanctimonious nose. Let him read that augury!" The king began to heave with laughter at the image, but his anger still crackled at the edge of it.

Puduhepa tried unsuccessfully to suppress a snicker. "As a priestess, I shouldn't find that funny." Then more gravely, she asked, "Do you plan to dismiss Tapala-tarhunta, my husband?"

"Not without a fight, by the thousand gods. Let Armatalli spend a little time sending me all his documentation. Let him consult the birds and see who it is that finds a good man and a loyal soldier so offensive. If he can prove this is the gods' will and not Arma-tarhunta's, I might consider letting Tapala go. But not without a fight." The king's mouth turned down in a snarl of defiance.

"Good for you, my dear. You don't want Armatalli to think he can manipulate you. I wonder if he couldn't be transferred to a less influential position somewhere. Augurs have a lot of power. We have to trust their honesty."

"Right. Let him go read oracles for the shepherds somewhere in the mountains. He can have his pick of sheep." The king heehawed outright and enjoyed seeing his wife catch the laughter. *Gods, but she's beautiful, even the inside of her mouth.* Then, growing serious, he said, "It would be cruel to take this post away from Tapala-tarhunta now, after awakening his hope. You should have seen his face in the festival procession. It's lent him a whole new zest for life. He's not a man to sit around feeling sorry for himself, but he had no motive for recovering. This gives him something important to work toward." He heaved a sigh. "Your uncle's a good man."

"So was his son," said the *tawananna* sadly. "That accident was such a waste. It wasn't an accident, though, was it? It could have been you dead, my love, or crippled forever. The Lady of Shamuha protected you yet again."

"I wish she'd gone a little easier on Tapala's family," Hattushili said with a wry twist of his mouth. He stood up and shook out his skirts. "And I wish she'd reveal the name of the bastard who sabotaged that chariot. I couldn't help thinking of it when our fat friend Armatalli was here a moment ago. Do you think it's one of that brood?"

Puduhepa rose in her turn and stepped down from the dais. "How can anyone know, My Sun, unless some witness comes forward? But after three years…? Anyway, Armatalli claims to support you, although we all know how solid a truth that's likely to be."

"Some support," growled the king, following his wife. "Tries to thwart everything I do."

The *tawananna* gnawed her lip. "Do you think Tapala-tarhunta is really up to driving again, though, my dear? It takes a lot of strength, doesn't it?"

"Don't you nag me, too." He eyed her knowingly. "You're still thinking of Tashmi-sharrumma, aren't you?"

Several weeks passed, during which the king waited for Armatalli to return with his documentation. The augur didn't disappoint. He showed up with a whole battalion of colleagues ready to swear to the honesty of their oracles. Tarhunta Pihasshashshi himself was offended. Tapala-tarhunta's presence in the king's chariot box, a very public service of the king, something that any citizen might see, was an offensive *hurkel*—taboo—and the patron god of charioteers objected.

"Why, any citizen might be scandalized by such a flouting of purity laws," Armatalli said.

Furious though it made Hattushili, who could smell political manipulation like the presence of a sewer running under these pious words, his hands were tied. The *labarna* was the high priest of all the thousand gods of Hatti. Hattushili couldn't afford to incur their wrath. He was seated on a precariously legitimate throne.

Armatalli's father Arma-tarhunta was Hattushili's uncle and bitterest political enemy. Hattushili's brother had fined and exiled the old man, but Urhi-tesshub had brought him back to honor. *Why? Just to flaunt in my face that he could? Was he hoping that the old plotter could really neutralize me, the young king's regent?*

Armatalli pretended he was above partisan politics, but it couldn't be true. His brother Shipa-ziti was the active leader of Urhi-tesshub's supporters. That whole branch of the family was a pack of mad dogs.

"Why did Muwatalli finally exile your uncle?" the *tawananna* asked as they lay in bed. "What exactly did he do?"

"He cast a spell on me, my dear," the king said, his mouth hard with contempt. "Black magic of the worst sort. It took forever to get it off, and meantime, I was sick to death. To be honest, he's probably been doing that for my whole life. And then he took me to court, pretending I had cheated him out of something. These people are completely ruthless. No doubt, some pact with the Lords of the Underworld has kept the old billy goat alive all this time."

"We must take every precaution, then, my husband. Call up the protection of every god to cover you with their invincible shield." She turned her adorable face to his, and her eyes were filled with flames of love and determination. "I don't want to lose you. We must walk carefully." She stroked his chest with her little hand.

He seized it and brought it to his lips with gusto. "Are you trying to tell me I have to let Tapala-tarhunta go, then, my doe?"

"It's not for me to tell you what to do, dearest. But we can't give those people any handle on you. I regret this as much as you. He's my uncle after all."

"We can call this the War of the Uncles, hah?" The king chuckled. Then he subsided, sobering. "Very well. I'll tell him myself. But it makes me damned furious."

Tiwatipara had intended to hire a girl for the evening and have a little fun, but he found that he could see only Lalantiwashha's delicate face and swanlike neck before his eyes. His desire was made to her shape—the coarse features of some whore would be an affront. Thus, when Zidanza mounted the stairs to the brothel at the end of the evening, Tiwatipara stayed sitting in the common room of the inn, dreaming. He watched the clients come and go. At some point, the kings' two sons rose from their table and disappeared.

Alone, he started to ponder who his father's murderer could be. It was someone who had wanted to kill the king. Someone, moreover, who knew the king was supposed to be on that chariot. Of course, Tiwatipara supposed, anyone who was even remotely acquainted with Hattushili could guess that he'd be unable to resist a turn with the new team. But still, it had to be a person who knew about the horses and the day's trial run.

Not for the first time, he steered his memory back to the afternoon of the accident. But this time, instead of following the unraveling of the chariot and the destruction of horses and riders, he let the eyes of his mind comb the crowd. Had the killer been in plain sight among them, coolly watching his plot unfold in the blood and screams of innocent men?

Prince Nerikkaili had been there. Could he possibly be so eager for the throne that he would send his father down the Great Way by violence? Lurma-ziti and Hishni had been there, too. Benteshina was there. Prince Zuzuhha, of course, was in charge of the stables. All the grooms and drivers were there. He knew all of these men and most of them well, and he could think of none who wasn't a loyal man of the king, risking life and limb for Their Sun every time they mounted and rode.

Lurma-ziti? Of everyone in the crowd, he was the one most likely to do mischief, Tiwatipara thought. He was a mean-hearted bastard, always mocking people and playing hurtful tricks on them. A person could see the hatred rolling off him in waves. The way he treated his little brother Tashmi-sharrumma was shocking. With his own eyes, Tiwatipara had watched the hunchback nearly beat the younger boy to death in a frenzy of bloodlust. He might well be the culprit. But what motive would push him to kill his own father?

And how had anyone gotten to the chariot after

Tiwatipara harnessed it? He had left it near the outer barn, only a few hundred *iku*s from the practice field. It hadn't taken him long to bridle up the two horses and lead them back out, and Zidanza had stood by the chariot all the while, leaning against it, watching the trials from afar. *But was he there the whole time? Did he step away for a crucial few moments? Go to take a piss? Move over to watch the team run from closer up?*

But even if Zidanza had left, it was no easy thing to crawl under the chariot box and take a saw to the hard ash wood of the axle. Surely someone would have noticed, of all those men standing around. Someone would have heard the sound of a saw… though, in fact, Tiwatipara wasn't sure. Everyone's backs had been to the barns, their attention riveted on the horses on the field. The thundering hooves, the rumbling vehicle, the shouts and loud talk, the exchange of wagers and laughter… the sabotage might have passed unnoticed. If an onlooker saw someone approach the car, he might have thought it was to make a repair.

Still, there had hardly been time. The perpetrator would have had to bring a saw and get it away without anyone seeing him—except, Tiwatipara suddenly realized, the toolbox was lying right there on the ground, with a saw in it. He and Zidanza had used the mallet to mount the wheels.

He ran his hands through his hair wildly. There seemed to be no way to find the person. Maybe it didn't happen after the wheels were mounted at all. Maybe the axle had been cut in the chariot room of the barn long before he and Zidanza dragged the car out and set it up. Tiwatipara certainly hadn't examined the underside of the box. *It's nearly hopeless*, he told himself, bordering on despair. *But I won't give up. I'll find him.*

Some time later, Zidanza came down the stairs, tying his belt. Tiwatipara waved to let him know he was still there, and his friend threaded between the tables toward him, bumping people occasionally in his awkward way.

"You thirsty after mounting your mare?" Tiwatipara grinned, holding up two fingers for the serving girl.

Zidanza laughed, blushing. "It was that old one with long teeth. She knows her stuff, but you were right to hold off. Lady Lalantiwashha is ten thousand times prettier."

They settled companionably over their pots of beer. Tiwatipara observed his friend. Despite his moon face, he was tall and slender, but there was a softness about him that predicted he would go to fat one day. He was lazy in some ways yet anxiously concerned to please. *Something is lacking in him*, Tiwatipara thought. *Much as I love him, there's something manly or firm that's lacking.* He thought of his own father and grandfather, so gallantly ready to accommodate the needs of others. Still, they would never flex in matters of principle. Zidanza was a wavering sort, as unsolid as a bowl of curds, falling this way and that. He was a great companion because he was always ready to yield his opinion. Tiwatipara had abused this moral softness often in their youth, dragging him, unobjecting, into all sorts of boyish adventures. He wondered if Zidanza *had* in fact left his post by the chariot for just that critical moment.

As if he felt Tiwatipara's considering gaze on him, Zidanza's smile faded and dropped from his face. His sleepy eyes looked guilty. "Tipa, I didn't want to spoil your good mood, but I need to tell you something you're not going to like."

Here it comes, Tiwatipara thought in expectation and dread. *He stepped away and let Lurma-ziti get at the chariot.*

"My father… my father's trying to get your grandfather out of Our Sun's chariot box again."

Tiwatipara stared, speechless, for a moment. "Why should he care? Does *he* want to drive?"

"No." Zidanza chuckled limply as if depressed by the content of his tidings but unable to resist the absurdity of the image. "He's an augur; he reads the signs the gods give us in the flight of birds and such. There's always one son in our family who is given to the gods."

That was typical, Tiwatipara knew. Even in the royal family, it was true. Hattushili had been the priest in his generation, hard as that was to imagine. But of course, Zidanza's family *was* the royal family—some cadet branch of it. He kept forgetting that. "So why is he against my grandfather?"

"He says that the auguries show the gods are angered by a lame man serving the king."

Tiwatipara stared at his friend, outrage starting to steam inside him. "Are you serious? Angered because my grandfather sacrificed himself for the king?"

"Don't kill the messenger." Zidanza held up his hands as if to protect himself from a blow. "That's what he says. And that's what the auguries said. I don't think it's anything personal, Tipa. But I figured you'd want to know."

Tiwatipara sat, wordless with growing fury. Finally, he burst out, "How dare they?"

"Who? The gods?" Zidanza sounded shocked.

"I don't know. The birds." Tiwatipara gave a short, brittle laugh. "I don't want to be mad at your father. He's just doing his job. But what does this mean? That my grandfather will have to step down? He's just started driving again after... after a long time. It's given him back his dignity, his reason to live. This will humiliate him. It will kill him." He could feel the rage mounting in his cheeks.

"I'm sorry," said Zidanza plaintively. "Maybe I shouldn't have said anything."

He looked so miserable that Tiwatipara's anger was defused. The *hashtanuri* heaved a sigh and leaned on his forearms. "Damn. Just when life seemed good again." With a fingernail, he absentmindedly probed a knife groove in the worn, greasy tabletop.

"Who knows? It may save your grandfather from danger," Zidanza suggested hopefully.

"Is it done, then? He's out for sure?"

"I don't think anything definitive has happened. It's just a reading Father took. Maybe Our Sun won't even act on it."

Tiwatipara made a dubious noise. They sat in silence, staring into their beer. Zidanza started suddenly to say something but, in his awkwardness, knocked his beer pot over. He reached out to catch it, and as his sleeve drew up, Tiwatipara saw his forearm. It was striped with deep-purple bruises.

"What happened to you?" he said in concern.

"What? Oh, my arm? I fell on... something."

But Tiwatipara didn't believe it. He took up his friend's arm and pushed back the sleeve. Thin bruises, some of them open gouges, scabbing over, barred the flesh as far up as the sleeve would fold.

"These look like whip marks. Did somebody hit you with a whip, man? What does your back look like?"

Zidanza hung his head and made a vague gesture of the shoulders.

"Did your father do this?"

He gave another noncommittal shrug.

"He did, didn't he? But, Zidi, this isn't right. You're a grown man. What's going on?" cried Tiwatipara in horror.

But Zidanza clearly didn't want to talk about it. He swung his leg over the bench and got up. "I'm tired, Tipa. I think I'll go on home."

Tiwatipara looked at him, his heart torn with concern. "Sure you wouldn't rather come home with me?"

His friend shook his head, his face shut. "Don't stay too long. See you tomorrow."

Tiwatipara watched him make his way to the door, his curly hair streaming down his back, concealing gods-knew-what ugly lash marks. *Who ever heard of such a thing?* The charioteer realized in retrospect that Zidanza's hide had often been marked with bruises, even in childhood. His friend was notoriously clumsy, and it had been easy enough to dismiss them as being the result of accidents. Tiwatipara was too innocent of such things to have recognized them as signs of brutality. No one ever raised a hand against him as a child—except for an occasional token spanking, because he'd been a pretty lively boy. His gentle grandmother, his kind father, his stern but fair grandfather—they would never have beaten him like a recalcitrant donkey. How blessed he had been.

I will avenge you, my dear father, he promised Pawahtelmah.

Tiwatipara rose from the table, too, and threw some bronze on it for the beer. He supposed he shouldn't say anything to his grandfather about the oracle. Maybe nothing would happen.

CHAPTER 6

THE LAST OF THE ROYAL councilors filed out from the council room. Through the open door, a chilly draft insinuated itself, lifting the tapestries that covered the shuttered windows against the winter cold. The biting wind of the capital bothered Tapala-tarhunta these days in ways it never had before.

"Tapala-tarhunta," said the king, his voice flat with suppressed anger. "Let's talk." He heaved himself up from his throne and stepped heavily from the dais. He looked gaunt and old, his long jaw skewed. He was troubled in his mind, Tapala-tarhunta saw.

Unease stirred in Tapala-tarhunta's middle. *What's this about that disturbs Hattushili so?* "Yes, My Sun?"

The king took him by the elbow and drew him away from the windows with a quick glance around, like a man who feared the walls could hear. "I'm going to have to let you go as my driver, friend. It kills me to say this, but the augurs are after me."

Tapala-tarhunta began to murmur something self-effacing, but the king pushed on, his voice descending into a hoarse rumble as anger mounted in him. "It's that godforsaken Armatalli, Arma-tarhunta's son. He's figured out a way to get at me though you. He says Pihasshasshi is displeased by a lame man in the royal box." Tapala-tarhunta opened his mouth, but the king cut him off. "No, don't apologize. This has nothing to do with you, Tapala. It's his cowardly, backhanded way of attacking me. If he gets everyone thinking some physical imperfection is a target for the gods' displeasure, then it's an easy step to calling for my overthrow."

The charioteer felt his heart sink, although he had fully expected something like this to come up. He said tightly, "I wouldn't be a liability to you for anything, My Sun. I'll resign—"

"But it's not right. May the underworld suck that smarmy bastard down. I wanted to defend you, but I dare not pick a fight over this when there are so many other issues that make me vulnerable."

You wanted to, but you didn't, thought Tapala-tarhunta sadly, *because I'm a very small and dispensable part of your life.* He honestly felt no resentment. He was old enough not to have many illusions left. But he had to admit to a certain sorrow. Here was the proof that his worth had been so diminished that he was no longer just lacking in value but had become downright burdensome. *Very well. I accept, Tarhunta, my lord.*

"But you understand that this doesn't mean I don't want your services in any other capacity, Tapala. You'll still be my man on the ground out there in the West, my *hashtalanuri* in the most important sense. I mean, we're old men, aren't we? This sort of diplomacy is more fitting to your dignity anyway."

"I guess we can't call back our youth, eh, My Sun?" The charioteer spread his lips humorlessly. "Anyway, thank you for wanting me. I'm yours to command; you know that."

"But it makes me damned furious nonetheless. There's nobody in the kingdom who is more constrained than I am. Those disloyal vultures are watching me day and night. Arma-tarhunta must be ninety, and he's still doing everything he can to bring me down. One misstep and"— Hattushili made an explosive sound—"they're all over me, pecking out my gizzard." The king's face had grown scarlet, his ugly mouth turned down.

"I understand, My Sun." The charioteer knew, in fact, that kings had different standards of loyalty than ordinary men. The favor of the gods was urgent to them in a way that ordinary men couldn't imagine.

At a loss for words, he bent and kissed the *labarna*'s hand. Hattushili clapped the other hand to Tapala-tarhunta's shoulder, gripped it, then turned and stalked out, his back rigid with anger. Tapala-tarhunta, numb of heart, laboriously let himself out of the empty council chamber.

That night, Tiwatipara stood before his grandfather, looking so stunned he could hardly close his mouth. "He's dismissed you? But he just brought you back. You said he told you he didn't trust anybody but you to drive him."

Tapala-tarhunta let a deep breath out through his nose, calling upon all his long life of self-discipline not to reveal to the boy how angry and hurt he was by the king's action.

"Son, the king—of all people—has to obey the gods. If the oracle said my presence was a source of pollution, then he had to take action, no matter what he wanted personally."

But in a voice raw with anger, Tiwatipara yelled, "After all you sacrificed for him? After all you've lost? To cast you off like that? I'm sorry, it's wrong. This is shameful."

He was taking it personally, his grandfather noted sadly. *If the lad only knew how much harder this makes it for me.* "Look, Tipa. Bad things can happen to the kingdom if the gods are angered." His grandson snorted, but Tapala-tarhunta continued. "And he didn't kick me out of the diplomatic corps. This is just a return to the way things were before." He forced a smile. "Think how happy this will make your grandmother."

"Nothing will ever make *Hanna* happy again. You know that," Tiwatipara snapped.

So this anger is still down there, thought Tapala-tarhunta, his heart heavy. *The guilt may be gone, but he's still gnawing on this sense of injustice.* In a stern voice, he said, "Look, son. We're soldiers. What we do is obey the king—when it suits us and when it doesn't. Suck up this self-pity, and spit it out. I won't have our family dishonored."

"Well, I'm quitting, too," growled Tiwatipara. "He can't treat us like that and expect us to do him favors." He clenched his fists and turned away, his shoulders taut.

Tapala-tarhunta felt all the fury and frustration of the last three years rising up inside him in a geyser of wrath that left him quivering. His last progeny refused to accept reverses like a man and a soldier. The Gulshesh had taken his only son. His wife had drifted away from life and now hovered, a pallid ghost, somewhere between him and the underworld. Tapala-tarhunta's dreams and dignity—his manhood—had all been scattered to the winds.

His face blazed, and his fingers crisped. His voice splitting, spittle flying, the old man roared, "He can do anything he wants, Tiwatipara. He's our king. You're not doing him any favors—you're doing your duty before the gods. Why is this so hard for you to understand?"

The boy spun back, his eyes wide, his dark, straight brows knotted. "You can't tell me what to do, Grandfather. I'm a grown man."

"Then act like one, by the thousand gods," snarled Tapala-tarhunta. He wanted to stalk away, but it was too laborious. What if he fell? All he had was the dignity of his age and his righteousness; he could not afford to surrender that. He might have struck the insolent boy if he had been a cubit closer. They faced each other in quivering silence for a moment, then the old man spoke more calmly. "Get out of my sight. Get out of my house. If you're a grown man, then it's time you set up your own household and live like an adult. Get married. Have children. Some responsibility will make you grow up, all right. But remember, if things don't go your way—if your wife doesn't please you, or your children rebuff you, or your health fails—you can't just run away. You have to bear the burden every day, whether it entertains you or not, because people are depending on you."

"Grandfather, I—"

"No, I mean it this time, Tiwatipara. It's long, long overdue."

"But how will—"

"Thanks to Our Sun's good grace, you have a job. I'll

be in the West, in Apasha. The king is sending me back to observe for him. Be kind to your grandmother, but don't you dare ask her for anything." Tapala-tarhunta was in control of himself now. The gods had given him this moment. He could see it was indeed a good thing to wean Tiwatipara from his grandparents' household at last. Pity had made the old man too accommodating, and it had hurt them all.

Yet again, as had become a kind of habit, Hattushili stayed behind the others after the morning's discussion while Tapala-tarhunta gathered himself for the least conspicuous departure possible. This time, the *tawananna* remained with her husband. She called out after the charioteer as he arranged his crutches, "Uncle, a word with you before you go."

Tapala-tarhunta turned carefully. He had come to dread these moments. "My lady, how may I serve you?"

"It's about Tiwatipara," said the king.

Tapala-tarhunta's stomach dropped ominously. He had to swallow before he spoke, bracing himself against the latest revelation. Had his grandson endangered the *tuhkanti* again? "Yes, My Sun?"

"Don't look so apprehensive," the king said with a grin. "He's not in any trouble. I just have a little job for him. How old is he now?"

"Twenty-five, My Sun."

The king looked at his wife, questioning, and she tipped her head in assent. "How do you think he'd like to teach my eldest first-rank boy to drive?" he said.

The charioteer nodded slowly. "I suppose he'd like that well enough. How old is your lad?"

"He's only eleven, but—"

Tapala-tarhunta made a skeptical little noise.

"But he's big for his age and serious."

"Yes, but it takes strength to control those brutes," said the charioteer. *An eleven-year-old child?* The Great King didn't know what he was asking of his boy.

Puduhepa shot her husband an uneasy glance and said to the charioteer, "We don't mean put him on with stallions, Tapala. Let him learn on some gentle mares or geldings."

The king added, perhaps for his wife's benefit as much as Tapala-tarhunta's, "The boy's got to get started sometime. I want him to serve as his cousin Ulmi-tesshub's charioteer when he's old enough—just for a while, the way I was a groom as a lad. Your grandson can train Ulmi-tesshub, too. He's fifteen and strong but not as mature as Tashmi-sharrumma. Still, anyone who is going to command an army needs to know what chariots are capable of firsthand."

What they're capable of—when a horse stumbles or a wheel hits a stone or comes flying off at a dead run downhill. What they're capable of when an enemy's vehicle broadsides you or clips the edge of the box and sends it tumbling over and over, when the driver is tangled in the reins and dragged by panicked horses. One could lose one's son so easily...

Stop it, he thought, forcing himself to look up at the room around him, solidly made of stone, painted plaster, and hewn beams of reddish cedar—real and present and concrete, far from the dust clouds and spraying blood of nightmare. *You're as bad as Mashuhepa. What's done is done. It's in the hands of the gods.* "Whatever you say, My Sun," he said aloud, keeping his voice impassive. "Tiwatipara will be honored."

The king beamed. He shot a smile at his wife and put his arm around her a little smugly, but her face was taut with concern. She said, almost pleading, "Remind him, Uncle, that he has every reason to want to live."

"You can trust the boy, my lady," Tapala-tarhunta said, his voice gentle in response to her motherly concern and full of pride toward his grandson. Despite their hot words, he *was* proud of Tiwatipara. The boy was a damned good driver—patient, painstaking, and kind with the horses. He would make a good teacher. The old charioteer just hoped the lad wasn't too obdurately steeped in his outrage and that he wouldn't somehow take out his anger on the king's sons. That wouldn't be like him, at least like the real Tiwatipara. But who exactly his grandson was these days, Tapala-tarhunta was no longer sure he knew.

Tiwatipara did not consider himself honored by the new assignment. He knew it was punishment for endangering Prince Nerikkaili. The king had found a way to keep him on the ground, trotting demurely around the ring. Gone was the thrill of flight, the rush of battle, army face-to-face with army, the chariot lines thundering at one another then passing through miraculously as if the very walls of the world had become permeable. Everything that made him love his life—gone. First Tapala-tarhunta had been dishonored, and now he. Their Sun had it in for his family suddenly.

In addition, he found the idea of teaching a couple

of children to do a man's job disturbing. He himself had mounted the box at an even younger age but with his father at his side, holding the lines with him. He couldn't see himself taking on that intimate role with the two princes. Still, the last word was that his family had been the *labarna's* men for five hundred years, and whether Tiwatipara felt honored or not, the king's command *was* his honor.

The charioteer was living, for the moment, in the dormitories where unmarried grooms and stable boys stayed if they had no family home in the area. It was only a walk of a few hundred chill, windswept *iku*s through the half-empty Upper City until he entered the gate of the royal stables and immediately breathed in the scent of the animals—the sharp, rich tang of their sweat and their sweet hay-scented breath and the dark perfume of leather and beeswax. He heard a bronzesmith clanging away at some piece of tack that required reshaping. The hooves of the animals clopped on the paving stones as they were led from their stalls, and somewhere, a horse blew out through his nostrils with a ruffle of air. Motes of dust hung in the beams of sunlight that penetrated the warren of wooden boxes, and a passing groom with a horse on a lead took on the magical air of some divine man-beast appearing in a flash of light until he walked on into the shadow. This was the world Tiwatipara had grown up in; these were the distinctive sounds and smells of his childhood. It had to be a good thing that the young princes would come to love them, too.

Prince Zuzuhha, the chief groom, was waiting for him by the hay wagons, as arranged. He waved at the youth, and Tiwatipara directed his steps between the clumsy vehicles. He clasped the older man by the forearm in greeting. The prince was a big man, tall and broad, with unexpectedly thin bowed legs and a protruding belly. Age had given his retreating hair the semblance of a charioteer's cut, high in front.

"Tiwatipara, lad," said the man who ran the royal stables, clapping him on the shoulder. "The *tawananna* herself has brought her son and nephew for their first lesson. Let's not be late."

"I hope they're not too young for this," muttered Tiwatipara as the two men made their way past another row of stalls into a broad, unpaved court more or less empty of other activity. The snow had been trodden into mud along the paths where men or animals passed regularly. Waiting in the shade of the wall, out of the wind, was the *tawananna* herself. She was dressed in the usual heavy pleated skirt and full-sleeved blouse that narrowed at the wrist, her dark hair partly hidden under the *kurasshar* and its veil, and over that was a woolen cloak as thick as a rug. But it was clear that the body underneath her clothes was exceptionally well formed. *A real thoroughbred,* Tiwatipara thought admiringly. There was no missing it. She fully lived up to her reputation for beauty, with big black eyes, a perfectly oval face the color of cream—the cheeks now, in the cold, flashed with red like mountain apples—and a little dimple in the middle of her chin. Although Queen Puduhepa was his cousin, he had not seen much of her for three years—since his father's funeral, when he had been too distraught to appreciate her beauty. And of course, she was the king's wife. His appreciation was purely professional.

Then his eyes started in confusion. Behind the *tawananna* stood a tall, slender, pale-faced girl, tranquil and poised as a princess. She *was* a princess. It was Lalantiwashha. She raised her eyes a little slyly, smiled ever so slightly, and lowered her gaze like the demurest of maidens. Her long slender hands held her cloak together at her collarbone, and her narrow feet were encased in boots. Now, *that* was beauty—not the queen's saucy, bossy, compact little beauty but the elegant lines of the finest blood filly. She looked as if she could float into the sky and fly. His heart groaned in longing.

"My ladies," said Zuzuhha and Tiwatipara both at once, each bobbing in a respectful small bow.

"Cousins," the queen greeted them cheerfully. "You know my stepdaughter Lalantiwashha, of course." She laid a hand on the shoulder of each of the two boys beside her and urged them forward. "Here are your charges, Tiwatipara. My son Prince Tashmi-sharrumma"—she stroked the younger boy's hair affectionately, devouring him with a mother's proud gaze—"and his cousin Prince Ulmi-tesshub. You've probably seen them." As she spoke, the older boy flashed his white teeth and turned out his hands with a flourish as if to indicate *Here I am!* "Our Sun wants them both to get a good grounding in driving, so this will be a charge that lasts for some years... if everything works out."

Her dark eyes fixed Tiwatipara's with a meaningful look. *Whether things work out or not depends on you,* they seemed to say. Clearly, she knew about Nuhasshe.

"I'm honored, my lady," the young man said. *Not so sure this is a good idea, though*, he thought. But the boys were kings' sons—they had the bluest of blood. Driving was something they had to learn eventually.

"I leave them with you, then. I know you have other things to do, and so do they. So, shall we say, keep them for half the morning for now, no more?" She smiled, and it was as if the sun had suddenly begun to shine. She seemed all at once very young and eager, her big black eyes pleading with him to keep her boys safe.

Tiwatipara was highly conscious of Lady Lalantiwashha's presence in the background. He found himself beaming broadly, full of gallantry despite his skepticism. "Yes, my lady."

The *tawananna* turned first to her son, speaking to him tenderly in Hurrian, and kissed him on the cheek. He was still young enough not to pull away from her demonstration of love and dutifully returned the kiss. Then she patted the elder prince fondly on the face. "Be good now, boys. Do whatever your cousin tells you, all right? He's in charge. His voice should be like the gods' to you." She turned to the charioteer. "Lalantiwashha has asked to stay and watch. I trust that won't be a distraction, Tiwatipara."

Tiwatipara murmured something incomprehensible, his thoughts scrambled by the proximity of his beloved.

The queen turned and made her way through the courtyard and out, her walk quick and full of energy that set her skirts swaying. Tiwatipara watched her go, fascinated in spite of himself. But in every woman, he saw the promise of Lalantiwashha. He tried not to stare too pointedly at Lalantiwashha herself, who remained silent and watchful, a satisfied smile on her long, soft mouth. Then he turned to his two charges.

Ulmi-tesshub, the older prince, was the son of the former king Muwatalli and the brother of the recently deposed Urhi-tesshub. He was perhaps fifteen or sixteen—tall, slim, and well-developed for his age, the beginnings of a beard smudging his lip and chin. He was the most gorgeous boy Tiwatipara had ever seen—like a young god, with his thick, wavy, dark hair and sensual mouth, and a hint of badness under his black lashes. No doubt every female—and perhaps male—heart in the citadel beat a little faster when he was around.

Ulmi-tesshub eyed Tiwatipara back appraisingly, a grin twitching up the corners of his lips. "Another cousin. What fun."

The younger prince, Tashmi-sharrumma, was ten or eleven. He was tall and coltish—all long, skinny legs and big hands—but still a child. He was manifestly his father's son, with old-looking hooded eyes and jagged teeth, but his face was just beginning to lengthen. His pink cheeks were still soft under light-brown hair that stood out in a bushy mane. The prince looked up at Tiwatipara then dropped his eyes again.

Does he speak Neshite? Tiwatipara wondered, remembering the *tawananna*'s conversation with the boy. He himself recognized Hurrian when he heard it, but he certainly couldn't speak it.

"Well, my princes," he began with a smile. "Tell me, what experience have you had with horses up to now?"

Ulmi-tesshub hooted and dug the younger boy in the ribs with his elbow. "Quite a bit, actually. Right, Tash?"

"Not so much," Tashmi-sharrumma said, his cheeks aflame.

Neither of them seemed inclined to explain, although Ulmi-tesshub could hardly contain his snickers. Tiwatipara seemed, in fact, to remember some awful event a few years before in which the boys had sneaked a pair of the chariot horses out of the barn. The king had verbally flayed the entire staff in his red-hot fury, but Zidanza in particular had been held responsible. No one who knew the groom had been surprised that he'd let himself be talked into abetting something like that by a couple of children.

"Well, we'll assume nothing and start at the beginning." Tiwatipara beckoned them over to the gentle bay mare he had tied up to a ring in the wall that morning. She sucked water placidly from her bucket then lifted her head to them, her lips dripping, her liquid brown eyes hopeful. Tiwatipara patted her on the neck.

He had opened his mouth to speak when Ulmi-tesshub interrupted. "Did you know it's legal to have sex with a horse?"

A stunned silence fell upon them. Tiwatipara gaped at the boy, suddenly afraid to ask what their "quite a bit" of experience with horses had been. He was poignantly conscious of Lalantiwashha's presence only a few cubits away. Her eyes widened, then she covered her mouth with her hand to smother a laugh.

The elder prince was grinning broadly, his fist on his hip, satisfied at his scandalous effect upon his listeners. "But not with pigs, dogs, or sheep. Isn't that funny?"

The damned lad was trying to provoke him, Tiwatipara saw, a wisp of anger starting to rise like steam from within him. *Snot-nosed little show-off.* He began dryly, "I should think that would be its own punishment, my prince. Now, if you can keep your mouth shut for a few minutes, I'll teach you a few things you need to know about the body of a horse—where it's strong and where it's not. And if you can't"—his hand snaked out with unexpected speed and grabbed the boy by the neck of his shirt, jerking him almost off his feet—"prepare to be struck by lightning, because as the *tawananna* said, my word is to be like that of the gods for you two. Is that clear?" Tiwatipara stared right into the lad's black eyes, his lips smiling but his jaw clenched, and gave him a shake. "Clear?"

"Perfectly clear, sir… cousin… sir… my lord." Ulmi-tesshub's eyes were round with shock.

Tiwatipara let Ulmi-tesshub's heels regain the ground and resumed in a normal tone of voice, "These animals are powerful and high-strung, and if you aren't going to be serious, I refuse to let you endanger your lives around them. Now, first off, I see you boys are wearing shirts and kilts. Charioteers wear long tunics. Always. It changes the range of motions you can make, so you need to get used to it from the first. Tomorrow, long tunics. And boots. Sorry, Ulmi-tesshub; no one will see your pretty legs. Get used to it."

He had their attention. For the rest of the lesson, the two boys paid rapt heed to his words, little Tashmi-sharrumma sticking his nose so close in that Tiwatipara almost had to push him aside. More than once, the charioteer made a grumpy comment that briefly sent the boy back a few cubits. Tiwatipara began to think the lad was making fun of him with this exaggerated show of fascination.

He kept the boys till shortly before midday, having let them feel the mare's body, open her lips, even sit upon her back. They practiced putting the bit into her mouth, tugging the bridle over her ears, and leading her so that she couldn't step on their heels. Lady Lalantiwashha watched everything with evident interest, never saying a word. Tiwatipara hoped he had impressed her with his mastery over the irrepressible Ulmi-tesshub.

After the lesson, Ulmi-tesshub came up to him alone and said, without the slightest rancor, "Tash can't see unless he's up close."

"What, are his eyes so bad?"

"Afraid so. How else could he stand to look in the mirror?" The boy ran off to join his cousin, and Tiwatipara thought gloomily, *A blind charioteer. What is the king thinking?*

But with greater cheer—*oh yes, great cheer indeed!*— he made his way over to the princess, who, after half a morning, waited in still and perfect patience against the stable wall, and bowed to her. He was exhilarated, his face aflame despite the frigid wind. "My lady, I'm honored that you find this interesting."

The princess's face was marbled with cold, her nose rosy. "I love horses," she said with a smile then looked up from under her pale lashes. "I love horsemen." Her breath made a little moist cloud that hung in front of her lips.

Tiwatipara's heart seemed to dissolve within him. A warmth spread upward from his loins to his cheeks. "And I," he said in a faint voice, "love ladies who love horsemen." They seemed to drift closer without even moving their feet until her lips were scarcely a finger's space from his. Then he melted into her kiss, sweet and soft and full of juice as a ripe mountain apple. When he fully realized how public their location was, he drew back, his cheeks burning. Miraculously, there didn't seem to be any grooms around.

Safe from the observation of others, his gaze drowned itself in hers, the carob brown of a horse's mild orb.

"You have a real talent for teaching, cousin," she said, although he was only a cousin of her stepmother.

"I thank you, my lady." They fell silent and filled their eyes with one another.

"Don't you think it was clever how I found a way to talk to you like this?" she said in a dreamy voice.

"Brilliant, my lady. You have a real talent for… finding a way."

She laughed, and he laughed with her, quite spellbound, not his usual saucy-tongued self at all. Her teeth were pointed and uneven, but somehow, that tiny imperfection added piquancy to her pale beauty.

"Are you betrothed to anyone, my lady?" he said, and although his tone was playful, he felt deadly serious.

"Not that I know of. Not that anyone has told me. But the *tawananna* is in charge of such things. What if you ask her?"

"If you help me find a way," he said. "Because you have a talent for such things."

She lifted a hand to his face and stroked his cheek, the gesture like the passage of a feather against his burning skin.

He found it hard to breathe. "My grandfather has told me to get married."

"What a wise man." She smiled, dipping her head a little. "I'd like to help you obey, Tiwatipara."

Did she just say yes? He seized her hand and crushed it to his lips, but gently because it was a very delicate hand.

He thought his heart couldn't hold so much happiness and would surely explode.

She arched her long, fine neck over him and whispered, "Until next time… my love."

"My love…" The words repeated themselves, beginning with his mouth and echoing down, down into his innards, warming him like a magical fire that was both hot and cold at once, fluttering like snowflakes down the length of him, covering all his anger under a soft, beautiful blanket of white.

CHAPTER 7

S PRING WAS THE BUSIEST TIME of year for the king and his court. In addition to the endless festivals, over which the land's high priest presided, the turn of the new year meant the royal family had to make a pilgrimage to the Stone Houses—the mountain-peak tombs—of their ancestors. Hattushili had offered sacrifices at his father's *hekur*, and now he and the *tawananna* and the older children of the king were in Tarhuntassha, Muwatalli's capital, to honor the king's late brother.

"There are some things I'll never understand about Sharri-tesshub," Hattushili admitted as he and his wife shared dinner.

"Who's that, my love?"

"Muwatalli, as he incomprehensibly chose to call himself. He had a fixation on the Luwians. What in the name of all that's holy possessed him to found a new capital down here? Is the capital of our ancestors not good enough?"

The *tawananna* gracefully sucked a bone of the roast young goose they had polished off between them, mostly through her husband's application. "Well, it had one excellent effect. When he moved the capital south, that meant he had to leave you to rule the north."

"He said Tarhunta Pihasshasshi appeared to him and told him to do it." The king made a whooshing noise and rolled his eyes. "Ever the mystic."

"But my love," Puduhepa reminded him with a barely suppressed smile, "Shaushga of Shamuha has appeared to you and me numerous times in dreams."

"In dreams, yes. That's normal. Although I guess the first time she appeared, when I was a dying child, was to Sharri-tesshub, wasn't it? And lucky she did, or I might not be alive. I'd wager my weight in silver that Arma-tarhunta and his sorcerers were already at work."

"Oh, don't talk about him, Hattushili. Let's have one meal without talking about him."

The king made a gallant effort to change the subject. "Where's Nerikkaili? I thought he was eating with us."

"When he comes, he'd better bring his own food with him. We haven't left him much." She reached out to pat her husband's guilty stomach, but laughing, the king shrank away, being hopelessly ticklish about the middle.

"Nerikkaili has given me some dark looks lately," said the *tawananna* once they had stopped laughing. "Has he found out somehow about Tashmi-sharrumma?"

"Yes, he has, or at least he suspects. I think Lurma-ziti has been bearing tales." Looking for the biggest fruit, the king prowled with his fingers through the bowl of dried cherries and popped one into his mouth.

"How does *he* know?" the queen demanded, unable to clear her face of the distaste that the mention of Hattushili's second son always provoked in her. "He's probably been listening at doors or hiding in clothes chests. That man makes me very uncomfortable."

The king's cheer sank into a puddle of gloom. His second born was a cause of deep sorrow to him. "It splits my heart to see how he's turned out. The poor boy..." He thought of Lurma-ziti as a spindly little toddler, flailing about in convulsions.

But his wife gave a bark of hostile laughter. "Poor boy? He's a piece of bad work, Hattushili, and always has been. He was only Tashmi's age when I married you, and he was already mean and spiteful. Some people are just bad."

"I have to disagree, my love. If you torment any dog long enough, he becomes vicious. The other boys were terrible to him and still are. The poor sickly little thing. They called him hunchback and wouldn't let him play with them and made his life miserable. And he's not even a hunchback, by all the gods. A bit twisted is all."

But she reminded him gently, her hand on his, "You were a sickly child, and it certainly didn't make you go bad. No, dearest, he is who he is, just as you are who you are. But enough of that." She sat up, returned to briskness, and selected a cherry stem. "Ooh, look, two little balls!" She dangled the twin cherries as she flashed her husband a suggestive smile, and he roared with laughter. "So what do we do about Nerikkaili?" she said more seriously. "He could be very dangerous to Tashmi-sharrumma if he's upset about losing the succession. It could mean civil war again. We have to keep him friendly."

"Why do I have to keep my own son friendly? He knows I love him." The king helped himself to more fruit and washed it down with the final drops of *walhi* beverage in his cup.

With a dubious quirk of her mouth, the queen said, "He doesn't know *I* love him. He thinks I'm working against him."

"*Do* you love him?" The king bared his teeth in a wry smile. "If not, you should."

"He's my age, Hattushili. I'm never sure just how it is he looks at me. He's respectful, but, well… I sometimes feel he's looking through my clothes." Her brows wrinkled a bit but not so much as to disfigure her face. "It's a little hard to feel motherly toward him."

The king watched her closely, a crooked smile lingering on his lips. "Then feel some other way."

She looked up, her eyes round with something approaching alarm. "What do you mean?"

"Do you find him attractive?" he pressed.

"Dear gods, Hattushili! Yes, I find him attractive in an objective way. He's a fine-looking man. But he's my stepson."

"And yet you don't feel motherly." He poured himself and his wife another finger of sticky, sweet, very intoxicating *walhi. Gods help me for being a totally amoral old dog*, he thought. *But this is a problem of state that needs to be resolved.* "Win him over, Puduhepa. Make sure he knows you love him and would wish him no harm. Make sure he realizes that Tashmi-sharrumma is no threat to him."

She gaped at him, discountenanced in a way he seldom saw her. "Are you telling me to have an affair with your son? Shaushga help us!"

"She's just the one whose help we need. The goddess of

love. All I ask"—he bared his lopsided grin—"is that I don't have to wonder whether my children are my grandchildren."

His wife stared at him, aghast. Then her expression melted into admiration, even awe. She seized his hands and whispered breathlessly, "You are the most wonderful, ruthless, self-confident, lawless, amazing person I've ever met, my dear. May the gods preserve you forever in the lap of Halmashuit." They stared at one another for an instant, the king enjoying greatly this moment of extravagant esteem, then they both burst out laughing—deeply, hilariously, and complicitly.

The king's chamberlain stuck his head in the door. "My Sun, the *tuhkanti* and the lord Benteshina are here."

"Send them in." Hattushili cleared his throat and gave his wife a wink.

With a disappointed expression, she mouthed, "Benteshina, too?" and snickered, beginning to grow slightly drunk.

"Good evening, son," the king said cheerfully. "Who is this with you, hah?"

With his accustomed dry sarcasm, Nerikkaili said, "Oh, some fellow I ran into in the antechamber. He insisted on coming, too."

Benteshina made an extravagant bow. "I represent the small peoples of the south, come to pay you homage, My Shining Sun. Plus, I was told there would be food." He eyed the table with its picked-over bones and emptied plates. "Clearly, the large peoples of the north have eaten it all, however."

"We'll order up more. Chamberlain!" the king called,

and the eunuch bobbed into sight. "Another round of all this, my man. And plenty of *walhi*."

"Can you honestly call a eunuch 'my man'?" wondered Benteshina, a pensive finger to his cheek.

"He can call him a walnut tree if he wants. He's the king!" Puduhepa was almost giggling. Hattushili found his wife illuminated by *walhi* quite delightful. She could be a little prim when sober, at least in public.

Nerikkaili seated himself beside his father and looked around with a smirk. "Seems we've missed quite a party." He picked up a bone and examined it in vain for meat.

The king eyed his firstborn and found that he *was* attractive, more so than most of his brood—a really big young fellow with mass to him and a smooth, imposing manner. Nerikkaili was a little pompous, as big, good-looking men often were. He had a strong jaw, a substantial nose of an aquiline cast, and straight dark hair. *He got that from his mother's side of the family.* A fond smile curved the king's lips. *Shaushga's tits, I'd be mighty sad to think he was alienated.* He reached out and cuffed his son's head affectionately.

A slave brought a fresh tray of goose and bread and bowls of lentils and greens, and the two newcomers helped themselves.

"We've heard from Washmuaria at last, through his queen," said the *tawananna* as the others ate. "He swears Urhi-tesshub is not in Mizri."

"He's lying," growled Hattushili, his face starting to flush. "Where else would the pretender have gone? You saw him heading south, didn't you, son?"

"If he isn't there anymore, it's because he's come and

gone. That's certainly where he was on his way to," said the *tuhkanti* around a mouthful of food.

"I want him back, damn it. We have to make Washmuaria extradite the boy."

The queen shrugged. "Washmuaria's queen claims he's somewhere on our territory already."

Frustration poured over the king in a drenching wave, taking away his breath, blinding him. He slammed his hand on the table and roared, "Then who, by the thousand gods, is hiding him? Who, of all those misbegotten vassals down there who are no more loyal than a… a…"

"Walnut tree?" suggested Benteshina.

"Shut up," snarled the king.

But Benteshina was irrepressible. "Those people are too small for the job, My Sun. Replace them with more loyal men. Take Amurru, for example."

Hattushili couldn't keep from giving a reluctant laugh, although he was far from appeased. That nephew of his was a canker on his empire. "As soon as this campaign in the West is finished, Benti. Patience, all right? Washmuaria just doesn't want to bother himself to look for Urhi-tesshub. He's no friendlier than he has to be, may the Innarawantesh take him. We need a real treaty with him, with a mutual extradition clause."

"At least he recognizes you, Father," said Nerikkaili. "So far, that's had a good effect on some of the Luwians. Kupanta-tarhunta of Mira, for example. He seems inclined to come over to your side, and I think it's because Mizri recognizes your legitimacy." He picked up a fistful of dried cherries in his big paw.

"Well, we should know before long. As soon as I leave

here, I'm going to Waliwanda. No reason you can't come, too. It's still on our territory. We'll meet Tapala-tarhunta there, and he can tell us the latest from the West."

"I'm coming, too," said the *tawananna* in a tone that bore no contradiction.

Hattushili's lips formed a silent *Oh* of mock surprise. "Aren't you wanting to rush home to the children like a good little mother, my dear?"

"The only reason the children aren't with us now is that I didn't want you-know-who to be the only one denied access to his father's *hekur*. That would be too cruel. Explaining why he couldn't offer prayers to Muwatalli might raise questions we don't want to answer."

"*You-know-who* being Ulmi-tesshub?" Nerikkaili raised an eyebrow.

"He must never, ever know he's first rank, Nerikkaili. Dear." The *tawananna* shot a sideways glance at her husband. "He might become a threat to Our Sun's heir. He's a strangely unpredictable boy. He blows hot or cold very easily."

And right there's another reason the heir has to be Tashmi-sharrumma, the king thought a little sadly. *Ulmi-tesshub would never rebel against the boy. They're closer than brothers.*

"Well, I have things to see to. Come on, Benti. The others are still eating." The king rose and stretched. He tapped the Amurrite on the shoulder.

"But I'm still eating too—" Benteshina caught Hattushili's eye and pushed away his plate. "Now I'm finished. Let's go, My Sun."

The king smirked at his wife as he moved toward the door. His son's back was to him, broad and rippled with muscle, with dark hair hanging to the belt. The king made silent kissing motions at his wife and closed the door quietly behind him. He heard Puduhepa say, "Can I pour you some more *walhi*, Nerikkaili, dear?"

It occurred to Hattushili that there was something he needed to tell his wife at his earliest opportunity. But now wasn't the moment. He headed down the hall with a crooked smile on his face, feeling rather like a spider bobbing pleasantly in the center of his web. At his side, Benteshina gave him a penetrating stare and grinned.

CHAPTER 8

T HE KING'S PARTY LEFT FOR Waliwanda soon
after the spring equinox, New Year's Day. Prince
Nerikkaili accompanied his father. If Hattushili
left the boundaries of the empire, the prince would turn
back, because the *labarna* and his heir were never both
absent at the same time. No more were they ever in a
battle together. Someone had to be left in case the worst
happened. Nerikkaili tried not to think about Lurma-ziti's
insinuations. For the moment, the king's firstborn was still
his heir.

They'd put aside their traveling carriages and mounted
official-looking chariots to enter the town, a smallish but
well-fortified outpost near the border between Mira—which
was part of the empire—and Karkisha, which wasn't. The
exact nature of the Karkishans was never clear from one
day to the next. Their suffering at the hands of Piyamaradu
had united them with the neighboring vassals, and they
appeared friendly at the moment, hopeful that the Great
King of Hatti could protect them.

Nerikkaili had agreed to put Tiwatipara back in the box

with him. Standing next to the charioteer, Nerikkaili let his mind drift backward over the days before their departure from Tarhuntassha, to the night after the sacrifices in particular. Shaushga help him if he knew what the *tawananna* was up to, but he felt little inclined to complain. To be sure, Puduhepa had been mildly drunk, enough that her inhibitions had been impaired. She was all over him as soon as her husband had left the room. Nerikkaili had held back at first, shocked and uneasy. But his stepmother was undeniably gorgeous. What a body, moreover—plump and curvaceous and soft as rose petals. *Succulent* was the word. Not that he had seen her completely naked. Yet.

Besides—without offense to his father, who, while not handsome by any standard, was certainly attractive to the ladies when he chose to be—it would be no surprise if a man Puduhepa's age held some allure for a young, beautiful wife whose husband was thirty years her senior. And the prince had to admit that he was a pretty fine specimen; it would be false modesty to pretend otherwise. He had yielded happily to the pleasures of the moment.

But in retrospect, Nerikkaili wondered if it might be a trap of some kind, a test of his loyalty. He considered warning Hattushili what his queen was up to. All he needed was for Lurma-ziti to find out and tell the king first. Nerikkaili blew out a blast of air from his mouth as if that might help him make a decision, and Tiwatipara grinned sideways at him.

Their cavalcade approached the gate of the town. Soldiers stood at attention on either side and over the scalloped parapets. The governor and his functionaries waited inside the flag-draped, flower-strewn portal. Somewhere a band was playing. Still, this was an informal entrance. There would be no long procession with choruses and priests and half the court trudging along between the chariots. The king wasn't decked out in the splendid garments of the Sun God. He was here as commander in chief and only wanted to see his ambassadors and local commandants.

Nerikkaili drew in a deep breath of warm spring air. There was that mildness of the sea nearby, despite the mountains. It was good to be alive at a season like this. It was good to be young. He remembered the fleshy curves of his stepmother, the warm weight of her breasts. It was damned good.

"Do you think it will come to a battle?" he asked his driver.

"I don't know, my lord. If it does, I'll just be glad to be part of it." Tiwatipara was smiling, his cheeks glowing with exhilaration.

Nerikkaili smiled, too, but with more acerbity. "Don't tell me you prefer this to teaching my little brother how to drive?"

"It's all right. He's a quick study. But that's not what I'm trained for." Tiwatipara looked a little guiltily out of the corner of his eye. "I mean, whatever Our Sun commands, I'm happy to do," he said. But he was happiest to be doing the real work of a charioteer. That was clear.

After a moment, unable to detach his thoughts completely from the pleasures of the flesh, the prince said, "Did you ever ask the *tawananna* about Lalantiwashha?"

The charioteer's face grew red, and he bit his lip. "No, my lord. Some things are scarier than going into battle.

But I'll do it. Maybe while we're here. I'd like to know my future before we meet the enemy, if it comes to that."

"Understood, Tiwatipara. Good luck." Nerikkaili cleared his throat. "I, uh… have some influence with the queen. I could put in a word for you, if you want."

The driver turned to the prince with joy written all over his honest face. "That would be too kind, my lord. How can I thank you?"

"By driving like a sane man, my friend. I'm glad to have you back, but I hope we won't have any repeats of Nuhasshe."

Tiwatipara looked at him earnestly. "I swear to you, my lord. It won't happen again. I have every reason to want to live now. I… I guess you're aware that the chariot that killed my father was sabotaged."

Nerikkaili nodded.

"I want vengeance, my prince." Tiwatipara's jaw clenched, and his nostrils grew taut. "I want to find who did it and make him pay."

"That would please Our Sun, I'm sure," said Nerikkaili smoothly. "Whoever did it was trying to assassinate *him*."

They passed under the crenellated wall of the town, through the double-leafed doors of the gate, and made their way in sedate procession up the street to the governor's palace, where the king and his entourage would be lodged. Grooms came out to take the vehicles and horses to the stables, and Tiwatipara went with them and the king's stable crew. Nerikkaili waited until his father and the *tawananna* had dismounted and followed them into the governor's audience hall, trailed by Benteshina. The Amurrite had found a flower lying somewhere and stuck it into his headband over one ear, like an Egyptian dancing girl.

The governor waited for them at the door of the hall. The small but lofty room had two rows of wooden columns up the sides, forming three aisles. Although he appeared to be a good ten years older than Nerikkaili's father, the man fell nimbly to his knees and kissed Hattushili's hand before regaining his feet, with the aid of Benteshina's arm. "Welcome, My Sun, to your stronghold of Waliwanda. Make use of it as you will. Have you any needs, I am at your disposal."

The king growled his praise, and the man left them. Within, Nerikkaili saw Tapala-tarhunta rising from his seat. The royal party made their way inside with a heavy clatter of boots. The hall was dark and was smoky from lamps, its two windows still shuttered against the chill.

"My Sun!" the charioteer cried. "Welcome."

Hattushili strode forward, as Tapala-tarhunta, clapping fists to chest in a military salute, bent. But the king forestalled him, instead gripping his forearms in a friendly man-to-man greeting. "Forget the pomp, old friend. I spent fifty-one years of my life not being *labarna,* and all that fluffery doesn't mean much to me," he said warmly. "I hope you have good news for us." He looked around for a seat, but there was only the governor's throne, the chair Tapala-tarhunta had vacated, and a bench. The king threw himself into the throne, his wife leaning against his knees like a little dog, and Nerikkaili and Benteshina sat at either end of the bench.

"Are you tired, My Sun? Have you drunk and eaten? I know your party's just arrived…" Tapala-tarhunta began.

"Benteshina, go order up some drink," commanded the king. The Amurrite slipped out. "Let's hear what you have to say, man. That's why we're here."

"I wish the latest news were better, My Sun," said the old man grimly. "Piyamaradu has been on a frenzy of raiding, striking up and down the littoral, from Lazpa—off the coast of Taruisha—to Apasha in Mira. And what he's after seems to be men."

"Men?" echoed Puduhepa in confusion. "What do you mean? He's looking for ransom?"

"Not at all, my lady. These are working-class men taken from their farms, their forges, their construction sites."

"What sort of numbers are we talking about, Tapala-tarhunta?" asked the *tuhkanti*.

"So far, they number around seven thousand, my lord."

"By the thousand gods," murmured Nerikkaili in shock as his father exploded with the same disbelieving words.

"How's he going to feed seven thousand fucking captives?"

"I don't know, My Sun. But in fact, they don't all seem to be taken by force. He's also offering gold to anyone with building skills who will join him."

"Shaushga's tits," muttered the king. "Seven thousand men at sowing time? Who'll get the crops put in?"

"What does he want building skills for?" Nerikkaili demanded suspiciously. "Is he constructing himself a fortress?"

"I wish I could answer that, my lord. Prince Kulana-ziti confirmed the picture from Taruisha, but he had no more idea than I about what's going on."

Nudging the door open with his derriere, Benteshina

backed into the room with pitchers in both hands while a servant followed him, armed with cups.

"Time for a party; here comes the juggler." The prince smirked.

The Amurrite unloaded his pitchers to the floor and proceeded to pour everyone big drafts of wine. He settled himself back on the vacant end of the bench. "You're welcome. What's been going on?"

"Piyamaradu has rounded up seven thousand of our vassals with building skills," said Nerikkaili.

"Now, that's going to be some party." Benteshina nodded appreciatively.

"With building skills," stressed the *tawananna*. "Do you have any guesses as to what's going on?"

Benteshina let out a low whistle. "My guess is… he's building something."

The king had slumped down in his throne, tugging pensively at his nose, his brows knotted. "Something exceedingly strange is going on," he muttered. "Tapala-tarhunta, keep your ear to the ground. I'd give a lot to know more about this. Where are these men being taken? What's Piyamaradu constructing? It must be enormous, or else he wants it very fast." He fixed his eyes on his cup and seemed deep in thought, his long jaw outthrust.

"Any more demands that he become a vassal?" asked Nerikkaili. "Or has that finally fallen by the wayside as the transparent ploy it is?"

"Not at all, my lord. He stipulates that he will come to Hattusha to sign a treaty but only if my lord the crown prince comes in person to accompany him."

Cries of dismay and outrage arose.

"The arrogant bastard," sneered the prince. "Does he think I'm his pet dog, to come when he calls?"

But the king didn't rage and shout as Nerikkaili had expected. He still seemed absorbed by the mystery of the builders. "If that's what he wants, go, son. We just need to get his seal on a treaty—by any means whatever. Because if he swears fidelity in front of the Oath Gods, and then we find he's up to something, we can smash him to the ground without worrying what the other vassals think." He stood and stepped over to the charioteer to help him rise, saying grimly, "Tapala-tarhunta, mobilize your spies. I want to know what the bastard is really up to."

Nerikkaili got abruptly to his feet. The bench flipped up and deposited Benteshina on the ground, and after an instant of shock, Hattushili began to laugh, a deep, gurgling, hilarious peal of laughter that rocked the rafters of the hall.

While Hattushili met with his advisor, Tiwatipara had joined the king's men in the mess hall of the governor's garrison. There were around a hundred of them apart from foot soldiers—officers, drivers, grooms, translators, and scribes as well as civilian sutlers, cooks, and barbers. The charioteers and grooms considered themselves above the rest of the crowd, he saw; they and some of the princely officers had ranged themselves together at a single table, where they were talking loudly and laughing in a way that implied, *You people don't know what we do.*

Tiwatipara made his way over to the gathering of his peers. He found Zidanza seated quietly by himself. The driver squeezed himself across the bench and sat next to his friend, who looked up with his sleepy eyes and said, "Tipa. What news?"

"Nerikkaili encouraged me to ask the *tawananna* about Lalantiwashha," the charioteer said, unable to suppress a grin. He felt very light at heart and tried not to notice how weary Zidanza seemed. "So I'm going to do it, first chance I get. Puduhepa's here, too. I think they won't send her and the crown prince home until there's a danger of battle."

"Will you go back with the *tuhkanti*?"

"Oh." Tiwatipara's buoyant mood toppled to the ground. "I hadn't thought of that. Shit." He stared at the table, conflicted between grief at missing the battle and joy at the prospect of finding himself once more in Lalantiwashha's presence in the capital.

"Better get some food before it's all gone." Zidanza slid a bowl of thick porridge with vegetables down the table to him.

Tiwatipara ladled out porridge into a bowl and dipped in his fingers, but it was hot. "How're things with you, my friend? You look tired." He sucked his fingertips and grabbed a piece of bread to wipe them.

"I am. It's been a hard trip. I mean, any trip is hard if you're not used to it. *You* travel all the time. That's your job." Zidanza laughed but without much juice. "There's so much more work than just taking care of the horses at home." He reached for the bread. "Guess I'm lazy."

Something was wrong with Zidanza, Tiwatipara was sure. His friend wasn't himself and hadn't been for a long time. "Zidi, if there's a problem, please tell me. We've never had secrets from each other," the charioteer said quietly, even though he now knew his friend had plenty of secrets.

But the groom shook his head with a drained smile. "Just tired." His eyelids fluttered as if he couldn't keep them open.

"Zidi," Tiwatipara persisted in a low voice that tried to isolate the two friends' conversation from the buzz around them. "You know that after family, friends are the most important thing to me." He laid a hand on the groom's arm then withdrew it, remembering the healing lash marks.

"And after horses," Zidanza corrected with a smile. He continued to eat, his eyes on the food.

"What is life for if not to help the ones we love, right?" Tiwatipara said earnestly. "You've been at my side through all this awful anguish after the accident. Do you think I won't hear you out if you need to talk about something? It's been a long, long time since we really bared our souls the way we used to do."

His friend's face froze. Zidanza looked down, his mouth unsteady. Then he glanced up at the charioteer from the corner of his eye. "There's nothing wrong. I'm just tired. Why do you always want to talk about things—life and death and all? You're not a priest."

"But priests aren't the only ones who have to figure out how to live. Look at us. Bad things happen sometimes. How can you make good choices unless you think about them and know how you need to respond to them?" Tiwatipara gestured with his bread. "I admit I haven't always done a very good job, but I want to be better."

"Personally, I prefer not to think too much about life. Seems easier."

But Tiwatipara felt an unaccustomed relentlessness. "My father thought about these things, Zidi. Pawahtelmah was always ready for anything because he thought about things. He was ready to die because he expected to give his life for Our Sun eventually. And he left behind the most admirable example of—"

"I know, Tipa," cried Zidanza, his face crumpled, almost in tears. "I know he was a good man. He shouldn't have died, all right?" He swung his legs around the bench and got to his feet, knocking his neighbor's spoon from the table with a clatter. Heads turned their way.

Realizing he had overstepped, Tiwatipara reached out and grabbed at Zidanza's hand. "Sorry, my friend. I shouldn't talk about him all the time. And I can't force you to do anything. I just miss the way we used to be."

But Zidanza muttered, "I need to get some sleep," and he made his way clumsily through the tables to the door and disappeared into the night. Tiwatipara was left staring after him, empty as an old hay sack and ashamed. He set back to his meal with hanging head and cheeks afire. *Have I driven him away by harping forever on my own perfect father when his is such a bastard?*

After having spoken so boldly about making good choices, Tiwatipara realized there was a big hole in his courage. He made up his mind to speak to his cousin about her stepdaughter as soon as he had eaten. Perhaps the day after a tiring journey wasn't the best moment, but he had put it off again and again, always saying to himself that such and such a day wasn't the best time. He knew he was just afraid of asking, afraid he'd be told Lalantiwashha was already betrothed. He thought of Nerikkaili's offer to approach Puduhepa on his behalf, but he felt shy of exploiting his friendship with the crown prince in that way. And if, by some awful chance, Lalantiwashha were already betrothed, Nerikkaili's presence wouldn't change that outcome; it would just increase Tiwatipara's embarrassment. He remembered Lalantiwashha's sweet, conniving smile, the way she'd maneuvered herself into the driving lessons so she could talk to him every day, and how she'd said she wanted him. *Up, soldier. Into battle*, he told himself.

The royal party was lodged at the governor's palace. Tiwatipara presented himself to the chamberlain and requested to see the *tawananna*. "Please tell her that her cousin Tiwatipara son of Pawahtelmah would like an audience."

A moment later, the chamberlain returned and bade the charioteer follow him. Puduhepa came to the door of her chamber, smile overflowing, arms extended. "My dear cousin. I see you so rarely these days. What can I do for you?"

He could see ladies-in-waiting unpacking in the room behind her, hustling about, laying things out. He was afraid he was interrupting her. He stammered apologetically, not knowing where to start. "My cousin, I… uh, I wanted to ask you about the king's daughter, Lady Lalantiwashha."

"What about her, Tiwatipara? Does her presence distract the boys at their lessons?" Her smile stretched out, guessing, no doubt, what he was up to.

"I wondered if anyone has asked for her hand. Because she and I, we'd… we'd like to be married."

But her eyes widened suddenly in alarm, in horror even. She had *not* guessed why he was there. Her mouth fell open, and she cried hastily, "Oh, no, Tiwatipara. No. Not her, dear boy. Anyone else. Not the king's daughter."

He felt as if a spearpoint had struck his coat of mail, not quite killing him but knocking him to the ground, bruised and gasping. "W-Why?" he stuttered. "My family is as good as any in the kingdom, isn't it?"

"You can't. No, no, no. Just forget her. I'll find you someone else." His cousin's face had gone quite white. She stared at him intently, and her features hardened. "Forget her, Tiwatipara. You can't marry Lalantiwashha."

Anger began to crackle in his breast. Here was one more act of disrespect to his family, on top of so many others. Stubbornly, he demanded, "I'd like to know why. Am I not good enough? You married a prince. Why can't I marry a princess? Is she betrothed?"

The queen seemed to grasp at that idea. "Yes, that's it. She's betrothed. Just forget her. If you're ready to marry, I'll find you a nice girl."

"I don't want *a nice girl*, my cousin," he said loudly, his pride stinging with the blow she had administered. "Lalantiwashha and I are in love. She never said she was betrothed. She thinks we're going to be married." Lalantiwashha's long, pale face with its secretive smile glowed before his eyes. *How could they take her away from me? How?*

Puduhepa turned away, gripping her hair at the temples, then she whipped back around. "Please, please, Tiwatipara. Don't do anything foolish like run away with her. You must leave her alone. Do you understand?"

He stood, quivering on the balls of his feet as if ready to attack. His teeth were clenched with the effort not to yell something irretrievable. "Is it the king who says so?" he growled.

"Yes. He says you can't have his daughter. Dear gods, no."

"Why 'dear gods, no'? Why is he after my family, cousin? Why is he bent on humiliating my grandfather and me? What have we done wrong? What have we not given him?" His words were getting louder and louder.

"Oh, my dear, he loves and respects you both, believe me."

"Then why can't I have Lalantiwashha?" His voice broke and shredded. "What's wrong with me that I'm not good enough?" He could feel the tears of rage mounting to his nose.

The queen put a hand on his chest and said, her face anguished, "I can't tell you why, Tiwatipara. But trust me, this marriage cannot take place. Stay away from her, please."

Suddenly Nerikkaili, perhaps drawn by the shouting, emerged from the *tawananna*'s room. "What's going on?" he asked in his rich, deep voice. Glancing at Tiwatipara, whose face no doubt looked as red and twisted as it felt, the prince raised his eyebrows.

"I asked for your sister's hand, my prince, as you encouraged me to do, and it was thrown cruelly back in my face. It seems I'm not good enough." Tiwatipara's mouth was a slit of bitterness and humiliation.

Nerikkaili looked at the queen in surprise. "Is there some reason?"

"Of course there's a reason," she cried aggrievedly. "I'll tell you, but I can't tell him."

"May Tarhunta smite you, cousin," Tiwatipara shouted,

his teeth bared. "I don't have to put up with this disrespect! You can tell him but not me?"

Nerikkaili stepped between the two with a warning hand outstretched. "At ease, man. I'll sort this out. You'd better go for now."

Tiwatipara made a furious hissing noise and spun on his heel. He stomped out of the palace, his boots clattering on the stone floors. Once outside, he stood in the street while his face steamed in the fresh evening air. Anger lapped him up and down like a flame. *Enough, by all the gods. I've had enough.* No one could keep him from his beloved. He'd run away with her. They'd go… someplace where no one could find them. Some corner of the empire. Or to Mizri. He'd drive for the Egyptian king, and his precious Lalantiwashha would be with him.

Tiwatipara strode toward the stables where their horses had been picketed. He saw the king's grooms and some of the governor's men drifting about, doing their work, and he was filled with misery. Why did joy always seem to elude him? Just when he was happy again, he received this slap in the face. In Pawahtelmah's name, he wouldn't put up with it.

He saw Bright Warrior, one of his team, near the end of the picket line, his white-flashed nose in a feed bag. Tiwatipara put an arm around the stallion's broad, powerful neck and rested his face against the warm hair. The animal turned a bit, his big eye searching for his driver. The horse's calm began to invade the tormented human. Little by little, tears began to dribble from Tiwatipara's eyes against the animal's solid body. They were like pus flowing from a wound; he felt better as they left him, carrying off his rage.

He breathed in the smell of the horse, letting the slow beat of its heart mellow his frenzy. He listened to the measured crunching of Warrior's teeth in the grain bag and smiled finally when the horse shook its crisp, soft ears. Horses forgave. They didn't worry about human disrespect.

Night was falling, stars beginning to sparkle in the indigo sky. The charioteer stood up straight and patted his companion gratefully. "You're my best friend. Sleep well, Warrior."

He passed through the courtyard of the stable, heading to the personnel dormitory, where he and the rest of the chariotry unit had been quartered. *You, too, sleep well, Tiwatipara*, he told himself wearily. *You'll either think of a way to change the king's mind, or you'll get over this.* He could hear his grandfather's voice saying, *You're a soldier, and what a soldier does is obey.* He climbed the stairs to the long room over the stalls of the governor's horses. Pallets were made up all over the floor, where some men were already sleeping. Others threw knucklebones or chatted. He and Zidanza had spread their beds side by side, and the groom was already rolled up in his blankets, his curly hair lying all over the pillow, his face buried in it, mouth open, dead to the world.

These men were all his brothers, Tiwatipara thought, his heart swelling, whether he knew them or not. They were united by the singularity of their calling, by the trust placed in them, by the lives of the priceless horses in their charge, and by the danger they faced without a thought every day. They were strong men, brave men. Some were smarter than others, some more charming. But every one of them was ready to face death for the king, who was the gods' chosen vicar on earth. Tiwatipara, taught by his father and grandfather, had always been deeply devoted to the idea of the nearly divine *labarna* and to Hattushili in person. He had fought at a tender age to put his king on the throne. His loyalty was almost mystical. But he had never expected that loyalty to be so hard. *My father, you died for Our Sun. Help me be like you.*

Had all Tiwatipara's loyalty been nothing more than a desire to be respected, thanked, praised? He couldn't hate the king just because Hattushili didn't grant him what he wanted. The charioteer thought of his brave words. How childish they seemed. *Run away together to Mizri, indeed.* He had been rejected. That was the end of it.

He slept well, sad but at peace—the sleep of a good soldier… until, in the wee hours of the morning, he awoke to a voice crying, "No! No!"

Tiwatipara struggled to shake off the remnants of dream and sat up, his heart hammering. The dormitory was dark and silent except for Zidanza, who was writhing on his pallet. "Don't hit me, please! Please, no!" Zidanza's voice was anguished with fear and pain, but his eyes were closed.

He's asleep, thought Tiwatipara. He watched his friend, horrified. The groom raised his hands as if to protect himself, whimpering and moaning, "No, please!"

Finally, overcome with pity, Tiwatipara leaned over and shook his shoulder gently. The youth started, perhaps awakened, perhaps not. Then he rolled over and subsided into a more peaceful sleep.

Tiwatipara blew out a heavy breath and lay back down. No wonder his poor friend was so tired all the time. How well the charioteer remembered the years in which his own slumber was wrenched by terrifying nightmares, the bloody events of that distant afternoon played and replayed in even more grotesque form, himself smothered, suffocated in guilt. Zidanza had comforted him with never a mention of his own suffering. *Poor old Zidi*, he thought sadly. *You deserve better than this.*

Prince Nerikkaili had reached the mountain pass where Piyamaradu had said he would surrender his person. *No, that's not the word,* the prince said to himself snidely. *This is where he honors me with his company for the journey back to the capital.* A more arrogant bastard had never walked the black earth than Piyamaradu son of Piyama-kurunta. And that was an earth that had been walked by Urhi-tesshub.

"So here we are," Nerikkaili said to Tiwatipara, drumming his ringed fingers on the chariot rail. Behind them, a small party of soldiers and princely diplomats milled in the oppressive heat of the coastal mountains. The day was young, but cicadas already blared in the pines. Nerikkaili, in his ornate formal garb, was dissolving with sweat. He pushed back his skullcap and mopped his brow with a forearm, trying to avoid the worked edge of his bracelet.

"If my lord thinks well of it," said Tiwatipara, "perhaps we should dismount. I'd like to turn the horses with an empty car so we'll be ready to leave when that son of a dog shows up."

"Fair enough." The prince jumped down, followed by his charioteer, who gathered the long lines up short into one hand and began to lead the team by their bridles in a semicircle. The road was barely wide enough, and there was much backing up and throwing of fearful heads in protest. It wasn't the sort of graceful process that Nerikkaili relished displaying to the recalcitrant Luwian.

Nerikkaili stared down the road in the direction of the coast. The forest and the gray rock-paved clearing festooned with broom were still empty of human presence. The mountainside rose like a wall to one side of the pass. To the other, he gazed out through a break in the vegetation to where the river and its valley stretched below. The jagged coast, with its bays and headlands, was bounded by the sea, a plate of deep lapis-lazuli blue. Only the pale fan of the river's alluvium inflected it. On a finger of land in the distance lay Millawata, a patch of white, as though crystals of salt had dried on the gray-green earth.

That city belongs to us, he thought grimly. *When I'm king, I'm going to kick those Ahhiyawans out and take it back.*

He heard a few restless murmurs from his party behind him. The horses had begun to crop weeds with a scything swish of their teeth. The prince's stomach growled, reminding him that it had been a long time since they'd broken fast in camp and started up the mountainside.

Prince Kulana-ziti slid up behind his nephew and murmured, "You don't suppose he's going to refuse to show up?"

Nerikkaili smirked. "What? Piyamaradu act arrogant and insulting? What an idea."

The older man gave a snort of disgusted agreement and drew back.

The *tuhkanti* turned and cast a quick glance over his party—a dozen soldiers, the ambassador, a handful of dignitaries and clerks, and a translator. *As if anyone needs to translate Luwian, which every Hittite speaks, especially me, whose mother is from Mira.* But diplomatic pomp imposed its own superfluous demands. They even had a banner of the imperial two-headed eagle and several standards of patron gods hanging limply in the unbearable humid heat.

Suddenly, a faint noise made the prince lift his head. Tiwatipara and the horses looked up simultaneously, as if the three of them were of the same species. From afar came a clopping and jangling on the rocky road that could only mean the approach of vehicles.

"Thanks be to the thousand gods," mumbled Nerikkaili. He took a deep breath and put on his diplomatic face—firm but smooth, never ruffled, a little cynical. He had it down to an art, despite his youth, and was secure in the knowledge of the impressive figure he cut.

Out of the trees a few *iku*s away emerged a pair of fine bay horses, tossing their richly caparisoned heads with spirit, and a princely chariot. In it stood a driver and a solid-looking man in his late thirties, his dark hair in ringlets spread over his shoulders. He was dressed in ceremonial armor—a plume-bedecked helmet and a gold-studded leather cuirass. *Show-off. Atpa must have paid for that getup*, Nerikkaili thought caustically. Behind the chariot marched a handful of soldiers in uniform. *Whose, I wonder? Probably Atpa's, too.*

"Greetings, my brother," called Piyamaradu in Luwian. "Welcome to the lands of Tarhunta Pihasshasshi."

"The lands administered by Our Sun, in fact, as the Lord Tarhunta's vicar. It should be I who welcome you, Lord Piyamaradu." Nerikkaili had a sense that the two men had just drawn their swords and begun to fence. *Attack, parry, attack.* "Have you decided to submit to the might of Hatti in order to taste its generosity as well?"

Piyamaradu dismounted from his chariot with a flourish of his cloak, but he kept his distance. *He's shorter than I am,* Nerikkaili saw. *He won't get any closer lest he suffer by comparison. The man is incorrigibly vain.*

"Tempt me." The renegade grinned. "Why should I surrender my independence?"

Haggling, the son of a mangy dog. Anger began burning its way slowly up Nerikkaili's cheeks. He said with studied smoothness, "It was my understanding that my lord had already comprehended the advantages and that he was ready to draw up a vassal treaty. Our Sun was obliging enough to humor your request to send his heir to accompany you to the place of signing."

Piyamaradu stood there, still grinning, a hand on his hip—not far from the ax that hung at his belt—in a pose relaxed and more than a little insolent.

He has no intention of coming today. No one goes armed to a treaty signing under the eyes of the Oath Gods.

"A man can change his mind," said the Luwian. "Seems to me I should sell my freedom a little more dearly than that, my prince."

"And what price have you in mind, *my prince*?" said Nerikkaili, a match for anyone in insolence.

"The restoration of my kingdom."

The scene seemed to freeze for an instant. They stood still and silent as figures in a wall painting, while the cicadas razzed in mocking chorus. An explosion of fury crept closer to the surface of Nerikkaili's face. He controlled himself with a costly effort and said levelly, "I see my lord is a man of jest."

"Not at all," replied Piyamaradu, his teeth bared in what might be interpreted as humor or threat. "The restoration of my kingdom in exchange for my oath of vassalage."

Nerikkaili sneered. "And what kingdom might that be, my lord?" He remembered Benteshina's description: *a one-man kingdom, a peripatetic kingdom.*

"Arzawa, my lord. The kingdom of my father and grandfather before me."

"There *is* no Arzawa, Lord Piyamaradu. My grandfather put an end to it because it was ruled by lying swine."

Piyamaradu's grin faded, and his ruddy face grew livid.

Attack, parry. The next move is yours, you sheep fucker, thought Nerikkaili, his breath steaming in his nose as if his swordplay were physical. Silence fell again. There was a rustling among the Luwian soldiers as if they needed only a word to fall upon their enemies. Nerikkaili could feel the tension radiating from his own men.

"The power of Hatti in the West may no longer be quite what it was in your grandfather's day, my lord prince," Piyamaradu said in a barely controlled voice.

Nerikkaili replied sleekly, "Our intentions are benevolent, my lord. We have given you sincere credit for your desire to become part of our Great Kingdom. I see now that perhaps you do not share that sincerity, since the terms you present are… unlikely to be met." *Ridiculous.* "Perhaps my lord needs more time to reflect. I caution him against proposing further conditions, facetious or otherwise. Our Sun's patience is not endless."

The Luwian cast a smoldering glance at his advisors,

who looked as furious and frustrated as he. He turned back to Nerikkaili and sketched a mocking outline of a bow. "As my lord suggests. Your Sun should be aware, however, that any treaty we agree to will not be unilateral."

"No treaty is unilateral, my lord. The gods go with you." Nerikkaili nodded and turned his back, a precisely calculated insult. Otherwise, they might exchange courtly goodbyes endlessly. The *tuhkanti* made his way at a quick but dignified pace toward his chariot. He mounted without so much as looking back. Behind him, he heard the chaotic clatter of harnesses and scrape of hooves as Piyamaradu's driver maneuvered his horses around in order to head back west. Nerikkaili laid a hand in silent command on Tiwatipara's arm, and the team trotted off in a neatly controlled departure, the Hittite soldiers and diplomats peeling out after them. Perfectly choreographed.

Yet, the crown prince realized once the tension of the showdown had drained from him, *the mission failed*. He had been charged with getting Piyamaradu to the treaty signing, and he didn't have him.

"The double-dyed bastard," he snarled under his breath. "Can he honestly have expected us to make him king of Arzawa?"

"Surely not, my lord," answered Tiwatipara without taking his eyes off the road.

"One condition after another. He's just testing us. Oh, he had to have the *tuhkanti* take him to Hattusha; no one else would do. And look—the dog turd already knew he wasn't going to go through with it." Nerikkaili hissed in disgust. The more he thought about his father's likely reaction to this debacle, the angrier he became. Another failure. The old man would flay him alive. But what else could he have done? Piyamaradu hadn't come in good faith.

"You carried it off well, though, my lord," the charioteer assured him. "You stayed calm while he lost control. It was really our victory."

"Except we didn't get the fucking treaty."

The two men were silent as the chariot rocked and bumped down the narrow stone-cut road. The horses picked their way carefully; occasionally a hoof would slip on the wheel-worn rock. Nerikkaili noted that only the length of the chariot's rigid draft pole kept them from overrunning the animals' heels on the down slope. *A man risks his damned life every time he steps into one of these things.*

He observed Tiwatipara's calm, concentrated face. The charioteer seemed to be exorcised of his frenzy, poor fellow. Nerikkaili was happy to have him back as his driver. Despite the fellow's youth, he was steady and experienced. *Look how calloused his hands are from the leather lines at only twenty-five.*

At last, the forested flank of the mountains fell behind them, and the road leveled out upon the plain. Ahead stood the brown-and-white cluster of tents, pennants rippling, that marked their base camp. The wind hit them as they left the trees. The horses' heads jerked up in surprise as their own banners lifted and snapped. They closed the distance at a sedate pace, the foot soldiers taking their place at either side of the vehicles so that they entered the camp in three columns.

Officers and secretaries came out to meet them. The *tuhkanti* could see the questions upon their faces. Was the news good or bad? Was the renegade with them? Was he going to sign the treaty or wasn't he? Their curiosity fed his anger... and frankly, his sense of doom. But the encounter with his father would be some weeks in the future.

They dismounted before his tent, and Nerikkaili sent Tiwatipara and the other charioteers on to care for their animals. He called to Kulana-ziti and the rest of the dignitaries to join him inside—and immediately regretted it. At barely midday, the interior of the tent was like an oven.

"Bring us beer and something to eat," he instructed his valet, who hovered around him solicitously. "And lots of water. We're parched."

Nerikkaili threw his cap and heavy, embroidered cloak onto the camp bed, only to find that most of his tunic was soaked through with sweat. "Feel free to unhitch," he said over his shoulder to the men who had followed him. The valet returned with a ewer and a half dozen cups on a tray. The prince poured himself a drink and drained it in a gulp. "Help yourselves. No ceremony here."

The others, some of them elderly, gratefully quenched their thirst and cast off their formal outer garments. Someone said, only half jesting, "Remind me why we want this land again?"

There was a ripple of laughter, but Nerikkaili, still thinking of his father's disappointment, said, "Metal, gentlemen. Metal and manpower. And ports."

They sat in a circle and, after a brief prayer, reached out for the simple lunch, drained physically and emotionally by the morning's confrontation. Nerikkaili, always a hearty eater, was positively ravenous. He felt as if he had done hand-to-hand battle—he was empty and dehydrated.

They stuffed themselves in near silence on bread and cheese and green figs preserved in honey until finally, the prince said, "I'll have to make a report to Our Sun. Tell me what just happened."

Kulana-ziti shook his head bitterly. "The man didn't come in good faith, my lord. You played it well, but there was nothing you could do. If we meet with him again, he'll have some other impossible demand. And another. And another."

"So what must we do, my uncle? Give up negotiations? Go to war?" Nerikkaili looked around at the other dispirited faces. "How long do we let him play us before we say we've had enough?"

No one seemed eager to answer. At last, a chancery official—little more than a scribe—asked, "What do we get out of a treaty with him, my lord? Is it worth losing face?"

"You'll have to ask Our Sun that."

Kulana-ziti nodded slowly, considering. "If Piyamaradu represents only himself, he's just an annoyance. But if he has the support of legitimate rulers, if he's really their mouthpiece…"

"Yes," said Nerikkaili. "Who prettied him up like that and gave him a dozen soldiers in uniform?"

There were some evil laughs about the Luwian's meticulously arranged hair. "Atpa supports him?" someone speculated.

"Atpa's not our subject. His opinions hardly matter. What about the pieces of old Arzawa?"

"Piyamaradu attacked Taruisha a few years back and drove their king out. They aren't likely to be behind him," said Kulana-ziti reflectively.

"But Mira? Sheha River Land?"

"Manapa-kurunta is sound. He'd never go over. Who's on the throne of Mira now?"

"But, my lord," Nuwanza said, "even if the king is loyal, what of his brothers? His vizier? His army? Kings can be overthrown, as was Alakshandu in Taruisha."

"So, what does all this come down to?" the *tuhkanti* finally said in exasperation. "What recommendations do I make to my father?"

"One more try," said Kulana-ziti, pounding his fist in his hand. His long, pockmarked face was forbidding as a wolf's. "If he pulls back again at the last minute, take him out."

Nerikkaili nodded grimly. "Gentlemen, I think we have our answer."

CHAPTER 9

T HINGS DIDN'T LOOK QUITE SO clear, however, when Nerikkaili found himself in the king's presence. He'd been warned that his father was suffering agonies in his feet again and was in a dragonish mood. Hattushili was propped up in bed, the *tawananna* hovering at his side. The king's face was gray and whittled with pain. His mouth was downturned, the muscles around it bunched.

"Arma-tarhunta is no doubt at work again with his sorcerers." Hattushili indicated, with a contemptuous hand, his sickbed, the medicines at his bedside, and the propitiatory braziers of incense. "He's been tracking me since I was a child. How long is the black-hearted bastard going to live?"

"I'm sorry to hear it, my father," the prince said uncomfortably. His father was already angry—not a good omen.

"So, tell me how it went," the king demanded. "Are we going to have a treaty?"

"Piyamaradu didn't come in good faith, Father. It was just like last time—" Nerikkaili began.

But his father repeated, his voice gravelly and dangerously low, "Are we going to have a treaty?"

"Well, no, because—"

The king shouted, "By Shaushga's tits, man. I sent you to get a treaty. Where the fuck is the signer?"

"I can't make a treaty by myself, Father." The prince's voice rose in spite of himself. "The other party has to be willing to negotiate, and Piyamaradu wasn't."

"That's what *negotiation* means, son. You talk 'em into something they don't want," the king yelled until the veins stood out on his temples. Puduhepa laid a calming hand on his shoulder.

"His conditions were unmeetable, Father. He demanded the restitution of his kingdom."

"What kingdom? He doesn't have a kingdom. He's just a fucking bandit."

"Arzawa," said Nerikkaili.

After a moment of stunned silence, Hattushili let fly with a roar of bitter laughter. "Arzawa? Arzawa doesn't even exist!"

"Exactly. Yet he was inflexible. Unless we make him king of Arzawa, he won't submit to vassalage. What could I do?" Nerikkaili's face was hot with humiliation, but he held his ground. Surely his father could see how impossible his position had been. "Everyone agreed we won the showdown. Piyamaradu lost his temper, and I didn't."

But Hattushili was having none of it. He shouted in the hoarse voice of a sick man, "Oh no, we didn't win. We don't have the treaty." He sank back against his pillows, eyes burning with furious frustration, chest heaving.

Puduhepa said, appeasing, "Don't upset yourself, my husband."

She stroked his hair, and he shook her off irritably. "Stop treating me like an invalid."

The *tawananna* drew back, unruffled. "Perhaps," she said coolly to her stepson, "Our Sun would like to reflect upon the *tuhkanti*'s report and consider his response to the renegade."

"In other words, 'Shut up before you make a fool of yourself,' hah? Is that what you're saying of me, my dear?" Hattushili chuckled, his anger disarmed, and he lay wearily, reaching a hand to his wife.

He looked aged and unwell, and Nerikkaili felt guilty for provoking such a rage. *But damn it, he can be a frightfully unfair old beast.*

"Perhaps I should talk to the *tuhkanti*, My Sun, and get the full details while you rest," the *tawananna* suggested quietly, petting her husband's shoulder.

"Fine," he grumbled, pushing his head back into his pillows with a wince. "Go sound the depths of his idiocy."

Nerikkaili flushed, but he knew his father was at least partly joking at this point. The storm of his wrath had moved on off as quickly as it had arisen. The prince drew a deep, relieved breath and tried to let it out unobtrusively.

Puduhepa came toward him with her brisk little steps and led him to the door. "I'll tell you everything, My Sun," she called back. "Get some sleep if you can."

The king muttered something that escaped Nerikkaili, and the *tawananna* pulled the door shut behind her. They stood in the semidarkness of the antechamber. Nerikkaili thought of the many things he might say and said none of them, just looking down at the extremely pleasant spectacle of his stepmother, enjoying the bird's-eye view of her well-fleshed bosom straining against her blouse. He let his imagination roam below her clothing and felt his anger float away.

"Well," he finally said, the heat draining from his face. "What a foul-tempered old bastard I have for a father." But it was said with more affection than rancor.

"Don't be so hard on him," Puduhepa pleaded, her hand on his arm. "He doesn't feel well. It's difficult for a man of his vitality."

"If, by *vitality*, you mean littering the black earth with his love children…" Nerikkaili gave her a dry, knowing smile.

She looked up at him from under her lids, pained. "I wish your father had told you earlier."

Nerikkaili traced the smooth oval of his stepmother's cheek with a finger. "Where do you want to go to… sound the depths of my idiocy, my lady?"

Two days later, the king was still confined to his bed but feeling better—and extremely impatient to be up and about. His wife and eldest son were standing beside him. "I think it's time the two of you went back to the capital," he said. "Somebody needs to keep things going at home; I'm not sure I trust that Walwa-ziti, and there are some things he can't do as vizier anyway. Besides, I expect we'll have to draw our swords against Piyamaradu before long."

"But, Father," Nerikkaili protested, "you can't even stand up. How are you planning to lead the troops? Why don't you go home instead and let me do it?"

"We aren't in battle yet, son," the king reminded him with a growl. "I don't plan to lie here for the rest of my life. And anyway, I don't have to go swinging a sword. I just want to be there to watch and direct. To confront the bastard and see him go down."

Nerikkaili exchanged glances with the *tawananna*. There was no reading the boy's face when he set his mind to being impenetrable. Hattushili's wife stood at the king's head, stroking his hair.

"And when you get back, my dear, send Hishni and Lurma-ziti," he said to Puduhepa. "I want to get that flag system into operation. Nuwanza will be glad to have him—"

"No one's glad to have Lurma-ziti, Father," said Nerikkaili with a curl of the lip.

"Then think of it this way: you'll be glad *not* to have him in the capital." The king grinned, but he felt bad for his second born, whom nobody wanted. Lurma-ziti was a smart boy, in fact. He had a natural sense of tactics, and he was devious, which didn't make him good company in real life but could be useful in plotting strategy. "And send me the two little friends. It's time they saw some action."

Puduhepa dropped her hand from his hair and pressed her fingertips to her mouth in consternation. "Tashmi and Ulmi-tesshub? You're determined, My Sun?"

"Absolutely, my doe. You can't keep them in the nursery for the rest of their lives. Let 'em get out there and see blood and feel the bite of bronze. Make men of 'em. Tiwatipara can stay and drive Tashmi-sharrumma. I want Ulmi to be on his own. He'll be a lot more serious if he isn't trying to impress his cousin."

Still looking skeptical, Nerikkaili took his leave to begin preparations for his departure. Puduhepa sat on the edge of the bed and took Hattushili's hand. "My dear, are you ready to go into battle so soon?"

"Who knows if I'll even have to? But yes, I'm tired of this life of the invalid. I've had more than enough of it in my day." He squeezed her little hand and put it to his lips. "I want you back in Hattusha to keep your ear to the ground. Things are too quiet with Urhi-tesshub. If he's really back in our borders someplace, he should be making more noise."

"You need Benteshina down there, listening."

"Eventually. I want him here for the moment, though. You don't think much of him, I know, but he's an extremely skilled commander."

"Of very small troops," his wife said, her mouth tight with the effort to suppress a snicker. Then the two of them laughed heartily.

The king finally grew pensive. "I'd give a lot to know what those seven thousand men Piyamaradu has taken are all about."

"That's a blow, isn't it? We're always so short of manpower—to farm and to serve in the army."

"Why can't we multiply faster?" He sighed then added mischievously, "I'm doing *my* part."

The *tawananna* laughed and bent over to hug him, her arms awkwardly under his shoulders. "You're such a naughty boy. That's what happens when the Lady Shaushga claims you for her own. You become irresistible." She kissed him on the eyelid and straightened up.

"And you're her priestess, my love." He felt a little sad suddenly. She was so young. His health wasn't getting any better. How many years before he would, in fact, be confined to his bed as he had been in childhood? What a life that would be for her. "Is the crown prince feeling any friendlier toward you these days?"

"He is, my husband. He's somewhat suspicious of the sudden turn of events"—she smiled thinly at the king, a blush seeping up her cheeks—"but he's not inclined to complain."

Hattushili chuckled. "Did you know he actually came to me to report you?"

"What?" Her eyebrows rose in surprise.

"See what a dutiful son I have? It makes me feel I can trust him. He said you were behaving with somewhat indecent warmth toward him, and he thought I should know." He gave a gurgling rumble of laughter.

"We never thought of that, did we? What did you tell him?" Her brows betrayed a kind of anxiety.

"That it was important we all be friends, for the good of the kingdom. That I trusted him not to carry friendship too far. He hasn't tried, has he?"

She shook her head, seeming amused. "No. He's a very courtly young man although… warm-blooded."

After a moment of silence, Puduhepa said, "What about Tiwatipara, my love?"

The king sighed heavily. "I was damned sorry you had to be the one to warn him away from Lalantiwashha, my dearest. That must have been painful."

"I felt terrible for him," his wife said. "He was so offended and kept saying, 'Why am I not good enough?' But he caught me completely off guard. She had asked to accompany the boys to their lessons, but I had no idea she and Tiwatipara were falling in love, or I would have told him she was betrothed."

"Well, it's true now. And anyway, from what Nerikkaili has told me, the lad has gotten over it. He's been a model of soldierly acceptance. You see, my dear?" The king stretched out an affectionate arm to encircle his wife's hips. "Hardship and disappointment make a fellow stronger. That'll be true of little Tashmi-sharrumma, too. He'll be a man by the time you see him next."

She sniffed, unconvinced. "A twelve-year-old man…"

In fact, the royal party delayed their departure from Waliwanda, so the crown prince and the *tawananna* did not leave immediately as foreseen. Instead, the king summoned by messenger Tashmi-sharrumma and his cousin. The former was hoping to see his first battle or at least learn, at his father's side, the art of war.

Tiwatipara's service had been changed from Nerikkaili to Nerikkaili's little brother, thus assuring that he would remain on the frontier. This came as a relief to him, not only because he looked forward to an eventual confrontation with the Luwians but also because he feared mightily having to tell Lalantiwashha that his suit had been rejected. How could he explain it, when he didn't understand it himself?

Rather than butting his head against the loss of Lalantiwashha, he applied himself to trying to figure out who had killed Pawahtelmah. Again and again, he let his memory roam the crowds that had stood around the field that afternoon. The king. Benteshina. Nerikkaili. Hishni and Lurma-ziti. Zuzuhha. All the grooms and drivers and stable boys not in service elsewhere. Fifty or more men, their eyes fixed on the field, laughing, yelling, and making noise. Then there was Zidanza, leaning with his back against the chariot while Tiwatipara led up the two horses. It was typical of Zidanza never to stand when he could lean.

I'm going to have to ask Zidi point-blank if he left the chariot for even a moment, thought Tiwatipara finally. They had avoided each other to some extent since his faux pas in the mess, and Tiwatipara hesitated to beard the groom about this lest he seem to be accusing Zidanza of laxity. He hated to trouble his friend, who seemed so troubled already. *What a bastard his father must be, priest or not. But if I don't ask him about this, I'll never get any further. I just don't see how it could have happened any other way.* He wondered whom else he could ask. Maybe the *tuhkanti* had seen someone slipping away as the first horses ran, but he had said nothing. In the back of Tiwatipara's mind also lay the possibility that Prince Nerikkaili was at the bottom of the attempt.

As soon as he had brought back his team from the morning's moving-archery practice, Tiwatipara roamed the governor's stables in search of his curly-haired friend. He found him cleaning out the boxes of the king's personal horses. His back was to the door, and he didn't turn when the charioteer approached.

Tiwatipara watched him raking at a dreamy pace and, in a sudden fit of mischief, shouted, "Attack!"

Zidanza jumped and jerked around, his round face agape with terror, the stallion shying away uneasily from the frightened human. Then the groom's eyes widened in recognition, and he laughed ruefully. "Gods, Tipa, you could scare a man to death. What is it?"

Tiwatipara clapped him apologetically on the arm. "Sorry, old man. I didn't mean to make you startle Wrath." His voice dropped. "Listen, I have a question to ask you about… the day of the accident." He drew his friend out into the aisle, and Zidanza carefully closed the half door behind him.

Zidanza's attention seemed to be on something in the distance. His face was pallid with brownish smudges under his eyes. "It's been a long time, Tipa. I don't know how much I'll remember."

"You were guarding the chariot while I went inside and harnessed up the team, right? You remember?"

"Not guarding, exactly."

"No, but you were there when I left and there when I came back. Zidanza, scrape your memory hard. Did you leave at all? Even for a little while?"

The groom's mouth twisted uncomfortably in the effort to recollect. Then he scratched his head, not out of puzzlement but in embarrassment, as if he feared he had let his friend down. "I went to the latrines. I… I was having trouble with my bowels, remember?"

Relief loosened the vise that anxiety had screwed around Tiwatipara's chest, and he exhaled a deep, easing breath. "That answers a lot of questions. Thank you, Zidi. Don't know why I never asked you before. So, it could have been anybody—one of the bystanders or even someone from outside sneaking over."

"Anybody… what?" Zidanza blinked his sleepy eyes at his friend.

"Who sabotaged the chariot."

The groom swallowed hard, his mouth drooping. He looked away. "They think it was sabotaged, do they?"

"You don't remember? I told you that," cried Tiwatipara in disbelief. "Why else would I be looking for a saboteur?" He was more concerned than ever about his friend. Was Zidanza losing his memory on top of everything? Maybe his recollections of that day weren't so useful after all.

"Oh, right." Zidanza's eyes met Tiwatipara's guiltily, almost fearfully. "You're not mad at me, are you, Tipa? I didn't know I was supposed to be on guard."

"No, no, my friend. I'm just trying to figure out who could have done it. If you'd been there the whole time, then it must have happened before we even put the car together, in the chariot room. But this way, anybody there could have cut the axle."

"With all those people around?" Zidanza said.

"They were all facing the other way, remember, completely caught up in the trials. And all that yelling and rumbling and laughter—it's quite likely no one even heard."

Zidanza looked dubious. "Pretty risky, though. Somebody could've turned around at any minute."

"I know, friend." Tiwatipara raised his eyebrows. "Yet it happened. Somebody took that risk."

Zidanza looked worried, his brow pleated. "If Our Sun gets mad at me for leaving my post, he may kick me out.

You know I've already been in trouble once. My father will kill me, and I'm not exaggerating."

Tiwatipara squeezed his friend's arm in compassion. "I won't say anything, Zidi. You know that. Gods, man, is your father such a brute? Leave home. Get away from him. It's not right to keep you in such slavery at your age."

But the groom heaved a sigh, dropping his eyes. "I guess I'm too lazy to leave."

Tiwatipara felt heavyhearted for his friend's sake. He hoped that at least Zidanza's bruises could heal while they were on campaign, far away from the capital.

"Thanks for your help, old man." He smiled sadly. "You can feed your horses now."

He drifted off down the aisle, lost in thought. *Anyone could have done it—anyone who absented himself from the circle around the track for a few minutes. Or anyone sneaking up from the barns.*

Tiwatipara saw ahead the king's two sons Hishni and Lurma-ziti. They were standing head to head in the shadows near the corner of the barn door, their voices quietly buzzing. Then Hishni gave a holler of laughter. Lurma-ziti shushed him with a spidery hand and peeked around the door.

What are they up to? Tiwatipara wondered, hostility chilling him. Hishni was a good-natured cipher by himself, but the elder prince could be counted on for being up to no good. The charioteer eyed Lurma-ziti, whose back was to him. Everyone called him *huwalpant*, but he wasn't a hunchback, just twisted unnaturally sideways so that one shoulder was higher than the other. He was thin as a wire and always twitchy as if some sort of painful energy crackled inside him, like the sparks of fire that skewered one on a winter day after dragging a woolen blanket off a horse.

Suddenly, in the doorway, Prince Tashmi-sharrumma and his cousin appeared in silhouette. Laughing wildly, legs pumping, they raced as fast as they could go toward the barn, the former slightly in the lead. No sooner had they crossed the threshold than the younger prince seemed to fly forward into the air, and he hit the ground chin first, sliding flat on his stomach across the hard dirt of the aisle. It was such a brutal fall that Tiwatipara could hear the thump from where he stood. The prince lay there, stunned.

Tiwatipara began to run toward the boys. Ulmi-tesshub had already dropped to his knees by the lad's side, crying aloud in dismay, "Tash!" Lurma-ziti and Hishni stood, watching and grinning, as Tashmi-sharrumma crawled painfully to his feet with his cousin's help. The boy's face was scraped, blood trickling from his lips and nose, and his knees were black and bloodied. He looked dazed and seemed to be winded, but he wasn't crying.

"My lord, are you hurt?" Tiwatipara cried, arriving at his side. "What happened?"

Lurma-ziti and Hishni were laughing. "You owe me a beer," said the elder to his brother. "I told you he wouldn't see it."

"You misbegotten dog turd!" Ulmi-tesshub snarled. He looked around at Tiwatipara and said, his voice shaking with fury, "That piece of crap stretched a string across the ground so Tash would trip."

"I'm all right," murmured the younger prince, his mouth full of blood. He stared first at his skinned palms and then at his older brothers, but Tiwatipara couldn't read his expression. He didn't seem to be angry, but he might have been.

Ulmi-tesshub, on the other hand, was quivering with rage. He charged at Lurma-ziti, his fists bunched, but Hishni reached out and grabbed him, stopping him in his tracks. "Easy, fireball." He laughed and locked the youth against him with a forearm across his throat. Ulmi-tesshub struggled fiercely, spitting out curses, scrabbling at Hishni's arm, and trying to stretch out a foot to kick Lurma-ziti, but the latter stood just out of range, smiling nastily, his arms crossed over his chest.

Tiwatipara felt outrage smoldering inside him. He longed with all his soul to plant a fist in Lurma-ziti's face, but he knew he must not yield to the temptation. He turned to Tashmi-sharrumma, who was drawing a few experimental deep breaths and feeling his tongue, which he had seemingly bitten. "Nothing broken?" Tiwatipara asked in a low voice.

The lad shook his head. His eyes were narrowed in pain, his lashes sparkling with unshed tears, but otherwise, his expression was inscrutable.

The charioteer faced Lurma-ziti, his contempt too strong to hide. "That was unworthy, my lord," he spat.

"Are you his protector now, too, Tiwatipara?" asked Lurma-ziti silkily. "Shed a few tears for us, won't you?"

You contemptible animal, thought Tiwatipara, snarling inside. *A grown man playing cruel jokes on a child? What sort of perverted thing are you?* He said nothing aloud, not trusting himself not to commit some terrible breach of etiquette toward the king's son, but his breathing had become dangerously heavy.

Lurma-ziti reached out and tickled Ulmi-tesshub's genitals through his tunic. The youth, spitting out imprecations, roared and bucked in Hishni's grip, murder in his twisted face. His tormentor smiled.

He's baiting him. Gods help Lurma-ziti if Ulmi breaks free. "Tashmi-sharrumma, Ulmi-tesshub, let's go and wash off those scrapes. Leave these *gentlemen* to their own pastimes." He shepherded the limping boy toward the door then turned back and shot Ulmi a peremptory beckoning jerk of the head. Hishni released Ulmi-tesshub and pushed him after his cousins. "Come on, Ulmi," Tiwatipara called in a voice that brooked no disobedience.

Lurma-ziti, his thumbs in his belt, watched them go. His face, long and narrow as a knife blade, was tense with some emotion Tiwatipara couldn't identify. *Pleasure? Hatred? Pain?*

"Go with your nursemaid, little boys," the prince said sarcastically and belched. Hishni snickered.

Tiwatipara walked the boys back to the spring-fed fountain that kept the horses' watering trough filled. Still steaming, he scooped water in his cupped hands directly from the spigot and splashed it on Tashmi-sharrumma's knees, trying to get the worst of the dirt off. Unfortunately, the boy hadn't been in his driver's tunic but in a short garment that exposed his legs to the full brunt of the dirt and abrasion. Pieces of gravel and manure were pressed into the shredded skin. The lad sucked in his breath as the mud and blood dripped down his shins, but he still didn't cry. "Good soldier," said Tiwatipara, clapping him admiringly on the shoulder. "Take him to the *tawananna*, Ulmi, and be sure she pours some wine over these. Did you bite your tongue, my prince?"

The younger boy nodded. He looked like he had torn into a piece of raw meat, red trickling from the corners of his mouth and down his bruised chin.

"Rinse your mouth out."

Tashmi-sharrumma obeyed, drinking from his hands and spitting bloody pink water back into the trough. "Thank you," he said thickly.

"I'll kill him," Ulmi-tesshub muttered, almost bouncing on his toes in his fury. "I'll kill the vile turd."

"He's not deserving of your attention, my prince," said Tiwatipara, scarcely able to keep the anger out of his voice. "Just stay away from him. He'd like nothing better than to provoke you to do something that will get you in trouble."

"What's wrong with that monster? Why does he hate Tash so? I'd like to get him in a dark corner one of these days and—"

"Stay away from him," Tiwatipara cautioned him again, this time roughly. He remembered the malevolent light in the prince's black eyes. "He wouldn't stop at killing you if he felt he could get away with it."

Then he realized what he had said.

Surely, he had found the man who had sabotaged the king's chariot. Hatred blazed like a fierce, devouring fire within his heart. *I've got you now,* huwalpant, he thought darkly, gritting his teeth. Only a few moments before, Lurma-ziti had stretched a string across the barn door while Tiwatipara and Zidanza had stood talking a few *iku*s away. They'd never noticed a thing. How easily sabotage could happen after all. He just had to prove it. Then he'd go to the king and get his vengeance.

CHAPTER 10

"MY DEAR, YOU CAN RAIL all you want, but I'm not going back yet. You won't be crossing the border immediately, and I'm not sure you don't still need me. You know you're not steady on your feet yet after your illness." The *tawananna* crossed her arms and stood with her little brow wrinkled stubbornly.

Hattushili shot her a look of annoyance over his dish of porridge. He rumbled, "Use the boys as an excuse, not me."

"That's another reason." Puduhepa banged her fist on the table. "You have to do something about that awful Lurma-ziti. He'll kill Tashmi if someone doesn't rein him in."

Her husband smiled appreciatively. "You're damned beautiful when you're mad, my doe."

"I'm serious, Hattushili. Neither you nor I want to interfere with the children's affairs, but—"

"You have to let them learn to sort things out for themselves, my dear, or they'll always be looking for someone else to make things right," the king interrupted around a mouthful of meat.

"I know, I know. I agree in principle. But this was quite serious. The boy could have broken his neck. And he'd never have said anything about it if Ulmi-tesshub hadn't walked him to my room to dress his cuts. This is probably going on much more often than we know."

The king sat up and heaved a sigh. "I can talk to Lurma-ziti, tell him to back off. I've done it before. But did that stop anything in the long run?"

"What did you tell him, though? 'Don't beat your brother'? So he hasn't done that exact thing again. But he still makes life miserable for him."

"And that's what Tashmi-sharrumma has to learn to deal with. There'll always be some bully after him. He can't go running to Mama."

"He'd be the last one to run to Mama. You know that."

"And I admire it. He's got character. Tiwatipara told me that he didn't even cry."

She fell silent, her lips compressed. She might have been proud of the boy, but Hattushili sensed that her silence was a strategic retreat and not an admission of defeat.

"I feel like you're defending Lurma-ziti, My Sun," she finally said resentfully. "You're the one who said mistreating a dog makes it mean. What if all this makes little Tashmi mean?"

"And *you* said, 'You are what you are.' Tashmi's not a mean boy. This will make him strong, believe me."

"If he lives."

The king's face began to grow hot. The woman could be insufferably stubborn. He growled in warning, "Enough, my dear. Life is dangerous, all right? The boy will soon be going into battle for the first time. Lurma-ziti is the least of his worries."

There was a knock at the door, and the king's chamberlain appeared. "My Sun, Lord Tapala-tarhunta is here. He said you had called for him."

"Send him in, my man." To his wife, Hattushili, all rancor set aside, said, "Puduhepa, you can stay, my dear, since you plan to be here for a while." He flashed her a meaningful wag of the eyebrow. She nodded with a prim smile, clearly content to have accomplished what she had come for.

The old charioteer maneuvered himself through the door carefully, his face tight with effort. He saluted. "My Sun. My lady."

"Tapala-tarhunta, sit down. I want to sound you out about a few things and hear your latest dispatches. Your niece"—he tipped his head at the *tawananna*—"desired to be present, too."

Puduhepa smiled warmly and helped the *hashtanuri* lower himself onto a stool. "How good to see you, my uncle. How does my aunt?"

"Well enough, my lady," he replied evasively.

She stepped back and seated herself on the bed beside the king.

Hattushili pushed aside his bowl and began without preamble. "Tell me honestly, Tapala. What do you think of my ambassadors in the West? Do they understand the situation?"

"They're good men, My Sun. Intelligent and loyal. Whether they take the Luwians seriously enough is another story. Did you know that almost everyone in our kingdom speaks Luwian, even here? Even to the eastern border, in Kizzuwatna. The only men who speak Neshite as our primary language are we, the royal family and the aristocracy. We float like a very thin layer of oil on the surface of the people. If there ever is a rising—if Piyamaradu or someone like him ever really does manage to get all those Westerners organized—it will be extremely hard to put down. Impossible. It will… it will be the end of us."

Hattushili shot him a glance, quick and intense, from under his heavy lids. "Is that so, Tapala? That's not good news."

The charioteer sighed. "No, My Sun, it's not. But it's what you need to know. Your father gave us a reprieve by dismembering Arzawa. For the moment, no one kingdom is strong enough to oppose us. But someone might just come along to unite them. They're not fools. And they're not happy."

"What is their relationship with Ahhiyawa, do you think?"

"Ah." Tapala-tarhunta scratched his chin thoughtfully. "Would that I knew. Piyamaradu seems to hole up there between raids on our shores. Is he in the pay of Ahhiyawa? Who knows? But he could certainly be useful to their king, who wants to expand his toehold in the Luwian lands."

"Of course," sneered the king. "His people are traders. And the West is full of metal—gold and silver and copper and lead. A trader's dream. Everybody wants metal."

"He wants to use Millawata as his beachhead. Its governor, Atpa, is some kind of relative of his and owes his existence to the protection of Ahhiyawa. Despite being our age, he's married to Piyamaradu's adolescent daughter."

"Oh, is he, now?" Hattushili chuckled darkly. "That explains why we can't get an honest word out of Atpa about the rascal's whereabouts. Any chance we can suborn him?"

"I doubt it, My Sun. We don't have much leverage out there. And anyway, Atpa isn't the real danger of the Ahhiyawans in the West, although he is the official face of it. The man we need to be afraid of is the king of Ahhiyawa's brother, Tawagalawa. He's his brother's roving ambassador, so to speak."

"So he's the one to negotiate with?" asked the *tawananna*.

"Yes, my lady. I would say so."

The king thrust out his jaw, musing. "We need a treaty with Ahhiyawa. Bind them to mutual extradition. Force them to turn Piyamaradu over to us so he doesn't feel he can strike at us and then abscond to somewhere safe."

Tapala-tarhunta grinned. "May Runda, the god of luck, run before you into that battle, My Sun."

The two men laughed but not with much humor.

"We need a peer treaty, though," said the king. "Is there any sense in which the king of Ahhiyawa could be considered a Great King?"

Tapala-tarhunta made a wry face. "I've never been to Ahhiyawa, My Sun, but from what I've heard, the kingdom isn't large or influential in its own region. Instead, there are many such kingdoms, all speaking the same language. Much like our friends the Luwians. Ahhiyawa is important to us chiefly because of its aspirations on our shores."

"Would it be completely cynical to write him, addressing him as a brother Great King, then?"

Tapala-tarhunta pursed his lips. "It would be cynical, My Sun. But you'll do it, won't you?"

"If that's what it takes to flatter him into a peer treaty with a mutual extradition clause, by Shaushga, I will!"

The three of them exchanged a knowing nod. Canny diplomatic maneuvers were more effective than brute force, but it seemed impossible to get an honest fix on what was going on out there. The Ahhiyawans were just one more layer of confusion.

The king gave a pensive tug at his nose. "And what about Piyamaradu's seven thousand builders, Tapala? Any ideas about that?"

The charioteer's face grew keen. "My Sun, that was something I wanted to tell you. One of my spies has reported rumors that the men are to be shipped to Ahhiyawa."

"What?" exploded the king, rage flaming up in his cheeks. "By the thousand gods! Ship my men to someone else? What is this? We've fought no battles; these aren't honest captives. What's that sheep-fucking bastard up to, colluding with our enemies?" He stood up and stalked back and forth, a little unsteady on his tingling feet, clenching his fists in fury.

"If it's true, this is an act of war," said the *tawananna* uneasily. She caught her husband's eye.

"It's only a rumor, My Sun," cautioned Tapala-tarhunta. "Words dropped in an inn, overheard on a corner. We can't act on such whispers, but—"

"But we'd damned better be prepared to jump if they turn out to be true," Hattushili snarled. "I'd rather they stole horses or silver than men. Shaushga knows how desperate we are to keep bodies in the fields. And on the battlefield."

"At least you can always hire mercenaries to fight," his wife murmured, but her eyes shifted toward her husband's with concern.

"I don't trust 'em. They cost us a magnificent hostage taking at Kinza. They're only a last resort." He dropped to a seat again and sat humped over at the edge of the bed, his knuckles on his thighs, elbows out. "It's the farmers… seven thousand men. That's like taking a city." The king sank into inarticulate imprecations, his face steaming, his jaw clenched.

Tapala-tarhunta sat in grim silence, able to offer no solution. Puduhepa, at her husband's side, was wrapped in concentration. Hattushili could almost hear the ideas clicking through her head. But she said nothing.

The king exhaled a harsh breath through his nose and said at last in a calmer voice, "Your network is the most valuable thing we have in our favor, Tapala. I hate to admit it, but Armatalli may have been right—the gods must have wanted you back in the West rather than in my box with me." He gazed ruefully at his friend, well able to imagine the disappointment the sudden demotion must cost him.

But the old charioteer dipped his head with perfect blandness as if he had no personal preferences. "However I can serve you best, My Sun."

The king got up, and Tapala-tarhunta gathered his crutches and heaved himself to his feet as well.

"How is Tiwatipara doing these days, hah?" Hattushili laid a hand on the charioteer's shoulder.

"I don't see him often, My Sun. But we've talked a few

times since we've been here in Waliwanda. He seems happier. He told me about being refused Lady Lalantiwashha's hand." Tapala-tarhunta glanced up at the king but without animosity, just with the amusement of an old man over a young man's broken heart. He nodded to his niece. "I apologize, my lady, if he was rude to you. He sees offense everywhere, I fear."

The king exchanged a sorrowful glance with his wife. She said graciously, "Not at all, my uncle. I know he was unhappy, but she's betrothed. To the king of Mira, in fact."

"A far more valuable liaison, for sure. You have Tiwatipara's loyalty with or without a marriage alliance, My Sun."

"He's getting over it, then? No hard feelings?" Hattushili asked solicitously.

"No, none. His obsession these days is to find out who sabotaged the chariot that killed his father."

"Ah." The king stroked his nose, thoughtful. "He can count on my help, whatever that might turn out to be. After all, the bastard was attempting to assassinate me."

"He'll be grateful for any aid, My Sun."

"Well, keep your ears open, Tapala-tarhunta. Send a messenger if you hear anything at all. I want a treaty from Piyamaradu before the spring is out."

The charioteer bowed, fist to chest, and made his way out. Hattushili turned to his wife. She locked eyes with him. Her expression was troubled.

"Well, in another month, I'll officially be a man." Ulmi-tesshub was in high good humor. He threw an arm around his young cousin's shoulders, and Tashmi-sharrumma gazed up at him in sleepy-eyed admiration. The boys were supposed to be harnessing up their team of mares for their morning lesson. "I'll turn sixteen and have my *hasshuma* ceremony," the youth explained to Tiwatipara.

"What's that?" the charioteer asked. He had had no *hasshuma* ceremony when he turned sixteen.

"It's only for princes," explained Ulmi-tesshub with a falsely modest grin. "They take you down to the soldiers' brothel and stretch you out on a bed." Obviously enjoying the recital, he mimed lying on a bed with his arms and legs spread out. Tashmi-sharrumma watched him, rapt.

"They put loaves of bread and jugs of beer all around you, and then twelve prostitutes come in, and then—"

"Ulmi-tesshub, dear, I think that's enough detail," a feminine voice cut in stiffly. "Your cousin is only eleven."

"Twelve," said Tashmi-sharrumma. No one seemed to hear him, and he didn't appear to care.

His mother had come unnoticed to the door of the barn in the course of her nephew's demonstration. The soon-to-be-man jumped in surprise then laughed uproariously, his face coloring with what might have been guilt or the pleasure of attracting someone's attention.

Suppressing his amusement, Tiwatipara bowed. "My lady." He had repented of his acrimony over the refusal of Lalantiwashha long ago.

"How are the boys doing, Tiwatipara?" The *tawananna* put her arm around her son and smoothed his hair affectionately. Her eyes were warm with love and pride, and the prince, who was every bit as tall as she, wrapped his arm around her waist. Suddenly, a pang of longing lodged in the charioteer's throat and seemed to choke him. He had never had a mother's loving embrace, never known a mother's gentle hand on his hair. As long as Pawahtelmah had been alive, he hadn't missed it. From the corner of his eye, he saw that a strange, sad look of yearning had invaded the face of Ulmi-tesshub, too.

"Well, my lady," Tiwatipara said, recalling himself to the moment.

"Please, we're family, Tiwatipara. No formalities. Can they give me a demonstration?"

"Of course, my cousin. Tashmi-sharrumma, you first. The two of you hitch up Little Pea and Shaushga's Darling."

The boys scampered away, laughing and pushing each other. The *tawananna* followed them fondly with her eyes. When they had disappeared into the stable, she turned to Tiwatipara, hope and anxiety warring in her wrinkled brow. "Is Tashmi-sharrumma really doing all right? He seems terribly young for this, but his father wanted him to do it."

"Oh, yes. He's strong for his age and very serious. He does everything I tell him. And he has a nice, gentle touch with the animals. He'll make a good charioteer, despite his eyesight."

Puduhepa smiled, her eyes lowered. Then she looked up. "And Ulmi-tesshub?"

"He has a man's strength, but he's less serious." Tiwatipara grinned. "He does *not* do everything I tell him. But he'll be all right. He'll probably concentrate better when the two boys are not together."

"They're always together," she murmured. "Our Sun wants Tashmi-sharrumma to drive for Ulmi-tesshub for a few years—when he's old enough, of course. He thinks it's a necessary part of becoming a good commander."

"He's undoubtedly right."

The clopping of hooves and the rumble of hobnailed wheels on the hard earth made them look up. The two princes were mounted in the box of a light processional chariot with a pair of mild-looking mares hitched before them.

"We're pretending these are real horses and that this is a real chariot," called Ulmi-tesshub. He stood to his cousin's right, his hands on the bar, grinning, while the younger boy had the reins wrapped around his knuckles and was guiding the two animals expertly toward his mother. His homely young face was very serious—no proud *look-at-me* smile, just a gnawed lip of concentration. The *tawananna*'s eyes crinkled with tenderness as her son brought the horses to her feet. The boy saluted with his whip like a real charioteer.

"We're just waiting till Tiwatipara shaves our foreheads," Ulmi-tesshub assured his aunt.

"Don't you dare!" she warned Tiwatipara then turned to her son. "Trot them around for me, won't you, dear? Tiwatipara will tell me how well you're doing things."

Tashmi-sharrumma obediently clucked up the team and began a brisk circuit of the court.

"So how's he really doing?" the *tawananna* said, her eyes never straying from her son's stiff little back.

"Fine. He keeps his hands up like he's supposed to, and his feet are well planted. Now, here he should lean into his turn a little less, take up the shift in his legs."

"Don't lean into your turn, son," she called. Ulmi-tesshub pivoted and waved, then elbowed his cousin and said something. He laughed, but Tashmi-sharrumma continued to concentrate on his driving.

"They're quite a pair," said Tiwatipara. "Couldn't be more different."

"Yes, it's so, isn't it? And yet they're inseparable. Or perhaps that's *why* they're inseparable." The *tawananna* smiled, watching her son take his turn without leaning.

Tiwatipara felt a sudden pang of sorrow for Zidanza, the boy who had been his own inseparable companion in childhood, adolescence, and now manhood. He'd thought they had shared everything—*he* certainly had, being a rather unreserved sort of person. But he realized only lately how little he had known about the groom and the suffering he had borne. *Poor Zidi.* He reminded Tiwatipara of his grandmother as he drifted further and further away, turning somehow thinner, less present, mistier—as if, at some point, he would become transparent and cease to exist. It was like part of Tiwatipara's own life fading away. *Dear gods*, he thought, self-pity creeping up on him. *Haven't I lost enough?*

He realized his face had grown somber. The *tawananna* was looking at him, her dark eyes penetrating. "What are you thinking about, Tiwatipara?" she said gently.

"Losing things," he said, forcing a smile. "Losing people you love."

"I'm sorry I had to refuse you Lalantiwashha's hand. She's marrying the king of Mira. But don't give up. You know, when you lose one person, the gods give you someone else."

He sniffed bitterly. "Actually, it was my father I was

thinking about. They don't give you another father, do they?"

She laid her hand briefly upon Tiwatipara's forearm then turned back to the court, where her son was trotting his team toward her. "Very good, my dear. Now, Ulmi-tesshub, you take a turn."

The king had decided that Nerikkaili, rather than he, would conduct the meeting with Tawagalawa. If the king of Ahhiyawa were not present, then some diplomat of rank comparable to the Western king's brother should represent Hatti Land. There was no possibility of the *labarna* in person negotiating with an inferior.

Nerikkaili had obtained Tiwatipara's services, since Tashmi-sharrumma would remain at Waliwanda with the rest of the royal party. The negotiations were to take place at the temple of the Sun Goddess in Iyalanda, a small town not far from Millawata—or Millawanda, as the locals called it—the colony of the Ahhiyawans. Iyalanda was just outside the vassal state of Mira and thus on neutral territory.

The town was on a fair-sized river, which ran in a narrow valley through mountainous terrain, but the road at the bottom of the defile was well maintained, and it was possible to make good time. By pushing the horses a bit, the prince's party had covered the distance in less than a day. Nerikkaili stared at the countryside around him with an evaluating eye. He observed that if it came to an attack on Millawata, troops could be moved easily through here but in columns no wider than two soldiers abreast. The forested cliffs and rocky, looming peaks to either flank would make excellent cover for an ambush. His father needed to know that. Nerikkaili noticed that the eyes of Benteshina, the third passenger in the chariot, roamed the mountainsides as well.

Nerikkaili's entourage entered Iyalanda at dusk, just before the closing of the gates, and proceeded directly to the temple compound, where priests came out to greet them and escort them to their quarters in the guesthouse. Benteshina and Kulana-ziti had accompanied the *tuhkanti* to serve as witnesses. The three princely diplomats had their own rooms, but Tiwatipara and the secretaries and translators and valets and grooms and other drivers were lodged in a large central hall that accommodated pilgrims at festival time. Still, it was comfortably fitted out, with camp beds, fine colorful rugs, and an array of refreshments sufficient for a light supper set up on a long chest. After all, even these lesser participants in the treaty negotiations were wellborn. A big sturdy table and benches stretched across one end, illumined by a row of oil lamps. Tapala-tarhunta was due to join them from Apasha; the priests told the crown prince that he had arrived earlier in the day.

It was pleasant to stand on a solid floor for a change, thought Nerikkaili, stretching luxuriously and drawing a deep, satisfied breath. His legs were still buzzing after a day bouncing over rocky roads. As soon as everyone had had an opportunity to clean up, the prince called a meeting of his men to prepare, over supper, for the discussions the following day, and they gathered in the lamplit common room while the grooms took care of their teams. He helped himself to some of the wine provided for their use. Kulana-ziti took up a plate and began to fill it with flatbread and cubes of steaming lamb.

"If this goes well," said Nerikkaili to his uncle, "Piyamaradu may find himself without a hole to hide in." He scooped up a mouthful of mashed favas directly from the bowl with a round of bread and popped it hungrily into his mouth. The depth of his appetite proclaimed itself with a rumble of the stomach; they had stopped for only the briefest of repasts at midday.

"It's the sole solution," the elder prince agreed around a mouthful of food. "Unite against the bastard and isolate him. As long as he can count on Ahhiyawa making excuses for him, we'll never see the end of him."

Tiwatipara, who had accompanied his team to the stable, entered with his grandfather at his side. The old man dragged himself laboriously on his crutches toward the prince and saluted.

"Ah, Tapala-tarhunta. Here you are," said Nerikkaili. "We need to rough out an agenda—the things we'd like to accomplish, the things we won't leave without, and so forth. Grab some food, and let's sit down."

One by one, the men served themselves and found a place around the long table. Tapala-tarhunta settled himself with care at the end of a bench. Tiwatipara stood solicitously at his back until his grandfather was seated but made no move to assist him except to carry his plate. Nerikkaili smiled. The lad knew better than to try to help the proud old *hashtanuri*.

"Kulana-ziti, Tapala-tarhunta, do either of you know this Tawagalawa? What manner of man is he?" asked the crown prince, seating himself next to Benteshina.

"I've met him, my lord," said the charioteer. "He's perhaps Our Sun's age or a little younger. A shrewd, observant man who tends to say little but see much. He's pleasant in manner, but I think he'll be a hard negotiator."

"So you recommend taking a businesslike tone, not going for threats or overwhelming spectacles of wealth, eh?" The prince grinned, thinking of the arrogant Piyamaradu and how their discussion had degenerated into a fencing match.

"Alas, I had so counted on an overwhelming spectacle of wealth," Benteshina said with a sigh. "I brought all my flashiest clothes for nothing."

"Go out and impress the fireflies with them." With a smirk, Nerikkaili got up, helped himself again to the wine, and brought the ewer back to the table. "Our Sun wants a mutual extradition clause. That means this has to be a peer treaty."

"And that means flattering Tawagalawa's brother," agreed Kulana-ziti. "We must speak of him as a Great King."

"Pallulla," the *tuhkanti* said to the plump, fortyish man across the table, "this puts a lot of pressure on you as translator. Be alert to nuances, all right? And keep an ear out for what this Ahhiyawan's translator tells him about us. Feel free to challenge him if you hear something that sounds inaccurate." He remembered, painfully, the dressing down his father had given him after the meeting with Piyamaradu. "We have to come out of here with a treaty—one that Our Sun will be willing to sign."

The men discussed a few more issues. Tiwatipara sat at his grandfather's side, listening with attentive ears but saying nothing. He was one of the younger men present. In fact, Nerikkaili was also one of the younger men present, but he thought of himself as more experienced than his twenty-eight years would lead one to expect. His father had entrusted him with delicate diplomatic missions from a surprisingly tender age. The king had confidence in his firstborn. *All you Oath Gods*, Nerikkaili prayed silently, *let this go well. Give me a success to present to the old man. Perhaps he'll forget about the recent failures.* He tried to imagine his taciturn little brother negotiating with wily foreign diplomats, but it was impossible. The boy hardly ever said anything. *Could he be smooth, sarcastic, flattering, menacing at will? Surely I'm safe in my succession to the throne.*

The following day, the crown prince's delegation and that of the king of Ahhiyawa met in the sanctuary of the goddess, in the very presence of her golden statue. The two long, louvered windows of the room were open to admit more light for the human beings, whose eyesight was less penetrating than that of She Who Sees All. The two negotiators sat in equally magnificent chairs at either side of the table, with their interpreters, scribes, and witnesses around them.

Prince Tawagalawa was a stocky man of medium height in his midfifties. Like the Hittites, he had long hair—a little balding on the crown—and a clean-shaven face. He was dressed in simple elegance in a rich, unbelted tunic decorated only at the seams. He wore no jewelry except the golden appliques across the horizontal neck of his tunic, which extended along its shoulders and down the short sleeves. Instead of slippers with turned-up toes, he had on elaborate mesh-like sandals laced high on the ankle. Nerikkaili, with golden disks in his ears and broad, expensive cuff bracelets, felt he came off well by comparison. But the Ahhiyawan radiated intelligence. His dark eyes seemed to miss nothing, and his craggy, strong-jawed face, despite the pleasant expression, gave him the look of a man who wouldn't yield much. The king of Ahhiyawa's brother was a formidable adversary.

After prayers to the gods of both kingdoms, they began their negotiations. Nerikkaili was quickly surprised by the lack of exigency in the Ahhiyawan's demands. A slow burn of suspicion began mounting in him, although it all seemed to work to his advantage. *Mutual assistance in case of attack*—that was more or less a formality, because Ahhiyawa only rarely circulated in the same world as the Great Kingdom of Hatti, and that mostly because of the Westerners' small outpost at Millawata. *Favored trade in both directions*—well and good, although Hattushili had no merchant marine to transport goods across the sea to Ahhiyawa or to their islands. All the advantage to the shipping trade would accrue to the other party, even though the coastal Luwians were sailors as well. Taruisha and Sheha River Land would be happy. *Will Father? They'll buy silver and copper and lead from us.*

And then came the issue of extradition. "Mutual, of course," Tawagalawa insisted.

But, thought Nerikkaili, *he has no offensive rebels running around on our soil. This works to our advantage.* "My lord, let me be frank," he said. "The first of our concerns here is Piyamaradu. Our Sun is not pleased that this renegade has been able to find a haven within your brother's borders. His family is safely established there. He can sail forth, strike at our shores, raid our vassals, and flee back to security whenever he wishes, without consequence. Is my lord your king aware of this?"

The interpreter chattered away, then Tawagalawa made a reply in his deep, measured voice.

"He says, my lord," Pallulla translated, "that his brother was only marginally aware of Piyamaradu's presence on his shores and not at all aware of his depredations here. He says that the king is quite happy to extradite him should we request it. Assuming the man permits himself to be found."

Well, then, thought Nerikkaili, with a growing sense of triumph. *This is what my father really wanted out of him.* He suppressed the whisper of suspicion at the back of his mind. In any case, a treaty was only words unless both parties committed to observing it. The words here sounded good, and that was all he could control.

They broke for lunch while the scribes of both parties collaborated on drafting up hard copies in the two languages. That afternoon, they solemnly signed the treaty in the presence of the human witnesses, who set their seals to the tablets as well, with the gods of both lands looking on in heavenly witness. Their curse would lie upon anyone who abrogated the agreement.

The two kings had yet to sign. The clay versions would be borne back to them by their emissaries, and official copies on metal tablets would be engraved and exchanged. But Nerikkaili's part was done.

The prince returned to his quarters in the guesthouse with a lightened heart. *At last. This could exorcize the Piyamaradu threat. The Sun will be pleased, surely.* Even now, Nerikkaili imagined himself restored to his father's favor. He found himself expansive and full of good humor at the supper his party shared that night.

Kulana-ziti was already a little intoxicated, his pockmarked face flushed, when he proposed a toast. "To our *tuhkanti* and the success of the treaty he has obtained for us!" The men raised their cups and cried out in ragged chorus, "To our *tuhkanti*!" Nerikkaili drained his wine and nodded around graciously, trying to maintain a look of cool detachment as if he weren't too proud of himself. He envisioned himself naming his firstborn Ahhiyawaili, just as his father had named *him* after the old man's victory at Nerik. But then he remembered that his children's mother would be Benteshina's daughter, and his satisfaction frosted over. Nerikkaili eyed the little man, who, to the merriment of those around him, was posing on a stool with one foot raised and both arms outstretched. The gods alone knew what he was doing; there was always some buffoonery swirling in his wake. Benteshina had, in fact, worn his flashiest tunic, woven with patterns all over and topped with a still more ornate kilt in the gaudy way of the south.

Tiwatipara sat at his grandfather's side, flushed and laughing. This was the young charioteer's first experience of witnessing a treaty. *Let's hope he'll still be bragging about it to his grandchildren*, thought the prince smugly. But Tapala-tarhunta had an ambiguous expression on his face. He seemed pleased but not without concerns, his brows knit and jaw outthrust in reflection.

Discreetly, the prince drifted over to the old *hashtanuri*'s side and took a seat. "Well, Tapala-tarhunta," he said quietly.

"Does the treaty meet with your approval? Be honest, now. Did we get what Our Sun wanted?"

"We did, my prince. You did well. The only thing that concerns me..."

"What, man?" Nerikkaili felt a chill moving up between his shoulder blades.

"The seven thousand builders, my lord. What if they really are destined for Ahhiyawa? Lord Tawagalawa might have mentioned that as part of the discussion of trade exchanges or indeed, of Piyamaradu. But he didn't. If there's anything to the rumors, he's purposely concealing something."

"Maybe there isn't anything to them," the prince said uneasily. "Damn it, if you'd mentioned that beforehand, I could have bearded him with it, made him go on record with a comment."

"Not on the basis of a vague rumor, my lord. It would have been offensive. He might have refused to continue negotiations. But still, I'd really like to know the truth of it." The old charioteer's dark eyes stared piercingly into space, as if he could see across the waters and make out Ahhiyawa's secrets from where he sat.

"Well, you're the man with the network of spies," Nerikkaili said, rising. His self-satisfaction was thoroughly chilled by the specter of some important factor overlooked. *Have I failed again?*

CHAPTER 11

T HE TREATY MAKERS RETURNED TO Waliwanda the
following day, and Tiwatipara went to bed as soon
as he had completed his duties, without seeing
anyone. But the next morning, on his way to take out the
horses, the charioteer stopped by the governor's tack room
to greet his friend.

"How was the treaty signing?" asked Zidanza. He had
a smile on his lips, but his sleepy eyes were untouched by
it. Tiwatipara's heart tightened with concern for the groom,
who struck him once again as drifting away into a vague,
somnambulant state.

"It was impressive," Tiwatipara said, enthusiasm for his
adventure pushing aside his uneasiness. "We signed right
in the sanctuary of the Lady of Arinna, Zidi. There were all
our diplomats here, with Lord Nerikkaili looking big and
smug and confident. And on that side, their prince—who's
rather older but quite splendid—and all their men. And
every time anyone said anything, the interpreters would
repeat it all, coming and going. They disagreed sometimes,
but everybody was very civil and smooth, and somehow,

they found a solution we could both live with. Then we broke for lunch, and afterward, the scribes had clay copies ready, and we all signed with our seals as witnesses, and they called on all the gods of both of us to guarantee the oaths." He shook his head, grinning. "I felt like somebody special, I can tell you. My name's on that document!"

"Sounds like fun. The king of Mira was here while you were gone."

"So that's where he was. We wondered why he didn't come to the signing, since Iyalanda's almost on his border."

"Our Sun met with him." Zidanza bit his lip uncomfortably. "I think he betrothed him formally to Lady Lalantiwashha." He looked up at his friend as guiltily as if he were personally responsible for this blow.

A cold, dull pain wrapped itself around Tiwatipara's heart. He couldn't speak. At last, he said flatly, "I pray she'll be happy."

"Not as happy as she'd have been with you."

"I'm afraid I couldn't compete," said the charioteer, trying to wring the bitterness out of his voice. "Who am I next to some king? Even you'd have a better chance than I would, my prince."

But Zidanza *tush*ed him in embarrassment. "I'm not anybody, Tipa. It was only my great-great-grandfather who was a king. Kings' sons are thick on the ground in Hattusha."

"Yes, but the great Tudhaliya!" Tiwatipara teased.

Zidanza laughed wanly, still uncomfortable with his praise. "You sound like my father."

That sobered Tiwatipara. A keen anxiety for his

friend burned under his breastbone. But at least here in Waliwanda, the groom was safe.

"The king has bought some new horses," Zidanza said.

"In the three days we were gone?" Tiwatipara laughed heartily. "Did the *tawananna* leave? He must have waited until her back was turned."

"In fact, she did."

"Lord Tarhunta help little Tashmi-sharrumma now. The *huwalpant* will make mince of him." He sighed. Then a cold, focused anger steeled his heart. "I'm almost sure Lurma-ziti's behind the sabotage, Zidanza. Look how quickly he strung up his trap while we were standing just a few *iku*s away, and we saw nothing."

Zidanza looked troubled in his vague way. He hung a bridle on its peg. "I can't see him dragging his skinny carcass under the box and wielding a saw."

"He could've paid someone to do it. Anyone. Some dogsbody from the palace or even a street urchin. He must have foreseen that the king would ride in the chariot with the second team. He and Prince Hishni were betting. The only hole in my theory is motive. Why would he want to kill his own father?"

Zidanza made an undecipherable little moue and smiled. Tiwatipara wondered if his friend could only too well imagine wanting to kill one's father.

"Could he be in the pay of Piyamaradu, do you think?" The groom bent to pick up another set of leathers and hung them one at a time.

"Anything's possible. I'm not sure I've gotten any closer to an answer, to be honest." Tiwatipara clapped his friend on the shoulder. "I leave you to your work, old man. I've got to take the mares out for the boys' lesson."

He turned to go, but before he could depart, Zidanza said in a hesitant voice, "Lurma-ziti's been hanging around the stables a lot in the last few days."

A blaze of triumph flashed in Tiwatipara's cheeks. *Got you,* huwalpant*!* But below his satisfaction lay a gnawing fear. *Is he about to strike again?*

Tiwatipara was under orders to continue the young princes' driving lessons until such time as the king's troops might have to move into action. Then he would drive Tashmi-sharrumma into his first battle while Ulmi-tesshub, on another car with his own driver and shield bearer, took a man's full part in the conflict. To the charioteer, it seemed like a demotion because he would certainly be expected to keep the twelve-year-old boy out of the thick of the fighting. But at least he didn't have to return to the capital.

In fact, Tiwatipara had been so pleased by his inclusion in the treaty signing that he had let himself dream of being appointed to drive the royal chariot. After all, his grandfather and his father had both been the *hashtalanuri*, the man chosen for the honor of transporting the *labarna*. Wasn't he the obvious choice to succeed them? But it hadn't happened yet. He still didn't know what the king thought about him and his grandfather. So frequently, Hattushili seemed to be punishing them, denying them the honor they deserved. Still, he was unfailingly friendly toward them both and almost deferential to Tapala-tarhunta. Tiwatipara suspected that the Sun still held against him his despairing recklessness in Nuhasshe. Everyone, even his partisans, said that Hattushili could hold a grudge.

He resolved to do a conspicuously good job of teaching the boys. Someday, they'd be grown men who would remember his expertise and patience with gratitude.

As he observed the young princes, his mind drifted back to his hunch about the king's second son. Tiwatipara had hoped to bring the *labarna* some concrete proof before he went to him—something heftier than a plausible supposition—but if Lurma-ziti was going to make another attempt on his father's life, perhaps Tiwatipara should speak up immediately.

He watched the rest of the morning's lesson in a state of preoccupation, correcting the boys' form automatically. He couldn't have recalled afterward a thing he had said, even if he'd been tortured to extract it. Finally, the youngsters ran off together, and Tiwatipara entered the stalls of the king's horses. His propensity for being careful had become a mania and would remain so until the would-be assassin was caught. He wanted to be sure every animal, every piece of tack, and every royal chariot was impeccably cared for and inspected daily.

Tiwatipara was just leaving Wrath of Wurukatte's stall, the bridle and his long whip over his shoulder, when he heard voices in the aisle of the stable—an adult's, speaking low, and the piercing, disgusted tenor of Ulmi-tesshub, crying, "Leave me alone, you animal."

There was a loud smack that could have been a slap, and the adult voice rose in a sharp, bitter snarl. It was, Tiwatipara realized, that of Prince Lurma-ziti. "Too good for us all, you arrogant little bastard?"

"Right you are. Too good for you, you twisted piece of garbage. How can you possibly think I'd be friends with you after the way you've treated Tash? Go find yourself a sheep."

He heard a growl of anger and the sounds of a scuffle. *What should I do?* Tiwatipara asked himself uneasily. *I don't want to confront Lurma-ziti. I don't want him to suspect I'm onto him. But Ulmi's just a boy—this isn't right.*

He took a deep breath and walked casually out into the aisle as if he had no idea anyone was there then stopped in mock surprise. He still couldn't keep the hostility altogether from his voice. "Ah, my lord Lurma-ziti. Good morning." Tiwatipara tapped the long whip on his shoulder in what might have been viewed by someone with a guilty conscience as a mildly threatening gesture.

Lurma-ziti was in a position that could only be considered compromising. He had the boy pressed against the board wall of a stall, with his tunic pulled up. The hair of both of them was sweaty and disarranged, testifying to a struggle. Ulmi-tesshub laughed heartily, but there was relief in his expression, too.

"Tiwatipara," said the older prince, drawing back. His long face was flushed, his currant-dark eyes a little crazed. He turned and lurched away, giving his young cousin a shove as he passed. "Whore," he muttered under his breath.

The two watched him go in silence. Once Lurma-ziti had turned the corner, Ulmi-tesshub gave a nasty laugh. "What a piece of shit." His face was red, his eyes bright with anger. He dusted himself down and rearranged his skirts.

"Did he hurt you?"

"Not him. I could break that turd with my bare hands," the boy snarled. He caught Tiwatipara's eye and forced a grin of bravado. Tiwatipara raised a skeptical eyebrow. He didn't much like Ulmi-tesshub, who was always showing off and full of bluster. And the charioteer was aware that he shared the prejudice of many men against one of their number who was so extraordinarily handsome. But the lad was clearly the victim here. Lurma-ziti, for all his physical frailty, wielded considerably more power than this brother of a deposed king, a mere hanger-on at the *labarna*'s table.

"Look out for Lurma-ziti, I tell you," he cautioned Ulmi-tesshub. "He's spiteful."

"He's already got it in for me." The boy snorted. "He hates me because I watch over Tash."

"Tell the *tawananna* if he keeps after you. She'll let Our Sun know."

"She's not here, is she?" Ulmi-tesshub flicked something invisible from the breast of his tunic and bared his teeth in a sour grin. "I can take care of myself." He gave the charioteer a mock salute and darted away.

Tiwatipara was left pensive. Was Lurma-ziti hanging around the stable because he was after Ulmi-tesshub, a desirable-looking boy who tended to flaunt his charms rather shamelessly? Or did he have something darker in mind?

The king was gathered with his councilors for their nearly daily discussion in the governor's small audience hall, his long frame slumped down into the governor's chair, his legs stretched out before him. Tapala-tarhunta had a fresh load of dispatches to lay before the Sun. Piyamaradu was still playing the I-want-to-be-a-vassal game.

"He's asked for a meeting, My Sun, to discuss the conditions of the treaty," said the *hashtanuri*. "He wants to meet us in Millawata."

At this, the king sat up, red faced, and exploded, "Millawata? That's on the territory of the king of Ahhiyawa. How did he get into this? And who is the governor of Millawata but Piyamaradu's father-in-law? Does he take us for fools?"

"Hardly a neutral site," Tapala-tarhunta agreed somberly, and there was a skeptical murmur among the councilors.

Kulana-ziti shrugged. "Piyamaradu claims to be afraid he'll be harmed if he meets on our turf, My Sun."

"And my ambassador won't be harmed on Ahhiyawan turf? Absolutely not in Millawata. Someplace halfway between us. Or even out in a field somewhere, if he's afraid of an ambush. But I will not be seen to be dancing to that sheep fucker's tune."

"My Sun, there was another condition," Tapala-tarhunta said apologetically. "He stipulates that… that there should be a hostage from our side held by the Ahhiyawans in Millawata for the duration of the talks. Otherwise, he fears for his life."

Even before the others could express their outrage, the king had surged to his feet, the veins bulging in his temples. "What in the name of the Oath Gods? That's not how civilized treaties are made! Everybody's watching. No one's going to try to do anything to the man. He's crazy."

"Completely crazy," echoed Benteshina, his tongue lolling and his eyes crossed.

The king said scornfully, "Why, Prince Ulmi-tesshub was in Millawata for the horse fair last year—a fourteen-year-old boy—and no one demanded the king of Ahhiyawa send us a hostage in exchange. This is unacceptable."

But that word, left reverberating in a sudden silence, sounded like a decision, Tapala-tarhunta realized. He spoke out again with urgency. "Can we ignore this overture completely, though? The other Luwian states will be weighing our every move. If they think we're not serious…" He stared around at his colleagues. Kulana-ziti, who shared his experience of the Luwian mentality, looked especially uneasy.

"What, does he think we're a bunch of assassins?" grumbled Hattushili, still steaming. He sank back into his chair.

And Tapala-tarhunta, reflecting on the sabotage of the royal chariot as the king had prepared to test out new horses, thought, *Maybe some among us are…* Or maybe Piyamaradu's supporters were the assassins. He had never considered that. *Who in the crowd that day might have been in the pay of the West?*

The *hashtanuri* was lost in thought—back on the field three years before, as he so frequently was—when he heard the king pronounce his name. He looked up. "Forgive me, My Sun, I was…"

Hattushili fixed him with a grave, almost pleading green stare. "I said, 'Perhaps Tapala-tarhunta would consent to being our hostage.'"

A thrill of reluctance bordering on fear sparkled in

Tapala-tarhunta's stomach. He was an old man, broken and ill; he had needs that might not be met in Millawata. And what of Mashuhepa if something should happen to him? But above all, he was a soldier. "I would be honored," he said, bowing his head humbly.

"Then set up a date, Kulana-ziti. And make it soon. We don't want Piyamaradu and his gang to have too much time to plan any surprises, if that's what they're considering." Hattushili turned to his secretary. "Shahuranuwa, get off a message to the capital. Tell them to send me an augur or two. I want to be sure everything is propitious for this meeting. We have to have that treaty."

Tapala-tarhunta waited until the others had left and then made his way from the hall. His heart sat like a sour rock in his stomach. He wasn't much given to presentiments, yet he had a bad feeling about this, as if he might never walk out of his captivity alive. But then, he was sixty-one years old. He didn't have that much life ahead of him anyway. Better he than some young man with children to support. If the worst happened, he would at least see his son again. *Pawahtelmah, my lad. How our lives have been overturned these last years.*

He was tired anyway. All this displacement on diplomatic missions—Apasha, Millawata, Waliwanda, back to the capital. *Our Sun has no idea how much it costs me to ride for days in a carriage, to sleep in a camp bed, to tramp from court to court. We both must have been delusional to think I could have taken the box again and borne the rigors of a campaign.* It was wearing him out. He wouldn't be so terribly sorry to stretch out in the fields of the Liliahmi and rest.

Tapala-tarhunta was laboriously crossing the courtyard on the way to his room when he saw his grandson striding along in the other direction. A warm tide of affection rose up inside the old man. He loved the boy, his only descendant. Perhaps he had never shown it sufficiently, but that was his way—he was a brusque old horseman. He loved his grandson deeply. It lightened his soul to see the lad coming out of those haunted years after the accident. Tiwatipara was himself again, sometimes preoccupied with his dreams of vengeance but once more full of laughter and enthusiasm. After the treaty signing, he had been all excited to think that he had been part of an event of such importance—full of the innocence and passion of youth.

Tiwatipara waved, brightening. "Grandfather!" he called and changed direction to intercept Tapala-tarhunta.

The old charioteer ruffled the boy's hair affectionately, and Tiwatipara put an arm around his shoulders. "Where are you off to, Grandfather? Do you want to eat in the mess with me?"

"Why not? We see little enough of each other these days." They directed their steps toward the barracks where the governor's soldiers were garrisoned and where Hattushili's troops now lodged. Tiwatipara solicitously slowed down his pace to accommodate his grandfather's laborious progress.

"How are the discussions with the Luwians going?" Tiwatipara asked as they entered the long mess hall and made their way toward the table.

A pang of regret caught at the *hashtanuri*. He would have to tell his grandson about the hostage exchange soon. "Piyamaradu's willing to talk yet again," he said. "He wanted to get together in Millawata, but Our Sun is demanding a neutral meeting place."

Tiwatipara nodded. He pulled out a stool for his grandfather and slid it under him, waiting there until he was settled.

A goodhearted, dutiful boy, thought Tapala-tarhunta gratefully. *Family is important to him.* "You ought to get married, son," he said with a smile. "Keep the family name going."

Tiwatipara's own smile chilled as he slid to a seat beside his grandfather. "I wanted to. But my suit was rejected, remember?"

"There are other girls out there, Tipa. I can ask around if you want."

But the boy shook his head, his long mouth tense at the corners. "I haven't given up yet. Something could happen. Our Sun might break off the betrothal. Lalantiwashha's the one I want to spend my life with. The one I want to bear my children." He reached out and pulled a dish of porridge toward them, offering it to Tapala-tarhunta first, and said, with a twinkle of humor, "Why? Don't you think her family is good enough for us?"

The boy is never one simply to accept, thought the old charioteer. *He has to fight first then come to some revelation of submission to the will of the gods.* It made life a lot harder. Age would knock a few of the sharp corners off him.

Tapala-tarhunta helped himself to porridge and passed the bowl. "Piyamaradu is demanding an exchange of hostages before he'll sign a treaty."

"What? Whoever heard of such a thing?" cried Tiwatipara with a bark of laughter. "I can't believe that man, with his curled hair all prettily arranged. He's the vainest, most arrogant bastard on the black earth. Who does he think he is?"

Tapala-tarhunta made no reply. They began to eat. After a moment, he said, "I'll be Our Sun's hostage."

Tiwatipara continued chewing, as if he hadn't heard. Then his grandfather's words apparently sank in. He looked up, his eyes round, his jaw hanging. "Y-You're… the hostage? What does that mean? They'll hold you captive? Where?"

"In Millawata. Not a captive, exactly. Just a guest until the treaty is concluded. Piyamaradu will send someone to us. He doesn't trust Our Sun not to play some trick on him, I suppose. He says he's afraid of being assassinated."

"At a treaty signing? May Tarhunta strike the man!" Tiwatipara threw down his wooden spoon with a bang and gaped at his grandfather. "And Our Sun is sending *you*? But that's not right." He refrained from saying, *You're old and broken*, but that was clearly what he meant. Tapala-tarhunta saw, to his regret, a wisp of anger, like smoke, rising from the lad's scarlet face. He was a passionate one.

"It's an honor, son. The king wants me to keep my eyes open, pick up any vibrations I can while I'm there. I'll be able to receive visitors and send mail. It won't be bread and water in a cell, I can assure you." He forced a smile.

But Tiwatipara was having none of it. He stared at his plate with a dark face and screwed-down brow. "Why does Our Sun have it in for us?" he demanded through clenched teeth.

First, Grandfather was humiliated by being taken from the royal chariot box, and now this. It was too much. Tiwatipara had thought Hattushili was Tapala-tarhunta's friend, but the king was treating him like a slave, selling him to the enemy. If anything happened to the old man, it would be the death of Tiwatipara's grandmother. The youth had to get the king to relent.

From a distance, the young charioteer watched Hattushili glad-handing the stable staff as he made his way through the aisle between the boxes. The king was surrounded by the gilded dust that hung like a divine aureole in the shafts of sunlight penetrating the dark stable. His rough, throaty laughter rose now and then. About him, grooms and drivers bowed and grinned, honored to be noticed. The sons of generations of kings, and their sons in turn, were a kind of race apart that populated the citadel and administered the kingdom. Their world was separated from the lives of their subjects, and the favor of the king was their meat and drink. An ordinary person did not approach the *labarna*. Clearance was needed, purification… *physical perfection*, Tiwatipara added darkly to himself.

He forced himself to move after the royal entourage until he was standing just behind the king, looking into the gray mane that billowed down Hattushili's back—the *labarna* was exceptionally tall and Tiwatipara barely average height. The king's attention was engaged by the fawning crowd that clustered around him. They were all laughing appreciatively at something he had said.

There was a momentary lull, and the charioteer sidled to the king's elbow.

"My Sun," he murmured, saluting and bending in a deep bow.

Hattushili turned, and his smile softened at the sight of his young kinsman. "Ah, Tiwatipara. What can I do for you?"

The helplessness of his situation choking his voice, the youth stammered, "May I have a moment of My Sun's time... at your convenience, of course?"

The king pinned him with a probing gaze from under his heavy lids. "Let's step in here, son." He pushed open the half door of the nearest empty box, and the two men slipped inside. The crowd edged discreetly away.

"Speak, boy," said Hattushili quietly. He looked down at Tiwatipara. The king's ugly face was as craggy and fissured as the rock upon which the city for which he was named had been built. He might be mercurial and ambitious, but he was acquainted with suffering, too, the charioteer saw. The old king's eyes were gentle. He knew why his young kinsman was there.

"My... My Sun," began Tiwatipara, clenching his fists, caught between respect and rage. "I beg you, don't send my grandfather as a hostage. It will kill my grandmother if anything happens to him." His voice broke in spite of himself. "Don't do this to him. Send me." He fell to his knees in the straw and dust and clutched at the king's legs. "Please, please... send me."

Hattushili laid a big hand on the young man's shoulder, and his voice was rough with emotion. "Don't *you* do this to him, Tiwatipara. Don't take away from him the chance to be of service to his king. He feels useless enough. Am I to replace him with a hale, young hostage as if he were somehow not good enough? No, he's just the one to go. He'll conduct himself with dignity and courage, no matter what happens."

"But my grandmother…"

The king smiled his crooked, fanged grin. "Your grandmother is the aunt of the *tawananna*. She's stronger than you think."

Tiwatipara realized his request was ridiculous. Tapala-tarhunta was a *hashtalanuri*. He went where he was told, did what was needed. But Tiwatipara's grandfather was all the boy had left. All the losses of his young life had come crashing down on him. It was not for Tapala-tarhunta's sake that he was here at the king's knees, he saw now—it was for his own. *Don't take him away, too,* he wanted to cry. *Don't leave me with nothing, no one.* His father, mother, grandmother, and sweetheart—they had all been snatched from his life. Even his best friend seemed to be slipping away. And now his grandfather, too. He began to sob, clutching his face in his hands as if he could pull it off like a mask and become someone less cursed.

The king will think I'm childish and weak, he told himself. But he couldn't stop. Too much sorrow had accumulated over the last three and a half years. He was once again the boy whose life was overturned with a chariot, whose dreams were dragged through the dirt and crushed by the galloping heels of panicked horses—the boy who was supposed to be on board that chariot but wasn't.

He felt strong hands on his shoulders, shaking him a little. "Easy, lad," the Great King murmured in his gruff voice. "You can endure it. He'll be all right." Hattushili lifted Tiwatipara to his feet and put an avuncular arm around his shoulders. "He'll have all the comforts of an honored guest. He won't be cut off from us. You can write him if you want."

"I can't write," said Tiwatipara, sniffing miserably.

The king threw back his head and gave a gurgling peal of laughter. "Neither can I, son! That's what secretaries are for. Are there no public scribes in the barracks?" He waited for a moment then added kindly, "Of course there are. And it's only for a few weeks at most."

"I'm not sure his health can stand it."

"What do you know about an old man's health, you healthy young animal? Let me be the judge of that, eh?"

Finally, Tiwatipara gave up. He saw there would be no convincing the king to change his mind. But neither was his own mind changed. He glanced up at Hattushili, whose muscular mouth was twisted with pity, his eyes fixed on Tiwatipara's.

"Whatever you say, My Sun," he murmured.

The king clapped him on the shoulder and opened the door of the stall. His secretaries and adjutants stood waiting in the aisle a few boxes down. He turned back to Tiwatipara. "Good soldier." He winked and disappeared around the corner into the aisle.

But Hattushili had run into more opposition to the choice of Tapala-tarhunta as hostage.

Prince Kulana-ziti was back from the West with Piyamaradu's response to the hostage transferal. The prince was perhaps five years his half brother's junior, with a long, shrewd, amiable face scarred by deep pockmarks. He was as lanky as the king but not as tall because of his unexpectedly short legs, which gave him something of the physique of a weasel. The ambassador stood at ease, fist on hip, while the king pondered the letter his secretary had just read aloud.

"So is the bastard refusing to accept Tapala-tarhunta? Or is he just griping so we know he has an opinion on everything?" Hattushili asked finally.

"The latter, I think, My Sun. The man is unbelievably arrogant. It was all I could do not to put him in his place more than once."

"Well, don't. We need to keep him sweet for a few more months, until we can get some sort of treaty ratified. Once we cut Ahhiyawa's support out from under him, he may find himself a little less inclined to arrogance."

Kulana-ziti chuckled. Hattushili turned to his secretary, an unranked cousin of some sort. "Shahuranuwa, write down this reply to that turd of a Luwian dog. Say that Tapala-tarhunta is not a 'broken-down old nobody,' by any means, but an uncle of the *tawananna*. And here, at least, the *tawananna* and her family are as important as anyone in the kingdom. Tell him that Tapala-tarhunta shared my chariot in our youth and that I would trust him with my life. What else should we say, Kulanu?" He turned to his ambassador, who shrugged, opening his hands in a gesture that said, *Whatever you think.* "I don't want to belabor the point. That's it, Shahuranuwa. Tell him he either accepts the hostage offer, or he doesn't. I'm not going to go around shopping for someone he approves. Piyamaradu has nothing to fear from us even without a hostage, by the Lady of Shamuha. He's just playing for time." *And why, exactly, I wonder?* This thought kept coming back to him. *Why is he playing for time? What surprise does he have in mind?*

The king rose from his chair, arching his back and stretching his arms, and stepped down heavily from the dais. His feet were still almost numb after his illness, and he had to be careful not to stumble; he never knew where he was putting them. "Bring me the good copy before you send it, hah?" He clapped his secretary on the shoulder.

The man bowed out, and Hattushili turned to his brother. His eyes narrowed a little, considering. They needed a more accurate reading on that sheep fucker of an Arzawan. "So what is Piyamaradu's setup? Does he even have a permanent headquarters?"

"I don't know how permanent, My Sun," said Kulana-ziti, "but he has a house in Millawata with all the trappings of kingship—furnished, one assumes, by Atpa. I saw many representatives of the Luwian kingdoms coming in and going out while I was there… as I was, no doubt, intended to do."

"So he's trying to look dangerous. Does he want to provoke us to attack him, do you think?"

"I confess, My Sun, I don't know. If he's sincerely intending to parlay with you, perhaps he just wants to make it clear that you can't roll over him without consequences."

"We'll see what he wants. I just hope he'll keep his word regarding Tapala-tarhunta. I'd hate to have to tell Tiwatipara that he's lost him, too." The king, who was no coward, found that the possibility of that conversation sent chills up the back of his neck.

"Piyamaradu's hostage has reached us, has he not, My Sun?" asked Kulana-ziti.

"He has. A thirty-year-old brother of his. The poor lad's clearly weak in the head." Hattushili chuckled grimly. "Dispensable, no doubt. Which concerns me a little. Is our renegade thinking of breaking his word?"

"Perhaps we ought to refuse him," Kulana-ziti suggested with an evil grin. "A 'broken-down old nobody' like that."

"The fucking nerve of that bastard," grumbled the king, his smile gone cold. "Let him sign that treaty, and I'll smash him flat."

There was a knock at the door of the king's chamber, and Shahuranuwa stuck his head through. "My Sun, the dispatch bag from the capital has arrived. Would you like to hear the messages?"

"Ah, yes, my man. Bring them." Hattushili turned to his brother. "Stay, if you want, Kulanu, and help me formulate a reply. The *tawananna* will undoubtedly want to hear the latest from the West."

The secretary carried in a large wicker chest packed with straw, from which projected a number of tablets in their clay envelopes.

"Does she know her uncle is our hostage, My Sun?" asked Kulana-ziti.

The king looked at him pointedly and said nothing, his mouth cocked to the side. *Of course she doesn't. Let him come home safe first.*

"Here's the longest one, from the *tuhkanti*, My Sun," said the secretary, drawing out a large rectangular tablet from its envelope, which he had cracked expertly with the hilt of his penknife.

Shahuranuwa read the news from the capital. There were the usual secondhand reports, which Hattushili would hear firsthand from other letters in the chest. But then something caught his attention.

"Urhi-tesshub has been spotted within our borders—"

"Wait," the king cried, holding out a hand as if to prevent the man physically from reading any further. "Slow down here. Now, what does the boy say?"

"Within our borders, in the Lower Land—"

"Shaushga's tits!" roared the king, anger mounting in him like a tide. "The rotten bastard! And why haven't my men nabbed him?"

"The Lower Land and in Kizzuwatna," continued Shahuranuwa. "My spies tell me that he is meeting with families loyal to him—that is, our enemies. Arma-tarhunta has emerged from his country estates and paid a visit to Tarhuntassha, where the pretender still has many supporters—"

"I knew it, the degenerate old sheep fucker!" Hattushili pounded a furious fist on his table, his temples throbbing. "They've trotted his mummified carcass out to conjure up the pretender." His frustration consuming him like an itching flame, he groped around for something to throw and dashed his water pitcher to the ground with a clang of bronze. Water splattered all over his feet and those of Kulana-ziti.

"My Sun, they've chosen this moment when you're out of the country," Kulana-ziti pointed out angrily. "That can't be a coincidence."

"Where's Shipa-ziti?"

Flustered, Shahuranuwa scanned the letter. "Uh, it says, 'No one is sure where Shipa-ziti has gone, and Armatalli has disappeared as well.'"

"Well, we know where *he* is. He's here." Hattushili turned to his brother and said snidely, "I ask the temple personnel to send me an augur, and who is it who comes? Armatalli. There are no coincidences, Kulanu. My government is rotten with traitors." He looked back to his secretary. "Anything else of importance in Nerikkaili's letter, Shahuranuwa? Then go on to Puduhepa's."

The *tawananna*'s message treated more or less the same array of issues. She, too, noted the presence of the pretender within their frontiers, the unusual displacement of the very old Arma-tarhunta, and the disappearance of his two sons all at once. "But the kingdom is in the capable hands of the crown prince," she reported. The king smiled dryly, suspecting the *tawananna* was in his hands as well.

Then she added a more personal note. "I inform you sadly, my dear, that my aunt Mashuhepa has died. Her slaves tell me it was very peaceful, in her sleep. Tapala-tarhunta and Tiwatipara will want to know. I feel bad for both of them, so far away. Shall we hold the cremation? Can either of them get back for the funeral? Otherwise, given the weather, I think we should go ahead and send her down the Great Way and let them say goodbye to her ashes when they return."

Sorrow descended upon Hattushili with the soot-black wings of a vulture. He looked up at Kulana-ziti and saw his own compassion mirrored in his brother's face. The king heaved a sigh, suddenly weary. Sometimes statecraft exhilarated him. He felt he was playing some fast-paced game of competition and cunning that drew out of him the highest degree of skill and strength, leaving him tingling with a kind of near-sexual pleasure.

And then there were times like now.

"Tapala, what have I done to you, my old friend?" he said sadly and tried to picture himself telling Tiwatipara, who was already raw over the danger to his grandfather, that his grandmother was dead. Tapala-tarhunta didn't need to know yet, Hattushili suspected. *I may call the* tawananna *back*, he thought with longing. *She has a gentle touch with things like this.*

CHAPTER 12

I T WAS NEARLY DARK—THE MILK-WARM darkness of a spring twilight, already rich with the song of crickets and the occasional call of the cuckoo. Pirinkir, the first star, pulsed over the crenellations of the city wall, the other stars beginning to outline his sparkling mantle across the sky. Tiwatipara had hung around the stables to talk to Zidanza, then the two of them had in mind to make their way to the local brothel, where there was good beer and better wine to be had. While the groom put away his brushes and gear at his usual lethargic pace, Tiwatipara began to whistle. Despite his snit over the king's treatment of Tapala-tarhunta, the energy and freshness of spring were too much to resist. The promise of a girl was pretty enticing as well. He felt full of sap despite himself. Soon the king's troops would move out into the Luwian countryside, and all such civilized pleasures would cease.

Zidanza hung his bucket on its peg and smiled. He had long ago forgiven his friend's insensitivity. "Ready, Tipa?" The two young men started across the unpaved court of the stable. Torches had begun to flicker here and there in the court, but never inside, of course, near the straw. A few grooms and drivers, late at work, crossed the open space, making their way by the last of the daylight that reflected from the pale mud-brick walls.

The two youths moved out into the unpaved, dusty streets of Waliwanda. Crowds drifted past, heading home after work. Soldiers of the king passed, laughing, no doubt bound for the brothel as well. Torches flickered on the city wall in the darkness above. Suddenly, Zidanza stumbled and froze, his shambling frame all at once rigid.

"What is it?" Tiwatipara stopped whistling with a start of fright. Zidanza's round face seemed to have gone lunar pale in the semidarkness.

"I thought I saw my father," the groom murmured.

Tiwatipara heard him swallow.

"What would he be doing here? It must just have been someone who reminded you of him. Just some native, probably."

"Dressed like a priest?"

Tiwatipara laughed and slapped his friend on the shoulder. "By the thousand, man! What do you bet they have priests here, too?"

They continued to walk, but Zidanza was clearly agitated, his eyes cutting around him as if he feared an ambush.

"Easy, my friend," said the charioteer under his breath.

It appalled Tiwatipara to see how frightened Zidanza's father made him. There was something unnatural about it. He thought how he longed to see his own father again...

Finally, infected by his friend's uneasiness, he said to Zidanza, "Does he know you're on the king's staff here?"

The groom nodded. He looked quite sick, his eyes slitted, his mouth slack and downturned. He put a hand to his belly and said faintly, "I need to find the jakes, Tipa. You go on without me. I'll see you in the morning."

"Zidi," Tiwatipara cried out after him, but the youth had peeled off into the darkening street and disappeared. The charioteer stared after him for a moment longer then pursued his own way, sunk in thought.

He sat with a group of drivers and grooms in the common room but had little to say. His heart was wrung for his friend. He didn't know how to help him. Tiwatipara had lost his appetite for a girl and was still on his stool, leaning dismally against the wall and pretending interest in a game of knucklebones, when Benteshina appeared in the doorway. The little ex-king stared this way and that into the dimly lit room heavy with smoke from torches and the big cooking hearth in the center. When his eyes met those of Tiwatipara, the Amurrite headed straight in his direction.

"My lord Benteshina," the charioteer greeted him, surprised. "Are you looking for me?"

"I am, son. The king wants to talk to you."

Tiwatipara disentangled himself from the gamblers and accompanied the king's friend to the door. They passed outside into the dark street.

"What's this about, do you know?" the charioteer asked uneasily. He could only think of his grandfather, captive in Millawata. *Please, all you gods, say nothing has happened to him.*

"Our Sun didn't entrust me with that information," said Benteshina at his side. "Where's your curly-headed twin?"

"He wasn't feeling well. He decided to go home." Tiwatipara blew out a nervous breath. "He thought he saw his father here."

"Who's his father?"

"I don't know his name. Some grandson of Tudhaliya. He's a priest. Zidanza is afraid of him."

Benteshina shot him a sharp look. "An augur? Armatalli?"

"I think he's an augur. Is that his name?"

Benteshina raised his eyebrows. "If it's Armatalli, he *is* here. And very likely his brother Shipa-ziti, too. There's a bad piece of work." He chuckled blackly. "I'd hate for *him* to fall on me in the dark."

Tiwatipara wasn't sure exactly what that meant, but there was no telling with Benteshina.

"My lord," he tried again, his anxiety growing, "does this have anything to do with my grandfather in Millawata?"

"I told you, I don't know, boy," said the little king. "But no, it doesn't."

Lightened, Tiwatipara listened to his footsteps, trying to shorten his pace to match that of Benteshina, who, with the effort to keep up, had begun to stretch out his legs like a horse in an extended trot, launching himself forward at each step to catch up to his own feet. The charioteer gave a snort of laughter despite himself, giddy with relief. "It's not like my legs are all that long."

"Not for you, perhaps," Benteshina admitted. "Nor is Shipa-ziti fat for him."

They gave the password, and the palace soldiers admitted them. The king's saffron-clad *meshedi* guardsmen watched over the entrance along with the governor's men.

Once again, a sense of anxiety infected Tiwatipara. *How often has the Sun ever called for me like this? Never.* Surely, it was important, but what could the news be if nothing had befallen Tapala-tarhunta? Could Hattushili possibly be planning to tell him he wanted him for his *hashtalanuri*? Perhaps that was it! The youth's heart began to beat in hopeful haste.

The two men made their way through the courtyard and into the corridor that gave upon the royal apartments. More *meshedi* guarded the precinct, standing at impassive attention in their fringed white or yellow tunics. Benteshina knocked at the door, and the king's gruff voice replied, "Come in."

Tiwatipara entered and bent, fists to chest, in a salute. His heart was in his mouth. He felt half-afraid, half-hopeful. Walking with an unaccustomed carefulness, the king came to him and drew him up. The charioteer's stomach dropped at the sight of Hattushili's face, which was pulled down into lines of sorrow, the muscles of his mouth bunched.

"Grandfather…?" the youth stammered.

But Hattushili shook his head once, slowly. "It's Mashuhepa, son. She's…"

"She's dead?" Tiwatipara could barely say the words.

Hattushili nodded. Tiwatipara hung his head, his eyes suddenly blurring with tears. He bit his lip. He found himself nodding, too. *I should have known.* She'd had one foot in the Tenawa for three and a half years. Perhaps this was the mercy of Lelwani. But he remembered his grandmother's sweetness, her piety, her delicacy of soul and how she'd loved him, sung to him, fed him little treats, and kissed him before Pawahtelmah came to his bedside to tuck him in at night.

Another piece of his life, gone. His chest heaved with the need for air, but he managed not to bawl. He felt the king's arm around his shoulder tighten.

He couldn't talk for a moment. Finally he said in a shaking voice, "Does Grandfather know?"

The king pushed out a sigh. "No, son, and I think he shouldn't. He'll just feel helpless. The slaves said she died peacefully in her sleep."

"She's with my father now," Tiwatipara reminded himself aloud, struggling to keep himself together. He dared not think of his childhood and *Hanna*'s place in it. It was better to remember her as the vague, ghostly presence of recent years, someone who wanted—in her gentle, undemanding way—to die.

"Thank you for notifying me, My Sun." Tiwatipara swallowed hard and sniffed back the tears he had overcome. "Have arrangements been made for the funeral?"

"The *tawananna* is seeing to it. I'd release you to go back for the obsequies, but it would take weeks to get home, and they can't keep her that long." The king blew out a heavy breath through his nose. "I'm sorry, Tiwatipara. I feel your family has suffered a lot because of your loyalty to me. I'll have sacrifices made for her."

"It's our privilege, My Sun," said the charioteer, somewhere between sincerity and bitterness.

Hattushili released him with an affectionate pat on the back, and the charioteer took his leave, dazed and leaden. He was conscious of Benteshina standing by the door with a mournful expression on his face, studying him with his dark eyes.

Two days later, after his day's work was finished, Tiwatipara overturned a bucket and sat down in the stall of Bright Warrior. At first, the horse prodded him, hanging around, expecting a treat, but little by little, the stallion drifted off to his own business, munching hay from his manger and scratching his nose on the frame of the door. His tail swished quietly, and once in a while, he gave a rippling exhalation. Zidanza had disappeared as soon as his duties were completed, so Tiwatipara was alone. He felt the need for solitude; sitting among the crowds in the mess or the brothel common room was too much to bear. He didn't want to have to talk to anyone or even touch them. He couldn't put a name to his mood. He thought he was resigned to his grandmother's death, but it seemed like a frightening presage of another death to come—Tapala-tarhunta's. His nerves seemed to be lying on the surface of his skin. The only company he wanted was the horses'.

It was still light outside but sinking into twilight within the dim confines of the governor's stable. At the bottom of the stall, it was already too dark to see much except the white stockings of Warrior, the white blaze on his nose, and an occasional roll of his eyes. Tiwatipara leaned against the weathered wood of the box and stretched out his legs. There wasn't much in his mind, but he felt peaceful and a little melancholy.

Out in the aisle, a man's voice said coldly, "There you are."

The words made Tiwatipara look up, but the man's presence was no surprise. Members of the governor's household used the stables as a place of assignation, just as the king's men did at home. Horses were discreet.

A lighter voice mumbled something in reply. Suddenly, the charioteer's ears pricked. That sounded like Zidanza.

"I don't suppose you've actually accomplished anything here," said the unidentified voice. It was scornful, diminishing, an unkind rasp meant to scrape off skin.

"I'm sorry, Father," said Zidanza in a weak monotone. Warrior drifted to the open half door, attracted by the voice of his groom. He stuck his head over, and Tiwatipara saw a hand extended to caress the animal's nose. He squeezed himself against the wall, grateful for the darkness. The other man had to be Zidanza's father, who so filled him with fear.

"You pitiful rag. Look at you. You look like you're asleep. Stand up straight, by the thousand gods."

Another voice—deeper, a rumble that seemed to bubble up through a very thick substance—spoke. "What have you managed to do, nephew? Speak up."

"Not too much—"

"He means *nothing*."

"I have no influence, Father," said Zidanza, almost pleading. "People hardly even talk to me."

There was a thump, and the wooden wall of the box shuddered. Warrior jerked uneasily, and so did Tiwatipara. He heard the cold voice say densely, as if through clenched teeth, "You insolent brat."

"We're wasting our time with him, Armatalli," said the deep voice, scornful. "Our lord is dishonored by such a servant."

"I'll deal with you later."

Shadows blocked the half-light from the aisle briefly as the three men crossed in front of the door, departing. As silently as he could, Tiwatipara got to his feet and peeked around the opening of the stall. Shoulders drooping, rubbing a cheek with one hand, Zidanza stood with his back to the charioteer, watching the other two men move away. They were tall—one of them portly and shaven-headed, dressed in the white homespun of a priest. The other, curly-haired, was gross, porcine rolls of fat hanging over his belt, his skirts swaying like the tented top of a wagon from his broad, quivering hips as he waddled away.

Zidanza heaved a shaky sigh, and Tiwatipara dodged back into the darkness. He wouldn't for the world have shamed his friend by revealing he had overheard such a humiliating exchange.

The royal party was preparing at last to move into Luwian territory, beyond the boundaries of lands properly ruled by the Great King as vassals. Mira had some vague claim to the region, but it as often adhered to Karkisha, a loose nonstate that informally acknowledged Hatti without benefit of a treaty. Hattushili was gratified to note that the local princes had sent troops to join him; that spoke long of their desire to please. The king of Mira, encouraged by his betrothal to Lalantiwashha, had decided to stand by his side after a lengthy soul-searching about who was the legitimate king of Hatti.

Nearly seven years now I've been on the throne. Isn't the debate over? Hattushili thought. But clearly not, if Urhi-tesshub had reappeared in the kingdom. It certainly wasn't to pay a social call on his uncle. He was trying to take back the crown, and there would be those who supported him, still unconvinced after nearly seven years.

And there's one of them right now. The king narrowed his eyes at the augur Armatalli, who, with his acolytes, was drawing lines on the ground, marking out the sacred field over which divinatory birds would fly. Rumor had it that his brother was in Waliwanda, too, but Shipa-ziti wouldn't dare present himself before the *labarna*. Hattushili couldn't arrest him for his opinions, and the prince hadn't actually taken up arms against the king since the showdown six and a half years ago, but everyone knew he was Urhi-tesshub's chief agitator within the empire—after Arma-tarhunta. Something was manifestly afoot. *Why are my two cousins in the West? It's not simply because I called for an augur.*

Watching the ceremony from afar, surrounded by his officers, Hattushili heard the orotund voice of Armatalli declaiming prayers from the end of the field. He saw the younger priests hammer in stakes and drape ribbons. *They'd better find the omens propitious, or I'll have something to say to that godforsaken birdwatcher.* The king was a priest himself; he knew how easily the signs of the gods could be tweaked. It was all a matter of interpretation.

Now the priests were coming back, solemnly walking one after the other, their fists raised in pious prayer. *Fucking fat hypocrites.* The king called, "Everything ready, Armatalli? We need to do this expeditiously."

"The gods cannot be rushed, My Sun," said the priest as pompously as if this truism, too, were a divine oracle. His round face and shaven head were flushed and glistening. The day was shaping up to be hot.

The king shaded his eyes with a hand, looking for the approach of any birds. At his side, Armatalli took his seat with pontifical dignity on the ceremonial chair, flanked by his subalterns.

Suddenly, a shuffle of footsteps made the king turn. Kulana-ziti stood at his shoulder, his pockmarked face grave, his eyes a little wild. "My Sun, a word with you, if I may?"

Hattushili walked him away a few steps, out of hearing of the priests and courtiers. His heart accelerated. What could replace his brother's usual cool aplomb with such a look? "Speak, my man," he said in a low voice.

Kulana-ziti said, "We've just received word that Manapa-kurunta of Sheha River Land has gone over to the pretender, My Sun."

"Lords of the underworld take the blackguard!" Hattushili exploded through his clenched teeth. *Long-time vassals peeling off. Nothing short of a damned disaster.* He forced himself to speak more quietly, but his face was aflame and his heart stomping around furiously in his chest, kicking things. "When did this happen?"

"Just in the last few days, one assumes. My messenger brought me word from the north as soon as he could get here, riding down several relay horses."

"Shipa-ziti has been at work, I see. I need to send a letter to Nerikkaili right away. He'll have to bring me more troops. He can deal with Manapa-kurunta while I'm trying to get a grip on Piyamaradu. Of course, this will strengthen Piyamaradu's negotiating hand." Hattushili snarled out some curses, frustrated beyond words. *Nothing lately but rotten luck. Runda, the god of chance, is toying with me.*

The king was aware of Benteshina, in the knot of officers around the augur, turning to look at him with a raised eyebrow.

"We can put Manapa-kurunta's son on the throne in his place; Prince Mashturi was one of my most outspoken supporters. Come on, Kulanu. We have work to do." Hattushili pushed the ambassador ahead of him, and the two men strode away back toward the city gate, Benteshina trailing curiously in their wake.

If anyone was surprised to see the Great King stalking through the streets of Waliwanda, his face purple with fury, followed by a handful of *meshedi*, they didn't stop him to discuss it. He and Kulana-ziti, with Benteshina a few paces behind, entered the palace in a storm of long strides, only to encounter the governor in the vestibule and, at his side, the *tawananna*. Hattushili's anger fell away, and he cried in delight, "My dear! What are you doing here? I just thought of recalling you, and here you are."

She stood on tiptoe to kiss his face, to which he surrendered only too happily. "I thought I'd come see if you were still here, My Sun, and if you needed anything." She pressed her cheek against his chest and embraced him tightly.

He was aware of his whole body responding, melting forward eagerly. "It's a journey of some weeks, my dearest girl," he said fondly. "I think this was more than a spontaneous trip, hah? Shall we go to my apartment? Our noble augur is waiting for birds, so we have some time."

"Kulana-ziti, Benteshina," the *tawananna* greeted

the men behind her husband as she took his hand. "Is everything well?"

Kulana-ziti looked sideways at the king, his eyebrows knotted uneasily. "Our Sun will tell you all about it," he said in the bland tones of the professional diplomat.

But Benteshina, with his most ingratiating smile, said, "I would love to hear the latest news from the capital. How is my wife, my lady?"

Hattushili frowned at him in annoyance and growled, "All in good time, man. I haven't seen *my* wife for weeks. Besides, you're only betrothed."

"Gasshulawiya is well," Puduhepa said over her shoulder as her husband shepherded her away. To Hattushili, she said in a lower voice, "Poor Lalantiwashha is crying inconsolably for Tiwatipara."

As they passed down the corridor to the apartment where the Great King was lodged, Hattushili said, "Kulana-ziti just got word from his men in the north that Manapa-kurunta of Sheha River Land has defected to Urhi-tesshub. And Armatalli and Shipa-ziti are here—you probably passed my messenger en route."

"Oh, no!" She looked up at him, anxiety crimping her shapely brows. "They've been active at home, too. That's what I wanted to talk to you about. Arma-tarhunta has gone to Tarhuntassha. What's the old buzzard doing there, by the Lady of Shamuha?"

"Raising supporters, what else? There, where my brother made so many Luwian friends sworn to support his son. His fucking second-rank son." The king clenched his jaw. "Tapala-tarhunta says the whole empire is essentially Luwian in sympathy—that only we, the ruling class, are properly men of Hatti. Given a leader to unite them, they'll all rise up against us."

"My uncle tends to be pessimistic," the *tawananna* said. "I'll be happy to see him. Is he here or out gathering information in Apasha?"

The soldier on guard at the king's door opened it for them, and they passed inside, Hattushili ushering his wife before him. He took a deep breath. "He's in Millawata."

"Oh? Preparing for the treaty with Ahhiyawa?"

"No, no. That's concluded. And successfully, I might add." He hesitated then said, "He's our hostage against Piyamaradu's safety."

Puduhepa looked up at her husband in surprise. "A hostage?"

"Yes. Piyamaradu sent us a half-wit brother against my safety."

She opened her mouth in anger and astonishment. "Hostages for a vassal treaty signing? He's leading you on."

"How well I know it," Hattushili growled. "I sent Tapala because he's experienced. He can send us back useful information while he's there."

His wife drifted in silence to the bed and seated herself, her expression puzzled. "Is he physically strong enough? This will be hard on him. And now that Mashuhepa has died…"

"He doesn't know about her yet. And sitting in a gilded cage for a few weeks is easier on him than traveling back and forth." The king felt a little defensive. No one seemed to understand why Tapala-tarhunta needed to be the hostage. These youngsters didn't grasp the imperatives of an old man's pride.

"How is Tiwatipara holding up?"

"Poor boy." Hattushili sighed. "He was resigned about Mashuhepa, furious about Tapala-tarhunta. He can be a little fiery tempered." He coughed, not daring to look his wife in the eye. "But he's goodhearted. And loyal."

She said nothing and finally stood to serve herself a cup of water. "When are you leaving for the signing, my dear?"

"As soon as Armatalli's birds give us the go-ahead. He should be delighted to send us out of the country, so I anticipate taking off tomorrow, perhaps. I need Nerikkaili to bring me more troops; we have to depose Manapa-kurunta. But I don't want to leave the rest of the country vulnerable, if Urhi-tesshub is stirring about."

"Can Hishni lead the troops in the east?"

"Perhaps, but he's young. Nuwanza can take them."

"Are Tashmi-sharrumma and Ulmi-tesshub going with you?"

"They are."

She was silent for a moment then turned to him, her eyes soft, and caressed his cheek with a small hand. "I've missed you, my love. You're so full of life. There's a great void when you're not around."

"Is there? I have something that would like to fill that void." He seized her hand and pressed it to his lips. Their eyes met, and he cackled naughtily.

The king's cortege moved at a sedate pace through the mountainous countryside. Tiwatipara knew the place slightly from his travels with Prince Nerikkaili. He had a good sense of direction, but he lost his whereabouts easily here in the strait gorges shouldered by towering mountainsides. The road was narrow but well tended. He kept in mind the landmarks offered by Piyamaradu's men, who had set the location of their treaty signing in a sloping field near the river at a point where the forest leveled off and gave way to a strip of agricultural land. They could see it ahead of them as they came down from the pass. Tiwatipara observed the snaking blue ribbon of the river— its name escaped him—hemming the green spring fields and lacy orchards. No one was there.

The royal party had carried their chariots of state packed up on wagons—the stallions, led on lunges—but before crossing the last range of hills, they put the vehicles back together and hitched up the teams so as to arrive in splendor. Wasted effort. They had gotten there first. Perhaps that was a good sign; it suggested there would be no trap.

Prince Tashmi-sharrumma was a silent little passenger, but he was clearly excited by this participation in his first diplomatic event. His cheeks were flushed pink, his odd dark-gray eyes wide. Tiwatipara wondered how much of the scenery he could actually see. He was a nice boy after all, honest and hardworking, not as prissy as the charioteer had thought at first. In fact, the real relief was not having Ulmi-tesshub on board, with his constant rejoinders and showing off and his veneer of hard sophistication over a core of desperate need for affection. That one glance Tiwatipara had caught of the older boy's face when Tashmi's mother had kissed her son had told the charioteer a lot. Ulmi was an orphan, too, from his earliest years.

The king, his diplomats, and their entourage in their processional vehicles entered the plains along the river, clopping and rumbling. The soldiers set up camp, Tiwatipara and the other drivers and grooms occupying themselves with the picket lines. Since the weather was dry, they left the chariots set up in the open. The king had assigned soldiers to guard them by night, and Tiwatipara passed by them as often as he could and didn't scruple to check the axles and poles and any other part that might give way under stress. Prince Lurma-ziti was part of the company; the charioteer didn't trust him not to wreak some mischief.

But as one day succeeded another, he began to get restless. Everyone wondered where Piyamaradu's party was. Had the renegade backed out at the last moment without notifying them, hoping to embarrass the Great King of Hatti Land? Finally, it was decided that Kulana-ziti and Benteshina would go the short distance to Millawata to lay down an ultimatum: either the Luwian show up immediately, or the deal was off. Piyamaradu's brother, held against his good behavior in Waliwanda, would become a captive instead of a hostage. And Tiwatipara knew what that would mean at the other end. He pictured Tapala-tarhunta deprived of the slave who helped him wash and dress, his medicine for when the pain became too much, and the ointments that soothed his aching bones. Perhaps he would even be consigned to some unhealthy lockup with little to eat.

After chewing on the degradation of the situation for days, an idea came to Tiwatipara. He would volunteer to drive the two diplomats to Millawata in order to pay a visit to his grandfather. Tapala-tarhunta had assured his grandson he could receive guests. But while Tiwatipara was in the palace, he would convince Atpa to hold him hostage instead of Tapala-tarhunta. Then, if Piyamaradu failed to make the rendezvous, it would be he, Tiwatipara, who suffered captivity, and not his poor old grandfather.

The king accepted his offer without suspicion. Since they were marooned on the plain with nothing to do, there was no reason why Tiwatipara couldn't make a quick trip to see Tapala-tarhunta—even to verify on the king's behalf that he was being treated with fitting dignity.

Anticipation tingled in the charioteer's stomach as he pulled his vehicle up for his two passengers to mount. The king and his older sons stood around to see them off. A chest with the men's clothing and even a few weapons was strapped to the side of the box of a fast, elegant processional chariot, where a quiver full of arrows might otherwise be stowed. Kulana-ziti exchanged a salute with his brother and climbed up. Benteshina, twinkling but for once minding his manners, ignored the stepstool and vaulted in spryly with the aid of one hand. They positioned themselves at Tiwatipara's right and behind him, in the stations of the *shush* warrior and shield bearer.

"Find out what's going on, you two, and get back here without adventure. Tipa, give your grandfather my thanks and admiration," said the king. At his side, the *tawananna* stood, looking businesslike—although no bigger than a child by comparison—with her arm in his.

"We'll see you in a few days at most, My Sun," Kulana-ziti promised. "Let's hope it will be with Piyamaradu in tow."

"May your lovely queen console you for the small hole

in your heart that my—" began Benteshina with a grandiose gesture, but the king guffawed.

"Out of here, you rascal. Try to act serious. I know you will," he added pointedly, "or I wouldn't send you."

They took off at a mild canter, a pace the horses could hold for a good while, and eventually, as the road became steeper sinking to the coast, they descended at a trot.

It was a magnificent spring day, already balmy so close to the sea. The scent of pine was in the air along with mountain-apple blossoms and fresh green grass and sun-warmed rock. Tiwatipara filled his lungs, a little giddy with the exercise after long stagnation and with the anticipation of his heroics. At his side, Benteshina managed to talk continually despite the bouncing of the chariot. Kulana-ziti had long ago ceased to try to answer; he pushed out a polite noise from time to time. Tiwatipara mulled over his own thoughts.

They made good time but still, by evening, had reached no farther than the little town of Iyalanda that sat athwart the road a few leagues from Millawata and the territory of the Ahhiyawans.

"What's your will, my lords?" said Tiwatipara. "Shall we press on, or do we stop here for the night?"

"Let's stop here," Kulana-ziti decided. "We need to eat, and it will be too dark to see before long. I'd rather know what I'm getting into when entering a foreign city."

"Who's the governor here, or do you think we should just stay at an inn?" asked Benteshina as they approached the walls of the small settlement.

No one knew who ruled it. "An inn it is, then," the Amurrite said. "Beer and girls."

"Girls? But my lord is soon to be married," Tiwatipara said with a snort.

"Ah, but my lady is in Hattusha." With a knowing wink, Benteshina dug his elbow into the driver's ribs.

"So is mine, come to think of it." Kulana-ziti laughed.

And mine? Tiwatipara thought, suddenly sobered. *She's probably suffering the courtship of the king of Mira. I should have run away with her after all.*

His high good humor was somewhat tarnished as they entered the city gates. The days were starting to get long at this season, but twilight was upon them. They asked one of the soldiers on guard what accommodations they could find, and he directed them to a place frequented by well-heeled merchants, not far from the double gate of the town.

"So this is a Luwian city," said Tiwatipara to his companions as he gazed around. The flat-roofed two-story houses that surrounded them seemed to be of mud brick and stone with exposed wooden beams and their protruding ends, like every city he had ever seen. The streets were unpaved, as were those of Waliwanda. "Doesn't look so foreign."

"No," Kulana-ziti said. He had been a diplomat up and down the Western coast for half his life. "They have pretty much the same style of architecture as we do. There's not that much difference at all except in mentality. We even speak their language for the most part."

"Why is that?" Benteshina mused. "You men of Hatti have the most melodious, beautiful, ear-caressing language on the black earth—"

"Liar," said Kulana-ziti with a laugh.

"So why would you abandon it for the cacophonous rattles of Luwian?"

"Which is almost the same as our melodious Neshite, you fraud. Besides, there are more of them than of us."

They found the inn the soldier had recommended but had to share the one remaining room among the three of them and only escaped another pair of roommates by paying exorbitantly. Tiwatipara made a pallet on the floor, while his more prestigious companions shared the bed.

"I hope there's a barber someplace." Kulana-ziti scratched his stubbled jaw with an audible rasp. "Can we have food sent up, do you think? I feel a little uncomfortable sitting around in a common room. We're almost in enemy territory, things being the way they are."

"I, on the other hand, can play the complete foreigner in perfect safety. I'll go down and get us something to eat. And cast an appraising eye over the house beauties." Benteshina straightened his tunic and brushed his beard with the back of his fingers. "See you soon, gentlemen."

Kulana-ziti unbuckled his sword and threw it on the one stool, shaking his head with a gurgle of laughter that reminded Tiwatipara of the king. The charioteer wondered how close the two men had been in their youth, the one first rank, the other the son of a concubine. Neither of them was much to look at—horse-faced men with bad teeth.

"I could shave you, my lord," he offered, realizing how much below the other two he was in station. "It would save you having to look for a barber."

"Roach my mane, eh?" Kulana-ziti chuckled. "I'll take you up on that in the morning."

A slave brought them a tray of grilled meat. Lord

Benteshina didn't return, so they ate it all between them, and Kulana-ziti decided to go to bed. Tiwatipara drifted downstairs to the common room, hoping to see Benteshina, but he was nowhere visible. The charioteer took a seat on a bench for a while and drank a pot of beer, but he felt uncomfortable among these Luwians, who were all but openly the enemies of his king. He heard other languages he didn't recognize, especially one that seemed to be well represented among the guests, and wondered if it were Ahhiyawan. After a short while, he drifted out to the courtyard where their horses were stabled. The moon was up, glowing benignly in an irised halo of milky light.

Lord Kashkuh. Or I guess you're Arma here, he addressed the silver disk. *Prosper my mission, Lord of the Night. Help me get Grandfather out of Millawata before everything comes apart.*

Thinking of the god Arma made him remember the augur Armatalli, Zidanza's father. The evil bastard—what sort of father talked to his son like that and inspired such fear? His poor friend was too pliant. He needed to rebel, get away from his domineering parent. Gods, he was a grown man of twenty-five. He should be married and on his own. *But then, so should I*, Tiwatipara admitted. *My father was married and a father himself by the age of seventeen. Instead, I'm still living in the bachelor dormitories with nothing to mark me as an adult. No household, no wife, no children. Still combing the inns for girls.* Pawahtelmah had been the father every youth should have, the man every youth should become. A wave of sadness washed over Tiwatipara at the thought that he would never again see that prince among men.

He drifted into the stable, uneasy at finding it unguarded. Here and there in the dark stalls, a few horses and a good many mules stamped and blew or munched peacefully on their rations of grain. Pack donkeys were tethered in the aisle for the night. He found his team by Warrior's white-splashed nose hanging over the half door. The animal greeted him with a nicker. Tiwatipara caressed his soft nostrils. Wrath of Wurukatte looked around from the next box, shaking his head up and down as if to say, *Me too.*

"You know me, eh, fellows? I didn't think to save you any raisins."

Reassured that the horses were comfortable, he strolled through the moonlit court and eventually went out the wicket gate into the street. The velvet silence of night in a small town enveloped him. Crickets pulsed. He could see a line of orange light through the crack of shutters here and there, where someone was still awake by lamplight, but for the most part, there was no sign of life in the deep darkness between the houses. An occasional torch passed on the parapet of the city wall where a soldier made his rounds. Tiwatipara heaved a deep sigh, feeling his losses painfully and less optimistic than he'd been by daylight. He needed to walk, and he hoped it wasn't so late that the local watch would challenge him.

He sauntered pensively in the direction of the gate, the only place from which he knew how to return. From the distance, coming in his direction, he heard a tramping, shuffling noise as of many feet. There was an occasional cough, but otherwise, the owners of the feet were silent.

Tiwatipara stopped, unnerved. Was a patrol coming?

The steps weren't marching in any kind of order, though. It sounded more like a mob yet was so unspeaking. He drew against the wall of a building, sinking into the shadows, to watch the crowd approach.

Across the intersection before him, heading toward the gate, stumbled a horde of men, shackled together, their wrists bound, their steps dispirited, lagging on the packed earth of the street. Row after ragged row shambled by— scores of them, hundreds, their shadows tumbling across the moon-whitened walls. He watched with sagging jaw as they passed and passed endlessly, stirring up a low mist of dust. Along the edge prowled guards armed with whips and sticks.

What in the name of all the gods? Are they a defeated army? Booty people, off to be resettled? He saw no women or children, just males of varying ages, some well-dressed, others in rough, tattered clothes, all weary and hopeless although they didn't look starved. They hadn't been captive for many weeks, surely.

For a long time, there seemed to be no end to the column of men, but finally, the last of them had passed. Tiwatipara could hear their disorderly footsteps shuffling off into the distance and a shout at the gate as someone gave a countersign. The great doors grated as they swung open, and then they fell shut with a clash. The men were gone off into the night, tramping along the road to their destination by the light of the moon.

A chill of unease ran up Tiwatipara's spine. He turned and made his way as quickly as possible back to the inn.

CHAPTER 13

ATPA AND HIS CITY OF Millawata were supposedly neutral, allies of the Great King by virtue of the recent treaty. But it was no secret that the governor supported and outfitted his much younger father-in-law, Piyamaradu. As long as Hattushili and Piyamaradu were talking—and only so long—Atpa would be friendly. Tapala-tarhunta might have begun to grow worried as the days passed and no word came about the signing of the treaty. If it had fallen apart yet again, what was to be done about him? But he'd always tried to live with the same calm resignation as the horses he loved. He was on assignment here. His commanders would tell him when he could leave his post. His life was the king's.

Meanwhile, the Ahhiyawans fed him well. Tapala-tarhunta was permitted to receive and send mail, though he couldn't say whether it was read by his captors or not. Atpa came to see him from time to time, conversing in good Luwian. He was a genial man about Tapala-tarhunta's age, eager especially to have the benefit of the charioteer's expertise regarding the horses Atpa bought and sold for his masters across the sea.

Tapala-tarhunta, in turn, was interested to examine Atpa's chariots, which were constructed rather differently from the Hittite vehicles. They were very light, like the southern version, but some had boxes that were a mere framework of yew wood, not even covered with leather. The draft poles were braced with a second bar extending horizontally from the front rail of the box.

"Beautiful workmanship," he said to his host. "You can hitch up younger horses—no need to be so strong to pull these. How many men do they hold?" He eyed the shallow box, a mere step, over the wide axle. The wheels had only four spokes, but then, they didn't have to support much weight.

"Two," said Atpa, rubbing the crimson rail of the chariot fondly with his hand. "It suits our style of warfare. In our country, there's no terrain suitable for grand charges of line against line of chariotry."

The *hashtanuri* nodded, pursing his lips in evaluation. "Thank you for letting me look at them. I'm always interested to see how other people do things." He thought, *They don't provide much protection in battle.*

The two men made their way at the charioteer's laborious pace back to the governor's dwelling, a small palace of considerable luxury with a double colonnade—brightly decorated with martial wall paintings—around a paved court. "I leave you here, my honored guest," said Atpa. "Let me know if you lack for anything."

Tapala-tarhunta wondered how independent his host was. Tawagalawa, the Ahhiyawan king's brother, was in residence at the moment, and as Tapala-tarhunta understood it, the real power of Ahhiyawa on Luwian soil lay in him. The man had arrived three or four days earlier, and the *hashtanuri* had not yet seen him in person.

Tapala-tarhunta sank with relief onto his bed and stretched out his aching legs and his spasming back. The humidity of the coast didn't help, but he wouldn't be there for long. He tried to relax his muscles and massaged his thighs, and at some point, he drifted off to sleep.

A knock at his door awoke him. "Come in," he said, pulling himself up and swinging his feet to the ground.

The slave who served as his valet and doorkeeper appeared in the opening. "A visitor to see you, my lord."

"Send him in," said Tapala-tarhunta, thinking uneasily, *Who, by the thousand, can that be? Atpa was just here.* He found his crutches at the bedside and pulled himself to his feet, straightening his tunic and running his fingers through his hair, conscious of how rumpled he must appear.

Suddenly, Tiwatipara stood in the doorway, his face all eager and full of smiles, his brown eyes wide. "Grandfather!" he cried, arms outstretched. Tapala-tarhunta was so shocked he could hardly speak. Of all the unexpected apparitions! He could feel joy like a cozy fire warming him up, flushing his cheeks and thawing his heart, which had grown fatalistic and cold. *Oh, the dear boy!*

"Tipa!" He laughed in delight. "What are you doing here?" He folded the boy in his arms and held him as tight as his battered old muscles could squeeze.

Tiwatipara, always a sentimental lad, clung to him, snuffling, and murmured, "Forgive the tears. I know they're unworthy—"

But Tapala-tarhunta, nearly in tears himself, ruffled his grandson's hair. "No shame, boy. It's just who you are." He had perhaps been too hard on the lad in the past, he realized with a pang.

"Oh, Grandfather, I'm so glad to see you. I drove Prince Kulana-ziti and Lord Benteshina here to talk with Atpa. Nobody knows where Piyamaradu is; we've been waiting at the meeting place for days. The king's getting impatient. If this attempt at a treaty doesn't work, that's it. He's going after the renegade." Tiwatipara guided his grandfather to the bed and helped him sit on the edge. Then the boy settled himself cross-legged on the floor. "Are they treating you well?"

"Yes. I'm an 'honored guest,' to quote my host. Still, if the treaty signing falls through…"

Tiwatipara's eyes dropped, a guilty look on his face. "I… I want to replace you as hostage, Grandfather. It's not right that you should run such a risk."

"What?" cried the old man, outrage rising in his chest. "What do you mean it's not right? Do I not have the right to serve my king?" He could feel his face aflame with shame, because he knew what his grandson meant. *It's not right that a broken-down old nag should run such a risk.*

"But things could get bad if Piyamaradu has reneged," Tiwatipara pleaded, his straight brows crumpled with anguish. "I know Our Sun plans to treat his hostage like a prisoner, and these people will surely do the same. You shouldn't have to endure that at your age."

"What in the name of Tarhunta does my age have to do with it?" Tapala-tarhunta roared hoarsely. "The king has assigned me this post, and I'll see it through. Do you think soldiers only serve when there's no danger, by the gods? What kind of *hashtanuri* are you?"

Tiwatipara drew back, his face sagging with ill-suppressed sorrow. Tears glittered in his eyes. "Please, Grandfather. How could I forgive myself if something happened to you and I was spared... again?"

"That's your problem, son," said the old man harshly. "A soldier has one duty: to serve his king. And this is my service. I'm not too much a useless old bag of horseshit to *die* for My Sun, am I? You'll find something else to do for him." He was breathing as hard as if he had come from the battlefield.

Tiwatipara hung his head, and Tapala-tarhunta could hear him swallowing back his tears. Suddenly, the boy threw himself at his grandfather's knees, clinging to his legs in the age-old gesture of beseeching. "Please, please. I don't want to lose you, too. Not after Grandmother." He began to cry.

Tapala-tarhunta felt the hot wetness of the lad's tears through the skirt of his tunic. A thrill of anguish ran through him. Had he understood Tiwatipara—had Mashuhepa gone down the Great Way? It was all she'd longed for these three years. His anger disarmed, he lifted the boy's face gently. "Leave me this one thing," he said in a tight voice. "This is all I have, Tipa. Leave me this." He folded his arms around Tiwatipara's head and let him cry. *Standards of manliness be damned. No one can accuse my grandson of lacking courage.*

At last, the boy sobbed his sorrow out, and he raised his tearstained face, managing a smile. "You and Father have been my heroes all my life, Grandfather. I hope Our Sun knows how lucky he is to have men like you."

Tapala-tarhunta, more moved than he wanted to admit,

gave a wry *hmph*. He gathered himself, thinking of his wife, then said briskly, "Now, tell me about your trip, son."

Tiwatipara's smile turned a little quizzical. "I saw something last night in Iyalanda that puzzled me, Grandfather. Perhaps you can interpret it for me. I was out walking a bit late at night when a huge horde of men, all tied together like captives, came past. Hundreds and hundreds of them, maybe more. I could hardly believe it. They were guarded by other men with whips. They went out by the gate and shuffled off down the road. I think they were coming this way. What could that have been about?"

A bolt of horror speared the old charioteer. He struggled not to show his shock and said carefully, "I have a feeling those are some of the workmen stolen from Our Sun's vassal populations up and down the coast. Remember I told you Piyamaradu had been raiding villages and farms from Taruisha all the way down here?"

Tiwatipara nodded, his straight brows taut.

"You think they were heading here, you say?"

"From the sound as they left through the gate, yes." The boy stared at his grandfather, infected by his fear. "Why are they coming here?"

Tapala-tarhunta's thoughts were spinning. *Why indeed? Because it's a port. The rumors were true.* He said tensely, "Go down to the docks, Tipa. See how many ships are there. Normally, there are no more than twenty or so. Let me know immediately. Or if they won't let you back in to see me, take this information directly back to Our Sun. The builders are shipping out for Ahhiyawa. He must act immediately."

Tiwatipara drew up in a salute, his smile thin but

eager. "I'm off, Grandfather. The gods protect you." He held out his arms once more, and the two men embraced as if it might be for the final time. *And that's very likely to be true*, Tapala-tarhunta thought, not in resignation but with a kind of exultation that made his heart pound. *War is coming.* "I have one more thing to ask of you, son," said Tapala-tarhunta gravely. "Leave your sword for me."

Tiwatipara drew the weapon and, like a priest with a sacred vessel, handed it on the flat of his hands to his grandfather, who held it up to admire. A long, slightly curved blade—the reflected light running down it like a lightning strike—with a wide crescent pommel. A wicked thorn of bronze that would rip out a throat or two before the old charioteer died. The boy detached his sword belt and dropped it onto the bed.

"Now go," Tapala-tarhunta said.

Tiwatipara attracted no attention as he wandered the streets of Millawata. It was a large city, a seaport full of merchants from everywhere around the Great Sea, and one more Luwian speaker drew no glances. Fortunately, he'd left behind his distinctive Hittite military sword. He followed the slope of the streets to the harbor, eyes wide, astonished by this whole other world that existed along the coast, where ships replaced chariots and linen sails the eager horse.

And there were a lot of ships—far more than the twenty that his grandfather had said was the norm. They were slim and graceful with black-painted hulls, high-curved ends, rapacious beaks, and great staring eyes painted on either side of their prows. The ships were anchored cheek by jowl so that one might have been able to jump from vessel to vessel without touching water. At the mouth of the harbor were still more, bobbing in and out, their oars extended like the legs of those insects that walk on the surface of a lake—a vast flotilla, a herd. Tiwatipara's hackles rose. Something was clearly happening.

The early afternoon was bright and warm, a strong breeze blowing back his hair. Sailors were at work on the quays, longshoremen loading amphorae packed in straw onto wagons. Sauntering in a nonchalant way like a curious man with nothing to hide, he approached a pair of the workers and called in Luwian, "What's going on here? Why so many ships?"

They looked up. One of them, his face split in a nearly toothless grin, said, "Slaves headed for the mainland." He had a beard without a mustache and an accent of some kind, perhaps Ahhiyawan. "Where you from, my lord, that you don't know?"

"Mira. Just here for a day with my father's goods." It wasn't wholly untrue. His mother had been from Mira, a lady-in-waiting to Prince Hattushili's first wife. He hoped that they didn't understand what his shaven forehead meant and that it might pass for incipient baldness.

"Yep," said the other sailor. "Our man Piyamaradu's been hiring, it seems." The two laughed knowingly. "They're gonna build the king of Ahhiyawa a fine new city wall."

"Is that so?" Tiwatipara tried not to sound too interested, but his heart was in his mouth. "So I guess I won't find any transport for my goods, eh."

"Not for the next week or so. No sirree."

"How many men are we talking about?" he persisted. "There are a lot of vessels here; surely some are available."

But the toothless one grinned. "There's more of them slaves than there are ships. Thousands, they say. These tubs'll have to come and go more 'n once."

"Incredible," Tiwatipara murmured. "Well, thanks for the news, even though it's bad." He drifted away, and the sailors went back to work. *Bad news indeed. Dear gods.* He needed to tell the king immediately, before so many of his subjects were shipped abroad. Piyamaradu had revealed his real face.

Tiwatipara made his way back uphill to the governor's palace, where he was to meet Benteshina and Kulana-ziti. As he approached the ceremonial entrance, he almost collided with a flamboyantly dressed, thickset man in his thirties, his long curls lifted from his shoulders with the speed of his passage. The man shot him a disgusted glance, and Tiwatipara murmured, "Forgive me, my lord." He stared after the other's departing back. It was Piyamaradu himself! *The faithless bastard.* A tingling began along Tiwatipara's spine. If he had been a horse, he would have been pawing the ground with nervous eagerness. He had to get back to the king.

In the antechamber, Tiwatipara took a seat on a bench and waited impatiently for his colleagues' audience to conclude. He could hardly restrain his fingers from tapping on his thigh. Around midday, the two men emerged from the governor's small throne room. The charioteer could see by their somber faces that their news wasn't good.

Benteshina spied him and said, "No luck. Nobody

knows where Piyamaradu is or whether he intends to come to the treaty signing."

"But he just left the building. I saw him with my own eyes!" cried Tiwatipara.

The other two men exchanged a simmering look. Kulana-ziti said with a snarl, "The lying dogs. That's it, then. Our Sun needs to know that Atpa is in with his father-in-law."

"There's worse, my lord," Tiwatipara said, his voice dropping to a whisper. He drew nearer to the king's brother. "They're shipping the seven thousand men out right now, as we speak. To Ahhiyawa. To build a wall around the city."

"Let's go. Now." Kulana-ziti spun and headed toward the court where their vehicle was stored. "Quick, before they try to stop us."

As they hustled into the stables, Tiwatipara told them about his fact-finding trip to the port and how his grandfather had counseled an urgent return to the king.

Benteshina nodded, watching the youth harness up the team. "Maybe if Our Sun acts quickly, he'll be able to catch Piyamaradu before he sets sail."

"He'll have to get the king of Ahhiyawa's permission to enter the city and take a prisoner. Otherwise it becomes an act of war," fumed Kulana-ziti.

Tiwatipara asked, "Isn't that what the extradition treaty was for?"

"Exactly. But all that back-and-forth takes time. At least Tawagalawa is in the city, or so they say—assuming that for once they're telling the truth. He probably has authority to grant permission to extradite our curly-haired friend."

The two diplomats settled into an angry, reflective

silence while Tiwatipara finished hitching the team. He ran an intent eye over every part of the chariot and harness, even crawling underneath. After all, it had lain in the hands of the enemy overnight. But nothing seemed to have been tampered with. "Our baggage?" he asked.

"Leave it," growled Kulana-ziti. "Get us out of here."

They clattered off across the court at a trot. The guard at the wicket gate looked up, but Kulana-ziti held up a friendly-looking hand of farewell and smiled, and the man opened the gate for them without demur. As soon as they were on the city street, the ambassador's smile grew terrible.

They carried out the same masquerade at the double gate then set out upon the road up the river at a hard run. After a while, the charioteer relaxed the pace to a trot. "Do you want to stop for food at Iyalanda, my lord?"

"No," said Kulana-ziti, grim. "Unless the horses need water. Take us back to camp as fast as you can, son. There's a moon; we can travel even after sundown."

They set off again, sinking into a silence broken only by the clopping beats of eight hooves and the rumbling of wheels over the stony road. At one point, Benteshina asked at Tiwatipara's shoulder, "Where's your sword, my boy?"

"I left it with Grandfather. He… he thought he might need it." The youth's stomach lay like lead, heavy with the awful realization of how quickly things had come apart. His grandfather's situation had become grave, very likely fatal. Just what he had hoped to avert. But he had seen Tapala-tarhunta's reaction, and he respected it, sad as it made him. Death in the king's service was all the old man had left. Tiwatipara's nose began to burn in spite of himself. His father and grandfather had been the finest men to walk the black earth. *But don't set that in the past*, he warned himself. *Grandfather's still alive.*

The emissaries entered camp at nearly midnight. The king, who was lying awake, heard the ruckus and, wrapping a cloak around himself, slipped on his curly-toed boots and left his tent without awakening his valet. The *meshedi* guardsmen who stood around looked up, but he waved them off and strode through the moonlight to the picket line. The king's brother and the little Amurrite had dismounted, and Tiwatipara led away the weary horses, their backs steaming, to unhitch them.

"Well? What's the word?" the king said in a low voice, rough with urgency. "Is he coming?"

"Let's go somewhere we can talk, My Sun. Everything has changed suddenly." Kulana-ziti's face was black, his mouth a furious line.

A wave of uneasiness crept over the king like nausea. Hattushili led the pair back to his tent, and to his valet, who sat up in his bedroll, rubbing his eyes, he barked, "Get these men something to eat and drink."

Once they were alone, he and his brother sat down on the bed, and Benteshina took a seat on a clothes chest. "What's happened?"

"In our audience, Atpa insisted he had no idea where Piyamaradu was nor what his intentions were regarding the signing. But then Tiwatipara ran into the renegade in the palace itself—Tipa's the one with the information. He should tell you himself." Kulana-ziti, despite his exhaustion, was crackling with anger, held in check only by the discipline of thirty years of diplomatic service.

"Go get him," the king directed his little friend. Benteshina scampered off and, a brief while later, returned with Tiwatipara in tow. The valet followed them with a loaf of bread and a slab of cold meat. He set it down on the king's folding table and came back with a ewer of wine and three ceramic cups. The famished emissaries bent and carved themselves off a portion of meat.

"Tell me what you learned, my boy," said the king to Tiwatipara.

Between bites, the charioteer recounted how he had seen the hundreds of shackled men in Iyalanda and how Tapala-tarhunta had made sense of them. He told the king how his grandfather had instructed him to spy around the port, how he had questioned the sailors, and what they had told him of the vast gathering of ships.

At the end of Tiwatipara's recital, the king sat in simmering silence. Then he erupted. "We've got to stop him! We've got to capture that blackguard red-handed and stop those men from being shipped out. It's a fucking act of war." He slammed a hand down on the bed with a *whomp*.

"Clearly, the whole business about a treaty signing was a smokescreen, My Sun," Kulana-ziti agreed.

Hattushili could feel his rage mounting inside like water approaching the boil. "We're going after him at dawn, pulling him out of his lair—"

"You'll need the king of Ahhiyawa's permission, My Sun. Piyamaradu is on his territory," Benteshina reminded him.

"We have an extradition treaty," snarled the king.

"Tawagalawa is supposed to be in Millawata himself. Somebody send out a messenger right this moment, a mounted courier. He can be back before midday."

Benteshina sniffed significantly. "Quite a little gathering of eagles going on there, isn't there? Coincidence? I think not…"

"And tell him we have a fucking army sitting a day's journey away, in case he doesn't feel like honoring his treaty, the scabby cur." Hattushili surged to his feet, no longer able to contain his energy. Kulana-ziti departed to pass the order, and his brother stalked up and down the confines of the tent, kicking his discarded cloak out of his way. He snapped at Benteshina, "Kill Piyamaradu's hostage. He's foresworn."

The Amurrite took his leave.

Tiwatipara had risen, too, out of respect. He said uncertainly, "What of my grandfather, My Sun?"

Hattushili stopped his pacing and came toward the boy, his face softening. "He knew what he was in for, son. He's a soldier."

The youth nodded sorrowfully, his mouth a compressed line, but he seemed resigned, no longer fighting it. "That's what *he* said." He looked up at Hattushili with his frank, dignified young eyes. "He kept my sword. He'll sell his life dearly."

A warmth of affection and pride flooded the king. He clapped the youth on the shoulder. "We can both learn a lot from him." His eyes misted in a wave of tenderness for the good boy and deep sorrow for the old charioteer, Hattushili's friend for more than thirty years. At last, he said, "Get some sleep. Tomorrow, we're going to war."

But it wasn't until nearly sundown of the next day that the horseback courier returned, drenched in sweat, his knees wobbling. He made his report to the king then described excitedly to his colleagues in the stable how events had transpired. Tawagalawa had granted permission to enter Millawata and take possession of Piyamaradu to stop his ships from embarking with the workmen, even by force. The Ahhiyawan had not even tried to explain his king's commerce with the renegade or the fact that his allies' men had been taken captive. One would have thought he had nothing to do with the shipping out, in contravention of the treaty between Ahhiyawa and Hatti.

The courier finally begged to go get some sleep, and the circle of grooms and charioteers surrounding him broke up, their curiosity assuaged.

"So, tomorrow we go to Millawata," said Tiwatipara to Zidanza as they returned to their work. He followed the groom alongside Tarhunta's Strike, carrying the basket of currying tools. "Have you ever seen the sea? It's beautiful. Too bad we won't do much sightseeing."

"I guess the *tawananna* is sending the rest of the troops still at Waliwanda," his friend said without much appearance of interest. He began to brush the animal's smooth chestnut flank with a handful of straw.

"I suppose. Someone said Prince Nerikkaili is on his way from Sheha River Land, too, but it may all be over by then."

"Who's left guarding the capital?" Zidanza laughed wanly, moving to Strike's shoulder.

"I bet Urhi-tesshub is having a good hee-haw over this," said Tiwatipara with an ironic snort. He leaned his hand on the pole that held the picket lines taut. "The king, the *tawananna*, and the *tuhkanti* all on the Western border at the same time. It isn't supposed to happen that way. I can't see that fat little vizier leading the home guard in defense of Hattusha."

Zidanza bent his attention to the currying of the horse's legs and said nothing.

"Did you ever figure out if that was your father you saw in Waliwanda?" asked Tiwatipara ingenuously.

"Oh. Yes. He was here to cast the auguries for the treaty signing." Zidanza laughed without humor. "They were favorable."

The charioteer brayed. "Nobody told Piyamaradu that." Silence fell again. Tiwatipara longed to ask his friend who the fat man was, but he didn't want to reveal he had been listening to their conversation. He watched Zidanza moving around Strike, brushing the dust and sweat out of the horse's hair. "You going to braid his mane?"

"Guess I have to, don't I? You know how slow I am, though. They'll be halfway to Millawata before I finish."

"I can do it while you take care of the rest of the work."

"Would you?" The boy looked up, his sleepy eyes grateful. He squeezed his friend's arm. "You're the best friend ever, Tipa." He winced and pressed a hand to his belly. "I'm going to have to run to the latrine for a minute. I'll be right back."

"It's really bothering you lately," said the charioteer, concerned.

"Something we're eating out here doesn't agree with

me." Zidanza hurried away, almost doubled over, and Tiwatipara watched him go.

I hope it's nothing serious, he thought. He parted the long hair of Strike's mane and began the finicky process of braiding each section then twisting up the tiny braids into knobs tied with ribbon and beads. He was nearly finished by the time Zidanza returned.

"I was afraid you fell in." The charioteer laughed. "You all right?"

Zidanza nodded. He looked pale and troubled, but he smiled. "Oh, thanks. You did all my work."

"So you can go lie down if you need to."

But the groom said vaguely, "I'm all right." He began to gather his currying tools into the basket. "Three more to go."

"I'll see you around, my friend. I have some things to do myself."

Tiwatipara moved off down the picket line to the area where the chariots had been assembled and left in the open until the order to move out. As had become his habit, he approached the royal vehicle and began a minute inspection, although he had been over it the afternoon before. As long as Lurma-ziti was with the army…

The pole and yokes seemed in good order. Nothing unsteady about the rails. Wheels, sturdy—no hidden cracks in the spokes, the felloes sound, their hobnailed leather tires starting to wear but certainly not dangerous. He lay down on the ground and pulled himself under the car. *Axle buttered with grease at the corners; seems intact.* He had started to slide out again when he pressed his hand down on a sharp piece of gravel. The charioteer lifted it to brush the pebble off, but to his surprise, his palm was covered with tiny, pale flakes of sawdust.

An alarm seemed to start trumpeting in his head. He flipped onto his stomach and hunted around in the dirt until he found a little sprinkling of wood dust just below the inside of the left wheel. He looked up at the axle but saw nothing. He felt across the top of it. Nothing. Then, with difficulty, he extracted his knife from its sheath where he lay upon it, and with the tip of the blade, he probed through the sheep fat where the axle moved through its socket. An indentation. Suddenly feverish, he scraped off the lubricating grease and pushed the wheel a bit so the axle revolved.

Now he could see a groove cut into the hard ash, filled with and covered by the fat. Someone had sawed the wood, rolled the car just enough to put the cut at the top, invisible, then regreased the area. Without a minute inspection, it would never be seen, but the instant the weakened axle broke—in a hard charge or on a bumpy road—that left wheel would be spinning off across the field.

A wave of fear that was almost literally sickening flushed up from Tiwatipara's gut. In his throat, a painful pounding began, and suddenly, he found it hard to draw a breath. The indelible image of his father's chariot—tipping, screeching, tumbling, striking the horses, sending the men flying before it into its path—illumined his mind's eye like a flash of lightning. He could see it happening again and again in slow motion. It would have happened once more. The king would have died the following day.

He backed out from under the box, his flesh crawling. He had to warn the Sun.

Tiwatipara ran as hard as his legs would take him toward the royal tent, his heart hammering with his urgency. The saffron-garbed *meshedi* stood in stolid watch at the entrance, spears in their hands.

He had just gone up to one to ask admittance when the tent flap opened and Prince Lurma-ziti emerged, a strained, weary expression on his thin face. As soon as he saw the charioteer, his mouth hardened and his black eyes ran Tiwatipara up and down. "Pony boy," he said and made his way off in his painful, crablike way.

Tiwatipara stared after him, his chest heaving. *You mangy monster*, he thought, clenching his teeth. *You unnatural, evil cur. I've got you now.*

The guard bore the charioteer's request into the king's tent and a moment later returned to say, "Our Sun will see you."

Tiwatipara entered, almost trembling with triumph and ferocity. The king was sitting at his folding table, preparing to eat. Before him sat a leg of some fowl and a bowl of groats. He smiled a crooked smile at the youth and cried out, "Tiwatipara. What brings you here? Further news about Piyamaradu, hah?" But after a sharp look at the charioteer, he beckoned the youth to have a seat on the stool across from him—the seat no doubt just vacated by Lurma-ziti.

"No, My Sun. I was just checking your chariot in preparation for tomorrow." Tiwatipara's voice almost failed him. "It's been tampered with. Since yesterday. Or since last night, because there were guards posted after dark. The axle cut through, just like before, and concealed with grease."

The king's long face went white under its ruddy tan.

"Shaushga protect us! Who could have done it right in the middle of the camp like this, with people all around?"

Tiwatipara gritted his teeth and plunged in. "I think it was Prince Lurma-ziti, My Sun."

But Hattushili looked skeptical, his jaw skewed, considering. His voice was almost cold. "Have you any reason for saying that?"

Tiwatipara told him about the episode with Tashmi-sharrumma, how the elder prince had managed to string up a trap right under the nose of Tiwatipara and Zidanza, and how ruthlessly he had let the boy risk injury or worse. He recounted how every time there was an attempt on a chariot, Lurma-ziti was present. He had to admit it all sounded very circumstantial. He could hardly say to the king, "Your son is a cruel, warped son of a bitch who would love to see someone killed."

Hattushili sat for a moment, staring sadly at his lunch. "He's extremely envious. He can hardly bear to see anyone loved." He looked up, his eyes troubled. "But why would he be out to kill me? He's several notches down in the succession. What would he gain?"

"Unless he's in with Urhi-tesshub…"

"That certainly wouldn't seem to work to his advantage. And anyway"—Hattushili's hard expression softened with pity—"he's physically incapable of having done such a thing. He couldn't get down on his back like that and wield a saw."

"He could've paid someone." Desperation made Tiwatipara a little wild. The king didn't believe him at all. And who *would* want to think his own son had tried to kill him?

Hattushili shook his head, disturbed but not convinced. "I'm deeply grateful that you discovered this, Tiwatipara. You've saved my life. Go change out the axle, and sleep by the chariots if you have to. But I think we need to keep looking for a perpetrator. The fact is, in his way, Lurma-ziti loves me."

You want that to be true, thought Tiwatipara hopelessly, *because you love him.* "May the gods watch out for My Sun."

"Anyway, if it's Lurma-ziti, he won't be any danger for a while. He's sick. Quite sick. He'll be returning to Waliwanda instead of going on with us to Millawata." The king rose wearily and accompanied the charioteer to the flap of the tent. "Keep up the good work, son. It makes me feel better to know my life is in the hands of men like you."

Tiwatipara left, downcast, his heart a ball of lead in his stomach.

The next day, the army finally moved. The troops Puduhepa had sent from Waliwanda had joined them the evening before, and they were a fair-sized force now. They had sung the old song, confiding their souls to the gods in case they should die that day and praying to be buried next to their mothers, and then they had massed in the road, prepared to move out.

His whip in its socket, Tiwatipara stood in his box, accompanied by a *shush*—an onboard warrior armed with a bow and ax—and Prince Tashmi-sharrumma, who would act as the man's shield bearer. Ulmi-tesshub was fighting in a separate vehicle, serving as the weapon-carrying warrior for the first time.

Tiwatipara remembered his own first time going into battle—the terror and the exhilaration and the sense of vulnerability as he, all but unarmed, guided the horses through a murderous melee where everyone was out to kill him. *May the gods preserve my little prince*, he thought.

The lad stood clad in a sleeveless quilted coat like Tiwatipara's; only the armed warrior wore a coat of scales. Tashmi-sharrumma rested his hands on the curved top edge of a tall shield, narrowed at the waist and covered in cowhide. He was strong enough to lift and maneuver it and had practiced that daily for much of his young life. His face was still and keen, ready to test himself against the enemy.

We're bred for this, thought Tiwatipara with awe as he gazed around over the assembled ranks, their standards rippling over their heads. *Just as the horses are. Generation after generation of us, cracking the whip, lifting the shield, wielding the sword in the service of the man the gods have chosen. And he, too, is bred to it. Fingered by divinity, generation after generation. He's of a substance a little more than human, for all his human flaws.* Something hot and sweet rose in Tiwatipara's throat, choking him, and he could barely hold back the tears, he found himself so stirred.

Hattushili himself had moved to the front of the ranks in his scarlet and gilt-bronze chariot. Tall and erect in golden scale armor and a lofty plumed helmet, he looked around at the men and vehicles massed behind him with their fluttering flags. Their bedizened horses were protected by quilted trappers, their heads and necks cased in bronze-studded hoods, their foreheads bobbling with panaches.

The thought that he should be driving the king flashed

through Tiwatipara's mind, but he told himself, *It's enough to get your prince home safely.*

The king gave the signal; trumpets sounded. Normally, they would proceed in mixed columns, with the vehicles flanking the foot soldiers, but the mountain roads were not wide enough. So the infantry moved out first, the chariotry pulling in behind them so as not to choke the men with dust. They moved at a quick march, the soldiers almost jogging.

They had nearly reached Iyalanda when the first arrow flew. A soldier dropped in his tracks at the edge of the column. Soon others were falling. A mass of guardsmen surrounded the royal box, and the king whipped out his ax. The archer at Tiwatipara's side had raised his bow and, upon his string, laid an arrow from the quiver mounted on the box. All eyes scanned the forested cliffsides that surrounded them. *What a site for an ambush,* thought the charioteer, all his senses on the alert, his breathing suddenly shallow. It seemed too quiet…

Out of the trees, with a ferocious cry, poured men bristling with swords and battle-axes. The archer let loose his string with a powerful twang. The sound of whistling filled the air, and some of the attackers fell to the dust. Tashmi-sharrumma lifted the shield overhead, and a bolt struck it so forcefully the boy staggered. Tiwatipara clucked up the team and sought the center of the troops, where the chariots were congregating to protect their horses. The archer had drawn his ax and swung off the box to fight hand to hand. Tiwatipara could see some of the king's troops forcing their way up the steep hillsides between the trees in pursuit of the Luwians. Before much longer, they returned, the archer among them. The attackers weren't numerous; the king's men managed to repulse them, and after loading the wounded on the supply wagons to follow, they took off at a goodly clip.

"Why were there so few of them?" gasped Tashmi-sharrumma, red-faced and winded, as they trotted away.

"That was some kind of diversion, my lord," said the archer, still panting. "They're trying to slow us down."

Before long, Iyalanda appeared ahead, its scalloped parapets sparking with helmets. The walls were manned against them. Tiwatipara felt a twinge of alarm as at death's near passage. Only days before, he had wandered the streets of this town alone, not dreaming it was so hostile.

A herald was sent out to demand passage. If not, he said, the Great King was prepared to invest the city.

"Who's your leader?" Hattushili yelled out in his gravelly voice.

"Lahurzi, brother of Piyamaradu," the enemy herald replied. "Long live the Arzawan Confederacy!"

Their request denied, the soldiers of the Great King prepared to besiege Iyalanda. They dismounted from their chariots and tied up the animals out of reach. Tents were set up, and a party trudged into the woods to cut a tree for a ram.

"This shouldn't take long," said the archer, shouldering his bow. "It's a piddling little place."

"But it's costing us time, and Our Sun is in a hurry. Every day that passes, he loses workmen, and the chance of missing Piyamaradu gets greater." Tiwatipara watched the walls with a throbbing sense of urgency. *My grandfather*, he thought. *We have to get there before Atpa puts him to death.*

They began ramming the gate. To the rhythmic booming of the ram, some of the soldiers set themselves to fashioning ladders and grappling hooks. No one had expected to have to besiege a city, only to sign a treaty. The king stalked up and down out of range of arrows from the town walls, crackling with murderous impatience.

Tiwatipara had nothing much to do until they were on the move again. Sometimes Prince Tashmi-sharrumma accompanied his father—at twelve, the lad was Benteshina's equal in height, so the two of them made a pair of miniature warriors trailing the king. Hishni had been sent to join his elder brother in Sheha River Land.

By the end of the second day, the town capitulated, its gates were thrown open, and its governor—a squat, ringleted youth, cocky and defiant—was taken prisoner. Like the attack on the road, the whole business had only been a delaying tactic.

The army hit the road again, pressed by a greater and greater sense of desperation. Tiwatipara kept the horses at a measured gallop until the sun was high in the sky. Before them, at the tip of its small peninsula, stood Millawata, white against the green of the land and the blue of the sea and sky. Kulana-ziti, bearing the letter of safe conduct from Tawagalawa, was sent ahead to negotiate an entry for the Great King's troops.

At noon, they thundered into the city through its double gate, pennants flying, some twenty chariots and hundreds of foot troops, the rest waiting outside the gate lest the Millawatans sense themselves threatened. Cracking his whip over the backs of the horses, Tiwatipara felt as if the pounding of his pulse were a countdown. *Will we get there in time to stop the shipping of the prisoners? In time to catch Piyamaradu? In time to save Grandfather?*

Some days after his grandson had departed in a flurry, Tapala-tarhunta became aware of a change in the pace of the governor's establishment. Atpa had not returned to visit him. There seemed to be hasty comings and goings of visitors and massing of wagons in the stable courtyards. The charioteer made it a point to continue wandering about, despite the effort it cost him. He suspected he might pick up useful information for the Great King if his mail were not censored—although he wondered if it would even be sent at this point. He passed through the corridors at his laborious pace—an unthreatening broken old object of pitying smiles—and saw attachés running in and out of the audience hall. More than once, he thought he saw Piyamaradu himself. *Wouldn't Hattushili like to know about that!*

Tapala-tarhunta realized that the urgency that had taken hold of the palace was also the drumbeat of his own impending death. If Piyamaradu was trying to escape overseas with thousands of the Great King's subjects seized by force, he was, in essence, declaring war. The hostages' lives would be forfeit. Tapala-tarhunta was ready, the gods knew. That was another pressure—the longing to see Mashuhepa and Pawahtelmah again in the green meadows of the blessed, to step out of this aching, mutilated body that no longer obeyed his will, to ride again, the wind in his hair…

He kept Tiwatipara's sword carefully hidden under his mattress. He would go down like a *hashtalanuri.*

Around noon perhaps five days after his grandson's departure—Tapala-tarhunta was no longer sure of the count—he stood in the stable court. He came here frequently; he liked to visit the horses. The calm majesty of the animals gave strength to his resolve. Outside the wicket gate, which opened onto a main artery of the city, he heard a growing rumble. His nostrils tensed. Any charioteer knew that sound: the thunder of Tarhunta Pihasshasshi's boys hammering down the hard earthen street, their heavy boxes bounding behind them. *Chariotry*! Was this the army of the Great King, come to strike the impudent renegade like a hammer of vengeance?

He could see nothing over the high wall, but he dragged himself toward the gate nonetheless and asked the guard, "What's that noise, son?"

"The Hittite king has come to take back his men." The soldier had a strange expression on his face—a little smug, a little crafty.

"Will he find them, do you think?" the charioteer asked with the innocent smile of an old man.

"No, my lord." The guard grinned openly. *So much for the neutrality of Ahhiyawa.* "The last of them have gone, and Prince Piyamaradu with them. Off across the sea."

"Ah," said Tapala-tarhunta mildly, but a black anger stirred in his heart. Hattushili didn't take kindly to humiliation, and he had been well and truly played. For all his suspicions and capacity for guile, the king was at bottom an upright man who played by the rules until he was forced not to. Piyamaradu had no such inhibitions; he was a creedless cur. The whole months-long farce of seeking to become a vassal had just been a distraction until he had his captives seized, rounded up, and shipped out. Tapala-tarhunta pictured Hattushili drawing up at the water's edge as the last ship sailed out of sight. A dreadful storm was brewing. Someone would pay.

It was only a matter of time now—and not much time. He limped back to his apartment, drew the sword from under his mattress, and sat upon the bed with the blade across his lap. In the corridor outside, he heard voices raised and the clanking of armor. He was poignantly conscious of his own chest lifting and falling with his breaths. Counting down.

Someone threw open the door, and Prince Tawagalawa entered with a pair of soldiers. The prince was dressed for battle, a helmet of white boars' tusks on his head, his shins cased in stiffened linen greaves. "Lord Tapala-tarhunta," he said courteously, but he sounded pressed. The urgency was growing. "I have one last task to perform for Prince Piyamaradu. It seems your king is unhappy with our part in that worthy gentleman's commerce, and we may have to decide the issue by combat. I fear we must say goodbye to you."

He gestured to his men, and they moved forward, swords in hand.

Tapala-tarhunta pulled himself to his feet then let his crutches drop. He hefted his weapon calmly. "I thank you for your hospitality, my lord," he said with the tranquility of a man with a clean conscience. "We knew it would come to this, didn't we, since Piyamaradu is a faithless dog who never intended to keep his word?"

The two soldiers drew near, raising their blades. *Hurry, hurry.* The old man swung, his breath sawing in his nose.

One of them parried. The shock ran up Tapala-tarhunta's arm; his heart was suddenly thudding impatiently in his chest, trying to burst free. He tried to raise his blade again, but his arm was too slow, too weak. His balance wavered, and he was leaning too far backward. *It's time.* The other soldier thrust under his companion's arm, and lightning pierced Tapala-tarhunta's breast. The blade fell from his nerveless fingers—a final, fatal disobedience of this body that had gone over to the enemy—and the last thing he heard was Tiwatipara, crying from the doorway, "Grandfather! No!"

Too late! Tiwatipara broke past the Ahhiyawans and rushed to the bed. He dropped to his knees over his grandfather, who had sunk backward across the mattress, crimsoned in his blood, the sword fallen beside him. "Grandfather!" he cried again, and the word shattered into a sob. Was it not only a moment ago that he had wept at the side of his father and grandfather as they lay broken and bloody? But there was dignity here, the high purpose of the king's man doing his duty. The old charioteer's body was still; it had ceased to breathe. It lay in perfect immobility, a holy shrine in which the highest sacrifice had been offered.

The Ahhiyawans stood, watching expressionlessly, while the young charioteer shook quietly with grief, his forehead on Tapala-tarhunta's chest, smearing his face with the old man's blood and not even caring. Only after a long space of time did he rise to his feet. Tawagalawa turned to the other Hittites in the doorway and raised his hands in surrender. Prince Tashmi-sharrumma and the archer entered the room and took up the swords dropped by the Ahhiyawans.

"You will not be punished for this, my lord," said Tashmi-sharrumma, his young voice as full of dignity as any grown man's. "The fate of hostages is understood." He stood tall and at ease, one fist on his hip, his sword in the other, as poised as a small adult. Tiwatipara was stunned at how the boy seemed suddenly to swell into the role of king's son. He must have been taking lessons from Nerikkaili.

"I thank you, my lord," said Tawagalawa with a slight smile crisping the edge of his lips. "To whom do I surrender myself, if I may ask?"

"I am Prince Tashmi-sharrumma, eldest first-rank son of the Great King," said the boy seriously. "My father is conferring with your man Atpa. No doubt, your presence would be appreciated. You're free to go."

The three Ahhiyawans bowed and made their way out the door. Tiwatipara gaped at his young shield bearer. "Well done, my prince. I don't think I've ever heard you say so much since I met you!"

The boy blushed and dropped his eyes. "It's my duty, Tiwatipara." He looked toward Tapala-tarhunta's wiry old body lying tranquilly with chin up, calloused hands outstretched, in a pose of flawless surrender. No doubt, the boy was thinking, as Tiwatipara was, *And that was* his *duty*.

Tashmi-sharrumma ordered his archer to find the king and ask him what to do with Tapala-tarhunta's corpse. Surely, they would take him back to Waliwanda for cremation. Tiwatipara gazed at his grandfather—a deep, filling look like a drink of cold water after a day's thirsty work. Filling his memory. Topping up his love. The noble old visage, square jawed and beak nosed, lay at peace. Tiwatipara felt tears starting once more in his eyes, and he turned away, his mouth twisted with sorrow. Tashmi-sharrumma put a shy hand on his arm. The boy's homely face was drawn down with a compassion beyond his years.

The charioteer managed a wobbling, grateful smile. "We were just too late, my prince. The Gulshesh were ready to cut his thread, that's all. Thank you for coming with me, though."

When the king's army had entered the city, most of the troops had pounded down to the docks, but a few had turned aside to confront Atpa at his palace. Tiwatipara had asked permission to free his grandfather, and his chariot mates had willingly joined him. But too late. It had been too late for everyone. The nerve-wrenching pressure was off now.

Piyamaradu had gotten away.

Nerikkaili had been in Waliwanda for several days by the time his father returned from Millawata. The prince was exuberant. He had driven the aged Manapa-kurunta from his throne and put in his place the old king's eldest son, Mashturi. The new king was Hattushili's brother-in-law, a man already the *labarna*'s age or a little older, who had been one of Hattushili's strongest supporters in the war for the kingship. Sheha River Land was no longer a problem. Nerikkaili looked forward to his father's praise and gratitude. It was about time he had something positive to his account.

The prince had just treated himself to a copious meal in the company of his stepmother and Hishni when they heard the clatter of the returning chariots in the courtyard below.

Puduhepa started up, craning to see out the window. "He's back," she said with such evident delight that Nerikkaili felt a moment of envy. He had yet to meet his betrothed. Would she long for his return with the same eagerness after nearly fifteen years of marriage? He tried not to think about his father in the smooth white arms of Puduhepa, pressed against her breasts. It seemed unfair, like so much else in life.

The three of them made their way down to the court, where the soldiers unloaded their wagons of materiel, and the grooms took away the chariots to unhitch. There was much milling around and shouting of orders, but the faces Nerikkaili saw were black with gloom. He spied his father's head above the crowd, the long hair matted with sweat and the pressure of his helmet. His expression was full of murder. The prince exchanged an uneasy look with his stepmother. She ran ahead and threw her arms around Hattushili, who bent and kissed her ferociously and spat, "The mangy dog got away, and so did seven thousand of my subjects. We missed them by fucking instants. Lords of the underworld take them all—that perjured blackguard. If he ever steps foot on my soil again, I'll chop him so small the Lady of Arinna herself won't be able to see him."

Puduhepa rubbed his back appeasingly despite the sharp bronze scales of his armor. "Don't upset yourself, my love. It's over. Those men could be the casualties of one battle. We'll do fine."

But Hattushili was still grumbling as they made their way toward the governor's palace. The two princes intercepted them. "My father. Welcome back." Nerikkaili and the king exchanged an embrace, then Hishni did the same, and Hattushili's anger seemed to disappear. He grinned affectionately at his sons. "How did it go in the north, boys?"

"It went well, Father. Manapa-kurunta is out; Mashturi is in," Nerikkaili said smugly.

"Well done, son," the king cried, as delighted as if it had been his own personal triumph. "He's a good one, isn't he?" he said proudly to the *tawananna* at his side. He threw an affectionate mock punch at Hishni. "You are, too."

The queen smiled ambiguously and cast a quick glance at Nerikkaili. Then she turned serious. "Is Tashmi unharmed, my love?"

"He is indeed. Tiwatipara said he performed like a seasoned warrior in his first battle. And listen to this." Hattushili flashed his crooked grin at the three of them in turn. "It was Tashmi who received the surrender of Tawagalawa! Imagine, a twelve-year-old boy! I told you he'd be a man the next time you saw him."

Nerikkaili tried to picture his silent little brother with the fangy teeth accepting a grown man's surrender. He found himself once again mildly frosted over with envy. *Don't be ridiculous*, he said to himself, disgusted. *Why would you envy a twelve-year-old child?*

"And Ulmi-tesshub rode into battle like one of the Innarawantesh. They're both fine boys. The gods have given me fine sons—and nephews." He ruffled Nerikkaili's hair the way one might caress a child, his ugly face so full of fatherly pride it seemed almost more than he could bear. Nerikkaili thought, not for the first time, *What an extraordinary person. He pours his emotions out all over the place, and it just makes him seem the more manly.* No wonder the prince and all his brothers were so desperate for their father's approval. It was like the kiss of the gods.

The four of them waited until Tashmi-sharrumma and Ulmi-tesshub ran up from the stable, flushed with excitement, eager for their share of the king's praise. At last, the *tawananna* hustled the youngsters off, her arm around her firstborn's shoulders, and Hattushili said in a subdued voice to his older sons, "This was a bruising defeat, boys. Urhi-tesshub and his sheep fuckers are licking their chops tonight."

Nerikkaili heaved a sigh. He was used to his father's wrath, but discouragement was something rarer. The prince said, concealing his desire to console under a glossy, diplomatic voice, "It was unbelievably dishonest. Piyamaradu is utterly without honor—surely everyone knows that."

Hattushili shrugged, his mouth downturned. "How is Lurma-ziti?"

"Suffering," said Nerikkaili, not much caring.

Hishni looked interested. "What's wrong with him?"

"That thing with his innards he gets. He was so sick he had to leave us at Iyalanda. I had hoped to use his new flag signals." The king looked genuinely sad over his son's illness. Suddenly, a wry smile caught up the ends of his mouth. "You know, Tiwatipara thought he was the one trying to kill me." Nerikkaili must have looked as confused as he felt—Hishni certainly looked that way—because the king explained, "There was another attempt at sabotaging my chariot."

"Are you so sure he wasn't?" Nerikkaili said, a bit caustic. He felt a strange kind of responsibility for his next-oldest full brother that was perhaps love, but he certainly didn't like him.

"I just told you, son, he wasn't there. He came back to Waliwanda."

"So, who *did* muck with the car, Father?" Hishni asked.

"Nobody knows. Tiwatipara has taken to sleeping in the chariot room. He's a good boy." The king's mouth suddenly twisted with sorrow. "We didn't manage to save Tapala-tarhunta, by the way. That was another blow. We've been friends for thirty years or more, since long before I married his niece."

"That's too bad," said Nerikkaili.

They continued walking in silence. He longed to speak to his father about the rumors Lurma-ziti had heard—or spread—about replacing him as *tuhkanti*, but he wasn't keen on Hishni being part of the conversation. Hishni would carry it back to Lurma-ziti, who would then know that he had gotten under his elder brother's skin.

But Hishni decided to head for the local brothel to celebrate, and Nerikkaili found himself alone with his father after all. They mounted the stairs to the royal apartments, Hattushili, heavy-footed with weariness, drawing himself upward by the banister. As they gained the corridor, Nerikkaili said in a low voice, "My father, there are rumors that you're considering making another of my brothers *tuhkanti* in my place." He watched his father's face carefully.

Hattushili cocked a wry eyebrow. "Rumors, hah? And who's circulating them?"

"People."

The king took his son by the arm and drew him into

his bedchamber. The *tawananna* was sitting inside, smiling at a piece of tapestry one of her daughters had made. She looked up at the two men.

"I want to speak to Our Sun in confidence," said Nerikkaili pointedly, and Puduhepa rose.

But the king motioned for her to stay. "I have nothing to hide from her."

The prince thought, annoyed, *Maybe* I *do*.

"Let's be frank, son. We need to think of the succession." Hattushili seated himself on the edge of the bed, his scales clanking, and his son, finding no other seat available, lowered himself at the king's side, the frame creaking under his weight. "The only objective in my mind is to find a candidate with the smallest possible number of vulnerabilities. We can't make civil war a permanent condition."

"I suppose you're saying this to prepare me for the news that you have, in fact, replaced me," Nerikkaili said, the heat rising to his cheeks. He had to struggle to maintain a civil veneer. *But I expected to hear this, didn't I?*

"I'm saying this so you'll understand the choices I have. You're my firstborn. You're extremely capable. I've never had a single reason to be ashamed of you." The king turned to his son, stared him intently in the eye, and gripped his forearm. Hattushili was still tired and dirty from his campaign, his hair a sweaty unbrushed cap.

I should've waited to say anything, the prince thought, guilty. *At least let him get a drink and take a bath.* "Thank you," he said. "I've always tried to be someone you could be proud of, Father."

"And I am. Whatever it looks like to you, that will be

true. But the reason I'm on the throne at all is because I'm a first ranker and Urhi-tesshub was only a *pahhurzi*."

"The reason you're on the throne is because you fought for it and won," his son said, unable to keep a driblet of bitterness out of his smooth voice.

"The reason he's on the throne is because the Lady of Shamuha wanted him there," the *tawananna* interposed tartly from her corner.

The king gave a smile as dry as his throat had to be and lifted an eyebrow. "Let me rephrase that, hah. The reason more people supported me than supported Urhi-tesshub was because I'm first rank. They accepted him only because I did. They were glad when I declared I'd had enough."

"Your Mashturi is a good example," Puduhepa said to her stepson. "He openly stated that he felt no loyalty toward a second-rank son when there was a first-rank brother standing by. It was a huge mistake on Muwatalli's part to name Urhi-tesshub his successor."

Nerikkaili's breath was starting to steam in his nose. That was all very reasonable, no doubt. But his life was falling in ruins around him. Was this the gratitude his victory in Sheha River Land had earned him? He didn't trust himself to speak right away. Finally, he said with more force than he intended, "So, I suppose Tashmi-sharrumma is the new heir."

The *tawananna* exchanged a quick, uneasy glance with her husband.

He said, "Not yet. Not until he's grown. A child on the throne is a whole other invitation to civil war."

Nerikkaili sat speechless. A mix of emotions seemed to squat on his chest, clogging his breath. Disappointment didn't tell the half of it—anger and helpless frustration fermented there, too. *Just because my mother wasn't the fucking* tawananna? He felt a growing resentment toward the solemn, silent twelve-year-old who was to be thrust before him into the arms of Halmashuit. After a long moment of struggle, he said, his voice quivering with bitterness, "So if someone assassinated you right away, I would still become king?"

Hattushili gave a grunt of laughter. "That's a calculated risk I have to take, son."

"I feel like you've slapped me in the face, Father. Both of you. I thought I had served you well, earned your favor—"

"This has nothing to do with my favor, boy. Haven't you been listening?" Hattushili put a fatherly arm around the prince's rigid shoulders and gave him a squeeze. "Don't think for a minute that you won't serve the kingdom in crucial capacities. Remember my grandfather, the great Shuppiluliuma. He made his firstborn not *labarna* but viceroy of Karkemish. It was that important to hold the south against Mizri. My father was a younger son; he was just a stripling when he came to the throne."

"So what viceroyalty will *I* hold?" Nerikkaili was sinking into snideness; he could hear it in his voice.

But the *tawananna* said quietly, as if someone might be listening, "And then there's Ulmi-tesshub. What if he should get ideas about claiming his father's throne? He's first rank, you know."

"He was excluded from the succession, banished with his mother," the prince said sullenly.

She shook her head. "So what? He could still get ideas. And you know this, Nerikkaili—he would never rebel against Tashmi-sharrumma. He loves him too much. Against you, perhaps. He's very impressionable; he could be manipulated. But against Tashmi? Never. Never."

Nerikkaili's anger had turned into sarcasm. "Perhaps I should warm him up as Lurma-ziti keeps trying to do."

Hattushili chuckled, but there was pain in his voice. "I'm sad to think you're hurt by this, my boy. But I trust your good sense and your loyalty to see why it has to be."

"Of course. It's crystal clear," Nerikkaili said, standing up. "Ulmi-tesshub gets to choose the next *labarna*."

He strode to the door, not waiting to be dismissed. *Well, I have been dismissed, haven't I?* He could feel his father's sorrowful gaze on his back. He passed the *tawananna*, who fixed him with her big, gorgeous black eyes like a pair of ripe olives, but he didn't melt the way she'd no doubt intended him to. At the opening, he turned and saluted and left, restraining himself from slamming the door behind him.

Nerikkaili stalked down the stairs and through the governor's courtyard, his breath steaming between his teeth like the Lord Tarhunta's bulls. He wanted a drink. And a girl. He could pretend it was his stepmother and throw her around a bit.

He saw Tiwatipara, who smiled and raised a hand in greeting, but Nerikkaili ignored him. *Yet another thing that was taken from me and given to Tashmi-sharrumma.* He strode through the streets to the brothel that served the garrison and, in the common room, sank to a stool against the wall. The serving girl approached, and he ordered up a pot of *marnuwan* beer.

Sunk in his thoughts, the prince sipped the brew. Hishni came down the stairs, grinning, and swaggered over.

"Nice ride?" asked Nerikkaili with no real interest.

"Wish we could take that one back to the capital." Hishni sighed in delectation. "Can't beat a Luwian girl." He settled himself next to his brother. "Lurma-ziti's up and about, by the way. I saw him at the palace."

"Marvelous." *He'll show up next, no doubt. Then my day will be more thoroughly ruined than it already is.*

But it was Tiwatipara who entered, his curly-headed groom friend in tow. Nerikkaili felt he owed the charioteer his condolences for the loss of Tapala-tarhunta, so he waved him over. The groom followed clumsily in Tiwatipara's wake, bumping stools as they approached.

"Tiwatipara, my man," Nerikkaili said, realizing with annoyance how much like his father he had made himself sound. *A pox on the old man.* "I heard about your grandfather. May his soul rejoice in the Liliahmi."

"Thank you, my prince." The charioteer smiled, his eyes a little too bright. "He died like a hero."

"Sit down." Nerikkaili raised two fingers, and the girl brought the newcomers their pots, filters, and straws. "My father says Piyamaradu got away. At least he won't be likely to come back now that he has what he was after."

"May that be so, my lord. Your mission was successful, at least?"

"Yes, may the gods be praised. Urhi-tesshub can't count on Sheha River Land anymore."

The curly-headed groom looked down, his polite smile fading.

He's an odd one, the prince thought. *Vague, limp. He's not all there.* "What's your name?" he demanded of the youth.

"Zidanza, my prince."

"You're Armatalli's son? Then you're a cousin of ours," said Hishni cheerfully.

Nerikkaili examined the fellow more closely. He could see a strong likeness to the augur in the round face, the height, the softness. But the son had none of the priest's arrogance. There was something crushed and abject about the boy.

"I guess we'll be going back to the capital any day, won't we?" asked Tiwatipara. "I'll see Lalantiwashha again." He hung his head. "I'll have to tell her I've been rejected as a suitor."

Nerikkaili chuckled. "She knows. She's been mourning your loss." His humor chilled, and he added more somberly, "We're all mourning something at the moment, aren't we?"

"Are we?" asked Hishni.

Nerikkaili knew he should keep his mouth shut. He was a trained diplomat, and keeping his mouth shut was a cardinal part of his job. But he was hurt and angry, and these men, his peers, were going to find out soon enough. He said in a low voice, very like the almost inaudible growl of a threatened animal, "Our Sun is going to replace me as *tuhkanti* as soon as Tashmi-sharrumma is old enough to take over."

"By the thousand gods!" Hishni exclaimed.

Tiwatipara stared, round-eyed, his open face compassionate. "My lord, I'm sorry…"

"We're soldiers." The prince shrugged, making light of it. "We serve at Our Sun's good pleasure."

His brother whistled. "Lurma-ziti was right."

"I'd thank you not to tell him, Hishni," the prince said, his mouth taut. "If there's anything more unpleasant than Lurma-ziti, it's Lurma-ziti gloating."

As if the mention of his name had conjured him up, Lurma-ziti appeared in the doorway. He cast his eyes around and lurched painfully toward his brothers. Since his illness, he had become skeletally thin, his face white as linen, his eyes dark ringed. Nerikkaili almost felt sorry for him.

The *tuhkanti*—he could still call himself that—said in his smoothest, coldest voice, "Look who's floated up from the underworld."

"Yes. All recovered. Thank you for your anxious prayers." Lurma-ziti lowered himself with an effort onto a seat next to Tiwatipara. "Why, it's the pony boys," he said with his sarcastic smile, eyeing the charioteer and his friend. He had a strangely pretty mouth as long as his teeth didn't show.

"My prince." Tiwatipara nodded, his face suddenly tense. "Perhaps we should be going. I didn't mean to cut into your private conversation, my lord," he said to Nerikkaili. "Thank you for the beer." He got to his feet, and Armatalli's son followed suit. They hurried off and climbed the stairs together.

"The tall one's some of Arma-tarhunta's spawn," said Hishni gleefully.

"I'm aware of that," said Lurma-ziti. "You bought them beer. Don't I get any?"

"Is beer good for you?" Nerikkaili asked, resignedly signaling the servant.

"Do you mean, is it good *enough* for me? I sometimes condescend to a beer, yes."

But Nerikkaili was in a foul mood, and his brother's endless sarcasm was more than he chose to tolerate. He snarled, "No, I mean you were sick, and I didn't know if you could drink beer without hurting yourself. Forgive me for being solicitous."

"I'm touched," Lurma-ziti said, smirking. The girl set a pot down in front of him, and he took the reed straw between his lips. After sucking in an appreciative draft, he belched. "I hear rumors flying again, big brother. And this time, they're more than rumors."

You godforsaken bastard. A wave of icy wrath washed over Nerikkaili. How had his brother heard? The king had only spoken to the crown prince minutes before. "Listening outside of doors again, are we?" he said, his voice a murderously sharp icicle.

"Sometimes our father and his lady talk as they walk together down the hall. You may want to reconsider my suggestion of a few months ago."

"Or not."

"Of course, the only sure way to inherit the throne is for the king to die before Tashmi-sha—"

In a rage, Nerikkaili lunged across the table and grabbed his brother by the front of his tunic, jerking him halfway over the boards. A grimace of pain flashed across Lurma-ziti's gaunt face, and Nerikkaili knew that he had hurt him, but he didn't care. "Don't let me hear those words out of your mouth ever again, you misbegotten lump of shit." He shook Lurma-ziti hard and pushed him back into his seat. Elsewhere in the hall, heads turned and then turned away again discreetly. He hissed between his teeth, "Torture the twelve-year-old all you want, but you leave me alone, is that clear? You don't push me, you don't try to tempt me to rebellion, you don't speak of my father disrespectfully. Is that clear?"

Lurma-ziti brushed himself down, his hands shaking a little. His black eyes were like holes. He said, tilting his head, "I know some things about you, Nerikkaili. About you and the *tawananna*…"

"And I know some things about you and Ulmi-tesshub. So we're even."

Hishni gave a low whistle. "Is that why you're always hanging around the stables, Lurma? I thought you had a hard-on for one of the mares."

Lurma-ziti grew livid, his face distorted, his eyes bulging, his teeth bared. "Shut up, Hishni," he shrieked, springing up and leaning on his hands toward his brother. Nerikkaili expected to see flames coming out his mouth.

This time, heads did turn. Nerikkaili rose to his feet. "I'm going." He strode between the tables with as much dignity as he could manage, breathing heavily, and regained the fresh, warm afternoon air of spring with the relief of a man who had come very close to drowning.

CHAPTER 14

I T WAS BOTH GOOD AND not good to be back in Hattusha. Tiwatipara entered the house he had grown up in—with its fading red walls, its hand-grimed banister, its cobbled floors—as a stranger might. In a sense, he *was* a stranger. The events of the past few years had changed him, he felt sure, until he was no longer the same man who had spent his childhood under this roof. The slaves were still there, sorrowful about the news of Tapala-tarhunta's death and frightened because Tiwatipara was their new master, and they didn't know what his plans were and whether the household would be dispersed.

But the beloved lords of the house, his dear grandparents, were there no more. Everyone was gone. Of the whole family, only he remained. He should have married. He should have had children. Then his return would not have been to empty beds, empty halls—the hollow, echoing sounds of rooms without life. What did it matter to him that he would inherit a substantial property—the house, fields, orchards, and chattel passed down for generations? His was the only human soul left.

A huge, suffocating loneliness descended upon him as he walked through the site of so many warm memories, of scenes so familiar, so dear. His grandmother's spindle and distaff still lay on her clothes chest, although she had not picked them up since the accident emptied her of her desire to live. They had cremated her with a fancier pair, it seemed. He hadn't even been at her funeral. Upon her bed lay the frayed coverlet that she herself had woven when he was only a toddler. His grandfather's ointments still sat beside it. Tiwatipara's childhood room—where he had slept until only a few months before, trying to pretend years didn't pass and rob him of all he loved—seemed so small.

He was truly an orphan now. Maybe the gods would give him another sweetheart, since they had taken Lalantiwashha from him, but he would never have another father, mother, grandfather, and grandmother.

The old steward approached him uncertainly. "My master, will you be living with us again now?"

The question caught him off guard. "I… I don't know. I need some time to think about it. But I won't sell anybody," he reassured the man.

What am *I going to do, now that I can't avoid being a grown-up any longer?*

The only thing he was sure of was that he would find his father's murderer and take his vengeance. *Lord Pihasshasshi, make me like one of your lightning horses: swift and relentless, swooping down with unforgiving power upon the miscreant and blasting him with your savage justice.*

But how? Nearly four years had passed, and Tiwatipara still didn't know who had sabotaged the chariot. They were yet alive and actively stalking the king, it seemed.

That much had been established by the attempt during the campaign in the West. The murderer was part of the king's entourage, someone in the army, in the stable crew, in the royal family. *Were other attempts made on Hattushili's life of which I was unaware? Poison in a drink? A push on the stairs?*

Again and again, he pictured to himself the crowd that day of the accident. The king, with Benteshina at his side. Nerikkaili, Lurma-ziti, Hishni. Zuzuhha—but he hadn't been in Iyalanda. The drivers who accompanied the king west. The grooms who went along—there were only a handful of them. Among those who were there at the time of the accident and also around on the campaign to Millawata—that was where his murderer would be found.

He tried to recall the events at Iyalanda, imagining who might have approached the royal chariot in those few hours between Tiwatipara's inspection in the afternoon of one day, the guarded night, and his discovery of the sabotage the next morning. *Benteshina, Nerikkaili, Lurma-ziti, Hishni? No, the* tuhkanti *had left by then, along with Hishni. Lurma-ziti had returned to Waliwanda.* But any one of them might have paid someone to act in their place. What would Benteshina stand to gain? The king had betrothed the little man to his daughter and was going to restore to him his throne.

Nerikkaili had been displaced as *tuhkanti*. Only if the king died before Tashmi-sharrumma was presented as the heir would Nerikkaili still become *labarna*. Right there was motive enough. But Tiwatipara had a hard time believing Nerikkaili would do such a thing. He was an honorable man, surely. Still, the king believed that all his sons were honorable men, yet maybe one of them was not. *Who else is there with a motive?* He kept coming back to Lurma-ziti but mostly because he was such an ass turd. *What would his motive be? He hates Tashmi-sharrumma. If the king died immediately, Nerikkaili would succeed, not Tashmi.*

Tiwatipara was almost dizzy with the possibilities. He needed more clues. He needed a witness. At the least, he needed to talk out his ideas aloud with someone.

He left the empty house and made his way to the royal stables, the magnificent city of horses. Here was his real home, he thought fondly. These men were his brothers. These animals were his friends and heroes, warm, solid, and majestic. He thought that even here, he should start to sleep in the chariot room. It was less lonely than the house.

Tiwatipara set back to his daily regimen of work with a sense of comfort that was almost physical. After the hardships of the campaign, the abbreviated routine, and the crowded conditions of the governor's barns in Waliwanda, it was good to be in the stables again—a real homecoming.

He made the rounds of the chariot room, smelling the good smell of leather, the dusty scent of wood. He'd go over the royal vehicles minutely in a while, now that he knew the trick of regreasing over a cut. Tiwatipara wondered if that was the sort of thing anyone who didn't know chariots pretty well would think of. Did that mean his perpetrator had access to grease? But the bucket always sat right there in the open.

He wandered down the aisle of the stable, greeting all the horses he hadn't seen since his return. The king's new purchases in the West had been assigned stalls. Zidanza had told Tiwatipara that a pair of the best stallions had been set aside for Benteshina's wedding gift. The ex-king's marriage was to take place before summer's end, and he and his bride would return to Amurru together to resume his reign after a fourteen-year hiatus.

Tiwatipara happened to be leaning against the stone wall of one of the barns, shaking sand out of his boot, when the Amurrite wandered in. The charioteer looked up and greeted the little king, toward whom he felt quite friendly after their shared adventure in Millawata.

"Tiwatipara, my lad," said Benteshina, brightening. "Our Sun has been so kind as to designate some of his new horses as my wedding gift. I don't know what the symbolism of two stallions is. Perhaps he meant them for Lurma-ziti." He grinned maliciously, his black eyes sparkling.

Tiwatipara chuckled. The mere mention of the *huwalpant* might have blighted his day, but he was too happy to be back in the royal stables. "I suppose Our Sun wants to say that you should always ride to his support in the chariot drawn by this pair, my lord."

"Show me my team. I want to make friends with them."

"Of course, my lord. Follow me." With Benteshina in his wake, he entered one of the long stone buildings, still mostly dark at this early hour, and made his way down the aisle. He could hear the stamping of hooves inside the boxes, and an occasional long face looked over the half doors in eager curiosity. "No, boy. I don't have any treats for you." He smiled, caressing the muzzle of Wrath of Wurukatte. "You'll have to wait for Our Sun."

They went to the second-to-last stall, and Tiwatipara turned to the former king of Amurru. "This is the first of them, my lord. Sand Storm." The stallion stuck his head over the door in response. He was a sandy golden color with a lighter mane but with a somewhat mulish nose.

"How appropriate. Did you blow out of the Southern Desert, my beauty?" Benteshina drew a shriveled apple from the pouch at his belt and presented it to the horse, who took it daintily with his lips and crunched it up, dribbling pieces into the Amurrite's palm. He turned to Tiwatipara. "I like to be sure they know I'm their friend. I don't want them harboring any grudges. Where's the other one?" he asked, wiping his hand on his hip.

"Right next door, my lord. This is Pride of Hakpish."

"Hakpish, eh? Why not Tsumur, eh, my fine fellow? Would you like to be the Pride of Tsumur?" Tsumur was the name of his own capital, whenever he should retake it. He laughed, and Tiwatipara laughed, too. The little ex-king was irresistibly good-humored. Benteshina dug out another apple and let Pride take it gingerly from his palm. Without taking his eyes off the horse's chewing mouth, he said quietly to the charioteer, "Have you found out who sabotaged the king's chariot?"

Tiwatipara froze. Did everyone know how feverishly he had begun to investigate? "No, my lord. Do you have any ideas?"

"Too many. Our Sun has a lot of enemies."

"It has to be someone who was there that day, though," said Tiwatipara, troubled. Again the faces in the crowd rolled past him in memory. "Someone who felt pretty sure Our Sun would ride along on the test run. And someone who was also in Iyalanda."

"Yes and no. The person who crawled beneath the box

and cut the axle was probably an underling. But almost certainly, a more important person was behind him. Don't you think?" Benteshina wiped his hand and faced the charioteer, who for once looked down at his interlocutor.

"That must be true, my lord," Tiwatipara said, still pensive.

"Who could have been in Urhi-tesshub's pay? Or Piyamaradu's, for that matter? Or Arma-tarhunta's? Almost anybody. Gold is an eloquent persuader."

Tiwatipara's voice dropped. He knew Benteshina was the king's best friend, and he felt he could say this to him. Any words that came out of his mouth in the Amurrite's presence would find their way back to Hattushili, and perhaps the king needed to take certain possibilities more seriously. "I've even thought of one of the king's sons. Could... could the crown prince be getting impatient?"

The Amurrite looked up at him sharply. "Do you have any reason to think that? You're around Nerikkaili more than I am."

Tiwatipara felt guilty even to entertain such a thought about his former employer. He spoke reluctantly. "Not really. But... he has said more than once recently that Our Sun is planning to replace him as heir. Although Lord Nerikkaili strikes me as an honorable man. Probably, he's perfectly loyal." A cogitative silence fell. "Prince Lurma-ziti? He hates Tashmi-sharrumma. If the king died before Tashmi was announced as his heir, then Nerikkaili would succeed." He added uneasily, "Gods forgive me for saying that. He may be innocent as the day is long, but he's done some awful things to Tashmi-sharrumma. Our Sun refused even to consider that he might be guilty, though."

Benteshina looked more than usually serious, staring into the semidarkness around them. "I've thought of them both, too. What about Hishni?"

"He's a follower, my lord. If one of the others initiated it, he might go along, but I don't see him acting on his own."

Benteshina said nothing for a moment then let out a sigh. "It would be a real blow for Hattushili if it turned out to be one of his boys. He loves his children deeply, no matter their rank. Even the bastards." He smiled affectionately and clapped Tiwatipara on the arm.

Something about the words, the gesture, struck Tiwatipara as strange. Benteshina was telling him something. He caught the man's hand. "What do you mean by that, my lord?"

"No offense meant, Tiwatipara. Royal blood's honorable on any side of the blanket. I've dropped a few bastards myself." He still had that amiable smile as if he thought the charioteer understood him. But Tiwatipara was confused and numbed by what the ex-king seemed to imply. *Is this one of his jokes?*

"I'm sorry, my lord," he said, loosing the king's hand in embarrassment. "I'm not following. What... what are you saying?"

All at once, Benteshina made a grimace of distress, his eyebrows rising. "Oh, he's never told you? Ba'al's beard. He said he was going to when Tapala-tarhunta died. Dear me. My, my." He chuckled uneasily, his face growing red. "I think it's not for me to tell you, then, my boy. Let's leave that to Our Sun, shall we?" He turned away, pretending to busy himself stroking the horse, but Tiwatipara, who felt as if he'd been struck in the face by a pair of flying hooves, wouldn't let him go so easily.

"No, wait. You're saying... what? That I'm a bastard of Our Sun?" His mouth hung open in shock.

"Talk to him, all right? Oh, look, the sun's coming up, speaking of suns. I'd better go get ready for... something." Benteshina held up a hand in apologetic farewell and walked away quickly through the twilight. He looked like a man who knew he was in trouble.

As the Amurrite's footsteps faded into silence, Tiwatipara continued to stare after him, his eyes unfocused. What was the damned little man saying? Tiwatipara felt as if he couldn't even understand his own language. The words simply had no meaning. He needed to talk to the king, but how did one conceivably approach the *labarna* of the Great Kingdom with a question like that? *What question?* What question was he possibly planning to ask him? Was he going to the Sun of Hatti Land and beard him with such a thing as, *Are you my father?* Did he even want to know? No, he did not. He was the son of Pawahtelmah, whom he loved and venerated with all his heart.

Lords of the underworld take Benteshina. What has he done to me?

Because the seed had been planted. He had to know the answer. Suddenly his whole identity had been threatened, and he had to hear the truth from Hattushili's mouth.

Tiwatipara realized it wasn't a good moment to confront the king, who no doubt had ten thousand pressing tasks to see to after so long an absence, but he couldn't hold back. People died without warning—hadn't he seen enough of that?—and he didn't want to go under the black earth without knowing the truth. A question that had never crossed his mind throughout the twenty-five years of his life suddenly became urgent. *Zidi would say I think too much,* he told himself. *But I have to know.*

His heart pounding, he made his way up the long causeway to the citadel. He chose to walk, needing the time to think. But he couldn't think. Still, the steady plodding upward, one foot after another, calmed him sometimes, and he needed calming. His breath was rasping in his nose, his fists clenched as if he were facing some rearing unbroken stallion with dangerously flying hooves. There *was* danger here. He could lose himself, find he was someone else altogether. He was disoriented, nearly dizzy. Below him, an eagle hung on the air, circling over the Upper City. *Pawahtelmah? Is that you? What does this mean, Father?*

Carved lions with lolling red tongues guarded the gate of the royal enclosure. They appeared suddenly menacing. *Who do you think you are to come here with such a question?* they seemed to roar. The sentry at the entrance to the palace recognized him as a *hashtanuri*, with his long tunic and shaven forehead, and when Tiwatipara gave his name and asked to speak to the king, the man hastened inside with the message.

A moment later, the sentry emerged. "Our Sun will receive you in his apartment." But he took Tiwatipara's sword.

The youth passed through the gate into a red-paved outer court. At the second gate, more soldiers, clad in the saffron and white of the king's personal bodyguards, conducted him across the public courtyard of the palace. The stone flagging was already bleached by the rising brightness of summertime. Scribes and slaves had begun their day's work, scurrying back and forth, casting long black shadows. Tiwatipara seemed to himself small and insignificant. Though a king's man, he was not familiar with this world. His world lay below, in the city of horses.

His guides took him through yet another gate into a smaller court, around which stood porticoed buildings of two and three stories. The place was bleak and sun swept as if unnaturally near to the sky. He was almost faint, his eyes burnt out by the glare.

They led him into the largest of the buildings, into the antechamber with its painted walls, tall, massive cedar doors, and floor of polished chalcedony. When the outer door clanged shut, the temperature seemed to drop. A shiver ran up Tiwatipara's back, but it might not have been the cold. A eunuch emerged, spoke to the guard, disappeared into the darkness of a doorway, and came out again an instant later, beckoning him. The charioteer passed through the door, and the slave closed it behind him.

The room was dim—its louvered windows not as large as one might have expected—but richly adorned with murals and rugs of gorgeous colors and priceless inlaid furniture. Hattushili son of Murshili, *labarna* of Hatti Land, stood leaning back against a long table, his arms crossed over his chest. He was dressed in a civilian tunic of deep red, with costly disks of gold in his ears and jeweled cuffs at his wrists—quite unlike the plain sweat-stained military garb in which Tiwatipara was accustomed to see the king. His gray hair lay on his shoulders like the mane of a grizzled lion.

"Tiwatipara," he said, heavy-lidded eyes crinkling

affectionately. "What can I do for you? I hope the boys haven't been acting up."

"Not at all, My Sun. At least not Prince Tashmi-sharrumma." Tiwatipara swallowed hard, suddenly seeming to himself very small in the presence of this impressive personage, who looked superhumanly tall to him at the moment. "I... I... someone said something to me that I felt I needed to hear from your lips before I believed it." He swallowed again with painful effort, as a man might swallow back nausea.

Hattushili tipped his head, an expression of friendly concern on his face. "Speak up, my man. What have they said?"

"Lord Benteshina said... he said... that you were... that it was you and not Pawahtelmah who were... my..." The charioteer could hardly put two words together. Anything he said seemed monstrously presumptuous. What if it weren't even factual and was just Benteshina's joke?

The king's face went through one expression after another as Tiwatipara struggled to speak—confusion, compassion, even shame. In a low voice, Hattushili finished for the charioteer, "Your father?"

Tiwatipara nodded, stricken. He whispered, "Is it true?"

After a moment of silence, the king said, "Yes, it's true," with a sad smile on his ugly face. He drew near to Tiwatipara, laid a kindly hand on his shoulder, and ruffled his hair shyly, as if he knew it might not be welcome.

The charioteer drew back, his cheeks aflame, suddenly filled with outrage. "You raped my mother? You cuckolded Pawahtelmah?"

"No, no, Tiwatipara. Dear gods, I may be a hardheaded old piece of ass shit, but I'm not evil. Sit down, son."

He had always addressed Tiwatipara like that, but the youth had assumed that it was just an older man's way of expressing avuncular affection. He didn't know what to think now. He *was* the king's son. He lowered himself, trembling like a man in shock, onto the stool Hattushili pulled up for him. He felt as if all the blood had run out of his head, leaving him white as a sheet and in danger of toppling.

Hattushili sat face-to-face with him, his tousled eyebrows crumpled in sorrow. "I didn't mean for you to find out like this, Tiwatipara. Let me tell you how it happened. It was before your parents were married. Your mother was exactly who you know she was: a Luwian noblewoman attached to my first wife's service. She was just a girl, sixteen or so, and had accompanied my wife from Mira. She was beautiful, son, so beautiful. So… so clean and genuine and full of joy. I was in my thirties, a younger brother of the king—useful to him but of no particular prospects. We were mutually attracted, but a mere prince can't put away a political wife to marry someone else as easily as a king can, and I wouldn't have made her a concubine."

Tiwatipara was listening, but even more, he was watching Hattushili's face. The king didn't seem proud of himself, but neither was he ashamed. He must have felt he'd acted honorably toward Tiwatipara's mother. *What did she see in this ugly man?* the youth wondered. But he knew how charismatic the king was, how his unaffected manners and honestly displayed emotions could endear him to people, despite his volatile temper and capacity for sarcasm. And

Tiwatipara had seen how the *tawananna* looked at him. Hattushili had been a man in his early thirties, not the weather-beaten middle-aged soldier he was today.

The king continued, "When I discovered she was pregnant, I found the finest young man I knew to make an honest woman of her—my driver's seventeen-year-old son, Pawahtelmah."

Tiwatipara tried to take this in. The big rawboned man in front of him—the man for whom three generations of his supposed family had risked their lives in battle six years before—was his father. The man who wore the habit of the Sun God was his father—he who ruled a mighty empire by divine mandate. It was too much to absorb.

Because that meant that he, Tiwatipara, wasn't who he thought he was. He had been the son of Pawahtelmah, shaped by him—by his father's love for him, by his familial circumstances and ambitions. He had *hashtanuri* blood in his veins—hadn't they told him that? Wasn't that why he was so good with horses? But he didn't. The *tawananna* wasn't his cousin. Tapala-tarhunta wasn't his grandfather. His world was reeling about him, pieces of it dropping off into the void.

After what seemed like eons, he managed to say, "Did my fa—did Pawahtelmah know his wife was carrying your child?"

"He did," said the king. "I wouldn't have lied to him. At first, he accepted the assignment like a good soldier. I dowered her well. But then he fell in love with her. He was grief-stricken when she died. When you turned out to look like her, he loved you with all his heart as his last little piece of her."

"So I wasn't just a... a cuckoo's egg in the nest?"

"Not at all. He could have remarried and had a child of his own. But he loved you deeply; you were all he wanted as a son and heir. Surely you knew that. Everyone could see it."

In fact, Tiwatipara had never doubted Pawahtelmah's love. The son of Tapala-tarhunta was still Tiwatipara's father in the deepest sense, perhaps more deserving of his gratitude and veneration than ever. Pawahtelmah had been a truly selfless man whose love had been pure and free of the vanity of seeing himself live on in a child.

Yet somehow, everything had changed with this revelation. Blood mattered. It wasn't just anyone who had begotten him but a man chosen by the gods—a man whose family had worn the *lupanni* crown for five hundred years. A man consecrated.

Tiwatipara could barely breathe. "Did my grandfather—Tapala-tarhunta—know?" *Why did he never tell me?*

The king shook his head. "I always intended to acknowledge you, but I would never have done it before Tapala died. You were all he had; I couldn't take my friend's only heir away from him."

Hattushili rose and opened his arms. Tiwatipara, confused and stunned, got to his feet and let himself be enveloped. He finally extended his own arms around the king's back. He was barely able to see over Hattushili's shoulder, and he felt like a child in the comforting embrace of an adult. He could feel the king's heart beating.

They two men stepped apart. Hattushili's green-brown eyes flicked up and down over the youth's face, perhaps seeking something of himself in Tiwatipara's features. He bared his crooked teeth in a smile of pride and affection. "You have a bit of my temper, I think. But thank the gods, you look like her!"

"That's why I couldn't believe it when Benteshina told me," Tiwatipara stammered. "All your sons look like you. They're so tall, and I'm…"

"Not," the king finished with a chuckle. "They're not all tall, son."

Tiwatipara fell silent. Questions bubbled up inside him—an urgent desire to talk, to explain, to listen to explanations. But the man before him was the Great King. A mere charioteer had no right to take up so much of his time.

"My Sun, I…" he began lamely. Then voices outside interrupted him. He heard the slightly mocking baritone of Prince Nerikkaili. The prince opened the door and entered with his aura of self-confidence, so big he seemed to shrink the room around him.

My brother, thought Tiwatipara, awed. *All these years, I've been driving my brother.*

"My father, I'm getting ready to—" the prince began, then he saw that the king was not alone. "Oh, Tiwatipara. Sorry, I didn't know anyone was here."

"It's all right, son. Tiwatipara was finished." The king gave the charioteer a warm, crooked smile that softened his hooded eyes. "We'll talk, eh, Tiwatipara? Soon." He clapped him on the shoulder, gave it a small shake of affectionate solidarity, and turned to his firstborn. "Now, what's on your mind, my boy?"

The charioteer bowed as if nothing had changed and made his way out while his father and brother—*my father!*

my brother!—continued their conversation. Tiwatipara walked blindly back through the courtyards of the palace and then out the gate, buckling his sword belt on almost without noticing. As he regained the stables, he saw Princes Lurma-ziti and Hishni crossing the practice field in the distance and thought, *They're my brothers.* Tashmi-sharrumma was his little brother. Prince Zuzuhha was his uncle. *Why, Zidanza is my cousin!* He'd thought he was an only child of a dwindling family, and instead, the black earth teemed with relatives. *How many of them know?* he wondered. *Would they treat me differently if they found out?*

Then it struck him—Lalantiwashha was his sister.

Dear gods, what hideous sin have you preserved us from? What if they had run away together before he found out? Tiwatipara suddenly felt defiled even to have looked at her with longing. He had imagined to himself her naked body. He remembered saying that he wanted her to bear his children, and he cringed. Her kisses burned on his lips with the lash of nettles, and he wiped at his mouth as if to cleanse it of incestuous desire. *Hurkel! The horror!* No wonder the *tawananna* had so brutally refused his request for her hand. *She knows. Surely, if Benteshina knows, she does.*

So why did the thought of losing Lalantiwashha forever still send his heart plummeting to his feet in a queasy lump? It was all too much to take in. Too, too much. He needed to talk to someone.

Tiwatipara drifted through the stable compound in a daze. Everything around him seemed to have changed, although it was he alone who had changed, in fact. How strange that even the awareness of royal blood transmuted everything. He thought of Prince Nerikkaili, so full of confidence in himself, always in control of his surroundings. He had grown up knowing the blood of kings flowed in his veins, even before his own father was a king. Hishni, for all that he wasn't very smart, had about him the same easy consciousness of his place in the world. Even Lurmaziti, who might have become timid because of his physical frailty, was downright arrogant. And Tashmi-sharrumma— Tiwatipara remembered how the shy lad had suddenly unfolded into a flower of princely dignity in Millawata. Would he himself have been a different person had he known all along that he was a king's son?

Tiwatipara wandered into the chariot room and sat down on the back edge of a vehicle that stood with its wheels already mounted. He stared down at his feet in their scuffed boots.

"Tipa, what are you thinking that puts that funny expression on your face?"

He looked up to see Zidanza standing in the doorway, his hands full of leathers. His friend's round face was lit with an anxious smile. "Zidi," Tiwatipara said.

The groom sat beside him on the chariot box but said nothing, just looked at him with his vague, sleepy eyes. Tiwatipara fixed upon him an anguished stare. He longed to tell his friend everything, but he didn't know where to start. "You're not going to believe what I'm about to say," he said. "I just found out that—dear gods, Zidanza, I can hardly say it." He wiped at his forehead as if to brush away cobwebs. "Pawahtelmah wasn't my real father."

Zidanza's eyes opened wider.

"My… my real father is… Our Sun."

"Really?" cried the groom. His jaw hung open for a moment, then he smiled. "That means we're cousins, Tipa!"

Tiwatipara laughed, a little breathless. "I guess so, old friend. But I can't tell you how shaken I am—rearranged. This overturns everything I thought I knew about myself."

He sat grinning at his lap, more discomposed than humorous, until Zidanza said with a seriousness that surprised the charioteer, "Does this mean that you aren't as set on vengeance for Pawahtelmah?"

Tiwatipara looked over at him. He felt the cold urgency creeping up on him again. "Far from it, Zidi. Pawahtelmah still deserves every bit of my love and respect. He raised me for all those years, knowing I wasn't even his. And besides, whoever killed him was aiming at my real father."

Zidanza nodded, his face pale and somber. He looked away toward the door. "I'm happy for you, my prince," he said in a tone that didn't sound especially happy.

Tiwatipara laughed, the cold dispersed. "Stop that, man. It makes me think you're addressing someone else behind my shoulder. Besides, I probably shouldn't have told anybody until Our Sun decided to make it public." He wondered, not for the first time, if the topic of fathers was painful to his friend. Zidanza seemed so uneasy.

The charioteer wanted to talk about his revelation, to wallow in it, to hear someone say again and again, "That's incredible," or, "I should have known; he always treated you so kindly," or... *something*. But now he felt Zidanza wasn't the one he should talk to after all. It gave Tiwatipara pain, making him feel there was something selfish in his news.

He slid to his feet. "Well, I still have to work, right? Do

you want to have a beer tonight after we're finished with everything?"

"Sure, Tipa."

Tiwatipara left the chariot room, Zidanza still sitting on the back of the box, his shoulders slumped.

Tiwatipara found himself increasingly disturbed as the days passed. He was caught between awe and distress. He felt he needed to apologize to Pawahtelmah for not being his son after all, as if he had betrayed him somehow. The fact that he'd turned out to be a bastard did not disturb him, because, as Benteshina had pointed out, even the bastard of a king had royal blood. Such men were the mainstay of the administration, and people like Tiwatipara respectfully called them "my prince" just like the *tuhkanti* or the first-rank sons.

Royal blood. That was what crushed him into a kind of disbelieving wonderment. The reverence in which he and the family he'd grown up with had held Their Sun, that consciousness of his divine election, of the presence of the protective gods of Hatti hovering over a human being, making him more than human, abased him with the awareness of his own unworthiness. What did it matter that Hattushili son of Murshili wasn't a perfect man? In fact—and Tiwatipara felt so guilty even thinking it that he tried to force the judgment out of his mind—Hattushili seemed quite conspicuously less perfect than Pawahtelmah, who had been calm and always reasonable and very adult. Could Tiwatipara say that he loved the king? He remembered how resentful he had been toward Hattushili recently. He liked the *labarna*'s warmth and enthusiasm, he supposed. *But that temper.* And it occurred to him, forcing a blush up his cheeks, that perhaps he wasn't so very different from his royal father in some ways after all. Still, he hardly knew him as a human being.

Nonetheless, what he had said to Zidanza was enormously true—he was more than ever determined to find the saboteur, because now he perceived more clearly than before that it was a matter of divine justice. Tiwatipara saw himself streaking down from the sky in a blaze of blue-white light to incinerate whoever had tried to lay a hand on an anointed king, in the process killing and maiming the innocent. He saw himself as a lightning horse.

CHAPTER 15

NERIKKAILI STRODE ACROSS THE INNER court of the palace in a black and reflective mood. He was managing to carry on as if his life had not just overturned like a basket of fruit, but it took all his skills as a diplomat to keep his real feelings from displaying themselves upon his face. In fact, he wasn't sure what it was he felt. He was angry but not at anyone, exactly, not even his father. Perhaps at the *tawananna*, that scheming little vixen. But perhaps not. She had been so sweetly apologetic, so full of self-sacrificing reasonableness, throwing her pretty arms around his neck, that he'd found it hard to stay focused on his outraged sense of being dispossessed. Maybe he was angry at Tashmi-sharrumma, but the boy knew nothing of the plans that were being laid in his favor. Maybe he was angry at the gods. The stars. The mysterious will of the Gulshesh.

His face steamed. The prince tried to keep his mind on the task his father had assigned him at the moment and not to think about that far-off hour when Tashmi would reach whatever magic age Hattushili foresaw as "old enough" for the boy to take up his duties as *tuhkanti* in Nerikkaili's place. What would everyone think when the king's firstborn was suddenly demoted? They would assume that he had proved himself unworthy in some way. *Piyasshili and the viceroyalty of Karkemish, indeed. I've been disrespected.*

He glanced up at a movement at his shoulder and saw that his sister Lalantiwashha had fallen in beside his steps. Her face was long with sorrow, her lids red. "Hello, my sister." Nerikkaili stopped and embraced her. He could feel her shoulders trembling with tears. "You don't look like a very happy fiancée," he said with a wry smile.

"Nerikkaili, how can I get out of it?" she begged him in a wavering voice. Her hands clung to his arm in pleading. "I've always thought of myself as someone who could figure things out, but I'm trapped. Father has his heart set on me marrying this awful old vassal—"

"Ah, yes. I can sympathize," Nerikkaili said with a gloomy smirk.

"And all I want is Tiwatipara. I don't want to be a queen; I just want—"

"Wait. No one's told you?" The prince drew back in shock. "Well, that's cruel." He chuckled darkly. "It turns out that Tiwatipara is one of Father's bastards."

She faced him in stunned silence, her eyes round, her jaw hanging. "What?"

He smiled a crooked smile. *You know Father. Why are you so surprised?* "Yes. The pony boy is one of our half brothers."

Lalantiwashha's hands flew to her mouth, covering it in horror, wiping at her lips. Her face twisted into a mask of disgust. "Oh no! It can't be true! Oh, dear gods!"

Nerikkaili laughed in spite of himself, a deep, pessimistic rumble. *Someone else whose life is overturned*, he thought. "Yes, dear sister. You've fallen in love with your own half brother. I'm amazed the *tawananna* hasn't said anything to you yet."

"Oh, Nerikkaili! How revolting! I swear I didn't know."

"Of course you didn't. And neither did he until a few days ago. Whereas Father and the *tawananna* have known all along and told you nothing." Nerikkaili patted her on the back with grim brotherly sympathy. "Our duty is simply to let ourselves be herded along according to the needs of the kingdom, without any personal feelings about anything."

"They may not have known how serious we were." The girl's expression was still fixed in a horrified grimace. Incest was something a person didn't play around with. It was one thing to marry an uncle, but a brother... Lalantiwashha looked up at her sibling with sudden understanding. "So that's why she refused his suit, isn't it?"

"Of course."

"She could have told me then."

"I think Father didn't want it to get around to Tapala-tarhunta, who still thought Tiwatipara was his grandson."

The girl was silent for a moment. Then she said, with a contortion of her long mouth, "To think we talked about running away together. What an awful thing that would have been."

Nerikkaili chuckled, feeling somehow lighter in spite of everything. There was such a dollop of black humor in life. "Just when you think you know how you fit into the world." He laid an arm around her shoulder. "I'm heading down to the stable. Do you want to tell Tipa you've found out? He probably assumes you were told long ago."

Lalantiwashha lifted her chin and blinked back her tears. She was a spunky girl. This wouldn't keep her down forever. "Yes, I think I'd like to do that. Take me with you, Nerikkaili."

They walked together to the red court and mounted a litter. The *tuhkanti* was impressed by his sister's resignation or flexibility or whatever quality it was that permitted her to adjust to a new reality with so little rancor. He suspected he could learn a lesson from her.

Tiwatipara was just coming in from the practice field, Tashmi-sharrumma and Ulmi-tesshub in his wake, as Nerikkaili and his sister emerged from their litters beside the first barn. The charioteer's face lit up with a friendly smile as he saw the elder prince, but then he froze, realizing who accompanied Nerikkaili. A tense silence descended over the three adults. Tashmi-sharrumma stood, alert and expressionless, in the rear, while his cousin eyed the others curiously. It was Ulmi-tesshub, in fact, who finally spoke. "Hello, cousins. Why does everyone look like they've seen a snake?"

"They've told me, Tiwatipara," said Lalantiwashha, her eyes fixed on the charioteer's.

"Told you what?" Ulmi-tesshub probed, still looking from face to face.

Nerikkaili growled, "Tiwatipara turns out to be our brother. Can you give them a few minutes to absorb this?"

But the boy elbowed Tashmi-sharrumma in the ribs and gurgled, "Another brother, eh, Tash? Oh, and he was interested in Lady Lalantiwashha! Oho! What a cock-up!"

Nerikkaili controlled his annoyance and shooed the youngsters away. "Go take care of your horses, you twerps. The grown-ups want to talk."

Protesting that he, too, was a grown-up, Ulmi-tesshub accompanied his younger cousin into the barn. Tiwatipara was still staring in pained silence at Lalantiwashha. At last, he said, "I swear I had no idea, my lady."

"That's exactly what I said. But now we know." She arched her long neck sadly. "We can still love each other, you know. It's just a different kind of love." She looked up under her heavy lids, her brown eye full of hope.

Nerikkaili watched the moonstruck expressions on the two young people's faces and suppressed a cynical grin. *Welcome to the royal family, where you can never do anything you want.*

"Always, my… my sister," murmured Tiwatipara with painful earnestness. He was such a nice fellow, so honest; Nerikkaili thought he must take after his mother.

The *tuhkanti* finally said loudly, "Well, I'm going to look at my new team. I leave you two to say your goodbyes or hellos or whatever is appropriate." He moved off into the barn, hearing behind him not a word. They were still staring at one another.

Tiwatipara was relieved that *he* hadn't had to tell Lady Lalantiwashha about the new reality. She bore up under it with all the strength of character one could hope for. What a wonderful girl. Someone would have a magnificent wife in her. Although, alas, not he.

He realized he still had the whip in his hand from the

boys' morning lesson and took off to the tack room to stick it back into its slot. A knot of grooms was laughing and chaffing one another in the doorway. They made room for him; someone pounded him on the back as he passed. It all seemed so unchanged from his old life. Yet he was different. *None of these men know yet*, he thought. Certainly he would say nothing. Not that they—many of whom were themselves the sons or grandsons or great-grandsons of kings—would be impressed. But in any case, it wasn't his news to make public. Zidanza was a case apart, his other self.

He looked around and noticed his friend wasn't among his colleagues. "Anybody see Zidi?"

"He's around someplace. His father was here earlier," said one of the grooms, an older man.

"Reading the flight of horses!" a younger member of the staff said, holding up pontifical fists. The others guffawed.

Tiwatipara squeezed out the door and wandered down the aisle of the stable, hearing their laughter grow distant. He saw Nerikkaili alone near the opening, a thick silhouette against the bright sunlight. Then the prince turned the corner and disappeared. Lalantiwashha must have left already.

From afar, the midday clapper sounded, and Tiwatipara watched the gathering of grooms disperse as they headed off to the mess or to their homes for lunch. He drifted toward the entrance of the barn, only to find Nerikkaili standing in the yard, talking to Lurma-ziti. He could hear the elder prince's deep voice and see his raptor-nosed profile, but he couldn't make out his words. The hunchback stood with his weight on one hip, his thumbs in his belt. His back was to

Tiwatipara. A chill of suspicion drifted over the charioteer. *What are those two discussing here, when everyone has left for mealtime?* Something made him step back into the shadows. He was so bent on hearing what the two princes were saying that he almost jumped when someone gave a tap on his elbow. He whirled.

It was Tashmi-sharrumma. He looked up at the *hashtanuri,* his young face serious. His chin was still scabbed from his accident weeks ago. "Tiwatipara, someone's in the chariot room," he whispered.

"One of the grooms? That's normal." Tiwatipara tried to smile, but he spoke almost as softly as the boy.

"He's under one of the assembled chariots. I couldn't see his face."

Of course not; the boy is hopelessly nearsighted. But a warning flare of doubt went off in the charioteer's mind. This could mean nothing, or it could be that the saboteur was at work again. He drew his knife from its scabbard at his waist and began to slip toward the chariot room quietly, the youngster at his side. He whispered, "Maybe you should stay here, my prince, just in case." Because he was Tashmi-sharrumma and not his cousin, the lad remained obediently in the aisle.

Tiwatipara was almost creeping by the time he reached the door of the room. It was ajar. He slid inside and looked around in the dim light, his eyes seeking the royal vehicles. He heard muffled sounds from the near darkness. He caught a glimpse of movement as someone straightened up and squatted again. There was another flurry of dampened noise. The charioteer moved forward with the greatest care, fingers tightening on the hilt of his long knife. His heart had begun to pound. Perhaps this was harmless, but he felt increasingly that it was, rather, something sinister. He could see a bent back, and he heard a muffled hammering as if someone had wrapped a fleece around the mallet. He drew behind the person, who rose up suddenly, facing away from the charioteer, his curly hair hanging down his back.

"Zidanza?" cried Tiwatipara in shock. The groom whirled, his face stricken. He dropped the mallet in his hand, and it hit the dirt floor with a dull thud. "What are you doing?"

Zidanza said nothing, his mouth open, his eyes wide with fear. He held out the cotter pin in his other hand. It was trembling.

"What are you doing?" the charioteer repeated, longing to hear a good excuse. He could see in the dim light that this was the king's war chariot with its red-stained sides and golden mounts. "You're taking off the wheel?"

Zidanza shook his head. He took the pin in both hands and opened it like a nutshell. It had been split and hollowed out and held back together with wax. Tiwatipara gasped, unable to credit his eyes. His heart seemed to drop to his feet. Disbelieving, he whispered, "*You*'re the one?"

The groom nodded, still wide-eyed and stunned looking. His chest had begun to rise and fall rapidly as if he were exercising hard. Tiwatipara stared at his friend—his best friend in all the world—and little by little, he understood what he was seeing. Zidanza was putting a tricked pin on to hold the wheel, so that with any speed at all, it would break right off. A variation of the sawed axle. "You were the one all along…"

Zidanza nodded. A pitiful mewl escaped his lips. His

face crumpled. Overcome with a surge of fury, Tiwatipara hurled himself upon the groom and knocked him off his feet. They slid against the chariot with a grunt. He dragged Zidanza to the ground and rammed the edge of his knife against his throat. He pinned him there, breathing hard, rage rising in him, mingled with confusion—and denial, a refusal to believe what he saw.

"You dirty bastard," Tiwatipara hissed through his teeth. "Why? Why are you doing this?"

"My father made me, Tipa," Zidanza whimpered, his eyes closed, the tears starting to flow sideways down his face. He made no effort to resist, just lay there with his eyes squeezed shut.

"But why?"

"To kill Our Sun. So Urhi-tesshub could be king. My uncle told him to make me do it. They thought I had access to the king's chariots, so they put it on me. So it would look like an accident. But I'm not clever enough. Nothing worked. You kept finding out after the first time. Something always goes wrong. I can't do anything right." His breath was quick and shallow; his chin trembled. He offered no resistance, just lay limp in Tiwatipara's grip, his hands open at his sides.

"But it was so stupid. You kept trying the same trick over and over…"

"That's what Uncle Shipa-ziti said. But nobody would help me. I could only do my poor best, and I'm not very smart." Zidanza chewed his lip as if to control his mouth.

The charioteer was so confused he could hardly think. "You killed Pawahtelmah…"

"I didn't mean to. I didn't mean to hurt Tapala-tarhunta.

I told you, nothing ever goes right for me. I'm so sorry, Tipa."

But Tiwatipara grabbed his friend by the neck of his tunic and jerked him up viciously, pressing the knife harder against his pharynx. The groom's head dropped back as if he were already a corpse. "Does that excuse you? You meant to kill the king." He threw Zidanza's head against the ground with a thud. Tiwatipara's heart was a hollow clinker of pain and betrayal. "How could you do this, Zidi?" Tiwatipara's lips drew back in agony as if he had been burned. "We talked about it over and over. You looked me in the eye and acted like you knew nothing about it. You acted perfectly normal. You *laughed*, by all the gods. How could you be such a fake? For three years? I asked if you had left the box unguarded, and you said you had gone to the latrines."

A sob ripped through Tiwatipara's chest, more pain than rage. "You pretended to be ill, you filthy dog turd, and I... I felt sorry for you. I actually felt sorry for you. But it was a lie. You lied again and again. You looked me right in the eye and lied through your teeth." His stomach lurched. He felt sick with betrayal and humiliated to have been so tricked. Tears mounted to his lids. *Anything but this. Anyone but him.*

"I lie all the time, Tipa. I do nothing but lie. It's the only thing I'm good at." Zidanza's brimming eyes opened a little, just enough to reach out to his friend in shame.

But Tiwatipara spat contemptuously, "I guess it is. What did they have over you to make you abandon everything decent like this—forswear your oath to the king—you spineless wretch?"

"They beat me." The groom's mouth trembled, drawing

down into a wavering crescent. "They beat me, Tipa. They turned me into a slave."

Tiwatipara was pierced with pity in spite of himself. But his friend *wasn't* a slave. He could have left at any time. The charioteer growled, "Why didn't you go, Zidi? Why didn't you just run away?"

"I don't know. I was afraid to. He wouldn't love me anymore. I… I wanted to please Father…"

"You let them turn you into a murderer. A regicide. An abomination to the gods." Tiwatipara could hardly breathe. Rage burned up inside his gullet, overtaking pity, as if the lightning bolt had started its fall, and he knew he couldn't contain it any longer. His fist clenched Zidanza's tunic, and the knife in his other hand pressed deeper into the groom's skin.

"It's been horrible, Tipa." Zidanza tried to swallow. His voice sounded stretched. "I've had to live with this guilt for three years. You were always talking about your guilt, and it was really mine. And then I had to lie to you, my only friend. It's been horrible, beyond horrible." His face was slick with tears.

"Am I supposed to feel sorry for you? Is that what you expect, Zidi?" Tiwatipara laughed in disbelief. "You kill my father and maim my grandfather, and I'm supposed to feel pity?" But he did, and he hated it in himself. He blew on his righteous anger, letting the flames burst out, letting himself be consumed by it. *Be the lightning horse, man. Strike.*

"There's only one pity I ask. Please kill me," whispered Zidanza. "Please put me out of my pain. I can't live like this any longer…"

Tiwatipara felt as if he were being torn in two. Here

was the moment he had prayed for, lived for, longed for. Here was the revenge he had dreamed of, the retribution for the blood, the agony, the overturning of his life. Part of him was an implacable predator, like the Zuwalli Gods, thirsting for the blood of vengeance—a lightning horse. But... Zidanza. His friend who was more than a brother. He wanted to savor the ecstasy of revenge but found it bitter as gall. *Why him? Why him?*

The knife was already making a deep indentation in the groom's throat; a few beads of blood began to well up along its edge. "I can't hate you," Tiwatipara said in wonder. "After all you've done, I can't hate you."

"It's not about hatred," said Nerikkaili's level baritone at his back. "It's about the king's justice."

And gritting his teeth as if against some terrible pain, Tiwatipara pressed in and gently drew the blade sideways, deeper and deeper. A fountain of bubbling blood washed over his hand, drenching his sleeve. With a gurgle and a horrible spasm of his limbs, Zidanza sagged lifeless on the ground at the charioteer's knees. *This can't be happening*, marveled Tiwatipara, numb. He slung the knife away from him all at once, as if it had become a viper, and he began to cry. "Zidi..."

Nerikkaili crouched at his side and took him by the arm, lifting him up. "We heard his whole confession, Tiwatipara. You had to do what you did."

Through his tears, the charioteer looked around. Lurma-ziti and Tashmi-sharrumma stood in the doorway. At Tiwatipara's feet lay Zidanza, his best friend upon all the black earth, dead in a tide of crimson, his round young face expressionless. *Now I have four deaths to mourn.*

Tiwatipara murmured, "I'm so sorry, Zidi…" Tears and mucus ran down his face. His shoulders shook with sobs he could hardly hold back.

"Come on, man," said Nerikkaili in a low voice, surprisingly gentle. "We'll get some soldiers to take him away. Our Sun will be relieved to hear about this. He'll finally have an excuse to go after Shipa-ziti and Armatalli."

The *tuhkanti* tried to draw him away from Zidanza's body, but Tiwatipara pulled back. "Wait. Let me see something." He reached down with gentle hands and turned his friend over onto his face. Then, with his bloody knife, he slit the back of Zidanza's tunic, exposing the raw scars and half-healed lash marks all over his ribs, the record of a lifetime of abuse. Death had indeed come as a mercy. A wave of nausea and pity rose up in him, and he leaned away and vomited on the dirt.

After he had wiped his mouth and managed to get himself together a bit, he left the chariot room, staggering, in the company of his three brothers.

Hattushili was listening with delight to the dispatches from abroad in the company of his wife when the chamberlain announced that three—four—of his sons had formed a delegation to see him about something important. He sent his secretary out and ordered the eunuch to bring the boys in. "I wonder what this is about," he mused, tugging at his nose. "I hope it's nothing bad. I hate to break the charm of all this good news."

Puduhepa cried out at the sight of Tiwatipara, who was soaked with blood to the elbows, but the king was more astonished to see Lurma-ziti in the company of Nerikkaili and Tashmi-sharrumma. Hattushili hoped that didn't mean that they'd caught the boy at something. They all looked quite grim, but there was something triumphant about his eldest as well.

"Tell him, Tiwatipara," said Nerikkaili, pushing the charioteer forward.

"My Sun, we've found the saboteur." Tiwatipara's mouth shook, and he gripped his lip in his teeth, his face stretched in the attempt not to break down. The boy's hands hung at his sides, but his fingers were twitching.

Hattushili bared his teeth in a predatory grin of satisfaction. He growled, "Well done, lads. Who is the sheep fucker?"

Tiwatipara hung his head for a moment then marshaled himself. "Zidanza son of Armatalli, My Sun. He's... he was one of the grooms."

The king and the *tawananna* exchanged disabused looks. "Well, well. So Armatalli *is* involved with Arma-tarhunta, as expected, hah. And he wouldn't even stop at this. I've told you all along, my dear, that Arma-tarhunta was responsible for more than one misfortune in this kingdom."

Tiwatipara continued in a flat voice, "Prince Tashmi-sharrumma saw him in the chariot room as everyone else left for lunch and called me. I found him... I found him putting a faked cotter pin in the wheel." He held out the wax-filled shell, which the king eyed curiously, raising an admiring eyebrow.

"Tashmi told me and Lurma-ziti, too," added the crown prince. "We were outside, so we came along in case Zidanza resisted. The fellow confessed everything. Said it was his father and uncle who made him do it, to give Urhi-tesshub a clear shot at the throne."

The *tawananna* had drawn Tashmi-sharrumma to her side and wrapped an arm around him. "Good for you, son." She kissed him proudly.

But the boy was strangely grave, and he looked at Tiwatipara with something that, on a more expressive face, might have been pity. "It was his best friend," he murmured.

"So where is he now?" demanded the king.

"In the Tenawa, My Sun," Tiwatipara said in a breaking voice. He hung his head.

Hattushili looked at his firstborn. "Dead?"

Nerikkaili nodded. He drew a finger across his throat. The king sighed heavily then said with forced good cheer, "Well done, all of you. That's one less danger to the kingdom. You've averted a civil war." He caught Nerikkaili's eye and tried to convey a little extra gratitude. His heir might have improved his own prospects by permitting his father's early demise, but he hadn't.

"I guess everyone can stop suspecting me now," said Lurma-ziti sarcastically.

"I never suspected you, son."

The king meant it wholeheartedly, but Tiwatipara looked ashamed and mumbled, "Forgive me, my lord. I had to consider everyone."

Hattushili walked over to the charioteer and clapped him encouragingly on the upper arms with both hands, not put off by the drying blood all over the boy—they would all need to be purified after this. His heart was brimming for the youth. "So Pawahtelmah is avenged, hah? And

Tapala-tarhunta can rest easy. You found your man." He gazed at Tiwatipara from under his lids. The boy looked up at him, and the king grinned, proud and full of love, and took him in his arms.

When he drew back, Tiwatipara's face was streaming again. He murmured, sniffing, "What will happen to his body, My Sun? Can he still have a funeral?"

"He's a prince," said Puduhepa from behind him. "He should still have the proper rites, don't you think, my dear?"

Hattushili made a dubious noise, but the charioteer pleaded, "My Sun, he had nothing against you himself. His father made him do it. Zidanza was tortured. He was no more responsible than a slave."

Clemency was a beautiful virtue, although it didn't always play out well in reality. However, Hattushili had to admit, dead men were rarely dangerous. "All right. But Shipa-ziti is going into exile sooner rather than later. All that crew—it's off to Alashiya with them, and I'm sequestering their property. Armatalli won't be doing anything more important than presiding over property disputes with his birds. I've had it with them all. I'm breaking them."

He stared around in approval at the young men who stood before him. "So go on, boys. You've done a good day's work today. Your king is proud of you." He let his eyes linger fondly on the bent head of Tiwatipara. "Your father is proud of you."

"Change clothes before you go out, Father," said Lurma-ziti wryly as he turned to leave. "You look like you've been stabbed."

Hattushili looked down at his tunic and saw that he was indeed covered in blood. He began to gurgle with laughter. "Most painless wound I've ever taken!"

The boys left. Puduhepa remained with him alone, as they had been before. The king sat down on the edge of his bed, remarkably cheerful. "This hasn't been a bad day."

"No, my love," said his wife. "Your faith in your sons is vindicated. And a very dangerous person is out of the way."

"And," he added, with a twinkle in his eye, "our apparent debacle in Millawata has had some positive consequences, hah?"

She smiled and rose and, coming close to him, stroked the side of his face, carefully avoiding the dark-brownish stains all over the breast of his tunic. "Kupanta-tarhunta has decided to side with you after all. And—"

"And the great king of Mizri is starting to show interest in a peer treaty. Ha ha! Who could have foreseen that bag of dispatches! I was afraid that after Millawata we'd look like goats."

Apparently, seeing how willing the king's forces had been to gallop right into foreign territory had made a few people think. What had seemed like a disaster had had some surprisingly positive repercussions.

He heaved a sigh of contentment and drew his wife against his side. "Maybe we've turned a corner."

"Careful, my love; you've gotten my blouse dirty!" she cried, drawing back and brushing at her bosom.

"We're both dirty. We'd better take off our clothes, hah?" He began to untie the neck of his wife's blouse.

Tiwatipara tried to concentrate on his duties, but his thoughts kept returning to Zidanza. Days had passed, and he still found himself wanting to tell his friend all about the events that had transpired. *Hey, Zidi, we've caught the would-be assassin.* But he would never again share his confidences with his childhood companion. Perhaps the most painful part of it all was discovering how little he had known the man. He had thought they were close, and he'd certainly laid his own soul bare to Zidanza. But the intimacy had only gone one way. Zidanza had had terrible secrets. *If only he'd said something and hadn't made light of his suffering, maybe I could have helped him.*

And now Tiwatipara was as alone in the world as a person could be, with no one at all to talk to. He'd found a whole new family in the king and his sons and daughters, but he was far from such a sense of familiarity—even with Nerikkaili, with whom he had worked for years—as to be able to unburden himself to them. He still thought of them as "My Sun" and "my prince." Perhaps comfort with his new identity would come with time.

He hung up the leathers in his hand and wandered out of the tack room, down the aisle of the royal barn. It was the end of the morning; the boys had had their lesson and run off together, and he had nothing pressing to do until after lunch. Tiwatipara passed through the golden motes that danced in the shafts of sunlight penetrating the barn from its clerestories. One of the stallions raised a curious head, and he scratched its poll with his knuckles. He drifted outside and, feeling idle and unhitched, sat on the back of a hay wagon with his legs dangling off the edge. The cicadas had started to razz.

He hadn't been there long when he saw Nerikkaili and Tashmi-sharrumma coming toward him. He looked up, thinking the boy had perhaps forgotten something. But the young prince said nothing, just hoicked himself up onto the wagon beside the charioteer and let his legs dangle beside Tiwatipara's. He was growing tall at an astonishing rate lately and starting to look like an adolescent, with his father's long jaw and thin, bony-ridged nose. He clasped his big hands in his lap, his wrists projecting from his sleeves. Nerikkaili leaned one hand against the chariot rail and flashed his ambiguous smile. He managed to appear impressive even in that relaxed pose. The muscles of his thick arm flexed a little under his weight.

Tiwatipara looked up at him. "Can I help you, my prince?"

"So, here we are, Tiwatipara," said the *tuhkanti* with an expansive sigh. "Our lives all overturned." He glanced at the top of the head of his young brother, who was probably ignorant of the exact nature of that overturning. "Even the most shocking changes become familiar over time, I suspect."

"I suspect so, my lord." Tiwatipara wasn't sure what he was meant to say, but he appreciated Nerikkaili's coming to him.

"You know," Nerikkaili continued, staring out over the barns, the practice field, and the citadel in the distance, "until I was older than Tashmi here, my father wasn't a king at all—not even that strange hybrid creature, the king of Hakpish. He's only been Great King for six years."

"That's so, my lord."

"So a good half my life, I wasn't any king's heir, was I?"

Tiwatipara grinned. "I see where you're going, my lord. No, you weren't."

Nerikkaili looked Tiwatipara in the eye, and his mouth

curled up at one corner. "We'll all manage, won't we...
brother?"

Tiwatipara returned his look, warmed by this oblique
admission of struggle, and gave a firm nod of solidarity.

Nerikkaili removed his hand from the wagon and
hitched his belt. "Well, I'm off to the south to lead
Father's troops against Arma-tarhunta's brood. Tashmi had
something he wanted to ask." The elder prince sauntered
off, his step jaunty.

Tiwatipara was beginning to feel brighter himself,
although he couldn't have said why. Perhaps the complicity
with Nerikkaili gave him a sense of being less isolated than
he had feared. Buoyed by a sudden fondness, he glanced at
the boy beside him. Tashmi-sharrumma smiled shyly, his
mouth stretched unattractively over his crooked teeth. He
was going to be even uglier than the king, Tiwatipara saw,
but without Hattushili's charm—and it made him love the
lad.

After a moment, Tashmi-sharrumma said, looking at
his hands, "My father said I could go with his troops to
arrest Shipa-ziti."

"Good. It was thanks to you we found out what he
was up to," Tiwatipara said warmly. Another silence fell.
Tashmi-sharrumma wasn't a talker.

But the boy finally said in a quiet, constricted voice,
"Zidanza was your friend. It would be like me having to
kill Ulmi-tesshub." He shot the charioteer a quick glance
from under his lids, and his muscular mouth turned down
sorrowfully.

*I do believe this lad understands better than all the
grown-ups,* thought Tiwatipara, touched. *He's deeper than*

we give him credit for. "Thank you for your compassion, my prince," he said sincerely.

They sat again, unspeaking, until the prince said, "My father said I could ask you to be my driver. For good, I mean." He glanced up briefly and looked back down. "If you want to, of course."

"I'd be honored, my prince. My brother." He clapped the boy on the thigh and felt real warmth stealing over him as he smiled. "But aren't you going to drive for Ulmi-tesshub at some point? Or are we wasting our time with these lessons?"

Tashmi-sharrumma nodded. "For a while. It's no waste. I love the horses."

"That says something good about you."

The boy slid off the edge of the wagon and bared his unfortunate teeth. "Thank you, Tiwatipara."

He jogged off on his long, coltish legs, and Tiwatipara sat there alone. But he felt less alone than he had been. Something as simple as a friendly word from his brothers had changed things.

Indeed, the charioteer wasn't a solitary person by nature. He was neither melancholy nor vengeful. That was a role he'd had to play for a few years—he'd had to be a lightning horse—but it wasn't who he really was. He was a cheerful fellow who liked nothing better than the company of his peers. And family was important to him. He remembered saying once in a rush of self-pity that while the gods could give him a new sweetheart, they could never give him a new father. He had been wrong. There was nothing the Great Ones couldn't do.

He dropped to the ground and brushed off his skirts.

Maybe I'll head to the inn, he thought, *and see if anyone is around who'd like to share a beer. Maybe find a girl.*

Maybe he'd find a girl to marry, in fact, and start his own family. He would name his firstborn Pawahtelmah, although it was an old-fashioned name. His new life lay ahead.

THE END

HISTORICAL NOTES

THE HITTITES WERE AN INDO-EUROPEAN-SPEAKING group who entered Asia Minor—today's Turkey—around 2000 BC. By the end of the Bronze Age, they had established a powerful empire that included all of Asia Minor and much of Syria.

The main part of our story takes place around 1250 BC, when the Great King of Hatti, Hattushili III, had been on his stolen throne for six years. Although we know practically nothing about any Hittite kings, Hattushili and his much younger queen Puduhepa left a kind of brief autobiography meant to justify his seizure of the throne. His troubles with his irrepressible deposed nephew Ulmi-tesshub (Murshili III) are historical. They were the cause of several generations of ongoing civil war between differing parts of the royal family, and Hattushili's uncle (actually a cousin once removed) Arma-tarhunta was indeed the leader of the opposition, even in extreme old age. Shipa-ziti, his son, carried on this animosity. The augur Armatalli, although a prince of some sort, is not known to have been the son of Arma-tarhunta.

All the episodes concerning Piyamaradu are historical, although without any dated documents from the Hittite Empire, we cannot be sure they didn't take place over several years. The Luwians, the natives of western Asia Minor—or rather, earlier immigrants, who spoke a language very similar to that of the Hittites—were in fact in league on and off with the people of Ahhiyawa, that is, the people whom we would call the Mycenaean Greeks, who had a colony at Millawanda. The seven thousand builders, lured or highjacked away to Greece, may explain the Anatolian character of the "Cyclopean" masonry of the Mycenaean citadels.

Nerikkaili was active as a diplomat for his father, but historically, he was displaced as crown prince in favor of his younger brother. He briefly served as the heir of the latter until Tudhaliya produced a son of his own, but Nerikkaili seems to have continued to serve in various capacities until a ripe old age.

Tiwatipara is a real person, although all we know about him is that he became the charioteer of Tudhaliya IV (Tashmi-sharrumma). Likewise, Tapala-tarhunta is historical. He was the hostage sent to Piyamaradu, and Hattushili supported him by claiming that he was a relative of the *tawananna* and that he had shared the king's chariot in their youth. Other elements of his life and that of Tiwatipara are fictional, including their relationship.

My principle has been to observe any commonly accepted historical fact (a concept which must be understood as relative when dealing with the Hittites), but where scholars are undecided or where we are completely in the dark, I have felt free to interpret.

GLOSSARY OF NAMES AND TERMS

(Personages marked by an * are fictional)

Ahhiyawa: One of the Greek city states of the Late Bronze Age which we would call Mycenaean, perhaps Mycenae itself or Thebes.

Alashiya: Cyprus.

Amka: An inland area of far-southern Syria. It included Damascus.

Amurru: A small kingdom in coastal Syria that marked almost the southernmost part of the Hittite Empire.

Apasha: A Luwian city in western Asia Minor, capital of Mira. Later called Ephesus.

Arantu River: The Orontes, in inland Syria.

Armatalli: An augur, that is, a priest who divines the will of the gods through the flight of birds. He was a member of the royal family.

Arma-tarhunta: An uncle or older cousin of Hattushili who carried out an ongoing enmity against the latter, including a lawsuit and an apparent attempt at witchcraft.

Arzawa: Formerly, a powerful kingdom of western Asia Minor which became the head of a coalition of Luwian states (the Arzawan League) that gave Hatti a run for its money in the late fourteenth century. Hattushili's father split it up.

Asshuriya: Assyria, a growing power in northern Mesopotamia.

Atpa: The king or governor of the Ahhiyawan colony of Millawata, married to the daughter of Piyamaradu.

Ba'al: A Syrian storm god, the chief divinity of Amurru.

Benteshina of Amurru: Coming to the throne of his Syrian vassal kingdom at a young age, Benteshina defected to Egypt when the latter was at his gates just before the Battle of Qadesh (1274). After a long house arrest in Hattusha, he was reinstated on his throne by the Hittites and married into the Hittite royal house.

booty people: The civilian captives of war, often deported to other regions to farm.

eshertu: A second-rank wife of the king, neither the official queen nor a simple concubine.

Gasshulawiya: Eldest daughter ("Great Lady") of Hattushili and Puduhepa, married to Benteshi of Amurru.

The Great Way: Death.

The Gulshesh: The goddesses of one's destiny. Like the Greek Fates, they were thought to spin out a man's life and cut the thread when it was done. There is now some debate about the actual pronunciation of their name.

Halmashuit: The divine personification of the throne.

Hattusha: The capital of Hatti Land, an impressive fortified city near today's Bogazköy.

Hattushili III: King of Hatti from about 1265-1235. He was the youngest first-rank son of Murshili II and the brother of Muwatalli II. After a sickly childhood, he became a priest of Shaushga and a successful general. Shortly before the Battle of Qadesh, his brother divided the empire, making Hattushili king over the northern half. He served as regent for his nephew Murshili III, but when the latter dissolved the northern kingdom, Hattushili revolted and deposed the youth.

Hakpish: A holy city to the far north of Hattusha. It became the capital of a kingdom of the north when Muwatalli divided the empire, and Hattushili was its king.

hanna: The Hittite word for grandmother.

Hapalla: A region in west central Asia Minor, formerly part of Arzawa.

hashtanuri: A charioteer, either in the sense of a driver or of an emissary. The **hashtalanuri** was the king's driver.

hasshuma: A ceremony of coming of age for princes of Hatti.

hekur: "Stone house." A peak sanctuary often associated with the burial place or cenotaph of a king.

The High Place: Kingship.

Hishni: One of the older sons of Hattushili.

hurkel: A taboo, especially sexual.

Hurrian: The language of the kingdom of Mitanni on the upper reaches of the Euphrates. Hurrian gods like Shaushga were eagerly embraced by their neighbors, and Hurrian names were popular among the Hittites and Semitic-speaking Syrians of the coast as well—e.g., Ulmi-tesshub, Tashmi-sharrumma, and Benteshina, which comes from the Hurrian Pentip-shenni. Because Mitanni had once held Kizzuwatna, Hurrian was probably spoken there, at least as a nod to heritage.

huwalpant: The Hittite word for hunchback.

ikniyant: The Hittite word for a lame man.

iku: A unit of distance of about ten to fifteen meters.

Innarawantesh: The Violent Ones, companions of the goddess Innara, one of the protective deities of the Great King.

Iyalanda: A small Luwian town near Millawata, later Alinda.

kalmush: A long curved staff like a shepherd's crook that was part of the Hittite king's regalia.

Karduniash: The Babylonian Empire under its Kassite rulers.

Karkemish: A town in inland Syria on the Euphrates River which was the seat of the Hittite viceroy of Syria.

Karkisha: An area in southwestern Asia Minor. It corresponds to the later Caria.

Kashkuh (Arma): The Hittite and Luwian names, respectively, for the god of the moon.

Kinza (**Qadesh**): A town in Syria on the Orontes River and site of a famous battle between Muwatalli II and Ramesses II of Egypt.

Kizzuwatna: A formerly independent kingdom in mountainous eastern Anatolia, later absorbed into Hatti. It was the homeland of Puduhepa.

Kulana-ziti: Hattushili's emissary in Taruisha. He was a member of the royal family—in this story, an unranked brother of the king.

Kupanta-tarhunta: The Luwian king of Mira. Like many vassals, he was undecided which candidate to the throne to support, but eventually came down on Hattushili's side. His son, however, would be a leader of the independence movement.

Kusshara: A city in Kizzuwatna, ancestral to the Hittite royal dynasty.

labarna: The title of the Great King of Hatti. It seems originally to have been a proper name, like "Caesar."

Lahurzi: Brother of Piyama-radu.

Lalantiwashha*: An older daughter of Hattushili.

Lazpa: The island of Lesbos, off the coast of northwestern Asia Minor.

Lelwani: Goddess of the underworld; the Sun at Night.

lupanni: The skull cap that served as the crown of Hatti.

Lurma-ziti*: One of the older sons of Hattushili.

Luwian: The language spoken by most of the inhabitants of Hatti and its vassals, especially in the west. Of Indo-european origin, it differed but little from the Hittites' language.

Manapa-kurunta: The Luwian king of Sheha River Land, who defected to the cause of Urhi- tesshub and was deposed by Hattushili.

marnuwan: A kind of beer.

Mashturi: The son of Manapa-kurunta, married to Hattushili's sister. A loyal supporter of Hattushili, he was set upon the throne of Sheha River Land in his father's place.

Mashuhepa*: A fictional name for the maternal aunt of Puduhepa who was married to Tapala- tarhunta.

meshedi: The corps of royal body guards.

Millawata (**Millawanda** to the Luwians): A city on the Aegean in southwestern Asia Minor settled by the Ahhiyawans. Later known as Miletus.

Mira: An important Luwian kingdom on the southwest coast of Asia Minor. Its capital was Apasha (Ephesus).

Mizri: The name given to Egypt by many of its neighbors.

mountain apple: Thought to be the apricot.

Nerikkaili: Hattushili's firstborn and sometime crown prince. Because he was not first rank, he was later replaced as heir but continued to serve in diplomatic capacities.

Neshite: The Indo-european language of the Hittites, derived from their first capital, Nesha.

The Night Sun: Lelwani, the goddess of the underworld.

Nuhasshe: A kingdom in inland Syria briefly governed by Urhi-tesshub.

Nuwanza: A member of the royal family (here an unranked brother of Hattushili) who served as a field marshal under three kings.

The Old Women: Priestesses of the Goddess of the Underworld and practitioners of magic. They presided over births and funerals.

pahhurzi: A second-rank child of the king, that is, one born of an *eshertu* wife.

Pawahtelmah*: Son of Tapala-tarhunta, hence a cousin of Puduhepa. He succeeded his father as royal charioteer.

Pirinkir: The evening star.

Piyamaradu: A leader of the Luwian resistance to Hatti. He is thought by some scholars to have been the grandson of Uhha-ziti, the last king of Arzawa.

Piyasshili: Son of Hattushili's grandfather, Shuppiluliuma I. Sent to conquer and divide the Mitannian empire, he was made viceroy of Hatti's new Syrian holdings and King of Karkemish under the throne name Sharri-kushuh.

Puduhepa: The young queen of Hattushili. As *tawananna*, she would hold office into the reign of her grandson, probably dying around the age of ninety. She was an involved and powerful consort, one of the best known and most extraordinary women of antiquity. She originated from a priestly family of Hurrian descent in Kizzuwatna, eastern Anatolia.

Qatna: An inland Syrian town, slightly northeast of Kadesh.

Shahuranuwa: Secretary of Hattushili. He would later become the chief scribe (vizier).

Shapili: The man who ruled Amurru for fourteen years after Benteshina was deposed and before he regained his throne. It is unknown whether he was a relative of Benteshina.

Sharri-tesshub: The birth name of Muwatalli II.

Shaushga, the Lady of Shamuha: A Hurrian goddess of love and war, doublet of the Mesopotamian Ishtar. She was worshiped throughout the Near East.

Sheha River Land: A Luwian kingdom just north of Mira. The Sheha River is probably the Classical Hermos.

Shipa-ziti: A son of Arma-tarhunta who continued the fight against Hattushili's kingship.

shush: A heavily armed chariot warrior.

Tapala-tarhunta: A charioteer in both senses of the word. A relative of Puduhepa, he drove for Hattushili in their youth, then served as an emissary, acting as hostage in the exchange with Piyamaradu.

taptara **women**: Professional mourners.

Tarhunta: The main god of Hatti, the god of storms. In his apostasis **Tarhunta Pihasshasshi**, he was the god of lightning and, in this story, patron of charioteers.

Tarhuntassha: A region in southern Asia Minor and also its capital, founded by Muwatalli II when he divided the empire and moved the seat of government there. Later known as Rough Cilicia.

Taruisha: A town in the far northwestern corner of Asia Minor. Later known as Troy.

Tashmi-sharrumma: The eldest son of Hattushili and Puduhepa, he succeeded Nerikkaili as crown prince and eventually took the throne as Tudhaliya IV.

Tawagalawa: The Hittites' way of writing Etewoklewes (Eteokles). He was the brother of the king of Ahhiyawa and a kind of minister without portfolio in Asia Minor for the latter.

tawal: A kind of beer.

tawananna: The political role of the Hittite queen. She held office independently of the life of her husband, thus might continue to be *tawananna* into the reign of his successors.

Tenawa: The grim part of the underworld, where all but the most privileged went.

Tiwatipara: A young charioteer who will later serve Tudhaliya IV as his driver. There is no known historical connection between him and Tapala-tarhunta or Hattushili.

Tsumur: The capital of Amurru.

Tudhaliya II: The father of Shuppiluliuma, the founder of the Hittite Empire. Tudhaliya had already begun the expansion and consolidation that would make his son's kingdom great.

tuhkanti: The Hittite crown prince.

Ugarit: A coastal kingdom of Syria, somewhat north of Amurru.

Ulmi-tesshub: The half-brother of the deposed king Urhi-tesshub. He was raised by Hattushili and Puduhepa with their son Tashmi-sharrumma. We know historically that they were "closer than brothers," and this no doubt played a role in the choice of Hattushili's heir. Scholars are divided over Ulmi-tesshub's parentage, and for this story I have followed I. Singer, who makes him the first-rank son of the deposed *tawananna* Tanuhepa, whom others believe to have been his grandmother.

Ummi-hibi*: A fictional name for the daughter of Benteshina married to Nerikkaili.

Urhi-tesshub: A second-rank son and the successor of Muwatalli II. He came to the throne as an adolescent, and after a reign of nine years, his uncle and regent Hattushili deposed him. He fled to Egypt, but seems to have returned and caused trouble for Hattushili for many years.

walhi: A sweet, powerful alcoholic drink, perhaps mead.

Waliwanda: A Luwian town in western Asia Minor.

Walwa-ziti: Vizier under Hattushili.

wannumiyash: The Hittite word for fatherless, orphaned.

Washmuaria Riamashesha: The Hittite way of writing User-ma'at-ra Ramesses (II).

Wurukatte: The Hittite god of war.

Wurushemu: The Sun Goddess of Arinna, Hatti's chief female divinity.

Zidanza*: Son of Armatalli and groom in the royal stables.

Zuwalli Gods: The gods of vengeance, equivalent to the Greek Furies.

Zuzuhha: Member of the royal family and Chief Groom of the royal stables.

ACKNOWLEDGMENTS

The author gratefully acknowledges all those who have helped her in the production of this book. To the wonderful women of my writers' group, for their critique and encouragement, my thanks. To Lynn McNamee and her editorial team at Red Adept—Jessica, Sarah and Irene— profound gratitude (and Lynn, for so many other forms of help). To the flexible and talented gang at Streetlight Graphics for the cover and map. To my cousin and her husband, my technology guru: thanks, guys. To Enid, who urged me forward by her support, I can't thank you sufficiently. And most of all, to my husband, Ippokratis, who put up with the months of fixation it takes to write a novel, many, many thanks.

Enjoy this book? Don't miss the next book in the **Empire at Twilight** series. Here is a taste of *The Singer and Her Song:*

W HAT DISTINGUISHED EVENING FROM DAY was the silence, Uqnitum realized as she stirred the watery soup that was meant for dinner. Only as the sun sank, listless, into twilight did the constant accompaniment of the daytime hours cease—the dull, rhythmic boom of the Assyrian battering ram as it swung again and again against the gate of the city. The noise itself had become a weapon, as relentless as the wind or the killing sun of summer in the desert to the southwest. How did they keep it up hour after hour, day after day? How many men were swinging that ram under the cover of its wood-and-leather "horse"? Day after day, on and on, they swung it, while the defenders hurled burning torches down onto the contraption in vain.

The real question for the people of the little Mitannian city of Kahat was how long they could hold out against their besiegers, and in her heart of hearts, Uqnitum daughter of Tapshihuni knew the answer: *not very long*. She would never say it out loud. Everyone was too close to despair—

her family, her neighbors, and maybe even the priests who ruled the city and directed its defense.

But nobody held out against the Assyrians forever. For nearly two months, the siege had dragged on—*longer than you dogs expected,* she thought defiantly—and food was dangerously low. They'd been penned inside before the wheat could be sown. All they'd had for weeks was a little porridge stirred up from the tiny daily allotment. A little dried fruit. The few sheep or goats within the city walls, shared out among the inhabitants. Then the final bits of dried meat from last winter's slaughter of pigs. Then the dogs. Now they were finishing the stored grain from the temple granaries. She didn't know what would come next. Uqnitum refused to eat a rat.

So far, she had kept her family fed. Little Wullu, her youngest son, was delicate; he wouldn't eat just anything. Her daughter, Tatasshe, had the needs of the pregnant. Uqnitum had stretched their sparse rations with wild dandelions, roots that grew between the stones, and a few straggly lettuces, already bolted and bitter, from the spring garden behind the house.

She'd brought her portable brazier inside so she wouldn't have to cook outdoors in the evening chill. And she could keep better watch over Wullu, asleep, exhausted, in his little alcove. They would simply have to live with the smoke. Crouched over the embers, she stirred a thin soup made with wild greens and a bone she had bartered from the neighbors—she didn't want to know what kind of animal it had come from. An onion would have been worth a king's ransom in Kahat.

The fact that they'd been the honored musicians of

the temple of Tesshub and Sharrumma wouldn't do them much good anymore. No one, not even the gods, had time for elaborate services and long hymns and incense and magnificent sacrifices these days, and what would they sacrifice? Everything edible had been consumed by the gods' starving people. Even the priests were manning the walls, organizing the making of torches, and filling jars of their dwindling water, ready to pour on any fire the Assyrians might lob into the city. She hadn't practiced her vocalizing for weeks. Who had energy for singing after a long day of hauling rocks?

With a shuffle of footsteps at the door and the scrape of the wooden bar rising outside on its lever and string, her husband, Ar-tesshub, entered, throwing down his borrowed pickax on the floor with a *thunk*. He was white with dust—face, hair, and clothing all the same color as if he had been hewn from the stone of the walls—a man of stone. Uqnitum rose, creaking, to greet him and exchanged a kiss, her spoon dripping in her hand. Ar-tesshub heaved an enormous sigh of exhaustion and forced a weary smile as he sank down onto the floor mat. He arched his back painfully, leaning against the wall. His dust-stiffened hair stood out around his head like gorse. Uqnitum remembered how Ar-tesshub's beauty had struck her when he first came to her father's house. She'd been—what, fourteen?—and Ar-tesshub nine years older, no longer a child. He'd already proven himself a better lyre player than her father.

"Good evening, my dear," Ar-tesshub said. "It smells good in here."

"Better than it tastes, I daresay. How goes the work on the counterwall?"

Like every able-bodied man in the city, Ar-tesshub had been reinforcing the weakening gate, piling stones against the inside of the panels so that if—when—the Assyrians broke through, they would encounter yet another impassable obstacle. If the inhabitants didn't starve first. The women, Uqnitum and her daughter included, had spent the day carrying stones from the site of destruction to the slowly rising counterwall.

ABOUT THE AUTHOR

 N.L. Holmes is the pen name of a professional archaeologist who received her doctorate from Bryn Mawr College. She has excavated in Greece and in Israel, and taught ancient history and humanities at the university level for many years. She has always had a passion for books, and in childhood, she and her cousin (also a writer today) used to write stories for fun.

Today, since their son is grown, she lives with her husband and three cats. They split their time between Florida and northern France, where she gardens, weaves, plays the violin, dances, and occasionally drives a jog-cart. And reads, of course.